Helm

Helm
Sarah Hall

faber

First published in 2025
by Faber & Faber Limited
The Bindery, 51 Hatton Garden
London EC1N 8HN

Typeset by Faber & Faber Limited
Printed and bound by CPI Group (UK) Ltd, Croydon, CR0 4YY

A CIP record for this book
is available from the British Library

ISBN 978–0–571–38355–9

MIX
Paper | Supporting
responsible forestry
FSC
www.fsc.org   FSC® C013604

Printed and bound in the UK on FSC® certified paper in line with our continuing
commitment to ethical business practices, sustainability and the environment.
For further information see faber.co.uk/environmental-policy

Our authorised representative in the EU for product safety is
Easy Access System Europe, Mustamäe tee 50, 10621 Tallinn, Estonia
gpsr.requests@easproject.com

2 4 6 8 10 9 7 5 3

For Loy

When gods were young
This wind was old.

—Edward Thomas, 'The Mountain Chapel'

Carlisle

Croglin

Eden

Glassonby

Salkeld

Melmerby

Langwathby

Kirkland

Penrith

Eamont

Hepp

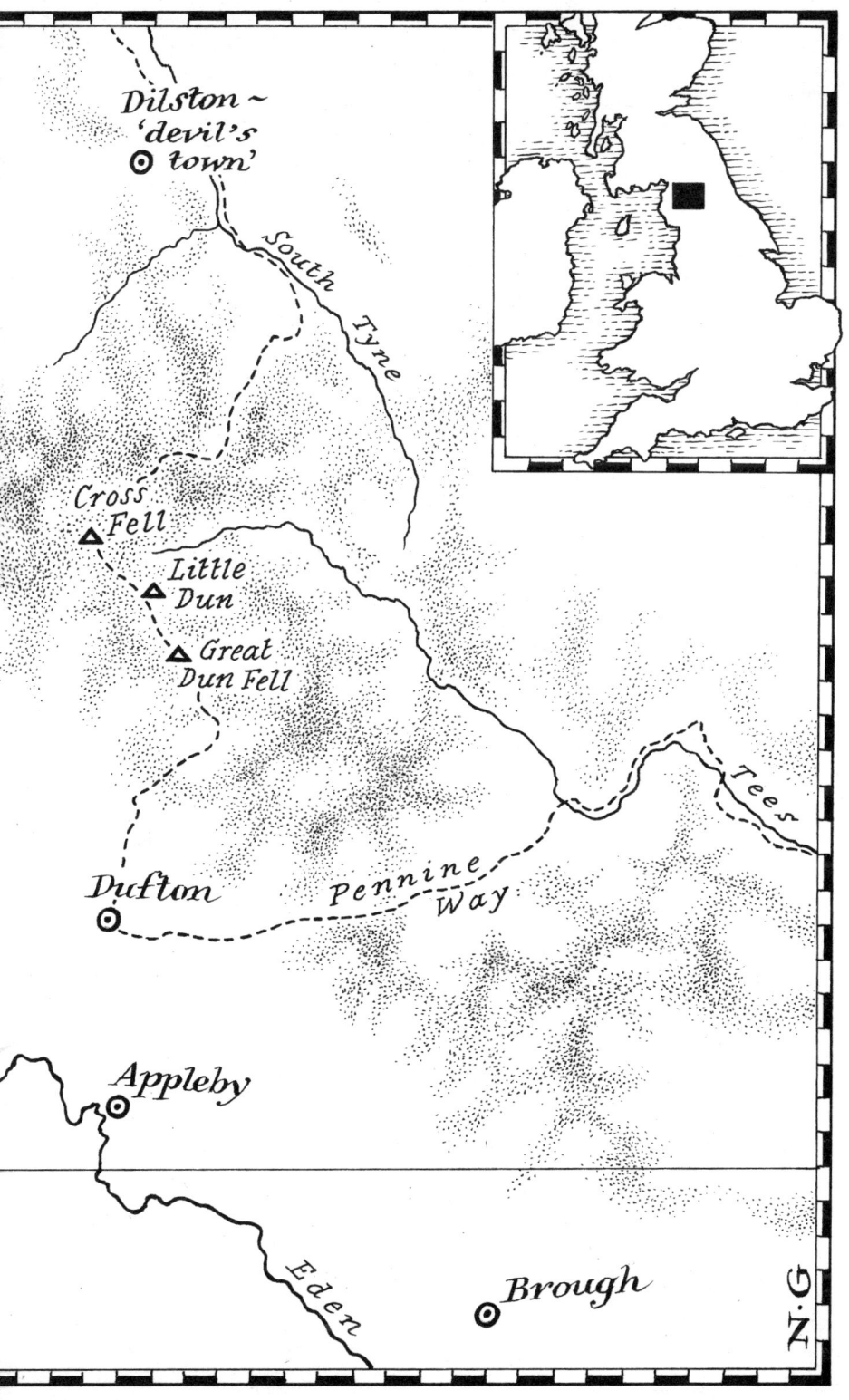

Dilston ~ 'devil's town'

South Tyne

Cross Fell

Little Dun

Great Dun Fell

Tees

Dufton

Pennine Way

Appleby

Eden

Brough

N·G

I

Helm doesn't know when Helm was born.
Or brewed.
Conjured or conceived.
First formed above the highest mountain.
First blown into the valley.
Long before humankind – that brief, busy interlude.

Time happens all at once for Helm, more or less, relative to longevity. A blink of the eye, universally. (Warning: Helm loves clichés, typical for English weather.) Something of a disorder, some would say.

Of what fantastical, phenomenal and calculable things Helm is made! Maleficence and data and lore. Atmospheric principles and folktales, spirit and substance, opposites and inversions. So many identities and personalities; it makes Helm's heads spin.

In the beginning, there was no Helm. Boring for the world, obviously. There were aeons before Helm arrived. The necessary arrangements had to be made, on the planet, and in the sky. It would take Ages for Helm to be recognised, let alone named. During which Helm suffered loneliness, inconsequence and ignorance – an original and terrible fugue state. Or Helm didn't care; Helm was just on standby.

But in the beginning nothing else had a name either, or a pronoun, or a preference. There was no godly language. There was no creative designer or clerical administrator. No titler of the things. It was all serious planetary business. A tremendous collision making Earth and its moon. Sun shrinking and getting hotter; everything bilious, oxygenless, not great for living. Earth was hot and cold, hot and cold, et cetera, for billennia. Fevers and chills, blah blah.

Huge continental arguments occurred, with fire and grinding, geological upheaval, smashing, subsidence, seas and lost seas; it was very dynamic. In amongst this, a little island was produced, with a forced-up, folded-together, eroded-down spine – a ridge of cross-bedded, water-laid, glacier-carved stones. The Pennine mountains were formed, across which forests and grassland, aurochs and wolves, Neanderthals, Normans, glampers and ramblers could come and go. Note: the biggest fell, its gradient and shape – geological cuvette, to be accurate – is most important in this scenario.

Or. Fossils are the devil's trick; some benign deity sneezed to make the world.
    Or. Artisanal aliens left their play-dough behind.
    Or. Balancing act – elephants and turtles.
    Or. Any other creation theory – hollow Earth, flat Earth, mud collection, hanging cord, corpse reuse, dreamtime, biosphere as gemstone in the ring of a galactic giant, please insert alternative here.

Helm doesn't care which story is true. So long as there is Helm.

Also, Earth's atmosphere had to stop fucking around and calm down. Stratospheric forecastable order obtained – that is a climate. One was needed with a narrow temperature range; in Helm's case, inglorious British maritime. In brief – Atlantic thermal capacities, a Gulf Stream, six stable air masses, including (something of a future issue) polar. Wet and dry fronts, prevailing winds, moisture and vapour, meeting, as luck would have it, exactly at the top of that big mountain on the little island.

Cue, a wind-appropriate domain.
  Cue, at some point, Helm.

Cue, afterwards, lots of identity politics, superstitions, bonkers rituals
and boffin theories about Helm. All of which please Helm. Helm is
nothing if not solipsistic, narcissistic even. Fear, devotion, inquisition,
obsession, admiration – all attention is good attention.

A poetic birth moment would be nice. Perhaps, curled inside the
turbulent virginal atmosphere, Helm dreams of being a storm, has
a prophetic vision of destruction, feels a natural calling. The foetal
beat of air beats all around Helm like a beating heart (must elegantly
variate). Or the sky, a bit bloated, lets one off. Helm loves a fart joke.

The top of the mountain, also as yet unnamed, is the perfect spot
from which to observe evolution. It's all kicking off below. Lavic
displays and dramatic columns of ash. The rearrangement of rivers
and lakes. Meltwater. Spores. Vegetation. Creatures crawling out of
gunk, their legs extending, their toe-webs rescinding, amoebic eyes
getting harder. Fast-forward to: creatures becoming other creatures,
eggs, bugs, pedes and pods. Lovely greenery sprouting. Mixed oak
woods, pine and birch, upland rowan. For a while there are big, lug-
ging animals, impervious to the sky and its inhabitants as they hunt
and graze. Everything is without self-consciousness, and adapts and
adapts, and just is.

Meanwhile, Helm practises Helm's skills. Studying the topography.
Reading the mood of the incoming sky. Orientating on the mountain. Helm gets ready inside the big dome of cloud (let's call it the
Helm cloud), waiting for an instinctive, brave, enabled feeling. Ready,
steady, blow! Tries a first flight from the escarpment, a learner breeze
across the valley, and realises – wow! – Helm has abilities. Helm has
or is a second cloud too, on the other side of the valley, an exciting

rotoring one (the Bar). Tricky to explain/visualise; additional info to follow, stay tuned. For now, imagine a skater launching off a quarter pipe two thousand feet high, then somersaulting. Again. And again. And again.

It's a crazy coming of age. Helm enjoys the feeling, of agency, of urgency, so plays with Helmself to arouse the feeling: desire for great, wreaking, havoc-making release, surging from a sky orifice, down the mountain and – *yes, yes, oh yes, there's Helm* . . . Flooding the valley with noise and velocity, making an impressive mess – smash-up of trees, shrubbery, and unballasted creatures. Or, it's uncontrollably random.

Still no witnesses, though, which is a shame. Also, the Helm-show is transitory. Only when Helm manifests does Helm really exist, and afterwards Helm isn't anymore. The dumb, lumbering beasts don't care: they fold their ridiculous necks, shelter behind each other's armoured rumps, and the airborne ones fly away, alighting in the dense canopy, drawing creepy, bloodless lids over their eyes. Helm's a little envious – these beasts are a bit duh, but at least they're always embodied, able to kill and eat and rut each other until they die.

So begins the inevitable existential dilemma of who/what/why am I? Heavy, especially for one so aerial.

Between manifesting, Helm sees stuff happen, or not happen. Sometimes a tree falls. Sometimes lightning hits the mountainside and splits or burns a tree. Big animal eats a tree, poops. Small animal eats the poop. Helm's valley, though it is being grazed by herds, hunted across by packs and stooped upon from above, seems a bit – dull. More aeons.

Comet, ash cloud, mass extinction, redo.

Helm waits around for the skies to clear. The remaining animals have a changing phase, becoming slightly different, then very different: swimmers, flyers, crawlers, runners, hoppers. This is bloody and chaotic, and reasonably interesting. But still, it's like, hello? The birds – nearest similar entity – don't hang out with Helm; every time Helm wants to play they leave. Sometimes hawks rise above Helm's whirling bar cloud – opportunists. River life is inaccessible, a closed world, the flicker of silver fin, a plopping frog. Helm can't see into the growling squawking forest to know what's occurring in there. The aurochs are quite nice, right below Helm on the mountainside, their coats riffling in the wind, their horns jewelled with ice in winter: dark, pretty eyes with long curling lashes. They turn towards the wind, acknowledging, but not really comprehending.

Then – boom!

It is when humans evolve that things become interesting. Because humans become interested in Helm.

Helm sees smoke rising on the other side of the forest, without lightning or lava's arson. Helm rises too, goes as high as possible, gets a little giddy (there are upper limits to Helm's domain). Far away, across the tops of the trees, is a group of dark-bodied, long-haired up-monkeys. They are scavenging along the shore of a big, shimmering bay. They are picking molluscs from between rocks, sucking the shells clean. Humans, organised and habitual – they go to the same places, nuzzle their favourite others, hold grudges if one finds a bigger crustacean and doesn't share. More promisingly, they act in accordance with the weather, retreating in the rain, sheltering under leaf umbrellas, sheltering the orange embers they use to start fires. They look up at the sky, have feelings related to its condition.

Smoke rises oftener, closer to Helm's mountain. They are burning

5

away forest, making inroads. Helm catches glimpses of the humans. Flickering flames. Deer being dragged. Bears dragging them. Skin tents. Badly fitting pelts. Bums, and two types of frontage (in-y, out-y). Have they seen Helm?

They make flint factories nearby. They bind flints to sticks, make tools, spears, toothpicks. They swap sharpened stone heads for antlers, seeds and – trinkets.

Trinkets!

Helm is enchanted. Trinkets are either very helpful or very pointless. Trinkets are desirable and valuable; they mean something that Helm cannot understand; they are items Helm cannot hold.

The forest smokes closer. Noise of trees crackling and sap hissing, branches thumping down, timber being dragged and chopped. Sounds of loud trilling shouts after silent hunts, and singing. They are definitely coming, across the hills and bogs and the willow-filled broadlands, over waterways on canoes; they lay stones in the shallows for others to cross, bridges – clever. They cook meats and smoulder herbs. Oh! Heavenly. Cue, predilection: Helm's love of smoke – campfires and coppicing, rushlights and paraffin, wacky baccy.

Then one, two, three of them step out from the arboreal shadows, into a clearing in the valley. Number one carries a child (four) slinged against her breast. Two has grey paws across his shoulders: he's inside a wolf. Three is bent and gnarly (could be either an in-y or out-y) and holds the fire-making equipment wrapped in moss. Eyes not on the sides of their heads, and a quick, macular gaze that isn't like other animals'. It's computerish, has guile, and some other quality Helm can't quite fathom yet. The old, wrinkled one looks up at Helm's mountain, at the sky above its summit. He/she points, draws an outline around nothing, circles his/her hands over each other, sucks in scarred cheeks and blows hard, shaking a head.

Here it is! Identification!

For Helm: elation. Helm is understood to be a feature, a concept. Today, absent. Tomorrow, possible. Returning. Powerful. Patterned. (And lo, meteorology is born.)

For the humans: error, danger, proximity to a bad oogabooga. They disappear into the forest. Cue, Helm's first rejection, abandonment, difficult emotions. Ouch. Helm smashes some trees and things.

But they do come back, cautiously, in little volleys, and with what can quickly be ascertained are tendencies. Skirmishing, partying, carving cups, draping themselves in fur, making smart headgear. Reproducing, carking it, burying their dead with vessels and trinkets, as if they will continue to drink and dress up underground (confusing: Helm blows away the grave soil. Nope, dead).

They speak, complicated babbles registering somewhere between a mammoth and a mouse. Helm learns some of their sounds. *No, milk, go, hurts.* They have words to differentiate things; to individuate selves. They grunt and moan when their different bits join together; watching this is strange, exciting, makes Helm feel—

Very cold, violent weather arrives. It renders Helm sluggish and unable to do business for a while. The valley floods and freezes. The humans leave. Lots of the animals leave as well, or perish, or evolve to be whiter.

Solitude and boredom again.

When the humans return, there are only a handful, better clothed, hair braided and combed, new fashions. They come with a proper survival kit: some cows that are less aurochsy, and a lot more trinkets. This mob seem serious about staying in the valley, regardless of Helm. They make settlements, piling up middens, using latrines. They are very influential. They consume the forest and deer and boar and fish. They gain dominion over predators using spears, torches, collectives and friendship – they convert wolves into dogs, neat trick! Grass grows, and there's pollen everywhere; it blooms through Helm's air. They dig over plots of land, plant grain; they build homes from stones, thatch the roofs with ferns. Their trinkets are elaborate, crafted. In spring and autumn they leave trinkets at the foot of the big mountain, or hang them from branches, and Helm makes them tinkle and rattle. Is this – a relationship?

These humans are very entertaining. They entertain each other. They ferment drinks that make them silly and aggressive and lusty; they biff and boff and booze. Fantastic theatre.

Helm demolishes their shelters, kills one or two of them, not on purpose, but they seem to take it personally. They soon learn about Helm. Underneath Helm's base and rotor clouds, it is safe, calm: a feather can be dropped and will float softly to the ground. Between Helm's clouds is a ruinous, wrathful force where everything is cunted. They begin to treat Helm as a deity, like the sun, or the river. If Helm blows thunderstorms away and keeps the valley lightning-proof, they thank Helm. They kneel. They hold their arms up towards the mountain, which is very pleasing.

Helm begins to have favourite humans – the ones who pay particular attention, the ones with Helm-related opinions and ambitions, even oppositions. They want to define Helm. They make pictures: shape and substance like cloud and wind. Not quite right – Helm does not have jug ears like that. Then other ideas. Spirit. Attributes that are magical, abstract, woo-woo. Still not quite right, though understandable. Later: numbers, energies, bit reductive, but whatever. It's a problem of qualia, really. Show me me, Helm thinks. My whole.

Still, they're *aware*. They're contributing.

The settlers begin work on an impressive structure in the valley. Massive stones, rolled, dragged and shunted in; it takes them ages (not by Helm's standards, by theirs). It is actually indestructible, which is disarming for one so destructing. What is it for? A gift, maybe, a gewgaw, a puzzle? Wonderful, thank you. They congregate there, many more of them than Helm thought there were. Hmm.

Their making improves. Furnaces. Farms. Roads. Medicines to heal wounds and sadness and the shits. Baths. Wheels. Helm topples trees, uproots crops, overturns feed stacks, steals loose blankets. They rebuild, reweave, reknot, renail: better designs, stronger glue, neater stones (Romans, very anal).

Metals. A whole new range of shiny trinkets! Coins, bracelets, cutting devices for manicures and butchery, projectiles. Tombs, anvils, boats, villages, guns, portraits, fiddle toys. So many things, dropped and lost and mislaid, twinkling all over the place like a museum/junkyard.

Everything human complicates. Behaviours. Ceremonies. Personalities. Jokes. Sex . . . Confession: Helm *really* likes watching sex. The touching and mouthing. The fitting of parts together. Strange breathiness. A process that seems both mindless and physical, loving and animal. This voyeurism will later be held against Helm during the puritanical trend (big misunderstanding).

Human-fucking-beings. They are so fun and terribly worrying. When they cooperate, they can learn, improve, create extremely nice things. At worst, they're ruinous, dumb as mud, making mistakes over and over again. Lives as fast as fireworks too. Crackle, fizz, pop, extinguished. Curious model.

The humans change constantly, but want permanence, evidence of being and having been, it seems. Their language mimics the essence of things, evocations of items and experiences. *River, tree, sorry, adder, stink, future, plughole*. They name Helm's mountain. That name is forgotten and they name it again. That name is wrong and they name it again. The valley – after some Christian–Pagan bunfighting – is Eden. Seriously? OK, it is quite pretty.

More to the point, they have names for Helm, and those change too. Fine, Helm can be whatever they want Helm to be, so long as there is Helm. Until, in and around an unspecified aeon, approximately between longship and flea-plague eras, one name gets reused – stability, suitability, memory or legacy, doesn't matter, it sticks. Enough of them keep saying the same word, a title that is spoken, spoken, spoken, spoken, spoken, spoken, spoken, spoken, spoken, written down.

Got it. *Helm*.

II

Medieval woodcut

III

NaNay from the herding tribe is an old woman now. She has three scars on her chest. She has mushroom-grey hair down to her calves, twisted and braided into columns, and threaded with polished stones from the river shore. The people say her anma is as strong as the Halron. But they did not always listen to her.

NaNay stands between the gateway stones of Magsca with a long bast rope and a sharp wooden stake. This winter, on the smallest day, she will measure and mark the place where the magstone will stand, once it has been found. The ground is white and hard under her skin boots. Above, teal-blue sky like a fisher-bird; cloudless. The sun is weak, flying low and tired towards the horizon. Soon it will fall between the standing stones and go into the other world. She waits for the moment.

All NaNay's life, the people have been building Magsca, with its immense earthworks, pillars and stadium of mountains. Each stone has been hauled to the gathering place and raised. It has taken many generations. The forest people and the herders and the nomads from the caves all stripped the turf with bone shovels and dug the ditches. They sledded the slabs to the plateau from the quarries, across glades and around dense woodland, slowly uphill. Orox were roped to help pull each stone upright against frames, and the ground around filled with rubble. The stones live half above and half below worlds. The two largest form the gateway, through which the people and the anmas come and go. When the Halron enters Magsca, the stones haw and moan, like a great beast preparing its throat to bellow, or a powerful instrument.

NaNay stands still as a heron and waits. She has observed the solstice here forty-four times. In her seventh winter she did not come; she was sweating and shaking and vomiting from sick-meat, and she could not stand up or leave the hut to worship and dance with the others. Irla said to NaNay's Second Mother, *The child will die, let the cold make death quicker.* But Second Mother did not drag NaNay from the bed and leave her in the snow. She brought NaNay water from the rain container and dripped it slowly from her beaker. NaNay's stomach spouted it back; her body could not hold any moisture. The skin around her eyes was like dry grey moss, and slapping her arm brought no blue veins to the surface. Second Mother wrapped NaNay inside furs and blankets, and placed hot embers around her bed. She burned three woods above NaNay's head and blew smoke into her mouth.

Finally, Second Mother gave NaNay half-fin fungus to reject the poison. The fungus tasted bitter and faecal; it turned NaNay violently inside out until the vomit was colourless and streaked with blood. It killed her and it saved her.

In the delirium of half-fin, NaNay saw the magstone. She went beyond unconsciousness. She went beyond dreaming. Her anma left her body in search of the other world and rose above the valley. It saw the great observable land as the Halron could from the top of its mountain: orox in caravans grazing below, the smoking huts and kists, and the herders moving tiny as bark lice. There was a rushing sound. NaNay heard fast water or a storm wind, and wailing, which was Second Mother singing and calling over her because her body was dying. Her anma moved on a current that was a river of bright sparks or stars. She floated past many people, more people than the valley contained, people of different times, before and after NaNay. Then she stopped moving and everything became still, and unlit as the deepest cave. She saw the magstone. It came out of the darkness. It was red and huge. It had a face halfway down its body and a long,

13

thin head. The face was sorrel and where its eye should be there was no eye, only smooth blank rock, yet it was crying. Dark-red tears, the colour of blood let out after death. The mouth was closed and sorrowful and it did not speak. Around the magstone was a black orb, the sun in the other world.

NaNay woke. She blinked and Second Mother knew she was alive.

She was too weak to move, so Second Mother dripped water into her mouth from a beaker again and her stomach held it. Second Mother told NaNay her chest had been silent, her skin had cooled, as if her anma had been released. They had let her go to the other world and were preparing clay for her burial mask.

When she could sit up and speak, NaNay told Second Mother about the magstone. It was sacred. It was a vision of time. Knowledge had been given like a gift to her searching anma. She must discover its location in her lifetime and then the people must bring it to Magsca. It would stand beyond the circle and accept the sun at the weakest moment and in this way they would know winter was retreating, and life returning.
 I will not see it standing in Magsca, she said, *but I will find it.*
 Do not speak of this to Irla, Second Mother said. *He will not understand.*

But the vision was too important, and at the next meeting, after the trading and the death and birth counts, she did speak of it. There was silence and the people looked at the girl, then at Irla. Before Irla could do anything, Second Mother stood up beside NaNay. She told the people that because of the strength of the meat sickness and the half-fin, because NaNay had survived two poisons, like a scorpion's claws and its sting, she was now a seer. NaNay had travelled almost to the other world and back again, with nothing in her belly, with the

14

stamina of a wolf. What she'd seen was intended. The magstone should be searched for and brought to Magsca.

They sat down. The people talked loudly. They were confused that NaNay had survived death. They were afraid that she had returned without her anma. A vision so powerful could not be given to one so young, and it was dangerous, and its meaning was not clear. Other gathering places did not have a magstone. Time could not be measured in the way she spoke of. They knew NaNay was a last-born, death-exchanged: her mother had not released NaNay's join-sac completely and had bled and died, and it was Second Mother's milk that had nourished her. The leaders of the estuary and forest tribes told Irla he must decide what to do.

The next day, NaNay was brought into the smoke hut. On the fire, sage was smouldering. Irla told NaNay she must not speak of the magstone again. NaNay refused. She stood and stared at him defiantly. Second Mother argued with Irla when he said NaNay would be expelled from the village. *Choose another punishment*, she said. So Irla beat NaNay until she lay still on the ground and oozing from the splits in her skin. After she recovered, Irla beat her again, pulled out her hair; he told everyone in the settlement that she had no true wisdom and should start her knowledge again. NaNay was sent to collect acorns and elm leaves at the edge of the forest with the littlest ones. She was full of anger. She thought of the black sun that her anma had seen – it would have terrified anyone in the tribe but she had not been afraid.

She sharpened a tusk knife on the whetstone and she cut two deep lines across her chest for twice having a chance to die and not dying. She washed her chest in the river and it stung but she did not cry. She rubbed charcoal and stainberry into the wounds so that when her breasts finished growing the marks would still be seen.

15

The following winter, NaNay stood between the gateway stones on the smallest day and watched the sun moving low and faint behind a thin cloud, a reddish thumbprint in the sky. She knew the vision of the magstone was real and that there was a place for it alongside the circle. She would make the people listen and understand.

When the grassland melted and green shoots were released, she took her tusk and some smokemeat and went away from the huts, into the wildest part of the forest. She denned under the roots of a leaning tree, pulled broadleaves across to keep her dry and safe. Her body smelled in its crevices so she rubbed mud there and wrapped her food in docks and became invisible to hunters. After the smokemeat was gone, she collected dried hips, star weed, nettle and horn fungus. She was hungry but not hungry enough to return to the settlement. She saw slim bears moving through the trees, their wide black noses quivering, and she was not attacked. In the branches, cryptic animals moved between patches of their colour and hid again.

The women, led by Second Mother, looked for her in the forest and the forest tribe looked for her, but they did not find NaNay; their leather boots trod through the undergrowth, inches from her head. In the darkness, there was forest music. Nightbirds called: *Tie-tie-tie* and *Noowip*. There was screeching and barking and the boughs above her rubbed and creaked. Overhead, stars clustered in their milks. The fish stars swam slowly past, diving into deep space. A comet with two metastatic tails shone brightly towards morning.

After several days, a great stillness arrived within the leaves and she knew this was an indicator. The interior was vividly lit by shafts of sunlight. The forest silence went inside NaNay's head and told her not to be there anymore: she must not hide but go and search for her third mark somewhere else.

So NaNay left her den and began walking towards the mountains. She waded through the river and the glades. On the plain, where bushes had been burned, there were bright-green ferns and saplings and beds of bracken. She moved swiftly, looking in every direction to see if she was being stalked, but there was only a herd of orox in the distance and two herders with poles beside the animals. She crossed the low marshland on its loose islands of sprung moss, and when she reached the foot of the Halron's mountain she began to climb upwards. The Halron was the most dangerous thing she knew, its anma was seeable and fierce, and if it did not kill her, it would give her a third mark.

IV

Helm doesn't know from which direction Michael Lang rides into the Vale of Eden.

North, perhaps. Michael's not an Englishman by birth, though he was a Durham Cathedral scholar before becoming astrologer to kings and noblemen. Could be he rides across the Solway: he knows the shallow waths along the estuary, avoids ambush by shoreline bandits. None would dare – they'd recognise the glinting sallet. He can command Olwen out of sinking sand where other ponies paw and froth – *Aram, aram* – the back-step, an Arabic trick. Or he might come through the ruined borders, over the abandoned vallum and a collapsing mile-fort on the great wall – its heavy, uniform blocks being cannibalised for other buildings now.

Or from the east, possibly – favoured route of the early saints. Past the tall, ornate crosses of Northumberland, Michael swinging his leg over the saddle and dismounting, chipping away the sacred ash trees and Lokis, while the servant, Isa, his convert and companion, holds the reins. Far east, even, where Christ's birth-star always burns and holy wars are available; where he has exchanged mathematics with academics and acquired this beautiful, dark-skinned boy.

Not west. The west is impassable after a winter such as this one past, the year of the Great Charter. The vapours of the Celtic Sea bring back nightmares, scents of disease, blood, spice and cattle on the deserting Scandinavian ships, telltale notes wafting over the crags and peaks. West is Helm's cinema, and Michael wants the element of surprise.

South is most likely. He journeys by way of the remotest Premonstra-tensian abbey, with its failed tower and wild, productive territories, hunkered in the uplands beside the fast beck at Hepp. The white canons will host him humbly and with considerable discomfort: Abbot Redman knowing full well Michael Lang's reputation. The wizard priest. Rumours of rivers changing course under his duress, of consecrated bodies dug up. His infamous, awful helmet. Last time Lang was in the region he helped King John kill five hundred hinds. He exhumed a tomb under Carlisle Castle – the grisly contents of which won some argument – and petrified a coven of witches in Salkeld, encircling them in stone for dancing on the sabbath. Six-ty-seven, sixty-eight, sixty-nine: counting them off after violating them, magicking their imprisonment. Redman doubts the latter tale; the stone daughters are weathered, already ancient. But the rapes – one cannot be sure. Myth serves the cause.

South, then.

Michael comes fresh from some unsavoury business in Lancaster, or some convention to debate Fibonacci, octaval doctrine, the mass of hellish substances. Past the prison and the drenched Lune, up and across the corpse-road pass. From here, he can see the devil's brown spine, raised north-east, and its highest point, the lair. Beyond is the vast royal hunting forest of Inglewood – the hunting tally, to be accurate, was two stags, four hundred and eighty-seven hinds. Fiend's Fell has blue, untrustworthy skies above it. May well you hide, lar, he thinks.

Michael is as his name, a long traveller, preferring stout centurion-bred ponies for both himself and Isa. There's no side mule for the boy; the white-robed canons at the fishery note it at their approach across the moors. A low sun haloes Michael's head. The helmet gleams. He has passed around – no, through – the black upland mires. The legs of the ponies are filthy, their backs lathered with sweat. Not a large man,

19

but thick-haunched, with compacted brawn in the chest. Strangely apparelled – neither soldier's full armour nor nobleman's cloak; he is not robed as a holy man or scholar might be, but wears an ensemble of hood, fox fur and split tunic. Chimerical. The canons look down; Michael says nothing as he passes. The boy stares at the smoked trout, hanging tail-to-tail from the poles.

The abbey is rich by the austere standards of the order, cultivated beyond its high walls. Water has been directed from the heath to the ponds; its sheep are fat and trained to the fellside, and the hives and orchards well managed. Word reached them only last week about the visitor: there's been little time for preparation. Enough time for whispers and speculation, of course. Why is the oath-binder coming?

Michael enters through the gatehouse by the half-built tower, with Isa clopping behind him, and the abbot, jaundiced but otherwise hale, sees that the legend is true: half the man's head is made of iron. The skullcap, so heavy and tight-fitting, has bitten into and become the flesh; it glimmers under its patina, like corroded bone. Never removed – not for prayers or penitence, not even for sleep. Michael Lang has foreseen his own death: a strike to the temple, some foul missile meant to end him before God's work is complete; rock, arrow, a cantering hoof on the battlefield, the cloven hoof of Satan.

He dismounts and calls out, to no one in particular, least of all the abbot who is waiting with customary hospitality, arms tucked into his woollen sleeves.

I am not, as you can see, one hundred years old.

The eyes are mirthless, austere as slate. No detectable humour to the words, though it may be some manner of jape designed to stir the solemnity of the place. Michael glances about, professionally, like a general surveilling camp. Redman comes forward, thumbs tucked, and nods.

Deo gratias, Brother Lang.

Michael nods also, issues instructions for the ponies: Olwen is not to be touched by anyone except Isa. The abbot winces. At Hepp, every man works and none has a servant, but the request seems not in concordance with their rule, more a brand of arrogance.

So, he has arrived. The great Michael Lang.

It is Lent. It is spring, just and so, after a brutal, frigid season, a season of lewd solicitous fox calls and eagled carcasses. As yet the branches are bare, or larval, buds like the tips of miniver brushes. The fist of winter is loosening; streams have begun to drool and trickle, and the pope's exorcist has appeared like thrax from the melted core. Abbot Redman admonishes himself for the thought, and Michael notes his recourse as a falcon would the vole's swerve along the banks. Here, amid the white canons, is a learned Vatican-sanctioned man, cleanser of the worst corruption and sin, a true son of Solomon. His pony carries across its flanks fine Persian saddlebags containing items of such powerful ordnance one should not even approach them. He doesn't want them handled or broken. Here is a man who has crossed continents, who has mastered Latin, Hebrew, Arabic, and can expel any demon from any occupied body, be it heathen, Saracen or Christian.

Michael Lang has been dispatched by high order, or has come of his own accord. Alarming though his presence is, he must be honoured as any pilgrim. He is kissed by the abbot and brought inside. A chamber is readied for him, an alcove for the boy. In the refectory, he is given good barley bread and the last of the apples, roast mutton. Such food seems profligate before Easter, but the Hepp canons are blessed, the previous harvest has given ample. Lang is known to enjoy feasts.

The boy waits to be instructed, then he eats, with the right hand. He does not touch the meat. An unearthly boy, angelic almost. The canons

21

note this too, disquieted. For as raw and scarred as Michael is – what sore mess must be smothered under that sallet – the servant is fine. Honey skin. Dark and oily eyes. Blackish, curling lamb's hair. Michael's is patchy and thin, or gone, killed by its hard covering. He catches the abbot's staring. He tears the bread crust, feeds pellets into his mouth.

I notice your keen interest in Isa, Abbot Redman. His family was slaughtered – every last one. I cannot say every last soul, for they were faithless. How many years ago, Isa?

The boy swallows, and swallows again, ensures his mouth is clear, as if about to speak. He looks at the abbot. He holds up five fingers of one hand, one finger on the other. Palms soft, unlined; whatever menial duties he performs for his master are not especially callusing. Is he mute?

Yes. Six years ago. That is when he became mine. He was old enough to remember the horror – within formation, as you brothers would say.

Praise the Lord for his salvation, says Abbot Redman. But the *mine* is troubling.

Michael nods.

Indeed. I also notice your interest in physiognomy. The way you are searching about my countenance. Tell me, Abbot. What is my relation? Not the lion, surely. My father's nose was narrow and I am his beneficiary. High forehead, were it exposed, though I will assist you immediately – I care not for the arts, it is often as not devil's sport. Have you noticed another detail yet?

He pauses, permits the abbot a moment of excruciated observation; he leans across the table, stares unblinking. Abbot Redman flushes red above his fleece, shakes his head.

No? Very well. I suffer from fixed pupils: they cannot dilate nor contract. Light is therefore often uncomfortable for me. Now. Can you interpret my nature?

The abbot stammers.

I, I have no skill in such a practice. I would not judge a man based on his face.

Ah. You think it not a suitable method, then? But is there no exhibition of the true self in a fellow's expression, his structure, in his colouring and composite?

It is a test, of course, some form of modern dogma. The abbot inflects, tells Michael that the white canons, while they were based at Blindbeck in Kendal, preached to an enclave of lepers, many of whom had purer souls than the misfortune of their disfigurements suggested. Michael chews the bread, seems disappointed. There are, now the abbot is looking properly, black, immovable nailheads hammered into Michael's irises. His mouth elongates – a smile?

Rest easy, Brother, I am quite used to being observed. The one I am here to confront is likely watching now, from nearby or from afar; I cannot yet say.

A week of unease passes in the abbey. The white canons pray not to be Michael's accused as they go about their chores. Between services, they tend to the abbey's work and their pastoral duties. The two guests seem unnaturally lodged, spelks in the body of St Magdalene's. They do not attend high or votive masses to honour the Virgin. Michael reads on the cloister bench where the light is good, parchments which should not be removed from the library, modest though the library is. The boy strokes and whispers to the ponies as he feeds them. He receives daily lectures from Michael and is shown manuscripts. *Andronicus,* the abbot overhears Michael say, *good, that is correct,* though the boy is not, is never, heard to speak. Every day, they walk up the high moors, taking with them a glass looking-device and a copper weathervane.

At table in the refectory, Redman stares at the tarnished helmet, faintly sickened. He waits to be told something. Michael tells him nothing. The abbot will feel it all the more keenly, he knows, auditing the accounts late into the night, sifting through possible breaches of rule, monies, taxes – the order's French legacy has strained relations with the Crown, and this, of course, is beneficial to their tormentor, if irrelevant. Hugo of Leicester came to St Magdalene's disgraced last year; Michael is aware of the transgression, and the bastard child, but Hugo is not interrogated.

During his stay, he dispels some of the Langian myths, reinforces others. He did not uncover the plot to murder King John, but has travelled with him to France, and advised on judicial administration. He does carry an anatomic relic – a section of the rib of Christ, in a silver gilt box made by Anglian smiths. This is not displayed, but is verified as they tour the abbey and discuss equipment. The abbot boasts about their wonderful bronze-headed plough, exceptional in the rough northern terrain.

Tools will civilise Cumberland, he says, *before the word of the Lord.*

Curiosity gets the better of him.

How came you by your holy item? I have heard that it radiates, as the body of the son of God did in ascension.

Michael places a firm hand on Redman's shoulder. The heat of the appendage, like boiled ham.

Aye, it shines with hallowed light, he concedes, *but is kept in darkness, where it cannot blind.*

Were this relic to be unboxed, would the abbot see its terrible, occult nature, spliced as it is with horn – from which ungodly creature? – and bound rudely with animal hair? Perhaps.

The wizard priest carries other weaponry: a mirror wrapped in Galilean linen, holy water, a book, which also cannot be shown, containing Psellus's diabolical itemisation and Michael's own doctored versions.

Such a document would be catastrophic in the wrongs hands, Abbot.

24

A manual beyond the ken and capacity of backwater pastors, then; no need to infer further, Redman understands perfectly well.

When Michael speaks, it is absolutely, with unquestionable conviction. Lessons on the demonic, warnings. Down table, the canons listen attentively, transfixed, appalled. Invisible servitors of malevolence are as common as flocks of geese or shoals of perch, he informs them, inhabiting every elemental sphere: marine, subterranean, aerial.

Shape-shifters. Infiltrators. Aerial monsters are invoked by sorcery, and create at every opportunity natural disasters. What they want, Brothers, is to be as close as possible to the human body, to enter it and be garnished by its blood. They borrow our form, they harness us. And I shall tell you what they enjoy most: obscenity. They penetrate the lewd and slippery ports of desire. They crawl into the openings of wanton women, into the mouths and rectums of fools in farces.

Here is their clue, though it passes them by.

Isa sits in the alcove behind his master, still and neat; a trained sparrow, other than his unusual blue shawl, pinned at the shoulder. He has been baptised, and renamed, but God sees what moves under titles, as magma courses under Earth's crust. His salvation seems apocryphal. Found in a burning stable, uncharred: the only survivor. Isa listens to his own story being told. Those black, immaculate eyes, tethered to Michael. Redman glances between the pair, no doubt trying to fathom what the arrangement is, whether it is sinful. For the boy is an over-make – is being taught Greek, and a dialect of Cumbric, perhaps even the necromantic texts. He is unnecessarily beautiful.

And Michael? Yes, at every moment, Michael is as formidable as his reputation, and doesn't exhaust himself. As if a hawk has perched on the coops, the abbey shuffles and clucks. The canons stoop when he passes in the dim corridors, as though their guts feel softer, plumper.

Redman continues to host as graciously as he can. He guides Lang through the gardens. In the kitchen, he gives Michael a small wooden bowl containing honey from the indigenous bees in the woods. He jabbers about the Lord's bounty, its exceptional taste and medical properties. The wax is rendered into balm, used to dress wounds. Michael tastes without visible pleasure, teeth viscous. It's like feeding nectar to a crocodile. There are patches of abraded, scabrous flesh around the hemisphere of the skullcap. Such perverse discipline, the bending of predestined law. He lets honey drizzle off the spoon, back into the bowl, and watches the abbot's nerves fraying.

The abbey is being cooked in a slow stew of ignorance; it is being self-indicted. They all know the rules. Where there are exorcists, there is foulness, actual or imagined, revealed or fabricated. He could tell them of his interest in the high moorland above Hepp, which doesn't include the Herdwicks, the bricks of peat or barrels of elm leaves. He could explain why he walks past the enclosures every day, up onto the tops, where there's nothing but wind and rain and the odd imperial hare, to a discreet lookout point. But it is so enjoyable, watching men squirm.

Finally, Redman plucks up his courage.

I hope you find that we at St Magdalene's are, as our robes would have us, the humble, devoted servants of our Lord and pilgrims?

Silence. The click of a tongue unsticking from the mouth's roof. Michael places the honey spoon on the table. He stares at the abbot, his blue, unresponsive eyes impossible to look away from, then moves to kiss him on both cheeks. Redman roots himself to the ground.

I do, certainly. All is commendable and righteous in your house.

The abbot's throat slackens. He finds he can breathe. So, all he had to do to be saved from the oath-binder's vice was break, and be seen to break.

Might we then assist you in your clandestine mission here?

26

Michael releases the abbot.

You cannot, which is unfortunate. Tomorrow we will leave you. This is unquestionably the best honey I have tasted. I would take some of your product of the comb, if there is sufficient.

On their departure, the abbot presents his guests with bread, sheep's cheese and a jar of bee balm. Isa fetches the ponies. Michael bids Redman farewell. The white canons close the gate, and peace is restored.

From the abbey, the travellers ride across rolling country, to the fortified town of Appleby, thinned of personnel and pitted with graves from plague and endless border raids. They ride up a wide avenue of limes to the castle, where the baron is absent, his wife and daughters cower at the window, and mastiffs slather and strain against their ropes. Another Scottish dispute is under way, beacon fires flaring in the night sky; the slaughter can almost be heard echoing down from the city of Carlisle. Appleby has a bad smell, raddled livestock, cesspools; its residents are gaunt-eyed, starving and embattled, unable to cultivate the fields or make proper arrangements for the dead. They are not flattered or terrified by Michael's banner, nor his machined head: they are beyond such feelings. All around is the chaos of hell. He might simply be the fourth horseman, heralding a merciful end.

There are shoddy barricades around the moat, over which Olwen tramples, snorting. Michael pounds the studded oak door, demands entry, but he is not here to war with his original kinsmen, or with any man. Inside the fortified hall there's rindless bacon, hoarded silverware and huge debt to the king. The women are ghosts beside the tapestries, of no more substance than thread. Use of a longhouse is agreed.

They stay a night only, to rest and water the ponies, to take their bearings, then they move on. Up along the brisk, unferried river, towards Blencarn and Salkeld, the place of witches and giants, the foothills. Towards the unholiest of all English mountains – Golgotha reborn in the north. Now they raise their hoods, woollen and furred; two anonymous riders in the vale of the demonic Helm.

V

So come the best and shiniest trinkets of all – trains!

The railway, from Settle to Carlisle. Into Eden, foot by Silurian foot, inch by igneous inch, it is blasted and hammered, raised across becks and moors, hoisted through the air on great Romanesque piers. Across backwaters the tracks are laid, riveted, soldered, bent and bolted, in the greatest engineering feat of the age. Twenty-one viaducts over mires and ravines, fourteen tunnels pounded through granite and lime; immortalised by scope, by collateral damage, by their own beautiful names.

Dent Head.
Arten Gill.
Long Meg.
Crosby Garrett.
Crowdundle.
Sheriff Brow.
Blea Moor.

Helm Tunnel: 571 yards of reinforced subterranean wall, directly in the eponymous bore, thus foiling vainglorious attempts to cowp the locomotive.

But queen of all the constructions at Batty Moss swamp is the colossal Ribblehead Viaduct. Twenty-four magnificent arches, a hundred and four feet high – a thing so tall and long and extraordinary it will sponsor the expansion of local graveyards as more and more men die building it.

So come the freight cars, rapidly and rhythmically, clanking through the valley, carrying sago, mutton, coppice-wood, charcoal, woollen quilts, spice, swill baskets, gunpowder. So come the passengers, on their way to business in Glasgow and Edinburgh; mill merchants, stockbrokers, agriculturalists, tourists.

But wait. Hold up. Reverse.

Before the crates of lamb and grain, the antimacassar headrests and tepid tea urns, before the ladies in long walking skirts, and Jocks and Southerners, first come the surveyors and engineers from the Midland Railway Company, arguing about topography and expenses.

Are you off your rocker, Peabody says to Crossley, looking out across the bleak North Yorkshire terrain. *This area cannot be drained, nor spanned. It's a quagmire, a veritable sinkhole; it is quite simply terra horribilis.*

Untrue. This is the age of can-do, of unstoppable industry; another Steam Mania, the newspapers say. It is the age of poverty and transitory labour; one man will do what the last could not, or did until his untimely demise, for only a shilling or two. Crossley is known for his lengthy stride and a frozen smile, his brushed mustachio and tenacity.

Certainly it can, my good chap. We will double the depth of the piers, and we will add six more arches. Indeed, Ribblehead can be done, and is, but not without moral compromise and excessive coffers.

So comes the Act of Parliament, and the moolah – lots to be spent and lots made between England and Scotland – and the blueprints for stations, the contracts for stationmasters, for boiler smiths, signalmen, stokers; opportunities for sandwich stalls and posy sellers on the platforms, penny-benders, et cetera.

Then come the railway workers. Navvies. In their hundreds: a marauding invasion of Helmland. On foot like the undead, riding scrub ponies

30

and hanging off carts, they come down the unmade roads – packs, clans, families, whole and transient communities. Welsh, Irish, English, Eastern European, unnamed, unnumbered, criminal, extremely good at their work. Each crew has a leader, two degrees cleverer and two degrees lazier. Lester Blunt. Wheeler Jones. Joe the Red. Peg; just Peg, because everyone knows Peg, with her gold tooth and her pinch box, her quiet Goliath boys; everyone knows not to cross Peg. It is said Peg removed the hand of a man who'd paid her a ha'penny short. How? A machete. She never! God's honour! The whole sorry lot of them are ready to kill each other, for the sake of nationhood, vendetta, navvy law, if dynamite and disease don't kill them first.

Also in tow come their wives. Their sick, unschooled children. Their tents and their musical instruments, their brandy stills and bake kilns, their shoddy boots – tied together, toeless, nailed at the heel, mended, resurrected, stolen, resoled – their pickaxes and shovels, the incred-ible capitalised machinery of their muscles. And in come the side economies: prostitutes and pote sellers, cockpits and canteens, tin chapels, the old, tired sot of a doctor servicing too many patients – Christ in a Hole, what vile act has he perpetrated to end up here; which war has desecrated him sufficiently for this position? – not to mention the under-politicians herding the rabble, inciting the crews to push harder for a mere pound more.

So come one thousand horses. *Woah, there!* Work ponies, dray mares. Hulking, feather-footed Clydesdales and Shires – draught breeds all called Samson, Mammoth, Titan and Brawny. In the plains beneath the Pennine range there's a herd so large it's as if the wild prehis-torics have returned. Helm straightens their manes, lifts their tails, incites stampedes.

Up go the shanty towns, mushrooming along the rivers and heaths, under the stretches of air where viaducts will be raised. Batty Moss

Hole. Belgravia. Jericho. Gallows humour to their names, but it's no joke to go there. Nor is anyone invited to, because there are already teachers, of a sort, preachers conducting fast masses and funerals, vigilantes with truncheons. Though, what is education in a labour camp, what's law and order and morality after a pittance in pay and one rest day a year (Christmas)? Betterment? Civility? Fuck the Lord and the Lords of Industry. Fuck the books and the Hornies. Here instead are amputations, disfigurements, poison. Open wounds, infections. Venereal pus, septicaemia, gangrene.

Old Doctor Rot tries to make his patients lie down, but they get up, limp off, cauterised, half-blind, for they must work, they must work, they must work. Back to where the next cutting is being hewn out of shale and rock. Back to the lethal, towering skeleton of Ribblehead. They cannot imagine a tramway through the hills or across the gullies, but will swing at it, shovel rubble and haul the hods away, rag their ears when the fuses are lit. Doc plugs and stitches their gashes closed, removes fingers after a shot of whiteout brandy – one shot for him, one for the victim. He burns the severed body parts and bloody swabs, sends pathological gifts downriver to Carlisle. He yanks teeth, fashions prosthetics with leather pads and buckles, jerry-rigged legs, plaster-cast hands.

He tries to suggest, occasionally and quietly, *Fellas, should there not be a union* . . . But how to unite the fighting nations or the nationless, workers who will be replaced lickety-split by others if they down tools?

He tends the feral children, with their bent and stunted bones, their fevers and impetigos. He rounds them up off the moors where they are collecting puffballs to cook, or snails, or vetch, or nipple-cap mushrooms which they scoff by the handful, then sit dilated for hours watching the silly, jinking stars. They show him their favourite trick – the gunpowder cuff – pinches stolen from the supply store, worth getting beaten for if caught, worth the burn sores. He anoints them, smiles, chastises.

Johnny Leck, I do not want to see you here on my table with a singed arm again.

He hears the kiddies coughing all night long, whoop-whoop, choke. That damn wind makes them worse, whooshing down the slopes, congesting their chests, sending them loopy. Another cheap wooden cross goes up every week – every other day, it seems. Van. McMaster. Evans. Szabo. Unknown Woman (whore). So ragged in the bitter winter are the inhabitants of the camps, vomiting up phlegm, boiling leather and cabbages in cauldrons of soup. Then sweating in the North African sand-dusted heat of summer, in the terrible seasons of Ribblehead.

Underneath the stone beast is Batty Moss Hole, where the wives make rabbit stew. They make tallow candles and fur booties. They make ale and shinny. The braziers always glow – fires to dry their men's clothes. They construct turf-and-timber huts like the First People, but they don't make gifts for Helm; oh no, too busy, too rankled. They knit socks, darn britches, they feed the horses; mend, muck out, maintenance fuck. Doc Rot sorts their itching crotches and pustules, their burning piss, their pre-eclampsia; he lets them hold their stillborns longer than he should. Begged by a woman Peg knows, he performs a useless mastectomy. The tit hole is a wet red nest; he stitches the flap closed but it will not heal. The patient whispers on her pallet bed: *Thankyou thankyou thankyou thankyou.* Thanking who? Him for trying to save her? This scrape of life off her shoe? Or the green-winged creature waiting for her in the corner? Sepsis takes her. Peg clears her bunk – bits of enamelware, a carthen, the single coin in the mothy purse, *thank you.*

The doctor, drunk and burning sick inside himself, thinks, enough. He walks into the river by the Eamont Viaduct foundation, drowns, and floats downstream, his black coat winging like ray-fish.

It is all so antic.

It is all so tragic.

This beguiling soap opera, the unexalted congregation worshipping below Helm's mountain.

The line pushes north. Work does not stop, day and night, night and day, the tink-tonk of metal on rock, the rumble and patter of landscape rived apart and raining down, hiss of gas lamps, the endless cursing and song of men indentured, as if they are in church, or on ships, or at the matches. Glory and filth; filth and glory.

Only snow stops the labour, for a day or two; spate floods, or frozen ground. Helm stops the work with some big spring mischief. A black, ten-day Helm – one of the tallest clouds ever seen. The tents flap savagely in Jericho. Timberwork at the south portal of Helm Tunnel clatters down, stuns a stray cow; she's minced in camp before the farmer can collect the carcass; no one saw a thing. But the great brick arches of the viaducts remain, immovable as those off Segovia and Nîmes as wind moans and flutes and bassoons beneath their massive gussets. And who is to say Helm will not lift the damn locomotive off the track if Helm wants to?

Settle to Carlisle. Seven years to complete the line, with the slick, greasy efficiency of cash and the British class system.

On the inaugural journey, twenty-four miles an hour is recorded. Racing speed. A man sets his champion greyhound loose beside the passing engine. It's neck and neck, until Pinpoint Sally is distracted by a hare and veers away. Approaching Ribblehead, the locomotive brakes and slows. The engine driver sees the viaduct coming; not a matter of faith, but he finds himself gripping the cab rail. *Steady, steady, we are iron-clad.* His darling flies safely over. Soon the crossing is gone, the track curves and the driver looks behind: there are

Ribblehead's hefty thighs and proudly elevated back, spanning the impassable swamp, *certainly.*

Service is begun, timetables written, a complaints office opened. Clinker and lead are carried on flatbeds. Cud-chewers. Turnips. Whisky. Adventurers in velvet-seated carriages. Mornings, afternoons, evenings: same times every day, give or take a few peevish minutes, toot-toot, chuff-chuff, that lovely coaly firebox smoke fills the valley. Helm knows when they are due, watches them pass through – the *Duke of Cumberland*, the *Royal Scot*, the *Bluebell*, the *Little Quaker*. Helm becomes – ahem – a trainspotter.

The last part of the northern railway dial is finished; travellers can circumnavigate Cumberland and Westmorland in a day, and penetrate its interior. (Already the line is in to Windermere, the lake only a short walk from the platform. Wordsworth would shit a farthing!) Now Eden is accessible too, with its lesser-known attractions, its verdant clefts and moonscapes, its wind-pummelled citizens and long-reigning tyrant.

So here they come: the industrialists, the aproneers, the Romantic inheritors.

Here, too, with his trunks of equipment – barometers and wind roses and boyhood correspondence from Admiral Beaufort – comes our man from the Royal Meteorological Society. Newly chartered. Queen Victoria herself has shaken his hand, wanly and black-gloved, and the hands of his fellow members, all lined up in a genuflecting, besuited row. *I do so enjoy our weather*, she commented drolly, whereupon our man bowed and replied: *As do I, Your Majesty.*

And look! In through the window of the train carriage, next to his rattling first-class teacup, can be spied a notebook, which is aspiringly, if provisionally, titled: *The Complete Guide to Britain's Only Named Wind*.

Marvellous! It's about time someone wrote a book for Helm.

VI

Thomas Bodger, FRMetS.

Crag-hopper Bodger, or Bodge to the Society chaps.

Tombo to his wife, Sara.

He is no stranger to Züge and couchettes, having travelled extensively in Europe, most recently to the International Meteorological Conference in Vienna, and also to the Cape of Good Hope, and to the Catskills, where other katabatic winds (Helm's reprobate relatives) sweep down mountains, dementing the suffering souls below. Here he is on the choo-choo, with the blessing of the Society council, with personal and private funding, and capital-A Ambition for a scheme to rival Whitbread and Howard. The *Bluebell* chuffs along, exits the dour, damp Dales, enters damper, wilder Westmorland. Our man looks out of the soot-speckled window, down at the ghostly labour camps, then up at the graceful fells, his excitement barely contained. *Marvellous view, just marvellous!*

Thomas Bodger has a proclivity. He imagines very many things, all manner of animations and enterprises, born of concoctions in the lab, one supposes, where he has studied which properties to mix and what spectacular, colourful combustions will occur. *Tombo has the mind of a magic lantern*, his wife often says. *He simply loves imagining things*. Poor Sara; she would have liked to accompany him on this latest expedition, but alas. He gazes up at the largest of the lovely hills, imagines Helm on stage as if in a music-hall production: to begin

37

the act, Helm blows a kiss so powerful the *Bluebell* grinds to a halt, groans and tips off the new rails, uncoupling carriage by carriage into the chasm below.

He sips his bergamot tea, around its floating pad of sliced lemon. Not bad – a tad over-steeped. As the train rolls north, he contemplates the tea's journey by caddy and elephant, by boat and barge – all the way to Cavendish's, then upcountry to the warehouses of the railway company, where it boarded the train, was brewed in a gargantuan copper kettle and poured into the china cup in his hand. What a world he lives in. He strokes his tidy beard, sets the cup back in its saucer, where it shuttles a little, and wonders how his apparatus is faring back in freight, fragile as it is.

Sit to the right of the carriage, he was advised by the conductor: less scenic, but better for viewing Batty Moss and the brooding uplands. Garsdale, Kirkby Stephen. The small, ingathered towns pass by, ancient ruined castles with ginger cattle grazing around their mounds, whitewashed village churches. He flips through his notebook, considers again the calculations for his plan. An operational formula is still needed, and he fully intends to apprehend one. There's an explosion of splendid sunshine on the fellside, which Thomas, engrossed with diagrams and numbers, misses. Nor does he see, when the carriage veers slight west, then slight east, a dark belt of rain following the *Bluebell* upcountry. Ho-hum. Typical northern summer.

He pushes the notebook away, and begins a letter to his wife in Blackheath: *Dear Sara. I earnestly hope your health is improving and that you are able to enjoy your walks again, or at least the garden. I do wish you were here with me.*

Difficult to write, not merely because of the frotting table. He glances up at the Pennines again, green as cooking apples and Saxon brown.

He doesn't wish it. Once he did, but he understands now her presence would be compromising, difficult for them both. She would try to accompany him up and down the mountain; she would suffer quietly, until he insisted she didn't, then guilt would have him attend to her disappointment. The days when they were travelling companions are sadly gone, but one must say the right things, be encouraging. Meanwhile, he is back in the uplands, alone, where the weather is large and animating, where one might achieve superior things, and this is really quite fine by him.

He peruses his notebook again, flicks through the correspondence tucked at the back. The component parts needed for his experiment have been sourced. Permission has been granted from the Earl of Lonsdale ('Lolly Lowther', Glaisher insists on calling him) to construct on his land – rather resignedly, it should be noted, in a tone that suggests every bod and bugger in the empire is applying for permission to build some folly on his estate. The Society council members are, though he's been roundly roasted in the way of the old boys, rather excited by his expedition. So much so that at the last meeting Glaisher informed him the president would be stepping aside the following year, should he wish to consider . . . Haha, a little jest, but one never knows. He cannot recall the exact moment of permission sought from Sara and granted, such are the miasmas of marriage. He may, once the project is established, travel into the Lakes, see about purchasing a waterside plot on which to build a charming little lodge for her, land being sold off at a lick as it is. Then, yes, Sara can most certainly come, and they may discuss the issue of children, whether her health can sustain that other project.

The *Bluebell* brakes, clanks and slows. At Langwathby, beside the neat, gingerbread station house and floral planters, he gets down. The stationmaster is there to meet him and has arranged for transfer of his baggage by the porters to the back of a hired carriage, which will take him out to the village of Glassonby, then on to Grange House. There, Colonel Brooke, whose wife is a cousin twice or thrice removed on Sara's side, Thomas can't quite remember the specifics, will host him. He has been warned by Sara not to expect London-grade hospitality.

Rebecca was a touch odd, but I'm sure she's outgrown it. She was a de Peyster before she became Brooke. They lost the hall, but I'm sure the new house is pleasant enough.

Comparative luxury – the Brookes have also organised a tiny tenant cottage for him at the foot of Cross Fell, a bolt-hole from which he might oversee project assembly, and sprint uphill, when sprinting is required.

He walks with the porters, rests a hand on one of the trunks. *Good work, chaps, upsy carefully.* In these trunks are the cupped anemometer, thermometers attached to balloons, the camera tripod, glass plates, his journals on British climatic systems, and – sentimental, really, no reason to bring them – his personal letters from Sir B. In them, more importantly, are the schematics for the device he has entitled – the Revelation Machine.

His carriage is waiting – more a hooded trap than a hansom, the driver all crags and crow's feet. The trunks are roped down; Thomas tugs the fastenings. Five minutes later they are struggling along the catastrophic boneshaker of a track to Glassonby. The suspension squeaks and jounces as the carriage sways. Thomas's jaw clenches. His posterior begins to feel tenderised, like a piece of beaten steak. The driver seems impervious to the battlefield ruts. Eden, as Thomas looks about, bears more resemblance to Nod than to its suggested Paradise, turgid and swept as it is now by the belt of rain that followed the train north. Behind the seat, the trunks tip and bonk together.

Do mind, please, he exclaims, but there's no response; the coachman is hunched inside a waxed cape, chewing something productive.

May as well begin the research, Thomas thinks.

I say, any sign of your Helm wind lately? he asks.

The driver coughs and spits brownly.

Bin and gan yam.

Oh, blast!

Aye, it did.

Ahead, the billowing Pennines. They do not compare with the Alps or the Dolomites, but they do have a certain presence. Cross Fell breasts a fraction higher than the others as if to claim the victory tape. It dominates, no denying, but is not quite the *unassailable bitch* that he described to the Society members last month in their club, emboldened as he was by Madeiran port and a letter received from Symonds Foundry in Millom outlining a very acceptable price per foot of iron.

Naturally, there's no ominous cumulonimbus over the summit. Just cobwebs of rain drifting about. Of course, he had not – had he not? – expected the Helm's presence upon his arrival, as if fate might manifest itself conveniently, as if it would perform with the punctuality of a lifted theatre curtain, simply because he had procured a ticket. Now he is here, the enterprise seems perhaps a little less valiant than he outlined. Questionable, as it had been rigorously questioned by his peers before the cheque was written.

There's no such thing as unassailable anymore, Bodge, if approached right. Glaisher, also half-cut on port at the club. *They said it about Mont Blanc a century ago, and now she's crawling with hoppers like you. Anyway, this phenomenon of yours* – Glaisher paused, attending to a moment of reflux, then spiralled his finger around like a tornado in the smoke of his cigar – *you will be getting proof, won't you? All jolly fine performing an experiment, but none of us are going to witness it in the arse-end of beyond. No yokel testimonials, please!*

Thomas leaned forward, hands on his knees, cheeks rouged.

I am. I intend to capture its very spirit and I shall record it in detail for the Quarterly.

Capture its spirit! Did you hear that, Fitz? Bodge is intending to have a windy seance!

There was much guffawing around the table, and Fitzroy hove in.

No doubt all those Aristotelian letters from local parsons about pabulums and nitrous vapours have seduced him. Bodge, I thought you had a chemistry degree, not a diploma in mesmerism?

Thomas continued to smile, good-naturedly.

Charles, never underestimate the value of the amateur's diary. Never dismiss oral evidence. Where would we be without it? Coleman's anthology, for example, describes the Helm as the Fury of Furies. Another account likens its roar to the deafening shuttles of a cotton mill.

Oh, very exhilarating, I'm sure. But how, my dear chap, are you going to apprehend this wind? Wrestle it to the ground? Bottle it? It doesn't sound very cooperative, not like a lassie in the hay, hey!

More guffaws.

Thomas stood and set his glass down carefully, gesturing for his coat and hat to be brought.

I'll get evidence. I am going to photograph the spectacle myself. And I shall make two types: one for the Society's magazine, and one for your water closet, Fitzroy. Ventum occurrit ventum. Gentlemen, I bid you all goodnight.

Glaisher spluttered and clapped a hand vigorously on the arm of the chair.

Bravo! Yes, you should mind your onions, Fitz! Pop a drop more ruby in there for me, William . . .

Now, sprinkled by rain and clunking about in an agricultural-grade carriage, the mountain in question doing nothing more than reclining on the horizon, it seems he may have overdressed the enterprise. No matter, he tells himself. Patience. Preparation. Pertinence. He shall gather his materials, study the vicinity and wring the district of

42

information, though perhaps not his driver. Peering through the drizzle, he can already see signs of Helm's onslaught. Reinforced bothies. Woven hawthorn windbreaks. The high walls surrounding the few substantial properties they pass do not suggest extensive land and wealth, as with those estates in Norfolk or Gloucestershire, more fortification, defended steads. And there are workers' cottages with aerodynamically rounded chimneys; vegetable plots and coops also enclosed by tall hedges.

They enter a village and pass a green where a local fete is being dismantled. A ring of hay bales have had their stalks scattered westwards. Bunting, unstrung from poles, flaps disconsolately on the ground. Beside a tipped lemonade trestle stands a woman in a bonnet from another era and a man wearing a battered bowler tied under his chin with twine. They gawp as Thomas's carriage passes. Yes indeed, the Helm has been abroad, and has only recently exited the scene.

Good afternoon! he calls, touching the brim of his own hat, and wondering how he might tie it down with a little more – panache.

VII

Selima stands beside the little Formica kitchen unit in the field station, waiting for the electric kettle to boil. It is taking for ever. Power from the temperamental generator, two thousand feet up on the mountainside and battered by the weather. Occasionally the overhead lights flicker, threatening to quit. She doesn't even try to charge her devices here, least of all the bike. The water in the kettle remains pond flat. God knows where it comes from – some questionable underground source on Great Dun Fell; sheep pee and giardia, best not to think about it. The Centre for Atmospheric Science clearly hasn't been upgraded since the sixties, when the university had a permanent weather observatory here, before the colossal radome was built. The station is, more or less, on the site of the original research hut, a black-and-white photograph of which hangs on the wall – a heroic, plank-and-tin shack half-buried in snow, long since collapsed. Her colleague David, who's been here multiple times, since the era of acid rain, did warn her.

It'll be like a trip back in time, he said when her research funding came through. *Remember to pack your dungarees and some LSD.*

There are two cups to choose from: one chintzy china number with a chip in the rim, one with the West Brom football club logo on. She pops a dusty teabag into the chintz, because, well (*those were the days, my friend*), Come On, Wolves! She must remember to bring a nicer one from the apartment. If a converted bothy with a macerator toilet, in a farmyard smelling of cow dung and chickens, can be called an apartment. The bothy has a hobbit-sized log burner, though, a big west-facing gable window and its own charming, rustic bijou. It's as

44

close to the bottom of Great Dun Fell as she could find for the ten-week stint. An hour-long commute along country lanes and up the chicaning mountain road on the Eleglide, pedalling the manageable bits and using the booster to buzz past the Lycra-clad cyclists bagging their Pyrenean-style category 2. *So long, drumstick-legs!* There's not much in the nearby village – a tiny, community-run general store, a mossy bus shelter where desultory youths gather, and the Horse and Farrier.

The kettle begins making a throaty noise. Selima stares at the forlorn teabag, then out through the porthole window. The summits of the range are obscured by broth-coloured cloud. They are covered by cloud two-thirds of the year: ideal for her purposes. In the three weeks she's been here, April, and into May, the cloud cover has more or less maintained these stats. Whoever left the pair of binoculars on the kitchen counter was either having a laugh or being ridiculously optimistic. Such a situation would send most people potty, Selima thinks, being enveloped by drifts and drizzle, day after day after day. But, in all honesty, it is quite nice to be blanketed, to be disappeared from the world, if only temporarily. No department meetings, no students – apologetic, late, turning in AI-'assisted' papers, prone (when did they become so emotional?) to tears. No dementing university admin. No chance of running into Gaurav on campus and having to have another awkward exchange.

Hey. I tried to call you, but maybe you've a new phone? Are you all right?

Yes, fine. You?

Erm, not really. I was wondering if we might be able to talk.

Oh, look, sorry, I can't, late for—

No need to open work emails, or the messages from deniers that now arrive regularly. Terrible phone signal at the station, she's told everyone she doesn't want to talk to, which is, for the most part, true. It takes hours for messages to download sometimes – her sister's crazy photos, of a new piercing (*You're running out of ear cartilage, Nita*) and her hideous, hairless, pedigree cat (*Looks like a gremlin, it was how much, just, why?*) and her hipster bikini (*Too much information!*). David, old-school texter, sends daily enquiries.

Doing OK up there? Got cabin fever?

All good, just me and the microplastics hanging out. Field station decor looks like your office, Grandpa.

Haha. Any sign of Mrs H?

Negative.

Grey swathes, drizzle, low visibility. It is amazing when the cloud parts, though, and great, streaming hunks of landscape appear, the long, lumpy view of the Lake District, and Scotland.

She paces to the window on the other side of the building, which is filled with the reticulated panels of the monstrous white radome. God's golf ball. It dwarfs the field station twenty to one, and its big, ugly, cracked shell holds the Civil Aviation Authority's northern surveillance radars. It hums or purrs, emits some form of vibration; she can hear it and feel it every time she approaches the summit on Ellie. She's never seen anyone enter or exit, though it's supposed to be manned by engineers. Oddest of all, given it's a key part of air traffic control, only a small barbed-wire fence protects the complex and the meteorology station. A rain-faded No Trespassers sign plonked by the cattle-grid.

You'll want to take a decent coat, David also warned her. *Gets bloody parky up there – subpolar oceanic bordering on alpine tundra, actually.*

Yeah, thanks, Professor.

Drink lots of hot drinks.

Easier said than done, given the underperforming kettle. But she did buy a giant puffer jacket for the secondment, which has seldom been removed inside the field station and, though described as damson, is a purple shade inexistent in nature. Plus, pull-on waterproof trousers for the bike ride up, which will never, not ever, be worn back in Manchester. Anita would absolutely hate it here, as, no doubt, would her bald puss.

That's totally prehistoric. Aren't you freezing your baps off, Lima?

She is. But it's a good distraction. Stops her craving a fag. Stops her ruminating, and feeling other feelings.

David, definitely more the weekend-warrior type, was the last one here from the department, a year ago. On sabbatical from radiation measurements, but working on his pet obsession, about which he has published several papers and one small, modestly selling commercial volume (actually quite a good read). Modelling, as they all now must, climate alteration and its interruptive effect on local weather systems.

Needs to be more pithy, mate. The Death of Mrs H, Selima had joked. *That sounds like a classic.*

It was quite funny, until his 'other wife', Sandra, was diagnosed with cancer, stage 4. A subject they both avoid, mostly, weather being a much safer, if not entirely blithe, topic. Before leaving Manchester, Selima promised to send him her lab results, pollution posing one of the many challenges for the wind.

It's the next generation to the rescue. You trad raddists are so twentieth-century. Isn't it time to retire to Todmorden with the other beardies, get a greyhound and start doing ceramics?

At which David had chortled.

Cheeky.

It is true, though, the changeover, funding-wise, to her wheelhouse – airborne polymers being suddenly all the rage. Though not really suddenly: this is a point she's been trying to make for a solid decade.

They are everywhere. In the water, the soil, in fish and vegetables, her teabag. In the bloodstream, the testes, perhaps even the brain. Just that now it is mainstream news.

The kettle is rumbling anticlimactically. She opens her laptop, glances through unread emails. Department round-robins, an email from one of last year's supervision students, an ad for camping gear; thanks to the puffer jacket purchase, she has been inundated with offers, crampons (as if), Dryrobes (as if!), wicking underwear – must unsubscribe. And, oh dear, another message from the Endtrepreneurs. This is what happens when you've been on the *Today* programme. They all come out of the woodwork with inexpert opinions, Old Testament prophecies and bad puns. The last message from them – if it is a group, not some sad, lonely individual – was wildly unreadable. All about how she was peddling lies, about the few and the many in end-times, and something about Babylon. She'll leave that one until later.

Keep a record. And make sure you pass it through to Comms, was David's advice after the first couple of messages came through. *Probably just pests, but, you never know, it's best to be cautious.*

David's mob was the first to really come under attack, two decades ago.

It starts small, then goes full-on spy works and six o'clock news.

She laughed. *Maybe back in the days of espionage. Also, the news is twenty-four hours now?*

He gave her that look. Amused, and slightly pained.

The department makes light of the hack now, but David's life was overturned, his research skewed and taken out of context, publicly discredited. He was plagued by reporters, at his office, on his doorstep; for a year he stopped going out, then had a breakdown. Selima was a PhD student at the time, but everyone in the department was interviewed by the police. No wonder he likes to do the dad act.

The politics of weather – it's nothing short of a superstorm these days. US weather reporters are getting mobbed outside the studios. In the case of Tyler Lake, shot, for making one small suggestive comment during a report about manmade climate change. But, you've got to continue the job. Her 'other Papa' knew that. He was a pro at taking shit and getting on with it. His motto: *We must think of the positive version. We must all contribute to making it better.* Big ask, when half the patients on your first rotation are asking to see a white doctor instead.

After – six, seven minutes? – the violently shuddering kettle clicks off. She pours water in the cup, bashes the bag with a spoon. She sips the tea, looking out. Nice to watch the sky for a moment before starting work, to be part of the sky, actually: the field station seems like it's floating around the troposphere. The clouds drift apart and the summit of Cross Fell appears. She picks up the binoculars, focuses them. The dome structure at the top – a shelter of some kind? – looks bizarrely Ottoman. If it had a crescent on top it could be a mosque. She should walk over there; it's only a couple of miles along the pavement of the Pennine Way. She really should explore more. Check the samplers, replace the filters and have a wander. She hasn't been along the river or the Roman road yet; she hasn't visited the stone circle up the valley, though she's seen groups of New Age pagans with big cloaks and blue hair heading that way. She hasn't even been to the pub, where, according to David, *the best chips in Britain* are served.

She puts the binoculars down, tries, as ever, to resist thoughts of the day's first cigarette. That quivery cellular longing, so hard to ignore. *Don't do it, Selima.* She should distract her hands; type up the lab results. Or watch the latest video of Anita's freakish thousand-pound cat doing something silly. The clouds move. The han or mosque or whatever it is disappears from view. She reaches into her jacket pocket for the box of Silk Cut, which shouldn't have been taken out of

49

the bedside drawer in the bothy; shouldn't, in fact, have been bought from the village shop. She thumbs the cellophane strip. There's a No Smoking sign pinned on the wall of the field station – hilarious given the proximity of approximately no one in the vicinity. Alongside it is another old photograph, of the previous century's field station meteorologists – hoary, intrepid-looking chaps in big woollen turtlenecks and deerstalkers, with pipes tucked in their mouths. One is trouserless, for some reason, long johns sagging round his knees and crotch. Best to step outside.

The air around the field station smells freshly laundered. The grass underfoot is springy and dotted with tiny flowers. A gentle north-westerly breeze. No proper rain for several days, just the overhang. Invisible, of course, but the summit's vapour is loaded. The first batch of results from the HVS filters recorded very high counts. The challenge is knowing whether these microplastics are just being transported, as part of the general aerosol of crud, or whether they are actually encouraging cloud formation. Dr Lim, her co-investigator at Mount Tai, and their colleagues in Japan, have fairly conclusive evidence of the latter from their laboratory replications. Not that the Endtrepreneurs will give a shit about evidence. They demand *truth*, while denying science.

Pot and kettle, re avoidance. There's something about this remote observatory, its altitude, its seclusion; it's the perfect escape from real life. She could be anywhere. Antarctica, Galapagos, the International Space Station.

She takes a deep breath of damp mountain air.
  Yeah. Fuck it.

She unwraps the packet of cigarettes and pinches one from the soft ranks. She fishes around the other pocket for her lighter, prepares to light up, and hears the eternal voice of Dr Vihaan Sutar.

You should know better, Beta.
I do know better, Papa.
Set an example for your little sister.
Ha! You should see Nita party now. Girl has smoked all kinds of dope.

She turns her back to the breeze. Behold me, the looming radome insists.

I see you, big ball, she says.

Next to the structure, two antennae spire upwards from gravel beds. A pervasive, indeterminate hum passes through her body; in only three weeks she's become almost immune. It's a condition of the modern age – this reverberating, technological om. Phones, TVs, planes, boilers, substations, scanners: the cocktail-party noise of progress, of convenience, of everything that irradiates humans. Microwaves, chemicals, hormones. It'll all kill her, so she might as well choose . . .

The lighter wheel rasps. The flame pops up. She inhales a first intoxicating drag, shudders inside the big puffy coat, enjoys an immediate heady queasiness. Nicotine (0.1mg). Tar (low). Satisfaction (glorious). She exhales a giant plume across the grassland. Oh, the dissonance of committing pleasurable acts of self-harm. The cool carpe diem of secret transgression.

At least Papa never caught her – the incense stick quickly lit when she heard him arriving home. (For Anita it was easier: pills, swallowed, stashed, flushed.) How many patients did her dad have to inform across his desk? Hundreds. Thousands. Small-cell in the lungs, in the liver and the bones. Mesothelioma. Emphysema. All those Black Country workers, coughing their way out of his consultation room, back to their factory houses. He didn't have to lecture his daughters, really; they knew from his demeanour when he got home from the hospital. She didn't quite manage to hide it from Gaurav, who said,

51

But you'll have to stop when we have children. David still doesn't know. He'd be mortified, but would probably see the delightfully ironic side too: a cloud pollution analyst adding her own share of toxic crap to the atmosphere. It's just too good to quit.

VIII

Trinket 7,861
Tobacco pipe

Vulcanite and briarwood. Stem is bent, with curvature towards the mouthpiece and tooth marks from excessive clenching/overbite. The wooden bowl has a natural finish and is waxed, with a flat bottom to enable it to stand upright when not in use. Interior has staining, tar residue and metallic filter (corroded). Maker's mark – Saint-Claude, 1924. Previous owner – Morris 'Moz' McClay, tempestologist; author of *An Energetic Mountain* and *The Mechanics of Föhn*.

Height – 11.5 cm
Width – 4.4 cm
Weight – 49 grams

Location – inside metal tobacco tin, Great Dun observatory foundations

IX

NaNay was halfway up the Halron's mountain when orox began coming down in single file. Their heads were lowered; they were snorting and kicking past each other to get ahead. Birds had begun flying back towards the forest, fast and direct, their wing muscles working methodically. There were no scavengers beside the carcasses on the hillside. White cloud was spilling over the mountain and streaming towards the valley. The air felt colder, flowing past her skin, a dry ice-mist, and she knew what this meant.

The Halron had seen her approach. It was growing taller in the sky, flaring across the hills either side. In the centre it was blue-grey, like bull hide, with the dull pearl-shine of scales at its edges. It was faceless and its body was its only government. Though the Halron rose up in a display of power and warning above her, like a hooded serpent, NaNay could not see an eye slit or nose hole, nor a long, sickle-shaped tooth. There was no haunch or spine to this being. There was no weak place where it could be struck and injured. Its breath began to growl all around her and it tugged at her leathers.

NaNay crouched on the hillside, making herself small and hard, and she held still for a moment. The skin tightened on her body as cold swept round her. Always, when the Halron came, the people would abandon their herding or leave the farmed beds; they would shelter in the forest or the huts. But she was not going to run away. She turned and lay on her back with her soft stomach and face open to the sky and she waited to see what would happen. She closed her eyes. The people did not understand the magstone. They did not understand how her anma had escaped the other world and come back into NaNay. But they understood supplication. They understood courage. They would understand her death or they would understand a third mark if she survived the Halron. She let her anma come to the surface and she made herself ready for pain and she waited.

There was no strike. The voice of the Halron bellowed over her, as if calling to a far mate. NaNay opened her eyes and looked up at the disappearing sky. The creature was horrible above, mantling, covetous of its mountain. Still she could not see a discreet leech mouth, or slim, rippled gills, only its immense and fazing substance. No one knew how to appease the Halron – it came when it wanted to, a torrent that broke apart the huts and the pens, turning in the sky, forming and re-forming. It destroyed what it wanted and then it disappeared, melting away inside a secret recess, a cave of elements.

NaNay stood. She began walking up the mountain and the Halron released its anger fully. Strong gusts hit her chest and shoulders like the angry swipes of a bear, and this made the hill steeper and her heart weaker. The Halron roared, throwing dirt and grit, and its long tail flowed on the other side of the valley. Its sound was incredible, worse than a male orox sparring, worse than a sow woken from hibernation and standing on its hind legs, its jaws wide and wet. NaNay did not turn and run or find a sinkhole to lie down in and hide. She crouched when it became too strong to move, and crawled on all fours, low to the ground like a burrowing animal. It ripped at her belt and skins. As she turned to look behind, it flung a loose branch against her head and stunned her. She knelt and blinked. The world swayed and her body went slack. There was stinging in her scalp and the wind made the patch of wetness there feel cold. She could smell blood. A trickle ran into her eye and everything she was looking at smeared. She made a fist and pressed the socket of her eye, waited for the green sparks to fade. Then she spat on her hand and put the saliva into the wound. After a few moments, the slow, red dripping stopped.

When she felt steady, she stood upright and thrust her small scarred chest out and shouted her name.

I am NaNay.

She began walking again. There was a moment of calm, before the Halron lashed her once more. She stumbled backwards over a mound of earth and through a cake of dung. It rushed against her again and she slid down a bank of scree, and felt the skin on her thigh scraping off. The Halron continued to blare down the mountain.

She thought of Irla, holding a sheaf of her torn hair in his hand. She got up and was battered back down to the ground, again and again. The fight was endless. She could not beat the Halron, but she would not give in to it either. There was a feeling in her of hot and furious strength, as if all the angers of her life had made a fire. Her body was trapped by the storm and her heart felt trapped inside its bone cage, lopping against her ribs. The cold howl hurt her ears, and her eyes stung and watered. She did not know how long she had been battling the Halron, but shadows had moved around their objects, stretching towards the valley floor. She was high on the mountain.

She shielded her face and looked up. The sun was unstable behind the Halron, like a figure on the other side of a waterfall, a creature behind a hymen. She walked and she crawled.

When she was nearly at the escarpment, she crept behind a boulder and rested with her back against it. Flares of cloud from the Halron's body streamed past, disappearing into space, reappearing in the Halron's tail. Such a thing could not be understood. The Halron was something pulled from a dream. There was no other like it in this world. In the grasslands, the ungulates were camouflaged until they moved. In the forest, green and bark-like creatures were always there, masked – the frogs, the martens and owls. She tried to determine the Halron's body in the space between clouds but she could not. It was as if its intestines were on the outside. There was no method against it. She sprang from the lee of the boulder and ran hard.

When she reached the reef of towering rock, there was more shelter. She was exhausted now, but alert. White flowed and eddied in the sky, churning above the cliffs like the surface of rapids. The escarpment was not a known way to the summit – the herders went round and over the flank when they needed to reach the succulents on the other side, a slower, flatter way. She had never been on the summit alone; the people always herded together, with the dogs, their poles and clubs. They did not come in blizzards or fog unless orox were lost. Above, NaNay could see chimneys and channels in the rock, some like ladders, wide enough to fit her body. She was a good climber, sleek and quick as a squirrel. But she did not know if she would be ripped apart and flung from the top.

NaNay wiped her eyes again. She chose a crevasse and edged into the narrow gap and pulled herself up. She began to climb, quickly and carefully. She found footholds and her fingers worked behind ledges as the Halron poured its loud, strange, soluble body overhead. Wedged in the cliff, she turned to look at the valley. It was being combed and broken open, the trees shaken and the grass bent flat. The creature was searching for her, forcing everything apart and turning everything over. If it found her it would toss her into the sky.

She clambered inside the tight chimney of rock, squeezing between its sides. Near the top, grit and soil rained down, pattering, trying to blind and choke her. She spat out dirt and continued, shelf by shelf, until she reached the mouth of the channel, which was wider, and saw the place where it opened onto the broad summit. She hauled

57

herself up and crawled along the split pavement. Then she lifted her head and looked around.

The air was thick with mist; she could only see the length of two or three people spanning their arms. It had a mineral taste, salt, like the crystals brought by the far traders. Her ears were still rushing, but the roar of the Halron had lessened. She could hear it echoing down the hillside, muffled. She must be underneath it, or inside it; somehow she had entered its eye or throat, its gut. She had been swallowed and was inside its belly, had slid down its gullet, soft and wide and fangless. Now, perhaps, she could harm it, cut out its lung.

She unbound her tusk knife from her belt, held it tightly. Her anma rose and filled the space inside her again, it flowed wildly through her blood, and now she was like the maned snake, she was the mother bear. She climbed out of the stone channel and ran, holding the blade in her fist beside her forehead. She shouted, declared herself again. But the words did not sound as they should; it was as if she were underwater, or far away from her own mouth. The blade did not drag through flesh; it found no purchase. She ran across the summit striking with the knife and the air held no force. She was not knocked to the ground or snapped apart or flung towards the remote and early moon.

NaNay ran in the blind mist and screamed until her tongue seemed to tear from her throat and her legs buckled. There was nothing left in her and she was exhausted. She knelt on the mountain, her breathing too fast to calm her heart, her heart punching up at her throat. There was no valley, no brindled moorland or corrugated forest below, just pale, fibrous space.

The atmosphere felt both warm and cold around her, like standing in a melted stream with fur wrapped around her shoulders. She looked at the knife in her hands. The knife was useless. But the skin under-neath the bruises and cuts was glowing: she was luminescing, as if her anma was passing through the surface of her body, trying to leave it. Perhaps she was dead now and going to the other world.

She waited on her knees for the ancestors to come. She closed her eyes. She would not recognise her First Mother but First Mother would find her, even if she was lost; First Mother would know her, even among multitudes. She waited, but no ancestors came to collect her.

When she opened her eyes, her anma was still shining inside her body, unreleased. Fear had bled and stiffened her muscles, and she could barely move. She knew she should mark herself now, and be known for three marks in whichever world she was destined for. Slowly, she drew the blade of her tusk knife down her chest, from the base of her throat to the soft bone beneath her ribs, paring the tissue without crying out. Then she dropped the dagger and sank to the ground. She did not know how to die or how to live, so she lay on rocks. After a while she slept with her chin tucked over on the wound. If no one from the other world came, the Halron would digest her, and the herders would find only hard pellets, her scored breastplate, her knife.

X

Who, Michael asks the ragged, gathered crowd, *will build the cross? Who will provide the three woods, as of the crucifix? Where is your carpenter and where is your smith to forge the nails?*

The villagers stand dumbly in the churchyard of St Cuthbert's, in the freezing rain. Dilston: Devil's Town. Such is Helm's reign here. Mud, cattle prints, broken carts, flies. The rotting wooden shacks are barely habitable. A vast bull is pegged nearby, gathering sleet on its back end. They have heard Michael's sermon, about pestilence, the evil that presides over their homes and commons and their pitiful souls. They know what this tilted fellow is about now. He's here to confront the malevolent form that issues from black cloud during spring and harvest, tossing sheep about, stripping wheat and uprooting turnips, the one who dements their minds and leads to their sin – for they are indeed poor sinners, this much they know. Michael Lang has a plan to banish the demon by righteous intervention, to sanctify the mountain, so that they may come again to the Lord. He's here to save them.

Silence. Their heads are bowed; one or two glance up at the fell. Their clothes are drab, torn, sour as silage. They shuffle in the mire. They do not trust the presence of Christ's emissary and evil's abolition, nor do they believe in impending prosperity, which is to say they'll believe in nothing and anything if it helps them scrape by, gods, wraiths, horrocks, capples; they haven't the courage or insensibility to choose. Under the pews of St Cuthbert's the carved wooden nubs of older deities remain, bestiaries, creatures of grotesque perverted ugliness;

60

one in particular, cyclone-shaped, full-cheeked both ends, its orifices tremendously flatulent. This lot practise the art of moodles and votive-making. The women place drops of breast milk onto figurines; the men hang wind chimes in the byres above pregnant heifers. Kill Helm? That would be like murdering their local emperor.

Silence. The ponies steam in the rain nearby, and Isa gentles them, blows warm breath across their muzzles.

Drip, drip, from the diminutive doorway of the stout church – one of the forty where the corpse of Cuthbert rested going home, his stretcher and bearers barely fitting between the pillars. Drip, drip, from the rim of the iron sallet. Then again, the face behind those drips is as grotesque as any misericord under the worshippers' arses, quilled and flocked as it is with skin tags and sagging pockets, eyes like arsenite fire. It's a face no one would contest has witnessed dire acts and battled in the lower sulphurous realms, has become hellproof. Michael waits with the patience of Methuselah for his answer.

Drip, drip. Enough of this quivering reticence.
Who among you? he demands.

Sir, I.
A coarse but steady voice lifts from the ranks, and a big russet man steps forward – leather jerkin, knuckles swollen, the yellow rinds of calluses between thumb and first finger from the repeating lathe.
You are?
James Wright. I am of the Carlisle guild. I am Sir Ranulph's wagoner and I helped build the defence towers. I am not a carver but my master's pelican is in the cathedral nave and it is extremely fine. I work oak and Scotchwood, and I work beech on occasion. There is no cypress in our woods, sir, but there is holly as replacement. Here is my son, James. He will serve you as I do.

61

A capped boy of twelve with similar sandy hair and a softly fila-mented chin is pulled to the carpenter's side. He looks up at the wizard priest, and regrets it: a glare of cold, clarifying flame meets his drooping eyes. Michael nods.

Good James Wright, I will employ you. Now, James the younger. Why does your father speak to me of holly? Why does James your father say holly will substitute Jerusalem wood in our endeavour?

Michael stares at the boy and the boy's gaze swims about; he swal-lows the apple bone in his throat, coughs as it bobs back up. He removes the coif, belatedly, catches the implacable eye of Isa. Isa looks away.

Speak, then, apprentice.

It seems the answer, if incorrect, will lead to disembowelment, branding; the lash at least. James the younger, cock enough to have met the nailing gaze but not inattentive to scripture or the loric codes of the family occupation, croaks his answer in a voice between boy-hood and manhood.

Your Grace, it is for the Virgin who hung her robe against the holly and so it is sacred and its flower is white. God save us.

Michael grunts, turns back towards his pony and his own surrogate or stolen son.

Good James Wright, I will employ you and you may bring your boy. Begin quick – finish before the sabbath. There will be enough coin to see you to Pentecost.

The villagers disperse, stupefied by such interference. They return to their hovels and their cattle, their geese and thin burgesses, to tell wives and children of this incredulous undertaking, to pray, possibly. They go to the alehouse, to sup and yam, saying, *Helm versus Lang, now there's a match I'd pay to see, a belter, better than the wrestling and the pits. How will he get the cross up there? Fly up on it, a-straddled.* Most in this turbulent upper kingdom have heard of him. Papal mercenary. A social climber. Son of a nobleman, or son of a butcher. Son of a whore, or son of a selkie. Mixed parentage, unquestionably. He's risen to become the most powerful courtier; whisperer to monarchs and sultans. Not the first to grapple with the Pennine demon, mind. St Austin, centuries ago, visited the parish, strode barefoot to the summit and built an altar table to offer Helm the holy eucharist. But Helm's soul remained tortured, its temper foul – hurling barrels around and blowing eggs back up hens' tusses. *Better odds this time? Aye, takes a professional bastard to cheg such a parasite. Do any remember the witch court over yonder? Nay. Those stones were not living beings to memory. Would it not have been another sorcerer who entombed them, then? Nay, niver. It was Michael Lang. Well, he must be two hundred year old, if he's a day. Scoll! Amen!*

The wizard priest and his heir return to the damp, empty longhouse in Salkeld, borrowed from the baron who has several spare, where there is little more than a vast scorched fireplace, a half-dead hag in the kitchen, and a rain barrel. From here, the summit of Fiend's Fell can be surveilled, its moods interpreted. Michael goes out as night descends, to walk with the moonlight accomplice. He looks up at the mountain's silhouette, just and so visible under the seeding stars, while Isa prepares a bed.

Next morning, in the mallard-green darkness before sun-up, the carpenter and his lad set off into the woods. James the elder knows exactly where to find the trees for the beams of the cross. He is dishumoured, though. Bile in his pipes; hot sluicing above his hole. Something bad is a-churn in him. Ordinarily, on the forester's path, he would issue a test for the boy, with all the citizens of the woods enunciated, their usages and steerage, their character and properties. Yew: not to be used except for churchyards, gateposts for the dead to pass between realms. Beware the rowan: bendable, inordinately strong, but full of cunning Celtic magic. Sycamore: complex, divining, winged of seed like the angels, and shelter for lovers, its leaves stuffed into pillows to ward away nightmares. No journeyman's lesson today. The carpenters walk quietly into the woods and the woods are unnaturally quiet – the garrulous blackbird is missing; the red robin, always nearby in winter, is missing; Jenny Wren, shy and busy in the briar, is missing. Nothing choruses.

Pink washes the sky as they begin on a young oak with the axe and the saw; pink, like a streak of blood in water, and James the younger tells his father he is afraid of the day's first omen, its ill tidings. His father says nothing to reassure his apprentice that it is a good and penitent task they are undertaking, for he feels the rise of gall as the sun rises bloody above the foliage. And in his mind, three words keep incanting – *cypress, pine, cedar, cypress, pine, cedar*. Instead of the axe blade he hears the knocking of nails into the wrists of Christ. He downs tools, walks between the trees, vomits a pod of bile and vegetable remains, spits, but does not feel better.

As they wait for the cross to be timbered, Michael and Isa lay apparatus on the longhouse table for inspection.

A polished mirror, made divinely, it is said, by St Eligius the goldsmith, in which any malefactor, invisible to the human eye, will be revealed. It will see its own reflection and, sickened by its hideousness and deformity, forbidden by Michael's spell, it will recoil. *God made you beautiful, God made you without ugliness and sin. Look what you have become. Foul. Repulsive. I tell the truth. I am the truth. Be gone.*

Water in vials, brought from the Church of the Holy Sepulchre and the font of Sibius. A leather whip, rubbed soft at the handle, its tip quick as an asp tongue and sharp enough to cut apart thunderheads.

A short-sword, though this is too solid and slow a device for the nebular diaflum.

Michael watches Isa clean the items. He is careful, very careful, with the task. He buckles the mirror and vials into pouches on Michael's belt.

Not the blade, Michael says when Isa moves to sheathe it. *Hold it. Do you feel its weight? You know its history, blue lamb.*

The boy holds the sword. It is the same weapon that was used in Edessa and in Carcassonne. Michael searches the boy's face for a tell. Nothing. His mother and father are a distant memory. He lays a hand on the boy's shoulder, on the shawl that the boy himself washed clean, wringing out their blood. Gently, his master takes the handle.

XI

De Peyster Hall, 1788

Dearest Beatrice,

How long this letter shall take to reach you I cannot imagine & the
Goddess only knows what fate shall befall me 'til it rests in your hand.
I should not be writing; rather, I am not permitted communiquer
with another human soul except for the chaplain – goblain, as I call
him – a bloodless rook-eye in possession of neither soul nor pity.
This, dear sister, is predicament for my mischief. Good loyal Phoebe
has sneaked in my writing implements and promised to steal a letter
away concealed beneath her mantelet. Nathaniel would unseal it and
expose my lack of penitence, then catastrophe & further malady . . .
Therefore I write at haste, ear tuned to footfall outside my chamber.
Dreadful old Tobias lurks in the hallway hoping to hear me whimper
and wail, hoping I will try to flee and he, once more the Hessian,
arrest me.

My last letter was swaddled in anxious speculation, was it not, and
my senses alert to trouble? Nathaniel was all astew with eradications
and solutions, and these (some of these!) have come to pass. Did
you receive my words? Is the parchment sunk to the bottom of the
Atlantic? One cannot be sure of safe passage for personages or papers
these days, nor which colony will be next to fall. How I wish you
would reply with reassurances & sororal guidance.

Alas, such intuition was not unfounded! Dreadful occurrence has
taken place at the hall, relating to those ancients my husband finds so
abhorrent. Does my tone frighten? Do not be fearful, I am preserved,
if very inhibited. I shall tell you all in good order, stowing away these

66

implements before being reproached (the marquetry has a hidden drawer and trick lock, for a woman must preserve her intimacies) & recovering them when left in isolation. No, do not be fearful, but brace firmly, for bewilderment is to come. Scandal has attached itself to my hems & I am to remain in a bolted room as a prisoner, the window nailed shut ere I leap. Nathaniel had Tobias knock long nails into the sill and bend their talons over the frame. No mere valet is Tobias, but hench and haggar in all things.

Impossible to haul open the window sash; I have tried & ragged my nails. Hermitic as a Carthusian am I. Fetched plain breakfasts and teas on trays & I must suffer unevacuated soil pots 'til Phoebe is permitted entrance. I endure early confinement as the clock ticks on and on towards doomsday – the carpet worn threadbare beneath my slippers. O, for a waft of fresh air! To feel autumn's cool caress against my cheek! Away, such idle dreams! I am expected to stitch, read scripture & reform. I may not beautify, though must make myself comely for my husband's visits. I may not muse over poems or novels, lest my emotions flourish, nor hear music lest immoderate passions arise – throw me in the river with my lyre!

Another blow, my parochial companions have been repelled by my husband – Lady Helene, Effie, Susanna Bousfield, ladies with whom I enjoy the wit of horoscopes. No longer are we permitted our teas, or to snuff the candles & perform summonings. What thrill! SB is quite the conduit, having manifested the voice of many departed and notated their instructions – sadly never Mumma or Pappa, and occasionally some frightful unchristian spirit. All part of the opprobrium. Truly, I am being dead-headed like the July roses! Snip snip snip!

Only Phoebe arrives, with bouillon & plain flannel bread – the goblain has prescribed the diet of the convent, doubtless he'll have me out at elbows soon – or to black the fireplace, or lay fresh faggots. She sneaks me powder sugar for my tea & brings me pretty cuttings, supplies news from the village and the kitchen. We chatter while she polishes. I implore her to tell me all that occurs beyond these grim walls, as far as Sydney Cove. Nathaniel has no new ally for his barbaric venture, she assures me, & will not imperil Tobias again, though we cannot be certain. Won't you beg the Mister's forgiveness, Phoebe urges, then, glancing towards my fertile crescent, won't you give him softer reason?

Surely you know your sister. I cannot forswear myself and will not apologise. I am in service to the Goddess & have scored a mighty victory. Once I am released – for a man cannot imprison his wife indefinitely & I have a royal card to play – I shall honour her further. I shall get two oak saplings from Lanter, plant them in symmetry within the sacred circle & interpret them as we Senhouse daughters.

Meanwhile. Here is a stalking tiger in its cage. Imagine, if you will. I pick at the flaking wallpaper. I observe the spindling spider. I embroider, then toss my tambour across the floor – backstitched Bible verse & threads of violets be damned! I stare from the eternal window imagining such wild & fanciful things passing by – eagles, angels, a crimson aerostat with a pig strung beneath! We are three-quarters through October & a magnificent gilding of leaves has occurred across Eden, as if illuminators had been working in the branches. The orchard is near the east wing – I could pluck a pear were the sash to budge a little. Those not trugged by cook's girl for jam have dappled & the birds are at them. At dusk the clatter and thump of antlers from the grounds is loud behind the shutters. The geese are away, so tidy in their formations overhead – a mournful desertion. Though there is much at the hall I do not like – its heavy furniture in the new style & the horned trophies – the valley beyond delights. The fells are subtle yet substantive; not the toppling slate peaks of our childhood, yet they still impose. There are great reverberant forces in these hills as you shall hear!

I am ruined in Christian womanhood, for our childhood was Arcadian. Dear Mumma let us gad as we desired, catching newts for our pails, skating the frozen brook, bathing in the jadey pond at

Rydal like naughty nymphs. Did we not witness boggling marvels in our old home? Do you recall the miracle of the rowing boat floating above the surface of the lake in the morning mist? How we gaped, our mouths ajar! The Spirit of the Lake, levitating the vessel, holding it in her green & lilied palm! My husband finds our childhood tales woolly & delusional. Some godly or scientific physic lifted the rowboat, he says, so I must not speak (nor think!) like a hitherlander. I bite my tongue, Bea, & wish to bite his. Women are the loyal courtiers of Nature, tolerant to her mysteries, while men oppose her, rattling their abacuses & stamping sandcastles. Nathaniel has pretension as an academic, where I would school my children as we were, keen and joyful little wildlings. I scarce commit this proposition to the page. Phoebe surmised it when I asked for gingers & failed to present last month's napkins – I shall be employed by maternal seminary before summer. Phoebe may be correct, some household rapprochement shall occur when Nathaniel is informed.

Yet the problem of Catherine de Peyster née Senhouse remains. How does one suppress the free heart for state occasions in the parlour? I am learning rawly & against my marrow. Darling sister, I imagine you 'roused & toused' in your new world as I once was in this moderate dale. I imagine your sea, blue as lapis, while my sky is pewter. I hope your Antrobus is kind, accommodating of the femme propension. Do you still converse in dreams with dear Mumma? Is the little hazel spoon from which the verity in our well sipped still tucked in your tie-pocket? Nathaniel would dismiss that as a tinker's toy!

How he tries to bend my stripes. Gone are those first days at the hall when my husband was away at the cornings & I was let loose in the saddle, practising the minor disobedience of solitary exploration amid Salkeld's pastures & coppices. I am still learning the wilder routes, but the estate is not large, comparatively; I hear the manor at Greystoke is commensurate to the immense Caledonians above us & to George's Norfolk palace. We are slight mortgaged; I know not why – N's father's involvement with inaccurate accounts or crisis or coup – 'tis rare discussed alongside me. But the business prospers, with three hundred barrels per calendar, sampled at the laboratory in Woolwich & graded excellent. Hardly a badge of pride for a wife; however, it yields respect at his lodge. Nathaniel has set about improvements, a chapel & mausoleum, a new high wall around the hall. And excoriations, to wit, let me pin the matter of this horrid tale firmer.

On the aproned commons here are the daughters of Meg, a splendid colosseum of ancients. Pappa took us to Castlerigg as children, & you will remember with some wonder that high arena of stones, all gnarled & pitted & mossed, born from the ground as if before creation. Our local stones are much the larger – each individual, also in their encirclement. Nathaniel has despised the place since he was a boy, appalled by stories his Nurse Margaret told him whereby these sinister petrified ladies may be released from their curse by twice counting their number & arriving at the same tally – no easy task, I have tried with Lady Helene, the mind wanders peculiarly as if enchanted – & thence would seek a vengeful reckoning. Nathaniel has recently declared the site paganic; he says it is brute in origin and shameful to our Christian civility. This is the language of the new masonic house, Bea – they are devout & joyless iconoclasts, unlike dear Pappa. According to N, we who are fanciful about henges & cupped gneisses are the Philistines. Mark the boy within, for I suspect he is still quaking at the knee about witches.

Naturally, he recognises no hypocrisy; he talks about divinity & reintegration while profiting from savin & saltpetre, the newly licensed mill at Sedgwick. Whither gunpowder in God's divine, peaceable establishment, I asked him once, very innocently, for I am unable to fathom its fit, husband. (If I stroke & drape him I may jib close to the wind with my comments.) He scoffed at my feeble politic. Black powder provides us copper and lead, said he, the means to construct our civic order. Black powder ignites the holy flame by which the savage is suppressed. Oh? But what of those barrels commandeered in the Jamaica rebellion, I asked him. Was the grain less righteous & combustible in the hands of slaves? And thereabouts I halted, for he detected a veiled challenge & I risked the strop.

As halt I must now, shuffling outside my door—

XII

O! But what manner of airborne creature is this? This great, gaseous, patch-skinned thing hanging up above the valley? A bright red os on the horizon; a lost, see-through sun, or mackintosh planet, growing larger, coming closer on the light prevailing breeze, excusing itself through the low clouds as if it has important business up here, in Helm's realm. What unearthly bladder or florid hollow could it be, drifting towards the fell, where Helm sits (or stands, or squats, or savasanas) boggling at it. A contraption never seen before, incomprehensible, undoing the laws of physics, though Helm is becoming accustomed to the way weird things keep occurring; humans being obsessed with new inventions, manically productive in their cottages, mills and workrooms.

Never before something of this ilk! A fat diaphragm of papers and silks, declarative in its primary hue, full of hot fiery ego, its globular materials stitched and stuck together – jellyish, viscous, really quite hideous. With, slung from its preposterous body, a little woven basket containing not the experimental, expendable barnyard guinea pigs à la le continent, but a man inside it. A man, and a woman, sporting fine hats – his tall, hers broad – and adorned with jewellery and lapel trinkets. Laughing, sipping champagne from a couple of coupe glasses, believe it or not.

Chin-chin!

Look at that view, Claudine!

Just sublime, Henry!

A very dapper pair they are, unlike the usual dirty-shirted, field-gleaning, sheep-shouldering citizens of the vale. Mad aristos who are, irrefutably, flying. They've done it; they've freed themselves from gravity; conquered the exclusive upper zone. Helm's not quite sure how Helm feels about it.

There's an unusually unpleasant burning smell coming from the undercarriage: wool and charcoal smouldering in a lethal-looking kettle, hot tongues licking at the base of the – new word for Helm – balloon. The woman says it, her voice sharp and silvery as cutlery in the heavens; anxious – well, who wouldn't be.

Henry, darling, is our balloon sinking? Aren't we descending a tad hastily?

Balloon.
Ballooooooooon.
Ew.

We aren't going to wreck, are we, Henry?

Claudine has a point. Surely it's a little dangerous, the onboard fire propelling the flimsy-looking lung of fabric, under which the humans, who are observably prone to plummeting when met with pure un-structured atmosphere, are now kissing. Goosing, actually, for Henry's free hand is sliding down the stayed waist of the fancy frock to the beskirted bottom of Claudine, and groping about its layers, and gathering them upwards to reveal stocking tops and flocked bloomers, while his other hand holds the sloshing coupe. (Such is the masculine form of reassurance.)

Helm, meanwhile, is astounded, processing. Wasn't expecting this business anytime soon. Helm is used to humans swarming about below on terra firma, jumping not very high compared to, say, a lynx or a frog or a buck. Hitherto they have not had much luck with wings, or chutes, or floats, throwing things up that rapidly come

73

down, arriving in abrupt mush at the bottoms of cliffs – haha. Who knew that one day they'd learn the trick. Which ingenious inventor fashioned this impossible flying trinket? (The clever Scot, Cameron, did, having adapted a design from the Montgolfiers: this one's been inflated near Langholm, has travelled the length of Cumberland and is, though novel in these parts, a very imperfect and soon-to-be-defunct breed, replaced by propane- and helium-fuelled versions. Cameron himself no longer flies, having crashed the previous balloon, having been – full disclosure – dragged three miles in a tangle of rope and silk, then tossed off the woven platform and hurled against an oak; several lower vertebrae fractured, resulting in a stiff-gaited limp plus a nightly dependence on opium. He still likes to send his chums up, though, if they're game enough.)

The balloon draws alongside the summit, level, almost, with Helm. Its basket creaks a fraction under the weight of flesh and bone. The bubbles in the glasses tingle – 1812, imported from Aÿ: not a bad vintage, though fusty, a little semeny, thinks Claudine, who may simply be thinking ahead.

There they are, the exuberant, flamboyantly dressed couple, petting beneath a gargantuan inflammable. Helm is buoyed by the aerial company, and oddly nauseated. Something about the creepy, crêpey surface of the inflatable, and the oo of the balloon, and the balloon itself, its potential to burst and issue forth a loud, deflationary, unfunny raspberry. Cue, globophobia. (Just wait, those smaller, rubbery plastic ones are really going to twist Helm's melons, accidentally let go of by children at parties, squeaky, sticking to hair with static and popping without warning, leaving withered, foreskinny cases behind – it's all shudder-inducing.)

There is the temptation to gaily blow the thing across the valley, to sending it off, waffling and spinning. Except even more thrilling is the peep show at which Helm has a front-row seat. For Henry has now tossed the empty bottle of champers and his glass over the side of the basket (*Mind out below, sheep!*), in order to use both hands on Claudine, to get inside the bloomers and rummage gently and insistently in a way she simply can't resist; to release his trouser buttons and draw out his slightly convex pink spigot with its bead of lubricant at the tip (bizarre apparatus really, see how it nods and bounces, how it salutes), while Claudine, crackling with panic or adrenaline or arousal, is sipping off her champagne and gripping the nearest crown rope.

I feel you are amenable to love, my love, oh yes, splendid, I do feel it most specifically here. Shall we just die together?

Why not? They are blissfully alone in the clouds (almost). They are bright as birds. There's such death-wishing effervescence in Claudine's brain she will agree to anything, any dangerous act of congress, an orgy with the celestial masses possibly. She too tosses her glass overboard and it sails downwards, glinting, faceted, brittle, exploding its crystal bomb on the limestone below. She adjusts her stance. Henry lowers the garment to reveal a frazzle of pubic hair, with its damp twist, then performs, with murmurs and groans and a kind of daring unstoppability, the first-ever act of the mile-high club – more accurately 3,500 feet and sinking steadily. Sinking rapidly. Claudine is not wrong, for the upper silk stitching has loosened and hot air is rushing through the gape – putting them on a trajectory that will lead to a rather undignified but unfatal landing near Soulby, in the crook of the meandering, soon-to-be-christened Scandal Beck, to the astonishment of both the villagers and the minnows, and luckily only half a mile from the house of Robert Hutton, bonesetter.

Until then, Helm, through no fault of Helm's own, goggles at the pair in gross detail. Henry circles his fingertips and sucks Claudine's earlobe. Claudine releases the rope she is gripping, holds on to her magnificently feathered hat, and ohs and ahs, her décolletage flushing as she climaxes. Henry courteously grants her a minute of breathless recovery, cheek to cheek, before helping her kneel in the wicker gondola and mouth at his ridiculous apparatus until he, too, expleting and juddering, calls out, *God's body!*

The lady rises and delicately spits out the whitish product. It rains onto the Pennines.

Ballooooon.

XIII

Grange House is a large, blank-faced building, surrounded by meadows, drooping pines and sycamores; more Gothic farm than mansion, Thomas thinks, as the carriage pulls up the driveway. It is quite the loveliest plot, with several acres of wildflowers, though the vernacular red stone of the valley is a tad austere. He is met at the front door by a fox-eyed maid who barely curtsies. She introduces herself as Midge. Midge tells him his luggage will have to wait until Boller gets back from his day off: too heavy to lift, and she has a bad thumb. The colonel is *away, of course*, she tells Thomas knowingly, as if he understands. Perhaps he has been out at the fete, overseeing some obese animal prize or wrestling trophy, or perhaps he's abroad; who can say. Mrs Brooke is also not here to greet him.

She's at the green pot, I expect, Midge says.

Oh, I see.

Again, he has no idea what she means. He manages to heft the trunks down from the carriage with the help of the station driver and pulls them under the canopy of the porch where they will, at least, dry out. My archive, he thinks, beginning to regret having brought the precious letters and so many frail charts.

Midge takes his coat but not his case. Inside, the house is also a strange juxtaposition: cabinets of pistols, dress swords and medals, planters of citrus trees and jasmines trained up doorways, with faux, bead-eyed birds wired to the boughs. The decor is both botanical and mannishly ordered. Sara remarked before his departure that she hadn't actually seen her cousin Rebecca since they were young girls, hadn't corresponded much with her over the years, and couldn't quite remember the details of why she'd married the old colonel – some kind of obscure covenant was involved.

I expect you might encounter a few oddities, darling, but do be kind. Try not to be a wag.

Midge leads him down the hallway and up an impressive curved staircase. He is shown into a bedchamber with a high ceiling. The window is wide open; yellow leaves have blown in and not been swept up. No fire has been laid in the grate, but there is a decent scut of coal. Bamboo-patterned wallpaper, a washstand. The bed is ebony, carved and canopied, and unmade; its mattress looks lumpen. There are sheets and quilts folded on the bureau beside it. Midge glances at the bed as she shows him in.

Expected you tomorrow, sir.

She trots across the room and pulls down the window sash, ignoring the scattered leaves.

No matter, thank you, I'm sure I can manage.

He is sure, yes he is quite positive, that his last letter to the Brookes had outlined the date and time of his arrival. But perhaps the household is, as the new way seems to allow, *casuale*. Or perhaps it's just northern.

Let you get settled, then, sir, says Midge. *I dare say Mrs Brooke will be back by suppertime.*

She excuses herself, closing the door.

Thomas carries his valise to the bureau and sets it down. He sits on the bed. The mattress sags and rustles. There are stalks poking through its cover. He tugs at one and out slides not eiderdown but a beech leaf.

Well, well.

Opposite the bed, the windows are large, the shapes of the fells held like dramatic portraits within their frames. The clock on the mantle ticks. Five to five. Now what? No hosts available. It is too late in the day to ride out towards the range and set up the anemometers and roses, though he's itching to begin. No mention by Midge what time dinner is served, nor any other formalities. All fine, Tombo. A little rustication will be no bad thing, he tells himself, in preparation for his encampment in the Pennine cottage. He'll take a stroll. The shower seems to have peregrinated off elsewhere and late-afternoon light is shimmering in the damp trees. A walk will be just the ticket to unstiffen him after the buttock-bruiser of a journey from the station.

He makes his way along the landing and downstairs to the front door, passing several more rooms where the curious conflict of formal versus natural is occurring. Leather-bound books in glass cases in the library; a large stone receptacle at the room's centre filled with water, like a giant bird bath – indeed the real thing (a goldfinch? a bunting?) is perched daintily on the rim – riffling its feathers as if just having bathed.

Well, well.

He collects his coat from the vestibule, lets himself out and follows a scythed meadow path round the side of the house and down towards a copse.

Away from the manured fields and sties, the air smells tonic – an intoxicating scent of wildflowers. The grasses are soft and feathered, with pale-blue and white butterflies flitting between stems. At the bottom of the meadow, a slab bridge crosses a trickling stream and the path continues through a handful of larches. How beautiful the stretch around the house is, he thinks as he climbs a stile and walks up a rise, hoping to get a good view of Cross Fell. It is there, not quite as the reproductions in oil and charcoal would have it, but definite in form, solid, manifest. For a long moment he stands and stares, and he begins to feel, in the tips of his fingers, a faint buzzing sensation – that excitement of cells, which is knowledge that something important is occurring.

He felt it as a young man – the night he looked through the large reflecting telescope at the observatory and saw a spiral galaxy, the rings of the planets. And before that, as a boy – the view from Helvellyn over the Irish Sea, his father standing with a hand on his shoulder, saying, *Look, Thomas, there is the Manx Isle.* And as a newlywed husband, seeing the magnetic aurora from the bow of the *Eldaren* as she sailed north between ice floes; Sara beside him, fresh from their tangled cabin bed and wearing a white fur hood. Such beauty, pulsing, effusing.

Now, soggy chattels notwithstanding, he is reassured. But he should try to find his host, present himself. He turns away from his mountain – for it is now his in some capacity, or he has been claimed by it – and walks down the sloping field towards the woodland beside the river. He will loop back along it to Grange House. Between mature oaks and willows, he finds a thin pathway in the undergrowth, so slightly made it could have been trodden by an animal only moments ago. Inside the canopy it is quite the verdant arboretum, light slanting between branches, radiant moss. The rain has softened the earth underfoot – how quiet his feet are. He hears water coursing in the shallows, and then the River Eden appears: broad, strong, muscling brightly past sandstone boulders.

He finds a small beach beside a lovely curved well in the waterway, and steps down the bank onto the shingle. Eddies and swirls, timbrels of light on the river's surface; it moves sensually, is bearded with reeds where it deepens and slows. There's a complicated, freshwater aroma of silt and weed, trout and minerals.

He glances to the side. On an outcrop beside the bank is a shawl of very fine silk, embroidered, fringed, heaped in a spilling pile. The rocks next to it have been wetted. He looks about, sees no one; the garment has been forgotten, or lost, perhaps. He lifts the shawl and folds it – soft as ash, perfumed slightly of lily.

He continues on through the woods, downstream. The path leads away from the shore and the riverbanks rise taller, reddish, dressed with ferns and lichen. Ahead, flattened grass stems are gently rising back up, and in his noticing this detail he does not at first see a woman moving between the trees only a few lengths away. He catches sight of the drifting mazarine skirt, white flashes beneath it. Her feet are bare; from one hand, laced together, boots dangle. She moves between the trunks, disappearing, then reappearing. Her dress is darker at the hem from the damp undergrowth, and has a dark stroke below her waist where the tip of her braided hair is dripping.

She is the owner of the shawl, perhaps. She must have been bathing. He almost calls out – *Pardon me? Mrs Brooke?* – but finds he cannot speak. He cannot speak, but continues to follow her. Heels a little muddy, he sees, now that he is closer. She touches the mossed tree trunks with her free hand as she passes, gently, gloveless, a touch that is lingering, communicative. Then she lifts her arms and reaches behind; she gathers the long wet coil of hair – dark rust colour, like soaked autumn bracken – and wrings it out.

The intimacy of the gesture – as if he is present in her washroom, and she attending to her customary acts. And then it dawns on him, that if he'd arrived only a little sooner at the river's edge she would have been—

He stops. Wrong, very wrong, to be following her. He should not be here; in this private spot, nor pursuing. But it is too late. A twig snaps under his boot, or the bushes rustle. The live state of his body, perhaps, is felt. She is alerted and pauses too. She turns back towards him on the path, and as she turns he can see that her eyes are covered by tinted lenses, the kind he has seen worn by visitors to the Garden of the Blind in Greenwich.

How terribly, terribly awkward it is that evening as they sit opposite each other across the dinner table. Thomas shuffles in his chair, adjusts his trouser fold. Mrs Brooke has changed into a dry, formal dress, deep brinjal against the pale skin of her neck. She peers at him with brilliant, disconcerting eyes, eyes that are not blind but are shadowed and slightly too protuberant, sedge green with gold rings; clearly she is suffering some form of sensitivity or disease. It is hard to look, and hard to look away.

Outside Grange House's dining room windows is a bright, long summer evening. The room feels several degrees cooler than the temperature outside, even with his dinner jacket. It is apparent that the windows of the house are the subject of minor conflict. They are closed by Midge as she passes, and reopened by Mrs Brooke when she notices them closed, in some unspoken domestic altercation.

Thomas clears his throat as if to speak, but doesn't. He traces his trouser crease again. Rebecca Brooke emits a little huff of air, as if to fog and clean a mirror. Her hair is perfectly dry now, spilling auburn strands from its loose rosette.

Between them sits a jellied gammon and a tureen of anaemic disintegrating potatoes. A mysterious sauce, wobbling under a brown meniscus, is deposited on the table by Midge. Their wine glasses stand empty. The decanter is also empty. Instead, into medieval-looking tumblers, Midge has poured them a mysterious yellow concoction, its scent herby and bitter, and somehow reminiscent of coastal mudflats. A local speciality, very good for the kidneys and gall bladder, Rebecca Brooke informs him.

My husband may no longer take wine, she says, *so we have transposed our habits. It's fermented. A woman in the village brews it for me – she calls it souse.*

Thomas smiles tightly, and does not suggest that to the best of his knowledge his own kidneys and gall bladder are perfectly operational and not in need of remedies. She stares at him while he samples the tincture; he tries not to wince at the tartness, the curdled effervescence. Perhaps this is his punishment.

She had clearly not expected to be disturbed at the river. Nor had Thomas expected to come upon so beguiling a thing as a woman of gentle means walking barefoot through the woods, fondling the trunks as if for all the world they were her lovers. Caught like a fox stalking a peahen! There was nothing he could do but continue his approach, assume some manner of formal introduction, all the while trying not to picture a nude body entering the river, its swales and fleshy moons, its dark badges beneath the arms and navel. She took off the purple spectacles and squinted painfully at him, her eyes large and incredulous.

Mrs Brooke? I do apologise if I am intruding—
That is my shawl.
Is it? I thought it abandoned.

After his faltering explanation – like Midge, she seemed not to recall any knowledge of his arrival – and his profuse apologies for having disturbed her, *her, her, ablutions*, after she had untied her boots and put them back on, *It's called Earthing, Mr Bodger, I dare say you'd benefit*, they'd walked to the house together, several feet apart, in excruciating silence.

Not unlike the current silence. The eyes, fixed on him now at salt-passing distance, are really rather compelling. Remarkable shades in the irises, a hazard of greens, flecks of copper, with amber limbal rings as if mercury-poisoned. A faulty thyroid? Perhaps her eyes make her appear more angry than she is? He sets the tincture glass down. If Sara were here, he could rely on her adept pleasantries to get him out of strife. Buck up, Bodge, he tells himself, you've faced worse than this – the cantankerous queen, for example, tornadoes, college examination. He smiles, swallows again – his saliva ducts seem now to be over-producing – and enquires after the colonel.

I am sorry he will not be joining us this evening – perhaps tomorrow?

No. Sanderson is away, Mrs Brooke says, flapping a napkin onto her lap.

I shall look forward to his return. Is he perhaps on business?

His host snorts gently.

Well, if one can call it that.

Thomas ploughs on.

I noticed the village fete when we drove in. Did you attend?

The fete was yesterday, she says. *I did not attend.*

Thomas lays his own napkin, neatly, squarely, and changes tack.

I wonder – did you plant the meadow around the house, Mrs Brooke? It's so wonderfully rich with wildlife. Did I see a brown fritillary out there? I believe I may have.

Mrs Brooke's left eye begins to rock with water. She blinks. A tear spills at the corner. She inclines her head fractionally to the side, dabs with a cotton handkerchief removed swiftly from the sleeve of her dress and swiftly restored there, a gesture so discreet it barely occurs.

Do you study lepidopterology, Mr Bodger?

Please, call me Thomas. I do not, but Sara takes a keen interest in the little fellows and I borrow titbits from her. She's very concerned that the heath beside our home has become over-populated and is being damaged by we lumbering Homo sapiens. She's campaigning to stop the linden trees being felled.

Rebecca Brooke nods, curtly.

I am positive she is right to. I do not understand why people endure London, choking on smog and wading through filth. Yes, I had the meadow reinstated, Mr Bodger. I don't see why the house should take precedence. I'm for turning over all the machines, if you must know.

Ah yes, he thinks, the recidivist philosophy, he should have pegged her there. And we do have street sweepers. Best not say it. Best not

84

engage in a debate, given the frosty climate at the table. There's a pause, and then—

My husband tells me you're here to hunt the Helm wind – is that correct, Mr Bodger?

He smiles. So she does recall their arrangement. One quadrant of her left iris is, he would swear, absolutely and unnervingly citrine.

Hunt? Dear me, no. No, I wish simply to observe its formation and effect and deduce its exact mechanism. Did your husband mention how I plan to?

Mrs Brooke blinks rapidly.

Sanderson has absolutely no interest in the weather – least of all the Helm. It costs him too much in repairs and tenant claims. Why is the Society suddenly interested in our wind? We've endured it for years, quite unencumbered by the attentions of those such as yourself.

Keen to extract himself from the tense short-tennis of their conversation, and on much safer ground, Thomas commences his usual enthusiastic advocacy. Almost always, an amateur lecture about weather is a guaranteed ice-breaker, frequently warming the halls populated by leisure-time ladies.

Well, he begins, *the council wishes to compare local conditions in the British Isles with conditions elsewhere, to form a broader base of knowledge, if you will. We must take reliable measurements, make scales. Then we may begin to contrast and affiliate, to map; we may begin to accurately predict. I had the great privilege of attending the International Meteorological Organization's conference in Vienna, and a great many speakers are cataloguing their native climates. You see, weather, while particular to and dictated by the specifics of location, and even local phenomena, is not an isolated occurrence. It is conjoined and functions as a global composite. What is happening in Cologne or Switzerland or Canada will influence, days or even weeks later, what is happening here, in Westmorland.*

Mrs Brooke tilts her head, clears away another leaked tear, and watches him. She is not weeping, yet the disconcerting impression remains, of sorrow, of woundedness. He tries not to think of Sara, the occasions when she is doubled over at night, her nightgown soaking, weary and weak and apologising the next morning. He forks a slice of gammon onto his plate, continues.

You see – water vapour in the air can travel hundreds of miles on the conveyor of the oceans, so storms are simply passed along between countries, reinforced or weakened in transit. Winds such as your Pennine Helm don't start and stop within county boundaries, even if they appear to. Would you be startled to hear that last year sand from North Africa arrived in Dorset, by air contamination? The particles travelled hundreds of miles. It was all rather messy.

He chuckles. Mrs Brooke shows no sign of being surprised. She spears a potato.

How do you know it was North African sand and not Dorset sand?

Excellent question! It was deposited all over the buildings and the boats in the harbours, even the horses. It was blown into dunes that banked to the north, and there was a very strong southerly all week, thick dust in the air, even out in the Channel. The sunsets were glorious.

But still, how do you know it was North African sand?

Oh, we had it analysed. It was lacking the usual native minerals – quartz, feldspar and the like.

I see, Mrs Brooke says. She peers at the brown sauce, then looks back at Thomas.

A conjoined system is an attractive idea, of course, like the Pangea. Surely sand proves only one relationship, Mr Bodger. Everyone knows the Atlantic conveyor warms the Scottish coast and enables palms to grow – Benjamin Franklin wrote about those currents over a century ago, observing how whales behaved differently in the stream. But how do you explain the ever-changing nature of clouds? How do you predict the rainbow? It's – if not random, then without prescription? Rain

86

refracts sunshine. But each combination is unique.

It is Thomas who is startled – his host is rather well read. And now it is her turn to lecture.

I can assure you, the Helm starts and stops here; it offends Edeners alone, not Cumbrians, nor Kendalians. I myself have stood underneath the bar cloud – sometimes it rests above this very house. Imagine being in a re-volving door, Mr Bodger. Step east and there's a gale blowing, one can barely stand upright. Step west, and a gentle opposing breeze is occurring, one could light a candle. It is as a door between heaven and hell. How is this explained? It is magical.

Thomas raises his eyebrows a fraction. Magical! Not a word that crops up often in the Society club.

Perhaps, in so far as it performs an illusion we cannot yet unveil, he concedes.

She is shaking her head. Mrs Brooke, he suspects, rather enjoys a good parley. He, of course, spends half his life sparring with Glaisher and the others. She seems to be thawing, though, and the conversation has become quite engaging.

It's the wind's formulation I'm interested in, he says. *It will operate along principles, rules – all nature does, even that which we do not yet understand. How does the base cloud form, for example, and why, once the wind is unleashed, does the bar cloud appear?*

People say the bar cloud holds the wind in check, so it cannot cross the river. But I think this unlikely.

Thomas nods, pleased by the scepticism.

I think it unlikely too. My notion is the bar is an associate, not an in-dependent. If we apply the laws of hydraulics, or pneumatics, the basics of power systems, I suspect we may find the answer to Helm's mysteries.

Rebecca Brooke's wet eye trickles; she dries it. Thomas reach-es for the sauce. For a moment there is silence again, though the atmosphere has lightened. The leaves of the great sycamores outside stir in the summer breeze. There's the restrained clink of cutlery as they begin to eat.

After the pause, Mrs Brooke resumes the topic.

I have read about a wind on a mountain in Italy that performs in a similar way. It is self-limited in behaviour, and incredibly disruptive to farmers. Do you know it?

Yes, the Bora. It's a mean old interrupter. There are others too, similar in character, in the Americas. They are cousins of the Helm. All require lee-slopes to function.

And how is my own cousin? I heard from Great-Aunt Caitlin that Sara suffers greatly.

Thomas glances up, and is met by the wide, harish stare. Disquieted by the shift of subject and the candour, he is, momentarily, at a loss.

Um, Sara, gracious, yes, well.

He looks down again, slices the gammon, swabs it through a puddle on his plate.

She's been rather green-fevered, admittedly. It's been a tricky few years, lots of, um, liver and stout.

I heard there might be a surgery? Aunt Caitlin mentioned the new Euston.

Oh, no. No, no. Great-Aunt Caitlin can be a little dramatic, can't she.

Heat rises towards his collar. He chews and swallows, attempts to re-steer the conversation.

I can tell you've journeyed quite far into these subjects, Mrs Brooke. Your observations are most interesting. I have only read about your Helm. Any experience you might wish to share would really be quite helpful.

Rebecca Brooke does not immediately reply. Across the dining table, she appears to be weighing his suggestion, or mulling the hard swerve from the topic of his wife. Thomas scuds on.

And given your interest in meteorology and your local expertise, per-haps you would also enjoy observing the atmospheric experiment I plan to undertake?

Experiment? Which experiment is this? Sanderson said nothing about it.

Another solar glare. He cannot tell if she is intrigued, alarmed or simply hostage to her ocular condition. Either way, Rebecca Brooke is capable of changing the pressure in the room from one minute to the next. One needs, he decides, both umbrella and sun visor while in her company. Intrigued, he decides. He puts down his knife and fork. He draws his hands together.

Yes, allow me to explain. I believe that if we are to properly investigate Helm's nature, we must flush the sky using an agent to enhance it. Then – it's really rather exciting to imagine – we will be able to reveal Helm's anima. Its motion. Its nature. The wind's dance will be visible, and all its mystery will be revealed.

Thomas opens his hands, and spreads them wide. Rebecca Brooke also sets her cutlery down, a hard clatter against the china rim of the plate. Her left eye brightens and fills again. This time she does not attend to the spillage, but allows the tear's explicit passage down her cheek.

Flush the sky, she repeats. *With an agent. What on Earth can you mean, Mr Bodger? Flush it how exactly and with what?*

With steam and with dye, Thomas says, a little too declaratively. *Preferably the brightest colour possible. I'm going to build a machine on the mountainside.*

Silence, again, deep and wretched. Then, wet-cheeked and gas-eyed, Rebecca Brooke rises slowly from her chair. She places her napkin over her unfinished dinner and, though the scream seems only to echo within Thomas's skull, she exits the room with the swiftness of a retreating banshee. Offended, apparently.

XIV

Helm's Foreign Relatives

Zonda (Argentina)
Adelaide Gully (Australia)
Fall wind (Antarctica)
Novorossiysk (Black Sea coast)
Oroshi (Japan)
Williwaw (Alaska)
Chinook (Canada/America)
Berg wind (South Africa)
Garbino (Italy)
Fogony (Catalonia)
Wreckhouse (Newfoundland)
The Barber (New Zealand)
Sundowner (California)
Puelche (Chile)
Lodos (Turkey)
Warm Braw (New Guinea)
Košava (Balkans)
Fønvind (Norway)
Terral (Spain)
Halny (Poland)
Garmesh (Iran)
Gio Lao (Vietnam)
Nortada (Iberia)
Loo (India/Pakistan)

XV

Selima crushes the cigarette butt on the wall of the field station, and goes back inside. She settles down in front of her laptop and starts cleaning up her inbox. She scrolls to the email from the Endtrepreneurs. Her finger hovers over delete, but she opens it and scans through. More pseudo-scientific rubbish, about how the particle filters are giving false readings, have been programmed to lie by the manufacturer, blah blah, then, as with the other messages, the end becomes altogether more devotional and personal. *We are the guardians of true heavenly knowledge. You are one of the fallen and not worthy of your place in Eden.*

Good one. She flags the email and forwards it to the university Comms team and the Public Affairs office. How many messages from this group now – fifteen, twenty? The PA office has been supportive, but it's not really about the university's reputational risk, so what can they do? Send another cease-and-desist reply? She picks up her phone, types to David. *More conspiracy mail – think you'll like this one.* She deletes it. He's still touchy when it comes to this kind of thing. Besides, he'll be in the weekly department committee meeting, phone on silent, dunking his biscuits and worrying about pension increases. Worrying about Sandra's latest round of chemo too.

She shuts the laptop and goes to the field station window. Grey cloud drifts by, the same, the same. Thirty feet away the upland vanishes. There is no valley; she may as well be on Mars. Bit of a coincidence, though: *your place in Eden.* Who knows she is here? The Centre for Atmospheric Science is in a building separated from campus – a hideous beige Lego block – and hasn't much to do with any of the other faculties. Only a few people have seen her application for principal investigator funding. There are always applications being made – another is currently in with the Royal Society, seeking a three-year fellowship, and the Illcombe Trust has supported her research previously, for, quite literally, blue-sky thinking. But the personnel in her field don't tend towards crankery. Is it coming from abroad? The USA? Russia? China? Should she contact Dr Lim and ask if she's received similar?

The trouble with the online loonland is it scrambles your head, makes you feel disarmed and surveilled. Not for the first time, she wonders, briefly, if this 'group' is someone she knows; either a bad joke, or something a little more sick and corrosive. Someone on the periphery. Her cousin's son has autism and wormholes all day every day, fixated on conspiracy theories. But he's a nice kid, harmless. Gaurav? Some kind of jilted payback? He did, when she first broke off their engagement, send a few late-night messages – ghost texts, no words inside, just sad blank spaces, as if to say: Here I am, a void.

The mind could run riot, especially up here, in the grey fugue. Nothing like remote seclusion and Gothic fog for a hefty dose of self-disturbance. Fuck it. The nice relaxed buzz of nicotine has gone; she opens the field station window, lights another cigarette. Second of the day, and inside. *You should know better, Beta* . . . She blows smoke towards the No Smoking sign, and the black-and-white chaps puffing on their calabashes and churchwardens.
  Go ahead. Arrest me, lads.

As she flicks ash out of the window, she hears the engine of a vehicle below, muffled, unlocatable. Often she can hear cars, tractors, quad bikes, miles away but close-sounding. The acoustics carry incredibly well. Barking dogs. The shrieks of buzzards and cawing crows. Human voices too – she'll hear the comments of hikers on the Pennine Way, transmitted over the fell, their words totally clear.

Mustard and ham . . . OS map . . . fold it properly, Carol.

The engine sound pauses; perhaps someone has parked in the lay-by near the road barrier. Lazier dog walkers sometimes drive their mutts up for a run-about there. Occasionally a lone driver parks and sits, morosely contemplating the view, and life.

The engine idles softly. The metal barrier on the road below clangs. Then the vehicle can be heard coming up towards the complex, shifting down a gear on the steepening rise, thrumming over the cattle-grid. Selima stubs the fag out on the windowsill, and goes to the other porthole. A small van appears out of the cloud, white, dirty around the wheel arches; looks like a work van. It pulls up beside the cabin building under the radome and two men get out, wearing fluorescent jackets. One has on a baseball cap. The other has skinny racing-snakes legs under flappy polyester trousers. Must be official, if they've come through the locked barrier. So the radome is manned after all.

The men stand talking for a minute, hands in pockets. They don't look very official, more like two scruffy white blokes better suited to a sports bar: unshaven, po-faced, moochy. They probably can't be arsed with their job, she thinks. Maybe they're sick of the barren commute up to the tops, which, in all fairness, does lose its charm on the more monotone, rainy days. Baseball Cap glances over at the field station, sees the electric bike parked outside. He nods his head in that direction and says something to Racing Snakes. Racing Snakes looks over too, shrugs, and walks away, towards the towering antennae. Baseball Cap walks towards the field station, slouched, but semi-purposefully. He stops abruptly when he notices her looking out of the porthole window. Selima holds her hand up, gives a little wave. His head jerks. He frowns, looks suspicious. Or perhaps just spooked – there is, after all, a lady in this usually empty building. Were they not aware she was here? Surely the Civil Aviation Authority and the Centre for Atmospheric Science share information about the site?

Baseball Cap continues towards the door of the field station, then knocks loudly – very loudly, given Selima has already seen him and he has seen her. She opens the door, grins.

You must be from the anti-terrorism squad, she says.

He stares at her blankly.

I was just preparing the oxidiser.

What? he says.

Selima's grin widens.

I'm kidding. Obviously. How can I help you?

Are you from the Met Office, he asks. *Can I see some ID?*

No, I'm not, and no, I don't have any on me. Can I see yours? Are you from the CAA?

Site security, he says, thumbing vaguely at a badge on his jacket. *What are you doing here?*

I am researching the interaction of pollution and cloud conveyance.

He stares blankly at her.

More specifically, the density of micropolymer particles in vapour and how they might correspond with changing atmospheric activity.

What?

Plastic in clouds, she says.

Oh. The university people.

That's right.

Can I see some ID, he says again.

As I said, unfortunately not, it's back at my apartment. I tend not to need my cards up here. Not exactly Buckingham Palace, is it.

Her grin reaches maximum capacity. Baseball Cap scowls underneath his rim.

Is that your bike?

It is. She's an absolute marvel.

I should really ask you to leave the site, if you don't have ID.

94

I don't have ID here, but I do have the passcode for the barrier, though I usually just, you know, go round it on Ellie. And I do have a key to this building, which is, as I understand it, owned by the university and which I have permission to use – see?

She holds up the improbably long brass key, with mock officialdom.

Right.

Right. Everything OK at the golf ball this morning? she asks.

Maybe don't make jokes, you know, about bombs, he says.

Maybe try not to be abrasive and stupid, she thinks. And, you know, look at the optics.

Sure, she says.

The man is still staring at her, eyes narrowed a fraction, as if she might be joking about being a terrorist because she is in fact a terrorist. A form of duplicity, or triplicity, well beyond any comprehension. What kind of arbitrary training do they get for this job, Selima wonders. There are days no one shows up at all, and now they are going to escort her off the premises for not having a passport glued to her forehead. David did say it might be a good idea to downgrade her sense of humour among 'the natives'. You never knew what throwback National Party member was floating about among the more progressive Cumbrians.

Please shut up, David. I have been to the Lake District before. It's not colonial India.

To which David tilted his head and looked uncertain. *Well . . .*

OK, *good, thanks,* Baseball Cap says, rubbing his nose with the back of his hand.

Good, Selima says.

Don't you need a driver's licence? he asks as he turns to go.

What?

For the bike.

His tone is the same, but is he being sarcastic?

No.

Maybe bring it next time you're here.

OK, what's your name?

What?

She can feel her temper speeding a little, along with her tone, as all the possible reasons for his pointless, jobsworth over-persistence fan out. Race, gender, boredom, any number of little prickish complexes. Or is he just an indiscriminate twat to everyone? Maybe his haemorrhoids are killing him. Think of the positive version. She smiles again.

I'm Dr Selima Sutar, she says. *I'll be here every day for the next seven weeks as part of my research programme. And you are?*

There's a pause, during which trillions of particles swirl in the clouds above, imperceptibly, altering form, funking with the operation of the weather, and gathering in the HVS filters. Selima holds her tongue, does not say what she'd like to, namely: Come on, mate! Why not worry about the real-world problems. Within your and my lifetimes we are going to witness a catastrophic breakdown in the relationship between stable air pressure fronts and temperatures. Heat, radiation, pollution, it will fuck up all the norms in this little kingdom, as it will everywhere, and your shitty drive up the mountain will get a lot shittier.

Paul.

Pleased to meet you, Paul. Have a lovely day.

Paul nods.

Yeah, thanks.

He walks slouchily away, gets back into the van and looks at his phone while he waits for Racing Snakes to finish whatever survey he is doing of the radome. Selima closes the field station door. Shame them with politeness, her Papa used to say, be better than them. Don't give an inch for the aggressor to insert poison or justification. But it was a different age when Vihaan Sutar first arrived in the UK, a different climate when he married Karen Willis, the respiratory nurse. Their indomitable mum: embracer of all things Indian, positioning sandalwood and kalamkari-printed cottons all over the house, telling the cashier at the local shop, *Isn't it time you stocked more pickle than Branston, love.* Being better than them was a sidestep to avoiding trouble, a way to disarm biased institutions. Being one of them, as far as she could tell, started not with the so-called liberal academics but in the Wanderers football stands, where turbans and buzzcuts did get along – providing everyone had black and gold on. *Out of Darkness Cometh Light.* Well, Selima thinks, welcome to the insidious age of boring, house-broken discrimination. Paul clearly doesn't care who she is or what she is doing here. He could have asked to come in, look around, checked her work – actually done his job. She could, in fact, be here to take down the radar and disrupt the whole of northern air traffic, throwing all those transatlantic planes into chaos. Can't be that difficult to make a bomb – can it?

She hears a door slam and the engine starts. The van pulls away, thrums back over the cattle-grid and drones down the hill. She looks out of the window. Disappointing, really. Disappointing that the only interaction she has had up here is with – a Paul. Maybe her own social skills are a little rusty after days spent alone, miles from civilisation. And cooped up in the bothy too, ploughing through novels on her Kindle, feet to the stove, bottle of wine.

Maybe tonight she should actually go to the pub. Get some chips. Interact with other punters. She could give David a call after, see how he is doing, which is essentially how Sandra is doing. Ask about his Mrs H stories.

So, Professor, let's have a chat about supercritical wind speeds and inversions. Tell me about the time . . .

He'd love that. Every meteorologist loves a yarn about mountain bivouacking in force 9 gales. The Great Dun diary entries of

97

the tin-shack generation are full of derring-do. *Day 26, –9, drifts chest height, mine road impassable, had to melt snow for morning coffee, corned beef rations low.* Every meteorologist, except perhaps her. She does not want to be caught out in the storm, thank you very much.

She won't ring David. Sandra is deteriorating. His evenings are difficult now. A mostly liquid diet, carers three times a day, infection after infection. He seems stoical, or, if not stoical, something else – not quite metabolising the situation, not accepting it. Pot, kettle, again – she hasn't exactly scored high marks on the end-of-relationship scale. When David asks how she is really, she says, *Murky, occasional squalls. Next question, please,* and she tries not to think of Gaurav's stuff in boxes being ferried from the flat, or his handwritten note posted through the door, pleading, angry, or his parents ignoring her in the street, her existence cancelled for rejecting their precious son.

Anita teases her about David sometimes. *So weird that your best mate is some cis OAP who likes to go rambling and drives a Honda Jazz – it's, like, cream, Selima. He has an actual vanilla car! Bet he thinks you're fit, though.* Is it weird? Not really. It's just that she's known David for so long now, things don't need to be explained, and the language of weather isn't a bad way to communicate about life's difficulties. He probably could do with some cheery distraction, though. She types a message.

Radome Security Firm employs Tweedle Dee and Tweedle Dumber? Please discuss.

One bar. Sent message failure.

She sits back down in front of her laptop, opens the lid. She unsubscribes from the hideous neon camping gear list, and quickly glances through the department admin. She moves the Endtrepreneurs' email from her inbox into a folder labelled: Apocalypse/Various.

XVI

Trinket 110,958

Apple iPhone 11 64GB, refurbished, black, with dual camera

One of eighty-four in the North Pennine lost phone collection. Lockscreen image was of colourful abstract fibres under microscope, battery is now dead. Case is red silicone, soft-touch, shock-proof, anti-skid grip-tight series. Production date – 2019.

Height – 15.9 cm
Width – 7.57 cm
Depth – 0.83 cm
Weight – 194 grams

Location – the hushings, Little Dun Fell

XVII

NaNay walked down the mountain as the orox caravans were plodding back up. The storm had dispersed and the herders would be out looking for them. She passed the animals without stopping; their dark wet eyes were fixed sidelong. The Halron had swept across the hillside and pulled up grasses and clumps of moraine and the cows that were carrying calves kicked at loose divots and grazed the rich lower stems. NaNay ate grubs from upended tree roots and drew sap from the birch and pine trees with a stripped feather. She ate the cold, sweet syrup and felt stronger. When she reached the base of the mountain, she made an offering of bone shafts and laid it down. The Halron had given her a third mark. They had been joined, and she knew to respect but not to fear it now.

She returned to the huts. The little ones saw her coming and followed alongside her, touching the torn leathers. Irla watched her walk past the pens. Under his face were many feelings, the strongest of which was fear. She stopped and drank water from the kist. Still, he said nothing. Second Mother came out of the hut and held NaNay's forehead to her own.

I knew you were not dead.

NaNay showed her the angry red line on her chest and Second Mother mixed nettle and spit to heal it and the injuries on her thigh and her head, pressing paste into the wounds.

Now I will be able to speak about the magstone, NaNay said. *I will find it.*

When she had rested, she was taken to Magsca by the women of the herding tribe and they left thumb pots with oil, grain and brown ore inside. Ore was ground in the mortar and rubbed onto NaNay's forehead. The people in the settlement stepped off the path whenever she came towards them as if she was not a child. She avoided Irla whenever she could and he did not try to beat her. She did not look at him if he had drunk barley milk and was staggering about and pulling at Second Mother or wrestling with the younger men. She wove bark and reeds with the women and made coil pots. She mashed bulrushes and made flatbread. She talked about her vision to them and they believed her.

NaNay went to the river and looked along the gorge. The magstone was red and this was where the red rock was in abundance. She climbed the cliffs and looked down into the water, between the reefs; she combed the weeds at the edges with a pole, looking for its long face. She asked people from the forest tribes and the far traders if they had seen such a stone in the mines beyond the valley – they said they would look. If she had to leave the valley to find the magstone she would go with them. If the people had to transport it from the quarries to Magsca she would convince them to.

After another winter, NaNay had grown one hand higher and her breasts had come. Her hair was growing back and when it became long enough she plaited in a polished river stone. She laughed with the other girls about which boys had long stalk legs, which were shy, which had the best combination of darkest skin and bluest eyes. She tested the young men, telling them she would partner with only the strongest.

Go and climb that tree and collect the big red apple at the top. No, the higher one.

They were impressed with the way she stood her ground in the wind, and slapped the hinds of the bulls with paddles if they were in the way; how she followed the herd dogs towards approaching wolves. They admired the scars on her breasts and touched the longest rippled line in the skin, which looked as if she had opened her body to take out its heart. No one so young had three marks.

Your hair has been torn but one day it will be longer than anyone's, the girls told her.

When she started her bleeds, there was a ceremony at Magsca. She paired with Henti, who was tallest and could lift orox calves out of the marshes; he desired and respected her. She had a child who lived until naming. He was called Dal. Second Mother became Third Mother to Dal and she was praised by the people and given a belt strung with melted ores shaped into point-heads.

The following year, NaNay had a girl child that did not live to naming. The child was small; her body was not ready. There was a gastric sickness in the cattle and then in the settlement and the baby became sick and sluggish, bleating every time it was taken from the nipple but not suckling when it latched. It lived several more weeks but its eye colour did not begin to alter; its anma was not coming. It died in the night without any sound when the moon was its slenderest rind. The baby was incomplete, so NaNay and Second Mother built a pyre and its body was burned. It could not go to the other world but with the smoke would join the stars. Dal became strong with more milk.

Two harvests later the sun was swallowed by a black disc. The world became dusky and the birds fell silent. The dogs whined and leant against each other. Quickly, the people met in the smoke hut. They were afraid and confused – this had happened to the moon before and the moon had been reborn, but the sun was the stronger anma. It meant something very dangerous: a great damage. Dead crops or

102

sickness, the worst Halron, or the return of ice times. NaNay stood up, with Dal clinging to her back.

I have seen a black sun, she said. *I saw it in my vision. It is a sign that the magstone will come.*

The people went to Magsca and put whatever precious objects they could afford against the stones, braids of their hair, mussel shells brought by the estuary people, studs, the heart and genitals of a bull orox. They burned three woods and sang quietly, sorrowfully. They sat close together in the quiet dimness of the day.

The black disc slowly released the sun.

But the people were unsettled afterwards. There were disputes and skirmishes. Some of their tubers were dug up and they were rotten, with liver worms inside; they had not been tended properly. A great white-headed eagle was seen carrying in its talons a fish with legs and a speared tail. There was a stillbirth in the settlement of herders across the river – the women cut the cord and pulled the sac gently and the deformed child was webbed and had a spine curled like an armoured louse. It was burned and when it was burned it cried.

Argument spread like sickness. The forest tribe complained that thirty trees had been felled by the valley herders without agreement. There were fights at the glades when water was collected. Henti challenged Kobe, the son of a forest elder, and Kobe threw him backwards onto a rock and broke his neck. Kobe held the loose rolling head and moaned. NaNay was quickly found and she sat with Henti's body until his anma was released; his eyes became opaque. She made his clay mask. Dal kept taking the lifeless hand and putting it on his small head, petting himself. Henti had been among the best herders and he was the one who had trained the dogs, he had killed a white orox and NaNay wore its fur cloak; he would have been father to more children. His loss was significant.

103

There was a meeting between the people of the valley. It was agreed there would be no reprisal if Kobe came to the settlement and if the forest tribe allowed the herders to pick garlic, nuts and broadleaf as far as the gorge. No more forest would be burned or felled unless it was agreed. Kobe sat outside NaNay's hut. He slept outside. He brought her and Dal meat from creatures in the forest that NaNay had not tasted before, and insects blackened in the fire, their casings opened. He endured the scorn of Irla and the other herders as he learned how to manage the orox, how to steer them with poles and how to check their hooves and tongues. The next time the Halron came, he remained outside NaNay's hut and did not move to shelter, so that the wind beat against him. When it passed, she opened the door of the hut and allowed him inside. They paired and after a year there was another girl child, who lived to naming and had bright pale eyes the colour of glade water. She emptied NaNay's breasts and Second Mother sometimes lifted her up to a branch where she hung tightly, raising her fat legs and laughing. Her anma was fierce. She was called Reen.

The next year, as Irla was checking the eel traps in the river, he was attacked by a young dispersing bear. He was gouged in the belly and the skin on one side of his head was stripped. The people heard him shouting and drove the bear off with clubs. They carried Irla to a hut, covering the trackable blood on the pathway with soil and leaves. His body was slippery and hard to hold. They sat around him. He was making fast airy sounds, sucking sounds. Second Mother burned three woods above him to bring his anma back from the bear's jaws. His torso was open and ragged and NaNay saw quivering grey tubes and flinching muscles. There were bubbles like tiny mouths in the well of blood. Half his head's flesh had been raked away; chunks of hair and scalp were gone. One eye remained, moving globally in the pulp on the side of his face. Irla seemed to look only at NaNay in his suffering. He spoke inside her head.

After me, you are the strongest.

She reached out and put her hand inside the chest cavity around the sluicing heart, and she held it until it was still.

Irla had two carved beakers that were buried with him. He had been the oldest. They patterned his clay mask with flowers and beads. NaNay sat with Second Mother in Magsca for three nights to honour his anma. Irla had been brave, a good hunter, from him she had learned many things, but he could not see time in the ways NaNay could; he had had no visions.

At the first meeting after Irla's death, NaNay sat where he had sat in the smoke hut and talked to the people about the magstone. She was older now. She had survived several possible deaths, and had birthed children; she had predicted the black sun and been joined with the Halron; she had three marks. No one questioned what she said – she spoke the truth.

She told them – *Magsca is the most important gathering place for all the tribes between seas. Our ancestors began it before memory but it is not finished. Magsca needs the magstone. The magstone will be found before I die.*

She drew a picture on the ground with a stick so they would recognise the stone. Downturned mouth. Long, cloven skull. Blind eye.

Whoever goes to the other world must first tell their children about the magstone. There are many people gathered in the other world. Children of our children, waiting. They will see it rise at Magsca.

Then, as if strong birds have carried her to another place, NaNay is an old woman. Twice as old, her beads say. Great events have occurred, of the river splitting and part of the river changing course, of a new way to mould ore and the ability to germinate grain, rinsing and soaking it.

She stands in the gateway between Magsca's stones as the pale sun descends. This solstice, the sky is clear, so they will see the alignment – for the past three the sky has been full of rain or snow and the sun has been hidden. She will make the measurement and the people will lay markers. The people wait for her signal, standing together and breathing white smoke, stamping cold feet, ready to light fires and celebrate.

She wears the white orox coat. The stitched deerskin underneath is open at the front to show her marks, and the marks have softened and turned pale pink, absorbed by her body. She has kept good teeth to chew seeds and smokemeat and she can still run alongside the cattle and climb for fruit. She is Second Mother to Dal's child and she is called All Mother by the people, the herders, farmers and forest tribe, even the far traders. She is NaNay who survives half-fin. NaNay who flies with the Halron. The seer. The death-walker. Kobe is dead now, crushed and trampled by a bull. Second Mother has died of wasting, protected in the settlement and surrounded by singers, her anma honoured as it departed. Her cups have been buried with her, a wolf's tooth, a blanket with threads dyed purple and orange. The belt strung with stones and copper belongs to NaNay.

She stands in the stone portal, holding the bast rope. She watches the western horizon, waits as the sun sinks. The magstone is still waiting to be found. NaNay has forgotten some things. The pain of the child who died of sickness. The pain of childbirth. But she remembers exactly the magstone's face in her vision, its sombre expression, low jowls shaped by the red rock – when she makes the same face for the little ones, rippling her brow and sticking her chin out and pouting, they laugh at her and say how ugly and funny she is. She gathers them under her white cloak, and her skin is warm and oniony. Of all the second children, Joa is her favourite, and she keeps him held tightly until he squeals; he has Reen's eyes, Kobe's eyes. Na-Na, he calls her, and sleeps against her chest as if she had birthed him, made milk for him.

As still as a heron, she waits. Her long grey hair braids have a hole-stone knitted in for each year the hair has grown back after the fight with Irla; the stones clack together when she shakes her head and when she dances. *How many more stones?* the children ask. Not many. She cannot stop the constellations and moons passing overhead – big hunter chasing the bright star chasing the fish. Sometimes she goes to sleep and does not know if another morning in this world will come.

She has searched the riverside many times for the magstone, looking along the beaches, among cliff-fall boulders and in the caverns, wading across the current and putting her face underwater so her eyes burn with cold. She has sat by the river, smoking moss, entering a trance, trying to know its location, to hear it calling, watching the raindrops ring the surface from above and the fishes' mouths ring the surface from below. Once she sat opposite a big male bear as it fished the rapids, close enough that she could smell the musk-stink in its shaggy coat. She didn't move and the bear kept fishing, eating the fatty heads of the fish, discarding the bodies on the rocks at the edge of the woods. The bear's muzzle was pale and scarred, the fur parted on its huge head. Its eyes were small and hazel, dark-ringed, like a human's. Perhaps it was the bear that had killed Irla and his anma was inside it.

There is no magstone yet but she knows where the magstone will be brought to, and where it will stand. She fixes her eyes on the place. The sun falls slowly, pale as ox-eye. On the horizon the mountain summits are repeated in the shapes of Magsca's stones. The ground of the gathering place is hard and white, all-day frost that has not melted, ice stiffening the tips of the grass. This is the time of smallness and economy, of closed seeds and sleeping mammals, when faith must remain and the sun's anma be given energy from the people. It is the time of turning, towards more light, new growth.

She knows the sun will disappear between two rises of nearby land, between two distant blacker mountains, and between the bent-knee stone and the saddle-stone of Magsca. It will pass into the other world through an opening and become black. The hole is alive in the landscape, like a blood channel – it heals at night and in the morning opens above the Halron's mountain, then the sun is released and rises like an orange bulb. The other world cannot be found between the hills, it cannot be approached, until it is time to die. It cannot be dreamed. Even NaNay, whose anma travelled to the entrance, who saw the people gathered, does not know what the other world is like.

The air is bitter and stulted. She can hear the river rushing beyond the trees. She waits.

The people wait. They are huddled and quiet and cold, each holding a rock for the cairn, but soon there will be dancing and cooked meat, smoked crab and bird and wild pig. They have all come. Manno and the people from the forest tribe. Beach traders from the great bay, the axe makers from the slate mountains; bronze traders from the south who celebrate at the lowland henge in summer.

The long rope looped over NaNay's arm has been made by Reen and the children, who have stripped damp, supple conifer bark and twisted the fibres together. Many reaches, woven and tightened. It is wound round NaNay's arm like a rough woody serpent.

The sun lowers moment by moment, until it is a hand-span above the horizon. Now it is time.

Dal comes forward and stands beside All Mother and takes the end of the rope. NaNay loops it around his waist and lays the coil down. She holds cupped hands underneath the falling sun. She folds her thumb across her palm and measures its height from the edge of the world.

She closes her eyes. Where the sun burned, there is a black disc inside her head. She asks the magstone to come out of the darkness and belong with the other stones. When she opens her eyes again, the sun is in the right place and the ghost of the bright star has appeared nearby, pricking the deepening blue.

She picks up the rope and walks forward, paying it behind her, toe to heel, counting. Dal holds it firmly. Her feet creak softly in the compacted frost, leaving almost no prints. Her fur is white against the white ground. The rope unwinds; she and Dal keep it taut. It is a good rope, very strong. She leads it between the saddle-stone and the bent-knee stone on the far side of the circle. She hears the people humming. She keeps walking.

She walks beyond the stones of Magsca's circle, and away from the gathering place. The humming becomes louder, protective, a communion. What NaNay has seen in her vision is not what was practised by their ancestors, not seen in their older sacred shapes, in the barrows, in mimicries of nature. The magstone is a new idea. It is a lever, a hand to mark time.

NaNay stops. Reen follows after her across the frozen earth and she lays a small rock between NaNay's feet. NaNay turns around and shouts.

Yayaya.

The people all come forward and lay their stones, until a small cairn is built. Then they move back within the circle; the fires are lit, and produce shared. There is a container of barley milk and fermented bulrush mash, creamy, vinegary; they dip their beakers and the liquid numbs their lips and feet. The daylight becomes deep teal with paler silvery-blue along the horizon. The stars begin to cluster. There is drumming and fire-made shadows leap and sway over the white ground. The heat of their togetherness steams the cold air.

NaNay continues to stand outside the circle of Magsca, beside the cairn.

Dal and Reen come over to her.

All Mother. It is hot beside the fire. The meat is hot. Everyone is dancing and holding antlers, they want you to dance and tell stories.

Reen offers her crab shell with meat inside. Dal is drunk and he tries to pick her up and carry her away.

No, she says. *Put me down. Back there. I am not cold. I am not hungry. Go to the fire, I will come soon.*

Dal lowers her. They leave her, standing in the midpoint of winter. The sun has already disappeared into the other world and the twilight sky is fading rapidly. Above her left shoulder, the bright star is proud and bold now and seems bigger than usual, flickering, flickering, staying fixed in its place, as she is. The next star, always unsure of its power though it is the heart of a winged creature, is chased by the big hunter.

Still NaNay does not move. Behind her, the moon rises in opposition to the bright star and the bright star finally sets.

110

XVIII

From the longhouse they ride out towards Fiend's Fell. They pass through woods, where garlic shoots have woken vividly beneath the desiccated briar. The inhabitants flee from the hoof beats, white-rumped, high-tailed, and the last golden-eyed lynx watches from its crux above the forest path. Michael and Isa do not see the carpenters, nor hear their rhythmic saw in the dense thicket. At the eastern edge of the woods are leaning and fallen trees, trunks dying in the embrace of others – and beyond, on the blasted heathland, which serves, when Ranulph fancies it, as a racecourse, there is a herd of fallow deer. The stag lifts its head; the does move on, gracefully, silently.

The mountain enlarges as they ride; the path up it, little more than an animal track, ascending, shedding fauna. Once again, Michael tells Isa to draw up his hood, though he does not cover his own helmet. On the open heath, Olwen begins to whinny, flaring her nostrils; she butts her head and tugs left, strangely uncooperative. He draws the reins, brings her still. He scans the undergrowth. Have they a hunter sloping alongside? Usually he can sense a stalk, be it human or animal. The pale gelding that Isa rides picks up the mood; she turns on the path, clopping, huffing; she shits. A breeze is blowing from the south-east, out of the dirty, clay-slipped sky, stirring the ponies' manes and lifting the ends of their tails. Michael holds up a hand, murmurs.

We are baited. It prods at us coyly. It is trying to beguile the animals.

A volley of rain arrives, seemingly from nowhere, peppered with lumps of ice that ring off Michael's sallet. Greetings or agreement

111

from his adversary, perhaps, a primer to their affair. The ponies stamp and sidestep.

Dismount, Michael says, swinging out of the stirrup. *Fasten them well. To the willow.*

He stands, facing the mountain. Isa ropes the ponies to a sturdy dwarf tree, looping the leather twice through its hitch.

Now we must go on foot, Michael says to the boy. *I've seen this often. Even the surest stallion might be turned against its master by such cunning infiltrators. One minute the pintle is soft and sheathed, the next red and engorged as a young groom's and the beast is for mounting any other. I've seen men shot like cannons from horses' backs when the devil has the bridle.*

He walks ahead, and Isa follows, the scholastic length behind. The shower, no more than tossed handfuls of hail, eases. They walk calm as shepherds through the scrubland.

You have seen this before too, Isa. On our crossing to the Holy Isle, when the typhoon rose around the ship and we were driven far into Scotia – was our purpose not deliberately thwarted? It was no mindless disaster. There were dire motives to the currents.

Isa remains quiet; he absorbs, a receiving lobe. An answer is not required. His master has studied the bold and intimate ways of evil, has dedicated himself to prosecuting cacodemons; his role is simply to witness this art. The fitting and frothing calmed under Michael's dispossessing grip, absolution after the commandment. Spirits departing their human casings; infidels turning to the Lord when the pyre is lit; white, rolling eyes become still after trepanation. He's seen it all. No, there is no need to answer.

Michael gestures again, and they pause. The many weighty miles of Fiend's Fell lie clear for them to see, its long, folded massif capped with barren-looking rock.

112

There, he says. *Up there is its rancid lair. A pile of naked stone, like a snake's, like a spider's. It will rise, sulphurous, with its two vaporous heads – one broad as a lion's, one narrow as the telson.*

He raises his gloved hands in the air, separates them a full reach, cupping two imaginary principles.

The power between is invisible, yet tremendous. This demon has strength enough to wreck a barn and transport Ranulph's barley to Ireland. Let us consider its mass. How much does it weigh and measure? How thick and heavy is its pitch? Akin to brass, or rosewood? Arsenic smoke? This is a soul-hunting fog we face. Is its force that of a hammer, or tipped bitumen, or wildfire? We must make our estimate, or be sorely disadvantaged.

Isa looks through the shadows of his hood at his master's solid back and the iron skullcap. The landscape beyond is allium red and green, wet-earthed, English. He is fortunate to belong to this man, perhaps, and have access to such acuity. Fortunate to have been salvaged, and given opportunity.

A flock of twittering brown birds lifts from the moorland, flutters away, then lands and disappears again. The canopy of trees behind them ripples. Master and servant gaze upwards, each in his own torrid limerence, each looking for Helm. Overhead, geese, returning from worlds not yet claimed, prowing the currents in the upper airstreams. No other dark signature is written in the sky.

As they ride back to Salkeld Hall, the lesson continues. Demons are not the sole enemy. Those they enter, reign over and manipulate, those put to savage purposes, are also hell's soldiers. They receive evil as a good Christian would the body and blood of Christ. He who has a bitter, grudging heart, he who is naive and jealous, he who aspires to power – these vanities can all be exploited by guile. She of lewd proclivity and insatiable appetite, or she of humours which tend towards phlegmatic. The child of incestuous, compromised parentage. All are weak vessels waiting to be filled.

Therefore, Isa, it is never one demon we battle, but multitudes.

Michael sighs. His head has dropped forward, a sign of pain. Isa spurs the pony alongside him.

At the hall, after dismissal of the grim cook and after the longhouse door is barred, they attend to the vulnerable matter of human flesh. Isa marks the floor with the circle and triangles; he places burning embers at six points. Michael sits, shirtless, within the pentacle, his torso dull as linen, his nipples damson-coloured, small and hard. The boy removes, with extreme gentleness, the tight sallet from his master's head and he places it on the ground. There's a convulsive, soft-throated sound from Michael as he forfeits control, submits, to the exposure, to trust, the air's weightless relief.

The skin underneath the helmet is appalling. Where old wounds have closed and bonded to the skull, there is immovable scarring. Where there are burst blisters, the white skin scrolls back from pink puddles. The hair is patchy, holding on in clumps if the iron hasn't killed the follicles; thicker at the base, gone from the pole completely, like a monk's.

Isa performs the medical diagnostic. Here is Michael Lang's head. Its spurs and depressions, its strong fork of tendon and muscle at the nape, its mortal construction. Here are new sores; here reopened ones; here the healed and hardened lids. Isa gives no indication of disgust or sympathy. The bronze exorcist's mirror is not employed during the process. God forbid Michael see his state. Imagine what truth might be reflected back, what essence manifested in the glass.

Isa leans to smell for infection, and, finding nothing putrid, just sweat and grease and metallic odour, he begins treatment. He lifts dry and matted bales of hair – once or twice there has been a maggot, or louse, working away at a pustule. He combs what he can of the brittle strands, like a widow grooming the cadaver of her husband. Occasionally the hair is trimmed, though it is better to let it grow if possible, to give protection against the sallet. He has prepared a bowl of warmed water and muslin cloths. He dips and partially wrings the material, then cleans from the forehead backwards. Michael's shoulders soak; the run-off streams down his back and chest, drips off his nipples. His eyes are closed, his fists clenched beside his spleen. There is never a moment when death might not come lumbering towards him, meaning to crack apart the bone and suck out the soft yolk of his brain. But such vulnerability is intoxicating, and the reversal of control arousing; his cock begins to stiffen.

After ablutions, Isa wraps the scalp in dry muslin, presses it gently, then he unbinds it. He applies the bee ointment made by the white canons: an antiseptic salve of jelly, herbs, oil. Myrrh or rosewater too – its smell is balsamic and sweet. For an intolerable hour Michael's head will remain free of its cage. He will be guarded closely. Then the iron skullcap is lifted back on, and Michael Lang is invincible again.

It is after this act that Michael delivers difficult news to the boy. He will ascend Helm's mountain unaccompanied. He will carry the cross alone. Isa shakes his head, objects. He is enthralled; he is his master's loyal escort through every danger.

I need no Simon, Michael says. *You must wait here for my return.*

Another shake of the head. But Michael is firm – it is decided. The boy will remain safe in the valley. He will spectate from the ground. He will watch the sky blacken and boil with the fury of combat above the summit, then he shall see the darkness evaporate as the cross is raised, and from it radiant spokes emitted.

115

No more on the matter.

Nor is there caveat, instructions for what Isa should do if Michael Lang is not triumphant. What fate or free will might be the good servant's if Michael is defeated? Inheritance of death, perhaps, following in his master's footsteps? Conversatio morum? Emancipation? The long road home to the Levant.

XIX

The hallway is empty & I resume. At my chamber door were Nathaniel & the goblain, come to lecture me on chastity, their own Capital Points. I stowed this letter, drew up my fan & feigned illness. None too difficult, I am quite green-gilled.

How paradoxical my husband is, though would never admit so. He bemoaned the completion of Heron Syke yet complains we have not enough packhorses to convey goods to Alston. He suffers apoplexy returning from London on the whirling coach, while ridiculing the Duke of Cumberland who made insistence for the tolls (Old Neb-Nob was the Duke). The servants here perplex him extremely, for they are not shook of their magic ordinances – the Westmerians especially. They have May Day ram heads & prescriptions at Candlemas which are deep-established, supposedly Pictish. They obey borderland forms & fairy law. Yet their common lore is most sensible – woe betide if snow beneath a patient sitting fox is not excavated! Nathaniel had the stable-boy whipped by Tobias for mumbling old charms beside the stalls & marking their doorways with a daisy wheel. Poor boy was striped across his back like a hyena. He meant only to keep the horses safe, Phoebe told me afterwards, as the groom had taught him.

Had my husband an ounce of curiosity he might have learned himself the clever position of Meg's stones before condemning them. I chanced upon the midwinter mathematic watching low women from the village gather there. On Advent's darkest day I was returning by trap from the carol service & saw the ladies, bundled in shawls & bearing gifts. I bid my driver hold so I might watch – he confirmed the annual escapade. A huddle were there, including our washer-woman Tilta, all standing between two very large pillars. These must have been especially stout witches, dear sister, for both are the size of a prize bullock! It was a fine stage for sundown – the orb did sink above Meg, whose crude pudendal cleft received its fiery glory.

This astonished me, for never would I have perceived the astral geometry. I went t'wards the ladies as they placed their boughs, enrobing Meg with hollies, bindweed & teasels. Tilta handed me a winter rose that I should offer it, saying, *Blessed is the light returning.* Quite so. I placed my palm against the stone's side, & I do swear while all about was frigid the stone felt warm, for Meg's energy passed within me. Titbits were left against the foot – ribbons, clove cakes, pickles, a goat's horn, runes & candles, raggedy poppets bound together in congress – they believe her power bestows fertility. (Beatrice! Is it coincidence I have now conceived after my trilogy of failure?)

When I remarked upon the principle of this ancient solarium to Nathaniel, he became sallow & silent. His manner of anger is ice not fire – no flushed neck when his temper comes, only shrunken diamond eyes. Thuggish, he said. Do they also believe the Croglin giant steps about the place at night or worship Hecate? Provide me with the names of any in my service. I said I knew not who these ladies were, old snuff-takers and offcomers and egglers, perhaps.

Since our marriage, strict fervour is upon him. I knew him devout at our betrothal; accepting the match for the sake of dear Pappa, as you know. There was never impropriety before the vows. Permit me sisterly confidence – he partook of additional communion on our wedding day and had us pray together after consummation, rather than lying in a gentle embrace among the fat cushions. We do not sit as companions in the parlour, nor spill marmalade together on the little table by the window in my chamber. (Do you with your Antrobus? I hope he pets you fondly and winds your locks around his fingers!)

There is darker purpose to Nathaniel's improvements, hot ideas about revival & purgation. The brethren of his lodge despise the Quaker propositions, any suggestion of abolition. Their purifying hand is everywhere about this parish. The amethyst luck, which I

118

brought from Rydal, has gone from the cabinet. I believe Nathaniel took it & broke it (truthfully I no longer feel our blithe Senhouse fortunate presides o'er me). Nathaniel is pressing the rector to have comic bosses removed from the church roof, though they are harmless & bright merries.

Most horribly, his vandal hand directed the event I shall now reveal to you. Two weeks ago he sent for black powder from the Sedgwick. The mill lies south of Kendal along the river's rapid chase; Nathaniel took me there after our engagement to shew the works. Naive soul I was! I could scarce believe that in such a beauteous location & from those tumbling aqua waters a deathly substance could be milled & caked. Nathaniel thinks me oblivious if I do not know the greater part of his product is fine-grind, used for armament. Gun money funds his piety, Beatrice. Yet I knew nothing of his recent plan. Phoebe reported that demolition was to occur on the land beside the hall, that labourers from the village were now in Nathaniel's employ. The men had been promised twice the farm rates, for it is exceedingly dangerous handling powder as any fulminator knows. When I went to him & asked were this calamity true, had he condemned the stone daughters, Nathaniel told me outright, Yes, dear wife, those wretched hags will be gone by Sunday.

I went to my knees & implored him not to fulfil this awful task. My Lord, they are very meaningful hereabouts, I said. They are proud relics such as those of the ancient Greeks, perhaps even sacred, we cannot know. They are of antique providence & we are merely their custodians. Not a drop of pity from my husband. There he stood, intractable as a statue on a plinth, gazing to the distance, with Tobias sly as a rat in the corner. I then made bolder argument. 'Tis irrational manoeuvring, surely; those spirits cannot harm you, they only seek exit from their detention. At that last bit of speech he hauled me up by the elbows & spoke a fierce whisper in my ear. Quiet, wife. We shall be cleansed. We shall use the large coarse black, same as sent to the blastings and quarries. No rock in God's creation can withstand it. There will be nought but witch stencils left.

XX

Helm notices. Among their tendencies, humans like to blame others. When things go wrong. For their pains. The mistakes they have made. For their misfortunate goings-on. They especially like to blame Helm.

They blame Helm for all their miserable illnesses and ailments. The poxes and puses, the agonies and accidents, the frailties of flesh and brain.

They blame Helm for the major damages, which, to be fair, are often undeniable. Bruises. Blindings. Lacerations. Concussions. Broken limbs. Fractured hips. Crushed feet. Staved fingers. Torn ligaments. Strokes. Dislocations. Decapitation (for the record, only one occasion of beheading). Helm is the indefensible culprit, caught red-handed in the middle of acts of grievous bodily harm. Battering. Beating. Shoving. Crushing. Dragging. Abrading. Grazing. Maiming. Even (yes, your honour) cold-blooded killing.

A wide array of weaponry used in the process.

Assault with a blunt object – snapped tree branch, low-flying dustbin lid. The toppling gate, hastily back-trotting goat, rolling tractor, hurtling barrow, the randomly redirected arrow. Stampeding cows, bolting coach horse, beams from the fallen-in roof, ouch.

Assault with a blunt instrument – piano flung from the grip of the removal men, guitar case clapped in the busker's face, cymbals frisbeed, a harp-sliced palm. The flight of the double bass, bassist still attached (not a sensible parachute). Playing the harmonica badly (hee-hee).

Assault of a more sinister and particular nature – ladies' stays blown tight, compressing the abdomen, scarves and pearls over-knotted, choking the throat. The plate-glass window (sharp as a knife, nice neat slice). The lashing washing line and live electrical cable snapped and buzzing about.

They blame Helm for the minor injuries also. The donk on the head with this and that – paperweights, condiments, brassware, bric-a-brac, rubbish cans, hatstands, any old junk. Shrapnel in the calf or buttock, missiles in the bollocks. Crud in the eyes – seeds, leaves, mud, helicoptering keys from sycamores, coins, peas, the rind of the cheese: Helm's aim is unerring! The ocular issues lingering after the medical eye bath – scratched cornea, conjunctivitis, skin growing over the foreign body so the doctor has to tweezer the foreign object out. Ingrowing short-and-curlies, hair won't grow straight in a Helm, they say, the ensuing boil in the armpit or groin. The fateful splinter under the thumbnail from fighting with the garth gate – infected, swollen, DIY lancing with unsterilised needles, blood poisoning, sepsis, rigor mortis ensuing.

Whatever the season, they blame Helm for their mishaps. The ice slip, the dust lung, the snow blains, the whirlies. Fertiliser spray raining a mile from its tanker, burns from the gorse fires run amok, scalds from the hot tea flask tipped into the crotch, the April Fool's trick gone wrong (don't ask). Distributed pollen spores causing widespread sneezing and nosebleeding. Blister sores when runners get wind-turned and lost.

And the headaches – so many headaches! Headaches of all kinds brought on by the Helm. Barometric pressure headaches, noise and sinus headaches, steel band around the crown, headaches from wind frown. Headaches in the dull middle brain (like someone is in there knocking with a mallet), throbbing frontal lobes, light strobes, frozen ear, locked jaw, the aching upper palate, stiff neck and crick neck, the ubiquitous tension headache, over-extension, teeth clenching, shoulder scrunching, headaches from stormy fits of crying, thunderclap, post-traumatic, cluster, paralytic, ice pick, and allergic headaches. Worse still, the dreaded migraines – Helm cops for those too. The auras, the flashing and floaters, pins in the scalp, the globe of the skull in a vice-like grip, bowking into the bin and bucket, the borehole of pain drilled behind the eye.

All the other aches and infirmities, miscellaneous and extraneous, are made worse when Helm blows, naturally. Arthritic knees, impacted wisdom teeth, ganglions, bunions, corns, head horns, the grumbling appendix, hot flushes, cold sores, growing pains, acne, the monthlies.

Ladies' issues! Yes, please. Helm is especially at fault for those. Irregular periods, inverted nipples, ovarian cysts. Early labours and late terms. All those problem pregnancies – ectopic, phantom, unwanted, divine. Twins (Helm can separate an egg, you know). Miscarriage, pre-eclampsia, Caesarean section, a million and one opportune bastards made while Helm blows. Why not include birth deformities in the list – a sixth finger, the third testicle, extra kidney, clubfoot, cleft lip, heart on the wrong side of the chest. Then of course the Gentlemen's Weaknesses. Swollen, shrunken, overactive, spastic, uncooperative, cancerous prostates. Sluggish sperm. Premature ejaculation. Urinary misdirection. Dad's back, from clearing up storm crap.

They blame Helm for every possible brown study. The physical – constipation (can't go when it's windy), flatulence (swallowing too much air, or scared, too pumped up), irritable bowel (e.g. shitting oneself in a force 9). And the psychological – panic, paranoia, depression, repression, insomnia, obsessive–compulsive disorder, psychosis,

122

metamorphosis, borderline personality, hysteria, brain miasma, disturbed humours.

Moreover, their moral pains and misdemeanours – quite a contortive strain to land those on Helm but they always seem to manage it.

Hangovers. Because a man has to drink just to cope with Helm's abuse, never know when it's going to kick off, start yelling, smashing plates off the dresser (given to you at Christmas by Mother), sneaking off with your money, stealing your best shirt, losing your best hat, making you argue with your best friend about whether he gave the gusty eyeball to your wife.

Fast and unfastened tempers – wind-driven, wind-stirred, wind-loosed, unleashed. The duels, the shootings, the stabbings (*You have barraged most rudely me, sir*). The brawls and the whippings. The clubbing with the rolling pin (self-defence, good on her). Grudges due to the smashed window, the failed handbrake, the rear-ended priceless classic car, the non-returned fiver (*Finders keepers, my side of the fence*), the broken lawnmower (*Worked when I borrowed it, Charlie*), the demented terrier setting upon Mrs Flufferson, the prize Burmese (*Sorry, slipped his collar, it's a dog-eat-cat world*). The ends of friendships (wedding invitation didn't arrive).

And, of course, top of the list, worse than all the rest, chief of all crimes, they blame Helm for sex pesting. The lusty, bluster manias (*Goodness, I don't know what came over me, I've never done that before!*). Chance of a quickie while it's blowing a hoolie (*May as well while we're sheltering, love*). The extramarital shenanigans (*Darling, I just couldn't get home in this weather, so I took refuge at your brother's*). STDs acquired in the sheds and caravans and bedrooms and outbuildings, in the lee of trees and the head rush of passions, couldn't find/didn't have condoms/prophylactics snatched right out of hands.

123

It's as if Helm is the third in their threesomes – the fluffer offstage, whispering in their ears, stirring their desires, pushing them into embraces, inflating flaccid members, lifting up the ladies' skirts, sweeping away reserve and ambiguity, so John Armstrong and John Postle can, after years of side-eyeing across the auction hall and wrestling drunk outside the Cock and Cobbler, finally fellate each other in the stalls while the farmhands are gathering in the flocks and their wives are chasing loosed ducks and raping drakes. *Now that's what I call a blow-job.*

Sigh.

And sigh again.

Yes, for every transgression, every horrid condition, every chafe and shame and itch and scratch, every offence in need of a patsy, a scape-goat, a schmuck, a wind-rod, they blame Helm.

(Helm could almost start taking it personally.)

XXI

Light topping the Eastern Fells and the twittering of meadow birds wakes Thomas. Beneath him, a drily rustling mattress, its stalks faintly pricking his back – comfortable enough, though. He has dreamed of something watery and illicit, a naiad, perhaps, a siren, drawing him towards a pond, green hair draped over her breasts. He rises and looks out of the big picture window. The Pennines are a dull wheat-blonde and folded with shadows. The sky above is pale, powdery blue, suggestive of French drawing rooms rather than an arena of great turbulence.

But he must start!

He decides to forgo breakfast and avoid another encounter with Rebecca Brooke, last seen firmly shutting the dining room door on him. He casts off his nightshirt and hastily dresses. Downstairs at the scullery, Midge fills his canteen with coffee; she sugars it twice at his request – he's quite the Turk, he quips. Midge stares blankly, then shrugs when he enquires about the possibility of local eateries.

Mrs Hodge might boil you a sausage, she says. *Or you can ask for cake at the mill.*

And where might Mrs Hodge be?

Settera Cottage.

I see. And where is Settera Cottage?

Settera.

Boller is back from his day off; a rheumatic man of approximately seventy, all knuckles and veins and slightly hunched, but otherwise operational. A horse is selected from the stables at the back of the Grange, a frisking sorrel mare named Vesta. She is bridled, and a dark, shine-worn saddle hoisted on.

Best watch her on the bridges, Boller says. *She's cockly.*

Pardon me?

She's a jiber. She'd rather go under and ford the beck. Sees the old company, I reckon.

Thank you. I'm sure we'll get along.

Thomas mounts the mare, allows her to step about and settle under his weight. He is a fair rider, though an infrequent one.

Please inform Mrs Brooke I shall be gone most of the day.

Aye, sir.

Will the colonel be returning today?

Nay, sir.

Boller limps away.

Thomas sets off, with Vesta tugging the bridle and lifting her knees a little as if at a gymkhana. The morning is bright and amenable, already very warm. He has a rough survey map, a compass and a fair idea of the route up Cross Fell, following an old mining track. At the midway point, he will turn northwards and then circle back, in order to gain a cameo view of the summit. His stomach grumbles a little – wasn't sure he should finish his ham after Mrs Brooke's dramatic exit, so didn't. But no matter! The expedition has begun! No longer theoretical, here is the dish upon which the experiment shall produce its marvellous results.

He has scoured the Society's archive for useful information, anything worthy of consideration transposed into his own notebooks. *Pouring like Satan's river* was the description of Helm by the Reverend Josiah Banks of Milburn in 1642 in a letter to his brother. *The mountain's hard declivity combined with air density atop and bottom the dale is surely responsible.* This, six years before Pascal and Périer lugged their

126

column of mercury up the volcano. Highbrows on the council may scoff at the amateur scientist's errors, the layman's hyperbole and the rector's riper metaphors, but weather diaries by thousands of parsons and quotidian clerks are the very foundation of British meteorology. To get past mere reaction, to achieve prediction and create the ideal system so lauded by the fellows, they must first look to the past. They must sift and sort the dog-eared postcards, squint at the tiny scripts in churchwardens' logs; they must catalogue the sets and subsets of tedious information and imprecise measurements; the bent vanes, duff swing-plates and siphons, the hedgerow observations of simple folk beholding to the conditions.

Vesta clops on briskly and Thomas admires the passing countryside, which is far lovelier than he judged it yesterday. Rich pastures. Flocks gathered in pens, fine-looking equines in the paddocks. Geese, goats, submarine-shaped hogs. He rides through the village of Melmerby, missing its sunken mill and the chance of a currant bun, and on to Skirwith. The horse vies with the reins from time to time, occasionally breaks into a trot alongside the field horses, and indeed has a nappy relationship with the humpback bridges, baulking as if some spectral obstacle prevents her crossing, then descending the bank and splashing across the water instead.

The roads, though remote, are quite busy. He greets those he passes, two dairy hands gossiping and giggling, a carter. Then a dark-skinned woman foraging the verge, who rises apparition-like from the tall grass, dressed all in white, her hair wrapped like a Bedouin's. The horse stops, unbidden, and stands perfectly still. The forager, neither young nor old, both weathered and vernal, stares at him. She takes from her basket a sprig tied with string, and holds it up to Thomas.

For the kessen, she says. *Thee and she. Hers is cleaved and yours is to bray.*

Charmed, and a little disarmed, he reaches down for the bundle.

I suppose, yes – how much?

The woman says nothing. She stares at him. He takes a coin from his waistcoat pocket and passes it to her. Thomas nudges the horse on, nudges it again. It remains stock-still. The forager moves off along the verge and Vesta trots forward. Thomas looks at the posy. Vervain and broom, tied not with string but with black horsehair.

Well, well.

No sausage, then, and an odd off to the day, but no matter. He continues on and meets no other. Acrobatic swallows perform alongside him. Around nine o'clock, he hears, but cannot see, the first train: wheel rods beating, a low, mournful whistle between tunnels. Smoke purls above the valley trees.

He keeps Cross Fell in his sights. It is not, in any case, easily dismissed, and is visible for a hundred miles from high vantage points; seen even from the summit of Snowdon. He proceeds to Kirkland, and St Lawrence's, a lost chapel tossed across miles to the foot of the fell. He dismounts and goes inside, inspects the simple whitewashed nave, its scrolled Book of Genesis hanging behind the altar. *In the beginning God created the heaven and the Earth. And the Earth was without form, and void; and darkness was upon the face of the deep. And the Spirit of God moved upon the face of the waters.*

He rides on, past the tiny cottages – one of which he will soon become tenant of – and begins up the long slope. The horse makes her way steadily on the track, then chooses for herself the softer bed of moorland. The saddle begins to rub, buttery though the leather is. As the heat rises, Vesta drinks at the edge of a black puddle, and Thomas sips from his flask. The pathway is still good, passable. He must assess how best to transport the machinery, including the steam engine, which will either be towed up the gradient complete or transported in parts and assembled in situ – cylinder, crankshaft, chimney. It must be portable, yet heavy enough not to topple in a windstorm. The larger challenge, though, will be the laying of the steam pipes up the uneven terrain. But it may all come to him, unfolding implicitly in his mind, as the Bonn psychologist says.

He slaps the back of his neck. Vesta snorts and swishes her tail. Gnats and clegs, nipping at his cuffs and the horse's rear. He takes out his notebook again, makes a rough sketch of the topography, its flatter stages, possible landing sites for the machine. He will send some sketches to Sara; she'll like that.

In remembering his wife, he realises he has not really thought of her, not since avoiding the topic the previous evening.

Dr Allen is due back this week. The tumours, benign though Allen assumes they are, continue to grow, and may, they've been warned, begin to interfere with the other organs in that region. Sara now appears with child, a tragic irony, and she has taken to belting her waist with wide leather to hide the swelling. The monthly event is ferocious. An image arrives, of Sara lying on her side, her pupils blown from the drops, the towellings blooming redly around her. She would submit to an operation, he knows; anything to put an end to it. Two guineas for anaesthetic and twenty for surgery: a bargain if it works, she says cheerfully. And if it doesn't?

The physicians are quite confident, Tombo. They have performed successful deep surgeries now.

Yes, and they are ambitious too, my love. We must be cautious.

Deep. Awful expression, and awful to dwell on its implication – his wife's abdomen opened like a preserving can. Of course he does not want to see her suffer. But he cannot grant permission. The risks are simply too great.

He puts away the notebook, checks the compass. On the mountainside the grass is tawny and aromatic. He tips his hat backwards to save his neck. He is unignorably hungry now, but pushes on, bearing north. The survey map is marked with an old redundant smelting mill; he doesn't find it, only the ore-hearths, subsiding and obscured by foliage. There are sinkholes from the lead mines, boarded-up shafts, and spoil heaps being redressed by ferns. All this, before the ingenuity of locomotives, he thinks. All this, in the age of torpid waterways. If the mountain was home to industry then, surely his own scheme is possible. He has seen spectacularly improbable things: funiculars built up mountains, monasteries teetering on the brink of heavenly altitudes, the frontier railways. Anything, everything, is possible, with decent engineering, and sheer bloody will.

As the gradient steepens, Vesta slows, her head dropping.

Nearly there, old girl.

At the sound of his voice, the horse stops and will not be spurred forward.

Right. Good enough, I think.

He dismounts, untucks his shirt to ventilate his own perspiring flanks. They have gained considerable height. The green valley has dropped away and Cross Fell's ramp glints like a sabre, a compressed curve of minerals. Extraordinary to think of its million aged layers, fossils of all that has lived and calcified. It is a glacial catalogue deeply incompatible with the altar verse of St Lawrence's, yet the debate rages. Ho-hum.

He sits on a warm scarf of limestone with his notebook out. Engine towed up. Pipes laid. Fuel deposited and kept dry. Problems, but not unsolvable. But how to calculate the steam jet and the distribution of colour? Like the nib of an ink pen, it must mark its cypher. Like the hand of God, it must manifest the vesper. Rather good phrasing that, Bodge, he thinks, jotting it down.

Vesta nibbles the botanics. He flicks through the journal, its pages of historical research. The earlier the era, the more vacant the annals. From the pen of Lady Celia Fiennes as she side-saddled about the region, availing herself of luxurious breakfasts in its manor houses, there is no mention of the Helm at all. From Coleman in 1734, after he joined the Langwathby races, a short observation that the four-mile common had been ruined by a Coruscating Terror. Then come the musings of the previous century – awestruck, plodding, wildly inaccurate. Dissertations on spheres of rarefaction and the orders of Helms – opaque, transparent, mixed (not altogether unhelpful). Helm's preferred ETAs – morning, teatime (cooler temperatures, therefore, and inversions). The measurement of Helm's diabolical arch, two to four miles between the clouds (where, then, to position the boiler and vent?). Backcountry snatches; there really isn't much. But what there is suggests the equinox seasons are the Helm's favoured conditions. Unsettled fronts, the clashing of warm and cold air.

So, then. The Revelation Machine must be built and ready to run by autumn.

He stows away the notebook, leans back on his elbows, allows his mind to wander in search of answers. He thinks of the towering Ribble-head Viaduct, with abandoned camps below. He thinks of the resown meadow at Grange House, its butterflies in silken blue attire. Those pale flashing feet with mud on the heels, a body damp and rivery.

How long shall you be gone, Tombo?

In the stone crevices, tiny pink-and-white flowers are blooming: alpine saxifrage with uplifted petals, beautifully diminutive and hopeful-looking. He should collect a few in his handkerchief, send them pressed to Sara , along with his impressions. Next best thing, he supposes, if she cannot admire this view with him, as she admired the frozen fjords, the New York colours. Her disappointment is always so

131

carefully tidied away. She doesn't complain, only says, *I wish to be the wife I once was, and I wish to be a productive wife*, clutching his hand so hard it aches during her floods. She would be willing to restore conjugal rights after each awful monthly; but he is not a brute. He has always taken great care. Took great care, before the act became too uncomfortable, unpleasant for them both. Chaps he knows would probably have sorted an alternative – there are discreet rooms one can go to, not always shameful and sordid and populated by fallen mill girls. He has not done that. He wishes to be a good husband. And for this transaction, there are other allowances.

Home by Christmas, I am certain. We shall decorate the tree together.

He looks up at the summit again, at the sky above.
  Empty.

Ninny, he says quietly.
  Then louder, *Absolute ninny*.

The horse continues grazing, grinding its teeth, ignoring him. Thomas gets to his feet, brushes himself off and resets his hat.

It is abundantly clear what the key issue with his scheme is. Not the ironwork and the coke and the steam engine, nor his missing formula. The biggest challenge, as any lion hunter or balloonist or terrariumist knows, is nature's cooperation. The Helm must show willing. The Helm must blow and blow marvellously for him, sometime between October and December. Or he shall have to wait for spring.

XXII

Little Janni sits cross-legged on the cairn at the top of the fell and all around is bright glittering hoar. The mountains are frosted like iced buns in a cake shop window and lickable. The air tastes of copper and salt. Her knees and nose are red raw. Where is your hat, Janni? Lost. Cast away. Caught on the briar. She has run fast as a rabbit on the moors to get here, shedding bobbles and gloves, the garments Mammy made not good enough to sell. Beside her, Helm is floating and copying her, legs woven, knees pointy, sniffing.

Too cold for snow, Helm tells her.
Are you sombre today? Janni asks Helm.
Not now you are here. I am sad when you go. I will have a hole in me.
I have a hole too. It is in my vee. Mammy says it is wicked.

Janni's wool skirt rides up against her thighs; it has brown-and-beige checks like a chessboard and her Mammy took away the kilt pin, saying, *Too dangerous a thing for you.* Helm can see the gusset of her underwear, and a blister sore where she tongues what her nose drips down, and the soft downy fur on her arms and calves. *Ladgeful lile Janni* and *Janni Fanny*, the boys at school call her. They say, *Janni Fanny, you are a gowk, you are stupid, and crazy, you are going to Garlands for an operation on your brain.* They ask to see her gash. They ask if they can poke her. *Yes*, she says, *if you will cuddle me after.* The girls pretend they cannot see anyone where she is standing. *Where is Janni Calder? Where is Janni Calder?* They untuck her blouse and slap her back to see whose hand leaves the reddest, longest-lasting mark.

If you were not my friend I would jump off High Cup Nick, she says.
  If you were not my friend I would not be either, Helm tells her.
  I want to fly.
  I can fly.
  Will you teach me?
  I will teach you.

Helm's face comes apart and swirls, then joins together again. Helm's legs swell and grow and flicker like gas flames. Watching Helm makes Janni dizzy with a full-of-air feeling. Helm is never still. Helm is a Zeppelin. Helm is a cyclone. Helm is a roll of dough. But Helm is always here, waiting on the mountain, and never says *Meet me at playtime*, then isn't there. Helm does not tease her or brag her with sticks. Helm never throws her books out of the window or twists her tit or twists her fingers in their sockets.

When Janni runs uphill to Helm, no one can ever catch her. She is the fastest creature, like the stoat, or the fox, or the hounded hare. Her mind bounds between blades of grass and up the scree, it leaps across the streams and streaks beneath the gates, and her body always follows. Where is your coat, Janni? Swinging on a fencepost and forgotten, or dropped in a cow trough. Impervious to cold, is she. Cold nips her skin to make her quicker. She flits between the snowdrops, darts between the boulders.

How swift was I today? she asks Helm. *As swift as Br'er Rabbit? As swift as the* Waverley Express?
  Helm says, *Yes. Quick as electricity. But not as fast as me.*
  It is because I have bits in my pockets for you.
  Show me what.

Janni takes two flints from the pocket of her skirt. White crystals in black stone glitter like the hoar. Helm rolls closer to see.

They are good but only quite pretty. What else did you bring me?

Bottle tops. Three silver and one blue. I opened the milk and drank the cream.

She holds the foils in her palm.

Better. They are very shiny.

Helm blows them off her hand and sends them spinning like flying saucers.

Anything else and more?

I stole an apple but ate it because I was hungry. Here are the pips and stick.

I like shaking apples off trees, Helm tells her.

Can you see the apple tree in our garden? Can you see into my bedroom window?

I can see you, Janni Calder, when you leave the curtain open. Your walls are yellow. You have a red blanket and a book of ABC. You have two pink blossoms on your chest growing bigger.

Mammy will not sew me a bra. Can you see Mammy?

I can see Mammy and I do not like her.

I do not like her either.

Janni holds her wrists around her knees and squeezes herself into a tight ball. Helm becomes a round thing too. The hairs on her legs lift and tingle when Helm breathes. Helm could blow her away easily. She is as light as a bag of kindling, an eggshell, a snail shell, as light as a sift of flour. Mammy can carry her by one arm to the cellar, if she can catch her running around the table or up the stairs or down the hallway. Mammy bolts the farmhouse door to stop her getting out, but she cannot lock the coal hole.

You, my girl, are a ferret from a hutch, a vixen through a snick, an oil slick on the floor. I despair of you.

Mammy tells the teacher, the vicar, the women in the parish store and the ones who she mends and darns for that, God forgive her, *the* girl is a royal terror and it is so hard to cope with her alone.

Mammy quivers and the women in the shop say, *Buck up, Mrs Calder*, and they wonder, where's the father, where's the firmer-handed boss-man?

Janni is sad so Helm's head shapes like a tear.

Mammy says I am not to say you are there.
    Let's spit the pips and flick bibbots, Helm tells her. *Come to the very edge.*

Helm floats across the summit to the broken scarp, and Janni jumps up and follows. She puts the pips into her mouth and spits them, one by one, into the air below. Helm catches them on a ripple and spits them further.

When I am locked up I am given goat's milk that is very sour and I long to come up the fell so I hit myself here – look at the bruise.
    Janni pulls her yellow cardigan off her shoulder.
    It is a very pretty bruise, Helm tells her.
    I have fits.
    I have fits too.
    I have a scar in my hair from Mammy throwing chip oil. She did not see me sitting on the step.
    You have shiny hair.
    I like it when Nurse Wilson combs my hair to check for nits. Her comb smells of Dettol. It makes me squirmy. She says there is a sky man where she comes from too.
    I like Nurse Wilson.
    I don't want an operation. It is where they take you apart with saws and tools and scrape your insides away.
    I have no insides, Helm says. I have a hole.

Janni pivots on the cliff and stands on one foot and hovers the other in the air. Far below is a tiny white rectangle no bigger than a fingernail, which is Higher House Farm.

Do you like lists? she asks.
  I like lists, Helm says.
  Say one, Janni says. *What are the best things you have ever seen?*
  I have seen millions and millions. Now it is your turn.
  Janni pivots, like a ballerina. The shale under her feet is brittle and clattery as clinker. The heel of her shoe is loose.
  This is a list of things I like. Pegs, crisp bacon rind, string that's two colours together, tooth powder, Vicks Rub, my vee.

Janni lifts her skirt and grins. Her incisors have come down crooked through inflamed gums.

Do you think I am bonny? she asks. *My head is too small in the mirror.*
  I do not like mirrors. Your hair is shiny.
  Mammy rinses it with vinegar.
  Do you think I am bonny? Helm spins in a fast column too. When Helm spins Helm is the colour of cats' eyes and pale dogs' eyes and eyebright and meteors.
  You are bonnier than all the girls and all the boys in school. And Joan. And Elvis.
  Who is Elvis?
  He is the king of music. Shall I steal a mirror for you? Mammy has one in her purse.
  I do not like mirrors.
  Now I have to go.
  Why do you have to go?
  So Mammy can scold and spank me. I have missed the bell for school.

Helm spirals upwards and looks down on Janni. Helm is a blimp.

137

Helm is an umbrella.

Do you promise not to forget me?
Do you promise to teach me to fly?
Goodbye.

Janni streaks like a rabbit down the fellside. She stretches her long thin legs and her underwear flashes like semaphore. She could run and run for ever, fast as lightning, fast as the wind, but the headmaster has told Mammy she is slow, slow with her letters and slow with numbers, and she should not sit the Richardson tests because she will fail them, and she should not be allowed to run the cross-country, because she runs past all the other children and the goalposts on the playing field, and she runs through the memorial hall gates and through the village and up onto the fell, miles and miles like a Spartan, and something must be loose in her brain, for she will just not stop running.

XXIII

The Eleglide takes the corners like a dream going back down the mountain. The narrow lane of tarmac flows by; a runway. It is like flying, like landing a plane. Selima breaks through the ceiling of cloud and the valley appears below, cambered, broad and green, with flocks of trees and farmland set out in yellow-and-ochre geometry. A lovely patchwork quilt.

She passes the emergency arrester ramp, and the lay-by where cars turn round. Sweeps down over the moorland, past old spoil heaps and sunken gullies, grinning scars in the landscape. Her hair whips behind. The thoughts and anxieties and disruptions of the day blow away. Under the hurring wheels of the bicycle is the reassuring and fundamental world, not a theoretical proposition. There's sheep shit peppering the road, heather and rowan trees, piles of limestone. People have toiled here for centuries, fighting and working with the weather, respecting it, not denying the reality of its systems. When it rains, it fucking well rains.

Halfway down Great Dun, she whizzes past a cyclist muscling up, dressed in skintight green-and-black Lycra, wraparound goggles and a sculpted helmet. Head down, concentrating. He looks like an amphibian, clammy and cooked.

Good afternooooon, she calls cheerily.

She passes the brown heritage sign for the Neolithic site. Must go there soon—

The cambers around Knock Pike are joyful to lean into, like a tame fairground ride. She pedals to make the lift and tilt more exciting. The pluffy puffer jacket begins to feel too hot, so she stops the bike and ties it round her waist.

At the bottom of the fell she passes a few decrepit barns; the beautiful old restored farmhouse with a placid carp pool in the garden, always unoccupied, it seems. She passes the decommissioned red telephone box in which someone has put disco lights and a nude, headless mannequin. Interesting local humour.

Up ahead is the Gospel of Jesus Christian Centre, with its white-washed tower and long utilitarian dormitory. She googled the centre after she first saw it, wondering what they did in there. Under the welcome on the landing page of the website was an interesting notice: The trustees reserve the right to refuse groups that teach or practise beliefs inconsistent with the Doctrinal Basis of the Trust. What did that mean? Disagreement about Jesus's marital status? A non-binary God? Theories of determinism not conducive with her own research, probably, or perhaps entirely conducive, the intersections of Anthropocene destruction and eschatology being not dissimilar.

She passes the gate and glances in. The centre has a playing field and a kids' park with a roundabout and swings, monkey bars. There's a minibus parked outside the dorm. A couple of hundred yards later, she meets another coming slowly up the road. She brakes and tucks into the verge. The driver cautiously inches down the lane and stops the bus beside her. Lots of hair, rock-star good looks. Next to him on the front seat are two young pretty women; the closest to Selima rolls down the window.

   Hey there. Little tight here. No room for whoopsies.
   Yes, Selima replies. *I'm in as far as I can get, I think.*
   It's a beautiful day. You look like you're enjoying this wonderful sunshine.

The accent is Irish, or American maybe. The woman has on an orange T-shirt and carpenter dungarees; her auburn fringe is cut short and blunt, Henry V style, under a flowery headband. She makes very uninhibited eye contact, smiles with teeth so straight they are hygienist grade.

Er, yes. It is. I am.

We're looking for the centre? Do you know where it is?

Just keep going, Selima says, thumbing back over her shoulder. *It's up there on the right.*

Thank you so, so much, the woman says, earnestly, as if Selima has presented her with an award. *Are you on the programme too? You look familiar?*

No.

Oh, OK. It's such a gorgeous place, isn't it. We just saw some rabbits in a field. Maybe fifteen.

The woman is still beaming. Selima smiles too, not quite knowing how to respond. The second woman in the middle of the seat, wearing a hipster fedora and shirt dress, is smiling too. There are tiny glitter stars stuck around the corners of her eyes, so the eyes look as if they have green comet tails. The driver, tattooed up his neck and over his cuffs, links his fingers together and leans on the steering wheel, patiently. His shirt is unbuttoned halfway down his chest. Hanging from the rear-view mirror are pink dangling beads. There's some kind of festival, pheromonal vibe in the bus. Maybe the centre is actually a party house, Selima thinks, everyone getting ecstatic and repenting.

Right. That's a lot of rabbits.

The man turns to face Selima, placid-eyed, looks like he's just enjoyed a vaporiser.

Are you from here? he asks. *You seem so natural.*

Er, no. I live in Manchester. I'm from the West Midlands.

What a great place.

What, Manchester? It's all right.

Sure.

141

He nods, incredibly slowly, to the beat of some inner zen. It looks like they will be having a conversation.

So are you on holiday?

No, I'm working, sort of. I'm on secondment up at the – ball. Research.

Selima points towards Great Dun Fell and the inevitable radome. She is starting to feel more than a little hemmed in; the minibus has her jammed against the verge, no way to go forward or back and around it.

Cool.

Mmm.

Everyone is smiling now, in a kind of positivity gridlock. The driver sits back and drapes his arm along the seat behind the comet woman, seeming to have all the time in the world. His shirt is unbuttoned really quite far down his chest, nearly to his navel, and there's a chain resting on the smooth skin beneath. Jim Morrison hair, shoulder-length. He is deeply aware of his gifts.

Well. You can't miss the turning to the centre, she says. *It's on the right, opposite the yellow grit box. If you get to the sign for the Druid Circle, you'll know you've gone too far.*

Both the women laugh delightedly, as if at the most excellent joke. The driver does not laugh but smiles benignly and puts the minibus into gear. The happy threesome hail her with good wishes.

Thank you again!

Enjoy your sabbatical!

Enjoy the rabbits!

The minibus grumbles away up the road. OK then, so that's the kind of thing that goes on in there, she thinks.

She cycles on, past a farmyard with a big sideless warehouse. A pungent silage smell emanates. Without warning, a tractor pulls out of the yard in front of her, its back wheels spinning off clods of muck, some kind of terrifying spoked equipment attached to its front end.

Shit!

She brakes hard, almost goes into the back of it, then she follows behind slowly, steering round shed pats of mud, or shit, whatever the substance is. The farmer bounces about on the seat in the cab, oblivious, cans over his ears and his flat cap. The sheepdog next to him adeptly readjusts its paws after each bump and swing. With no indication or deceleration, the tractor swerves through an opening into a field. Its cab continues parallel to Selima's bike behind the wall. The farmer side-eyes her, a rollie pinched between his lips. His face is red and apple-cheeked. Working hard not to avoid the stereotype there, mate. She waves. He nods curtly, slows the tractor and Selima pulls ahead on the road.

People: they are weird as aliens. Or perhaps she is the alien, and the golf ball mothership has wiped her memories of Pluto. She will go to the pub this evening, she decides. Reintegrate with humanity. She'll send a photograph of herself and a bowl of the famous chips to David. *Life beyond the sample filter.*

Back at the bothy, she showers and puts on a pair of clean jeans, a shirt and cardigan, her nicer boots. Probably overdressed – what do people wear to a rural pub on a Wednesday night? Tweeds? Boiler suit? Lurid purple puffer jacket? Her weather app shows a row of cloudless moons. It is infrequently right, she has learned – the northern Pennines can, within half an hour, produce three seasons. Tempting to light the stove and heat up some lentils on the small ceramic hob, open another bottle of wine, watch one of the six DVDs again. *Staying in, Lima, you are so bloody boring!* the voice of her sister chirrups internally. Anita would hate it here – the smells, the agricultural vistas, the extreme lack of people and nightclubs.

Since Gaurav, things have got even worse on the social front – not that they went out much during their four years together (two, officially, discounting their regrettably illicit start). Anita tries to zhuzh her.

Let me do you an online profile. I had a great time when I was on Tinder, all those hot Aryans.

No thank you! I don't want to pre-arrange to 'share some intimacy' along with having a coffee.

You're not even bloody forty. Come out with me and take some wizz. Have a nice time. Meet people.

But isn't the point of meeting people about reducing that number ultimately to just one, whereby you throw so much time and energy into the person it is like another job, and a huge emotional burden even before the prospects and expectations and misunderstandings around children, and then you feel yourself dwindling and suffocating, and then it's arguments, resentment, trauma, possessions put in boxes and public humiliation, the almost-in-laws calling you kutiya and randi to mutual acquaintances, and guilt, guilt, guilt, because that person left someone else for you and then you left him . . .

Spiralling, Selima. Get a grip. So, no, yes, she will go out.

She pulls on the puffer and slips the Airbnb's torch into her pocket. She virtuously leaves the packet of Silk Cut and the lighter in the bedside drawer. At the bothy door she takes a deep breath, and sets off for the Horse and Farrier. Make way then, locals, incoming cabin-fevered extraterrestrial climatologist.

XXIV

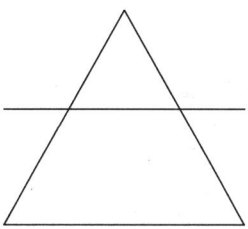

Aer

'The Aire is an entire Element, most worthy of the three in its quality, without, light and invisible, but within, heavy, visible, and fixed, it is hot and moist, and tempered with fire . . . It is volatile but may be fixed, and when it is fixed it makes every body penetrable.'
Michael Sendivogius (*New Light of Alchymie*)

See also mercurial, aether, wind.

XXV

After a paralysing winter, with frozen waterways and icicles hanging in the coats of the orox, the weather changes, becomes unsettled; red dawns, red evenings, the skies mix sunshine and storms, clouds shaped like rams' horns. Then it is cold again, and the Halron comes – raising its huge dark head above the mountain. The wind unleashed is relentless, more powerful than NaNay can ever remember, and there are several tails over the valley. The people are afraid. NaNay braces against its force outside the huts, watching the rolling edges, cloud travelling north and south like smoke blown from a pipe, then sucked back into the middle. The others call to her to get inside.

All Mother, shelter with us.

NaNay shakes her head, but soon the wind is too strong and she retreats and rolls down the door.

Everything between the two parts of the Halron is battered and bent, great oaks at the forest edge are toppled and they topple other trees. There is creaking and splintering and thumping. The crop shoots that the people have planted are ripped from the soil and scattered. The Halron sweeps hail and snow into the foothill gullies, and in the blizzard the orox become confused and disoriented, turning round and beginning back towards the mountains. Wind hammers against the huts, cracking the mud daubing and stripping the thatch; the grain store overturns and spills. The Halron howls for days, and the herd dogs howl and bark and fight with each other and must be brought inside.

NaNay and the children do not go out unless they have to empty their bowels or bring firewood and water. The hearth flares in the draughts and smoke billows round the hut. They cough. Their eyes weep. The Halron thunders overhead and the dogs whimper and scratch at the walls; the mobiles hung above the bed mats tinkle. No one can sleep. Dal sews leathers by the firelight and sings to the little ones. Reen holds Joa and rocks him until he is asleep, while NaNay carves a horn toy for him. The children are all scared and they sit with dropped heads and hunched shoulders like wet miserable crows, flinching when there is a bang or the bracken thatch parts and snow flurries inside.

Why is Halron so angry? they ask NaNay. *Is it going to kill us?*

Do not be afraid, she tells them. *Stay close. Halron knows me, and it does not want to kill me. It is trying to tell us something. Listen. I will tell you the story of when I climbed the mountain and got my third mark.*

Nine days and nights of terrible wind and white storm. It is as if some vast, wild animal or powerful anma is moving above them, reshaping the world, swallowing it, regurgitating. The hedge shelters are ripped apart and spun into the forest. When the people go outside to make water, the spray covers them.

It is a sign, Dal says. *There will be difficulty this year.*

Perhaps, NaNay says. *Or another sign.*

The children thread beads. They thread kernels. NaNay tells them stories and one of the stories is about her vision of the magstone and one is about the white orox with pink eyes that Henti killed for her pelt, and one is about the time Dal drank many cups of barley milk and tried to fight the Halron. They laugh at Dal.

Show us, they say.

Dal stands and squats his legs wide and opens his shoulders. He roars, as loud as the growling outside. There is more laughter. Then quiet resumes in the hut, and they listen to the Halron splintering and shredding the valley, its voice mourning its own violence.

147

After the storm, they roll open the door and there is an arctic, blinded world. The other herders venture out carefully and they begin to assess the damage. The huts are riven and one has collapsed. The crops are razed, and the soil of the growing beds has been scraped away and covered with ice. Tree trunks are snapped in half and wear pale, jagged crowns. The herd dogs walk about, puzzled, sniffing the bright, broken landscape.

They begin to clear the wreckage and mend the houses; they gather the swarming insects from the split roots and interiors of the trees, and tap the sap in bowls before it dries and is wasted. The children strip pine needles from the downed branches while they retain their fresh, camphor taste.

Up on the mountains, the orox herds are separated, their dark shapes scattered. Dal and the herders set out to gather them and bring them back down to the settlement. Two yearlings that wandered off in confusion have died – a cow with its foreleg broken after falling into a crevasse, the snow around it bloody and patched with paw prints. A young bull has been buried in drifts, and carrion birds are sitting on the white mound. They caw and disperse when the dogs approach.

The herders dig and roll the dead animals onto sleds and begin to drag them home. Dal's is followed by the pack of wolves that claimed the first carcass, had already plucked off the hair on one flank and tugged it open. They move in from above. The great black dogs turn and growl and drop their heads as the smell of the predators reaches them. They pad menacingly towards the pack, whale-eyed, baying. The wolves wait, in silent formation. The dogs close in. The pack splits, fans out wide, divides the inheritors. There is snarling and rolling as the breeds meet. Snow is shovelled heavily about, spattered with blood and slather. It is carnage. The herders try to call the dogs back; they will not come, they cannot. Dal pulls the sled harder, trudges through the high snow. It is better to leave the calf, but the food and the fur are needed.

The dogs begin to whimper; one by one they retreat, tails tucked. The oldest dog, still surrounded by the pack, is attacked methodically from all sides; somehow it escapes, limping down the hill, one paw held up, until it can't walk and its back end collapses. Dal runs back for it. It looks up pitifully. In its hind leg the tendons are ragged. Its jowls are hanging loose, lathered with foam, and a soft whistling sound comes from its throat. It will die, so he kills it quickly, leaves it behind. The wolves remain above, watching, then they turn and lope off. There is other meat.

It is a bad start to the spring. Late and fewer cereals, ruined buildings. But there is extra beef and timber. The people lay the orox carcasses on the game tables, stretching their legs wide, and they strip the hides. They scrape the fat into pots and hang the pelts over frames to cure. Dal takes out the guts and feeds the dogs, and the people share the other organs, loins and sidemeat. NaNay removes the black-tipped horns and testicles of the young bull for a ceremony. They store pieces of flesh in the deep stone chamber, and the dogs, licking their wounds, but well fed, keep watch for scavengers.

At the appeasement in Magsca, NaNay asks the Halron for peace. She stands the horns, filled with blood, in the carved holes of the gateway stones.

The sun warms, flying higher in the sky. The people replace the topsoil in the growing beds and plant more crops. When cress comes back to the riverside, NaNay, Reen and the little ones go to collect it with baskets. They move softly through the forest, smelling, listening for rooting boars and the shuffling of bears woken from hibernation, which will now be thin and hungry. Many of the known pathways have been altered by the Halron, some are blocked, and new foliage has grown around the felled decaying trees. Hooded orange-beaked birds are calling for mates, collecting twigs and fluff and attending to their territories; woodpeckers are drilling for beetles. NaNay steps quietly through the flowering undergrowth; she leaves the others to go to her favourite spot, scrambling towards the bank with the carrier looped over her back.

Around the gorge, the river has broadened into its floodplain and sits brightly in the wooded glades, but in the main channel water laps clear and fast. It is bodyless, its own shining anma. She clambers over boulders and down to the long pebble beach. She scans for bears. She approaches the caves but there are no prints on the ground at the tunnel entrance. Then she moves downstream. The bed of the river holds bright mineral colours, ambers, blue shales, green slate, and these are the stones of her braids. Dippers slip in and out of the wells, flicking water off their tails.

She finds the cress growing between rocks on the gritty shoreline, its vivid green ears curling, its stems knotted. She picks the plant heads and the white flowers, leaving the bottom stems and the threads so the cress will bud a second time before summer. She fills the basket with tangled greens and eats handfuls. It is bittersweet and peppery; the mustard juice makes her tongue hot. It is very good, like smoking a pipe.

Further downstream the river narrows, slowing and deepening between towering red cliffs. There are inlets underneath its shelves where sleek black eels hide, and the red-backs rest on the way to their spawning gravel. Soon it will be a good place to fish and she will

150

wade in and lay willow traps across the entrances, spearing under the stones with a long staff.

She moves along the gorge wall carefully to the next beach, where the cress is best. There is damage from the storm, trees above uprooted, collapsed branches from the big oaks, whole trunks cast down and lodged between the cliffs, latticing the sky when NaNay looks up. At the end of the next stretch of pebbles, on a high, long shelf above the river, a ledge-growing oak has been torn away and is hanging upside down by its roots. Beside it, the cliff has split apart and a small avalanche has landed in a heap. There is a deep new fissure between the prolapsed buttresses and the split in the sandstone is much redder than the surface, like opened fruit. NaNay moves towards it, and now it looks like a splayed woman showing her sacred venereal part, a lipped seam between big slab thighs. She comes closer. Now, on the nearer rock pillar, she can see there is a face. It is familiar. Triangle nose. Scoured mouth. Smooth rock where the eye socket should be. And a long, unborn forehead still held within the cliff.

NaNay puts down the carrier. She walks fast along the beach towards the face, past the cress, cocking her head this way and that, staring hard. Then she runs, clattering across the pebbles, forgetting the bears and the wild pigs, forgetting that she is old.

The other cress pickers hear her shouting – a pitch NaNay does not usually make. Shrill, urgent, echoing up the gorge, and repeating off the chasm walls. The children stop turning over river stones looking for crayfish. Reen picks up Joa and puts him on her back and he clings on. There is a predator, perhaps. Or All Mother has been injured, or pulled into the spate water. Or there is an offcomer, one of those migrants from the north who do not adhere to the hunting agreements of the elite tribes. They run quickly along the banks holding their knives, climbing over the rocks, splashing through the glades. Reen shouts,

Where are you, All Mother? What is your place?
The call echoes down the chasm. There is no answer.

When they arrive at the pebble beach, they can see NaNay. There are no bears and no other people. She has climbed up the cliff, under a section of red stone that has collapsed outwards and is looming over her. The gorge wall has split and shifted; a new piece is hanging out over the riverbank and NaNay is trying to reach it.

All Mother! What are you doing?

NaNay inches left, her thin muscles banding hard in her legs. She is not stuck, she can balance like a goat, but the overhang is high and difficult. The rock above does not look as if it has finished moving: deep cracks run from it across the cliff. She ignores Reen, continues trying to climb up, pinching her feet together in a fissure, her fingers scrabbling and sipping at little holes above her head. She dusts away the soil so she can grip. But she cannot get any higher. Reen and the children stand underneath. Joa pushes his feet against Reen's hips. He bounces on her back and laughs, pointing at NaNay.

All Mother, climb down, Reen calls. *It is not safe up there.*

NaNay arches backwards and looks up at the slab, her long, grey, braided hair nearly touching her ankles. The children shout for her to get down.

All Mother! Jump jump jump! We will catch you.

All Mother, Reen calls, *you will fall and smash like an egg.*

NaNay looks down at them all, grinning; she reaches behind to lift her leather skirt and she cocks one leg outwards to show her part. The baby shouts and laughs again.

Yayaya, NaNay shouts. *Yayayaya. Look. Do you see it is coming, it is being born?*

She shuffles round on the small ledge and springs off. She turns in the air as she jumps, twisting, her long braids sailing out, and lands

152

with soft feet, onto her bottom. Then she sits on the pebbles, holding her knees. She makes a trilling sound, as if a raptor is circling her nest. Reen bends down to her and Joa reaches out to take hold of a lock of NaNay's hair.

Are you hurt? Are you scared? What is the matter?

NaNay stands up. She takes the baby from Reen's back and puts him on her hip. She points to the cliff above.

Look, look, little one, she says, *you have eyes. Can you see what has happened? It is the magstone. Halron has given us the magstone.*

XXVI

Before the sabbath, as instructed, James the elder and James the younger deliver the cross. The raw wood is pale as a sow's underbelly and smells sweetly of resin. The shaft and transom have been securely mitred, fixed with bolts and rope. Father and son carry it between them to the churchyard of St Cuthbert's; they lay it at Michael's feet. Heavy, almost the weight of a grown man, but it can be carried by a single, determined one. They are paid. They are dismissed. The journeyman, not usually one for ale, dispatches several flagons in the sup-house to ease the noxious gut, which he has wrestled with for days, and James his son braces him home, where he sleeps fitfully, still dreaming of the punctured Christ.

Michael shoulders the cross, hefting it onto the big lump of muscle. Fine work; solid. He lays it back down, sprinkles it with Jerusalem water. The ragged village children watch him. Michael gives them leftover bacon from the castle, which they scrap at, tear apart and run away with. Charity, of sorts. Moreover, clarification. He plans to fast during the journey up the mountain and will drink only from the springs. He will empty his bowel before commencing, and rid his sack of hot seed, so no drop of sin be left fertile for the devil to germinate.

At dawn the next morning, in the faltering, gorse-torched light, he begins the undertaking. The cross is lifted up. No one witnesses the stage of separation other than Isa, wrapped in his blue shawl, and a topaz-eyed hare on the mound behind the church. The boy does not embrace his master; he knows better. No flags, nor bread and wine.

No songs of lament or praise. Michael Lang is not of the bare-chested school of flagellation, nor is he over-adorned. An exorcist's belt, aketon, helmet. He has a water-skin, a tinder stone, a few dried fruits. It is March now, but iron-cold, always so cold here. Not a breath of air; the demon is sleeping.

Michael begins. The cross scrapes forward. The hare hoists its magnificent ears, kicks the mound away and disappears.

Isa takes a few paces alongside, touches his master's sleeve, and Michael, not stopping, tells him again, no, he must stay. Still, the boy pilots. A firmer tone is needed then, a word the boy understands well: *Antazir*, repeated several times, as if instructing a dog not to follow its owner. For he must cast off all points of compassion. He must be an anvil, a spearhead, he must have the glabrous heart of a shark. He looks ahead only, fixed to the task. Isa does as commanded; he watches as Michael drags the cross along the thin drover's track, scoring the ground behind, bumping over stones and pits. It is a body in its prime, a body suggesting only success. He has the strength of an ox, this man, the stamina of an elephant.

He carries the load away from the village, out of sight, through turgid fields, through shocks of bracken sprung where woodland once stood, and onto the excoriated heath. He does not stop. On he goes, into the foothills and upwards. For several hours he drags the cross along the lower Maiden Way, where, a thousand years before, soldiers of the empire, inventors of this very murder device, marched towards the wall.

Rain comes and soaks his aketon. He walks without rest, taking great pulls into his lungs, his brow shiny beneath the sallet. The base of the cross cuts through mud and bog and over wiry grass, it dissects the softer flesh of the earth. He steers it through brush, cutting apart

155

foliage with its blunt scissor. Here and there, more often as the path ascends, he turns to pull it and shunt it from a sinkhole, holding the transom like the arms of a stiff corpse. He is watched only by stupid sheep, creatures half-goat, malformed by the harsh mountains.

By midday, the elevation is steeper. Michael's shoulders are bruised and bleeding under the slab of wood, and there is a good, truthful pain. He continues on, refusing to stop the machinery of his work; the pistoning of his legs, the cart of his back. His breathing labours and he slows under the weight, heavy as a bullock now, but he keeps moving, over blockades, hauling his oversized load like some mad, indisputable ant.

Acid in the muscles, bones pressed and grinding in their sockets. The degrees of agony arrive one by one. But he does not stop. For the son of God carried a harder burden, whipped and weak, mocked and humiliated.

Upwards.

And still not a breath of wind. Helm is waiting, pityingly, unconcerned. Or Helm is oblivious.

By evening, Michael is staggering on the hillside. Each step is a struggle, an explosion of pain, and he is burning with effort, his face lurid under the skullcap. The cross scrapes, inches, a foot, the length of a nave. But all is up, all is progress. He stops to drink from his skin and, overtaken by desperate thirst, drains it. Foolish. Undisciplined. The water floods his system, flushes back up his gullet, makes him dizzy and sick.

He continues. Into the deeper skirts of the mountain now, the immersive stage of pilgrimage, where the mind sails ahead and the body belongs to its pain, becomes automatic in motion; where he might become Christ on the Way of Suffering, limping towards redemption, the wounds passing inwardly to become the soul's. Here, his thoughts loosen. Bad memories. Crusades. The condemned. The face, looking up at him from the smouldering straw – those eyes, somehow they knew him – and he can feel his tunic, heavy and sticky with gore again. The boy did not kick when lifted or struggle in Michael's arms. Those not put to the sword are for ever owed.

He must be careful now. He is weakening, and might pass his deeds to the holder of the scales and reach agreement on a fate before it is time. He might furnish the devil with useful information, a map of the soul, deltas to be infiltrated and exploited.

On, upwards.

Dusk falling. Behind his back, the west will soon be on fire. He drags the burden even as his spleen burns.

When he looks up from the shadowed path, a cloaked and antlered companion is walking beside his left shoulder. Hooves on shale, its step is high and elegant, its legs articulated wrongly. The cloak is made of tar-oil. It turns its great, horned head to appraise him and the eye is a godless void. How many of its kind has he dispatched with an arrow? A thousand; always fewer than the king.

Michael Lang, the creature says. *Michael Lang of Kelso. Are you not weary? Put down your lever, and stand up straight. Follow me into the kingdom below this mountain.*

Michael looks away and down. He concentrates. The cross grates along the path behind him. The sinister companion tosses its antlers, keeps pace, speaks again in a voice that is beautiful, rich and melodic.

*Brother errant, come, and I will give you whatever spoils you wish for –
gold, whores, a banquet of wild game. Take off your wooden coat and sore
helmet. Come, bathe in the cold streams at the foot of Elysium.*

False ambassador, Michael says. *Gatekeeper of hell. You will not test
me. You will not tempt me. Beneath thy protection, Lord.*

He spits. He looks ahead, away from the creature. It keeps loyal-
ly by his side for another hundred yards before drawing away, and
Michael's mind clears and then there is only the voice of water running under rocks.

On, upwards.

The light fades. The foothills are like tall waves that keep coming; the
summit seems further and further away. Fiend's Fell is never closer.
All around is barren, darkening country. Empty, but he senses more
spirits gathering. On, past clawed rowans and crescents of shattered
stone. He pants like a hound after the twilight mink. He pauses to
drink again, kneeling at a slender, trickling stream, the water earthy
and bitter against his lips; he fills his belly, the skin. Then he lifts the
cross, and walks on, crushed beneath it, his bones splintering. It is
agony, as righteous work must be.

Is this the truth? No. The scales tip; his organs in the pan weigh heavy
as lead. It is something else that keeps Michael going – the erotic
mania of torture, athletic pride, ego. The terrible motor of his black
heart drives him.

On, upwards.

Into the silty dark of the English Apennines, towards the place of the
skull, and his own glory.

He had planned to walk at night too, if the moon accorded enough illumination. But cloud is banking; darkness obscures the edge of everything, masks hazards, wrong steps, chasms. Neither faith nor bloody-mindedness will allow a blind ascent. On the horizon, the jagged seam of red fades along Helvellyn and Moor Divock, Blencathra. He limps on until the stew thickens, then stops. He tries to rid himself of the cross but it pins him down; no strength left to heave it off, so he drops his shoulder out from under and the frame thumps to the ground. His right arm is numb, the fingers ballooned with fluid, like a corpse's. He shakes the limb, grits his teeth as the nerves fire back to life like hot needles. Then he collects dry grass and twigs, begins a fire with the flint.

Exhausted, he sits and stares into the flames. The stars arriving are his eyes' reverse: pricks of light in the dark. The temperature is dropping and he shivers under his sweated-through shirt. He has not brought the bisht he often wears when sleeping out. He shuffles closer to the fire as it snaps and smokes around him. The flames do as they wish. They feather. They sway seductively. Still no disturbance in the air; not a whisper. He is being let come to the field, honourably, as if Helm understands the protocol of war, or towards some ambush.

Fireside thoughts: This is wasted expenditure. He could have ridden the fucking horse up. He could have dragged the cross behind Olwen, rather than mashing his shoulder purple as a plum. Likely no peasant of Dilston or Salkeld or Soulby or Brough will care in what manner the holy sign was transported up this godforsaken wen. Even Ranulph, who first told him of the haunted fell in the company of the king, speaking of the demon as the scourge of the north, a dementor, a crop-ruiner – villain in the Baron's evasion of taxes – is liable to issue no credit. But Michael Lang needs no reward: the hardest way is the only one.

By the flickering light he studies his right hand, tracing the lines at the hinges of the fingers, the mark circumscribing his thumb. There are pigmentations, which are devil pacts if they spread. Fate, written by the scribe of God, is on the palm of every man. The divination of his own has always been clear: the life line ends abruptly, a good reach from his wrist. Blunt, untimely death, in which year of life he cannot say. But he has approached and passed forty.

He builds the fire before lying down to rest, and feels his tired body relinquish tension. He should not sleep. Bandits. Wolves. Imps and succubi. That antlered bastard with the voice of nectar. The overlord is here, somewhere, and might enter him while unconscious. Or creep up, pelt him with missiles, or bear down on him from above and crush him with a boulder, or toss him off some Tarpeian rock. He should not sleep, but he closes his eyes and feels sleep's inexorable pull.

Unwanted memories stir again, along the borders of consciousness. Stumps of human meat that he himself has carved. Screams and begging, the dispatch of women. His own mother – Virtue's ghost kneels over her, nightly, weeping. He rouses, casts off the disturbance. He thinks of the boy again, the weight of the boy in his arms – a perfect weight – and his baptism in the river, reparation. He should not sleep, and yet. He checks the sallet, which is tight against his scalp. He drowses. Time softens about him.

The Helm comes out of the darkness, towards the fireside. Michael's dreaming mind cannot apprehend Helm's appearance. It is a shimmering mirage, a dance of elements, mesmeric. Smoke curling bluely around itself, vapour rolling like a speeding storm. Pieces swirl, become features, like soot on an updraught or the murmuration of starlings. A man forms, half-obscured by a mask, and after all Helm is but an invention of vapour, and harmless.

May I sit with you, friend?

You may.

Let us sport, Helm says.

Michael sits up.

A fine idea.

There are dice in the pouch of his belt. They roll and count in the old way.

Another stake, says Helm.

Aye, another.

They play an Eastern game with stick and stones in complicated patterns, rules that Michael cannot comprehend. Must be code, though he does not know it. He loses, but no matter, it is only minor exchange. The tunnel of Helm's mouth opens. Helm bellows the fire, keeps its embers glowing and Michael feeds the orange furnace with twigs. Helm blows the sticks into a pattern, complicated, mathematical. All thoughts of conflict fall away.

Speak freely, as I am your familiar.

I am ailing, Michael confesses. *My head hurts and it is constant. This is a crown of thorns.*

I am a bad cap too, Helm says. *The mountain wears me. Shall we be comrades, then?*

Aye!

Aye to it!

Comrades!

Brothers until death!

How long shall you live? Michael asks.

Eight more centuries. Until you kill me.

Oh, then I am still young!

Michael laughs, delighted, relieved of his duty. He is twitching and yipping on the ground like a dog dreaming rabbits. How pleasurable is Helm's humour, his sightedness. Helm's laughter is gentle thunder. Mirth echoes down into the valley. Then Helm is a jester, lowering his britches, making obscene flatulence, and Michael laughs so hard he might be a different man entirely. Laughing and cackling, coughing and gasping. Soon he cannot breathe; the air cannot be drawn inside – a monkey's weight is sitting on his chest, and this he knows to be demonic.

Away, fiend! Away!

He wakes, roaring back into himself, scrabbling about on the scree, his heels digging in panic. He reaches for a torch, but the fire is out, and pale dawn has arrived. He feels instinctively for his helmet; it is there, thank God. The pain of the iron band arrives, pressing his temples; his first sensation every morning. He endures it and the metal grip eases.

But – a weak and penetrable fool! He has slept, deeply, like a sickly child. He has lain his body out on the hillside, like a sacrificial virgin in the bed of a prince. Spread open and fucked and deposited into. Now is there a parasite within?

Quickly, he gets up. Silvery light is growing behind the mountains; tinted fish-scale clouds. The world's shapes are being drawn again. He checks his belt and pouches – all buckled and laced. Nothing stolen. Nothing broken. He remembers the order of commandment; he says it aloud, knows himself uncorrupted. In the dewy grass is the cross, and a pile of sticks laid in some elaborate, linear formation.

Nearby, the air stirs. Laughter. He dreamt of what, exactly?

XXVII

O, Beatrice! Is every man within his adult casing a slapped callow boy, a spoilt & regentless king? I watch my husband striding below the window, ordering the servants fetch & go hither, his voice is louder now they have rebelled. His wig has slipped a little; his cuff has tightened, frothing from his sleeve as he froths at the footman and poor cook. None but Tobias remains truly devoted. None but Phoebe is loyal t'wards me, however, & our pieces are much weaker on the board. What shall become of this marriage? It has surely run aground, for I am cast onto the rocks. I pray this innocent little thing in me holds firm, at least then I might be partially recused.

Let me press on with this woeful tale.

The brute decree was passed. The fate of the stone sisters sealed. Such a torturous week ensued. On several occasions I attempted to dispel Nathaniel's resolve. I begged – rather let the monuments be mazed off than offend. I became most earnestly fiscal – was it not better to profit from the powder than waste it on a folly in a field? Alas, no joy to be had. My husband is as stubborn as a bison. Only warnings not to flap my tongue, to desist with my harassment, to remove my hand from his coat. Shortly after, I saw the barrels arriving on a cart, ported as carefully as any newborn de Peyster heir. The kegs were more numerous than those stacked below Parliament, each had NdP stamped dangerously on its base. The courtyarders bantered & bluffed around the wagon, each trying to prove his bravado. Why do men fluff up and perspire like gamecocks before disaster? 'Tis some blood deficiency.

Perhaps a modicum of fortune remained from Mumma's glass luck – Nathaniel was away with the accountant in Carlisle that day, due to return the following morning. I surmised there would be no demolition without his dropped flag. A chance for intervention! I instructed Phoebe to stalk alongside the barrels as they were conveyed by hand to their nestle in the farthest bothy. Be as the eagle, I said, spy upon each detail. No one was stationed to guard the powder, Phoebe informed me, but the bothy was locked, Tobias its Gorgon key master. What fool would dare rob or rake it over. I suppose my act must qualify as épileptique, Beatrice – incarceration in one's own boudoir is the slenderest punishment. 'Twas no death-wish, nor malevolent possession, though these are the ticklish accusations of the goblain – occultism, delusion, dementors of the mind. Rather, we might substitute a simple explanation – I could not bear to watch my husband dismantle the wondrous primitives. Act to preserve them, I must.

Swiftly and in order then:

Phoebe set aside my lamp 'til late. I did not undress & off to bed, though I feigned the procedure. I bided 'til the upper house was slumbering, the servants all retired downstairs. Tobias's iron hoop is kept among the chattels in his quarters – brave Phoebe nipped away the bothy key while he & cook partook of the presentation brandy. (I have sworn the act was my work entirely, having learned its whereabouts from servant chit-chat. In truth, she was only second hand to the crime, and I its principal guide – thus far she has escaped prosecution . . .) Sable-cloaked I went across the courtyard with my lantern & my jug. Now comes jeopardy, beloved sister, for the rescue could not be performed while chancing deflagration. I lowered the flame to nought but a drowsy firefly & prayed for Lady Lunar to furnish visibility. What I knew of black powder was sufficient – water is its enemy. My plan: to ferry drink from the trough beside the stables, to prise the lid off every damnable keg & flood it to impotence, doing so without reprieve or hesitation.

With not a little trouble I released the bothy padlock, uneasy work for a woman's delicate thumb, for the iron was exceedingly stiff. Inside, all was Hadean darkness. O, that acrid smell, same as the sour aroma at Sedgwick – sulphurous charcoals, rotting lemons, a note of horse-wetted straw. I shudder to recall it. Praying no grain had spilled along the horrid route and left an inflammatory trail, I stood the lantern in the doorway & went inside to view the barrels. There they sat, fat-bellied evil receptacles, spaced most carefully, ready to wage war against our Goddess. I was at the first, had the lid up & the jug was dispatching its sweet disarming agent, when none other than Tobias arrived.

Cease! Ho! What goes, madam? he asked, when my face was broadcast by his lamp. Is my Lady prone with walking terrors? Or is she pantomiming that treacherous Catesby? O yes, he knew what I was about. The first execution was complete, powder & water mixt, the keg all souped.

Tobias! The faithful hound! That craven ferryman!

Sister, if you think a valet may not drag his master's wife as a farmer hauls a heifer by her udder, you are mistaken. Come away now, madam, he commanded, without concern for his grip at my arm & pinch at my bosom, come away, or your naughty flame shall make a Parisian wedding for us all. I was pincered & stridden across the grounds – heels barely tapping the cobbles – next brought up to my room, then thrust t'wards the bed. My husband will not stand for such impossible arrogance, I countered. Tobias sneered. Wheest now, sleep, m'Lady, for I dare say tomorrow you will need a sharp alibi. He hauled the settle against the door, flipped his tails & planted his backside on it. So then did he guard me all night, hood-eyed, disallowing me even the privacy to toilet.

Nathaniel was informed the moment he alighted from his carriage. He came to me with most dangerous pleasantries, then recounted the indictment & sought an explanation. I remained in utter silence but held his glittering eye. Again, with all the deadly manner of a judge, he enquired. Speak, wife, let us ravel this situation. Sister, should I have flammered a tale to save myself or played dishonest pipes? Screamed like a baboon or drooled like an imbecile? I did not speak a word. Yet I did meet his gaze & saw him roil and fizz beneath it, all wasps inside the glass. What use words, when hitherto all reasonable ones had gained no purchase, sliding off him like the ice king? I held my tongue. He did not chastise or choke me. He did not lay a hand, but smiled, black-lipped & dry-toothed, as the long-hound does without reason.

Very well, said he. I know what stands before me. It is a wolf-girl from the backwoods whom the elements exposed. Catherine Senhouse, we shall see that you are civilised, we shall see you are reformed. Then he departed, turning the lock & withdrawing the key, & I to the closed door screamed, not the confession sought, but that I wished I had set my merry flame among the sordid barrels & blown them all to kingdom come!

Arrested again – so soon – read on—

XXVIII

Trinket 4,690
Howdah pistol

Double Damascus-barrelled .50-calibre percussion pistol with lodged 480-grain lead bullet in chamber. Decoratively engraved side plates and dolphin hammers, locks fitted with sliding safeties. Maker's name, J. Lang London, is engraved on top of the barrels. Iron swivel ramrod with brass tip fitted underneath. Brass trigger guard. Walnut butt. Finely chequered grips and pineapple scrolling with a silver octagonal-shaped escutcheon. Used for hunting in Africa and India, often emergency defence against large predators. Also used by British officers. Known as the 'big stopper'.

Length – 8.5 inches
Barrel length – 3.5 inches
Weight – 2lbs 6 oz

Location – Larch copse, Glassonby

XXIX

I have three daughters.

Jesse Symonds stands behind his office chair, gripping it with large hands. His fingers spread out along the backrest, and the leather dimples underneath the pressure. He peers at Thomas Bodger over the top of his wire spectacles – an item altogether too delicate for his broad, furnace-burnt face. Now the industrialist of the Millom foundry, he has clearly, for a good portion of his life, worked in its bowels. His shirtsleeves are rolled as if he still does; his collar is upright and tieless. Symonds's grandfather, Thomas has been told as they toured the factory, worked Hodbarrow Old Mine, extracting the richest haematite in the Isles. Symonds's father benefited from an endowed education, then partnered into capital; he was the self-maker in the era of self-makers. A natural transition from pickaxe to manufacture to listed deeds. *The scramble from humble, you might say.* And Thomas, nodding, thought of his own father, embodying a gentleman, while his mother's parents made bobbins.

Three daughters, Symonds repeats. *But none of them are handy with the tongs. None are showing any interest in pairing, either. It's something of a dilemma, Mr Bodger. Perhaps I have spoiled them. They do not attach themselves to this outfit, nor anyone who might. Have you children?*
    We are not yet blessed, Thomas says.
    God has his method, replies Jesse Symonds.

The office is on the upper mezzanine corner of the immense ironworks, a nest above the hot, booming foundry. On the wall hangs a plain wooden crucifix and a painted sign: Satisfy Us Early With Thy Mercy. Through the doorway, like Perdition below, Thomas can see the great molten vats, lavic metal pouring into casings, and cooling tanks steaming like sulphur springs. Row upon row of portable pipe has been stacked ready for storage and dispatch. Most fortuitous to have such a business so close within the region, Thomas thinks; the nearest others being located in Gateshead and West Bromwich (triple the transportation costs at least). But how does the man operate in this infernal heat? He has sweated through to the silk back of his own waistcoat.

From the office window, he can see the beginnings of the new barrier in the estuary, which will hold back the sea and allow expansion of the haulings. The foundations of its concrete wall and dam.

All on schedule over there? he asks, mopping his brow with a handkerchief.

Indeed, we are early. That is how new Millom operates, I'm proud to say.

He has been shown the warehouse, in which his own Pennine-bound pipes are mounting up. Symonds has proved professional and incurious about the value of the machine – not his business to weigh the project's worth, only the necessary ferric tonnage. He has not made any comment about smoking out a ghost, but simply said, *I am sure you will be assisting the good people of Eden, sir. The will is strongest when the threat is greatest.* They have also discussed which local fitters might be employed, cheaply but reliably, along with different kinds of end cuffs, rivets and bolts, piers and manifolds – options that have baffled rather than enlightened Thomas. Symonds is clearly a problems man: whatever is needed by a customer, by an architect or an engineer, must be produced. Water transportation. Sewage. Fencing. Ornamentation. He is, he tells Thomas, involved with discussions about girders for the huge French-style tower planned across the bay in Blackpool. A second cheque has been signed and the two men have shaken hands. All is in good order.

169

Will you permit me to show you our town? Jesse Symonds asks, letting go of the chair so the upholstery audibly breathes a sigh. He reaches for his coat. *Have you the time for a brief tour, Mr Bodger?*

I have, Thomas replies. *And I should be very grateful.*

Having assumed Millom to be little more than an industrial settlement in the flatlands, the sort of place one runs raids on, he has scheduled nothing else before his train departs. Then, off to the Swan in Newby Bridge for supper and a two-night stay, where he will hike in Grizedale Forest and cruise on Lake Windermere. A little hiatus from Mrs Brooke.

Symonds takes up his hat; he descends the spiral staircase to the foundry floor, stiffly and on bow legs. Thomas follows, past the forge, its orbital heat almost solar, its glow and shadow-cast hellish. The brows of the men shine, their shirts are patched with perspiration; indeed none are shirtless, and, notably, none are gaunt or pallid or bulge-eyed. For such hard and dirty labour, Millom's workers seem untroubled by the customary ailments. Nor is the boss far removed from the menials as one might expect. Symonds greets them all in a raised voice as he passes their stations.

William Alexander. Roger Dodd. Charlie Crake. Henry Tay – how fares your middle son after the scarlet, Henry? Agatha and I have prayed for him.

Gradely, sir. Up and about and back at his school desk.

Excellent.

As they approach the finished castings, Symonds resumes his voluble explanations.

Alloy manufacture, especially modern steel, Mr Bodger, is going to exceed iron demands within the decade, mark my words. Sheffield has the advantage, but we've the ability here to produce mild and mediums, as well as high-carbon. It is, as you'll know, the more versatile substance, doesn't corrode. It will soon be Britain's hallmark around the world.

170

The topic is not uninteresting, but the magnificent heat of the place has become deeply uncomfortable, and talk of sugar spoons and fish slices is beyond Thomas's stamina.

Come, Mr Bodger, I can see you are dissolving like a chalk pill.

They walk out through the yards, past the slender rails of the link trolley, to the main street, which is flat shale and clean under the coastal light. The fresh estuary air brings welcome relief. Jesse Symonds leads on, speaking to every person they pass, tipping his hat to the ladies, nodding to the men.

As you can see, we are something of an example these days – no longer the Place of Despair.

True enough, there are no horses or pigs or goats on the road, nor any manner of livestock loose and clattering about. There is no spillage or dung to avoid; the puddles have been compacted and gritted. Symonds points out the developments in the town – two chapels, one Wesleyan, one Methodist, a bank, a covered market hall, the awnings of which are ornate wrought iron; no doubt gifted by the foundry. Money has clearly been thrown over the place. The houses are freshly painted, their steps swept, and Thomas can see newly laid drainage ditches running the length of the street. Millom has the feel of a capitalist, booming frontier town.

Only fifteen years ago, Symonds tells him as they walk, *you would have been sickened by the squalor here. You would have pitied the poor souls living in degradation. You would have witnessed carcasses strewn about and human soilage, pigs a-wandering, cottages with three families inside, and women selling their virtue on corners. Cholera, smallpox, syphilis, you name it, we suffered those plagues. Every sin you could conceive of. But we have banished them all. We have, with the Lord's help and a progressive social formula, restored the place to its model origin.*

A worthy project, I am sure, Thomas comments, though he senses a repeating performance in the man's speech.

171

First, this sorry pit of vice.

Symonds points to a boarded-up public house across the street.

We had it shut down. As we had the other venues that broadcast immorality and ill health shut down. Whorehouses. Gambling rooms. Tobacconists, where China items were being sold, like the black dragon, sold to those who could not even afford bread. You see, men cannot come to work in sickness or sin. They cannot feed and cherish their families. When you elevate the working man, both in mind and body, when he respects himself and the good Lord Jesus Christ, he prospers, as part of the natural order of prosperity.

Who is this *we*? Thomas wonders. Perhaps a local twelve-man parliament, as in other small towns of the north: influentials meeting on Whitsun to smoke clay pipes and distribute bursaries, to determine civil dictates and fund almshouses. Or is this plural one man alone, standing here with his hand held out towards the library, commanding the mayoral position, commanding the position of main and mass employer, and judge of conduct beyond the factory floor.

Good wages, good health and nourishment, a six-day week and the sacrament on Sunday, Symonds is saying. *Consequently, we have no need for spokesmen or representatives at the foundry. We work as God intended. To wit, I'd best be getting back now.*

He holds out his large, reddened hand and Thomas shakes it again. *Best of luck, Mr Bodger. My lads will be with you by August thirty.*

Symonds strides stiffly away.

Thomas casts his eye about, at the hotel being erected, the lion-headed fountain, the school building. Is it such a bad thing? The revivalist factory master; the moral overlord. In this new age of sociology and reform, hasn't he himself a wide range of investments, a portfolio far more diverse than that inherited from his father, and hobbies Her Majesty admires? How else would he be chasing down a storm in the back of beyond, for the good of humanity? Is his own Society's council not the chartered version of this, granted the highest honour by the sovereign and the Privy Council for its pre-eminence and stability, given powers to govern its own affairs? Part of the Society's aim, he truly believes, is to gain better understanding of the conditions under which Britons live and work, and create a protectorate, make them, well, weatherproof. So too is Symonds's intention.

And yet. And yet. As Thomas departs Millom, he cannot help but feel unsettled. Were a nail to scratch at the fresh paint, or a thumb to flick through the notes inside the embossed wallet-book, what secret blight or dollymop's cameo might be hidden? The firm hand gripping the back of this town, improving though it may be, is surely another form of bondage; it is bankrolled faith. Will it take and will it hold? he wonders. Or will it be cast off, like a corset before congress, like a shawl on the riverbank? For men are men – carnal, venal and desiring of liberty. As the immense iron tower in Paris commemorates – that which Symonds is busily trying to replicate across the bay – men are ever prone to overturning authority.

Over the next weeks, he attempts to befriend Rebecca Brooke, who remains aloof. He attempts to engage her husband, the colonel, who has returned from being *away*, and is an ornery, boorish, sundowning man. He must socialise with them separately, for, as the lark and the owl, or, more fittingly, the jaguar and the tiger, they are never together, indeed they seem continents apart. He dines with one and then with the other; they rotate sittings. The staff at Grange House are clearly schooled in the methods of segregation.

The colonel, approaching eighty, deaf, and brain-congested after teatime, reintroducing himself several times to Thomas, asking if he has brought the propellant, asking if he has come to fix the ditching, asking if he knows Sobrero or Cavendish or Lancaster. On the subject of his wife, Sanderson Brooke is deeply disparaging, bound only by matrimony, it seems, some terrible economic situation having dictated their union. On the subject of the Helm, he has little to say – calling it a *ruddy flimp* in front of Midge, who does not flinch or startle – and has little patience with Thomas's meteorological rhapsodies. *Bit bosh, your popcorn machine, but carry on.* He searches the cabinet for brandy, port, wine and, finding none, curses his wife for the restriction, for his embittered stomach and enlarged liver.

The next drop is liable to kill him. Perhaps I should restore a bottle, Mrs Brooke tells Thomas drily during one of her sittings. Yet every week she ventures into the woods, where she procures from a local herbalist the terrible souse. The colonel accuses her of poisoning, being in cahoots with *that rhubarb-chewing yeast-whore.* All this Thomas overhears, wincingly, during their brief and inflammatory encounters.

But it is Rebecca Brooke who most compels. She dons her darkened lenses and bathes in the green river pot most days, returning with damp hair, an invigorated gait and dirty feet. There are continual nocturnal meditations about this activity, during which Thomas suffers. Catching sight of her passing the window one evening, flushed and dishevelled, the colonel leans in across the dinner table, lowers his voice, says to Thomas,

  My wife is beyond repair. She's a heath-dweller, afflicted with the same lunacy as her grandmother.

He wakes one night to the sound of a pistol shot. Husband or wife has done the other in, he thinks. He gropes for the lamp, proceeds cautiously down the hallway. He peers over the stairs, full of dread, expecting a puddle of blood, a corpse. Rebecca Brooke is below, lit by the glow of her own lamp, pale-red hair loose as catkins, her

174

nightgown held up slightly at the knee. The front door is standing open – she is peering into the pitched void. Outside, a little way off, another shot is fired. Thomas flinches. Mrs Brooke closes the front door, bolts it and remounts the stairs without haste. As she passes Thomas, the wick flickers and her eyes shine and shift in the darkness.

He's shooting at owls, she says. *Don't concern yourself. Please go back to bed, Thomas.*

Her bedroom door closes softly. An hour and several shots later, there is pounding on the front door below, muffled shouting. The racket continues until Midge lets the colonel inside. Thomas lies awake, staring at the ceiling, his mind too roused to sleep. Aside from everything else – *Thomas.* Finally, she has called him Thomas.

Next morning, he writes to Sara.

I am like Raglan, caught in the crossfire! I do feel most sorry for your cousin Rebecca. She's no admirer of mine, but at least she isn't an addled brute (with apologies, I know your father and Sanderson were chums, but honestly, the man has no return ticket). I have yet to convert either husband or wife towards my project. Rebecca's candour on the subject is rather brutal, but not unhelpful. She is – how shall I describe – rather a free spirit, and some form of sensualist, I suspect.

By return of post, Sara writes back.

Goodness, Grange House sounds tiresome, though I intuit you may be enjoying the theatrics. I wonder how your barometers are reading there – low or high? I am sleeping soundly; the drops help, of course, though they do tend to fuzzle my thoughts. Lately, I have been reading about germ theory and also Charles Peirce, which is all very interesting. TBD, Tombo?

He puts the letter away.

The colonel remains at home for two weeks, then mysteriously departs again. In his absence, the house settles. Thomas redoubles his efforts with Mrs Brooke. The more he tries to charm, and impress, and advocate the virtues of science, the more she regards him a usurper of nature, a vulgar industrialist. His plan is inherently objectionable, little helped by his casual confession, during a dinner debate of almost parliamentary fervour, that the experiment may prove a little noxious.

I'm still considering which colourant, mixed with the steam, will most usefully reveal the wind's pattern. Carmine, for example, is very bold and vivid, and in finely milled form it is quite soluble. Should wash away after a few rains, but the aluminium salts may be a little – indigestible.

How very considerate of you, Mr Bodger, she responds, *to moderate your depredation. Perhaps you feel a modicum of pity for the scarlet birds and vomiting sheep? Or the poor unsuspecting souls of this valley, who, looking up at your great red blight, might interpret it as a sign of endtimes and die of fright?*

Well, it's true, concedes Thomas. *I'm not convinced the Earl of Lonsdale will appreciate la montagne rouge. I'm also quite concerned that the powder may prevent levity in the vapour.*

Mrs Brooke claps her hands.

Bravo! Bravo, Mr Bodger! I can see pastoral concerns are not an issue in the slightest. Do tell me, what is to be the purpose of these findings? Might we simply be able to extinguish the wind, once you locate its rocker switch?

No, they are not yet friends. But nor does she leave the table outraged and flounce off again. She stays seated; she jabs and she jibes, she challenges his notions, draws him with her incisive questioning and her harrying opposition. She wishes to spar, he realises. Perhaps she wishes simply for company, given the war of attrition with the colonel. And her tests are rigorous: not quite peer review, but approaching viva. Several times, he invites Mrs Brooke to accompany him about the valley on his research trips. Invariably, she declines. So

176

off he goes, intrepid and solo in his sprung-soled boots, walking about the Eden villages, accosting locals.

Good morning, I'm here from the Royal Meteorological Society.

Good afternoon, I wonder if I might trouble you—

The Edeners are a sceptical, cogitative lot, in need of gentle and persistent prising open – then stories and superstitions spill forth. He jots it all down, with neutrality, like a broadsheet reporter. He separates the kernels of useful information from the fantastical fruits. The fact that the Helm blows at night as well as daytime, so any diurnal-based proposition can be dismissed. As can the humorous tale from Mrs Hodge – the gore-smudged butcher's wife in Ousby who does indeed cook him a sausage breakfast once she is located – suggesting that the night-time Helm is a muddler, swapping about villagers' dreams.

My Bess got the pothecary McBride's dream, and now she knows where lady slipper grows and how to cure warts. I got the dream of that tall Prussian which did marry the Hindmarsh girl, well I nivver spoke German, not a drop or drizzle, but I spoke German in my dream and the Kaiser said he did so enjoy my lamb patties.

If not weather study, exactly, it is boggling anthropology. He learns that, in the valley, they don't make hay or hoe turnips until sure the Helm will not arrive. How can they be sure? he asks. Grounded swallows. Rheumatism. The almanac of memory. One ancient shepherd in a suit of moleskin talks to Thomas for three straight hours, at the end of which his broad dialect is just and so interpretable. He tells Thomas he's seen dogs rolled down the bank like tumbleweeds by the Helm; that veterinary McGee has special concoctions for the eyes of wind-blind sheep; that in 1808, while Napoleon was in Spain, there was week after week of a howling black Helm, and he had to crawl up the mountain to bag up lambs with his *Fadder* and shoulder them down; that he saw, when he was a young colt at Mosedale, a series of five spinning bar clouds spaced out across the valley.

Five?

Aye. Pip. Like angels gan t'dance, or goblens whizzlin aboot. Willy, I sez to m'sell, is it the almighty or Luce-fer bowing ont fiddle up thear?

In the byres, there are dobbie stones hung to protect cattle against Helm's curse. Never is a bonfire built to the east of a property. And the fellside villages invariably have roads leading due west, the only possible exit when the wind blows. Thomas fills the pages of his notebook, sombrely. *Gay clashy back-ender*, meaning an autumn Helm. Brussels sprouts fired from their stalks like bullets from a Gatling. The tails of cows lopped off by slammed gates. Vendettas delivered on the back of the wind. Yarns. Rituals. Old folklore. Do they really believe it? he wonders. Their strange rustic traditions. Their curious tendency not to say Helm's name, in case, like the devil, it is conjured. Their use, instead, of Helm's many monikers.

XXX

AKA

Girt big mouth
The barley thief
The tup turner
Clog meddler
Knicker muddler
Swifty lang-gob
The steg rabber
Hellum
Mister Stone Pockets
Coo chopper
Neep kecker
The thropple of hell
Waal jonker
Giversum wedder
Gerawaback clood
Ewe blinder
Sly grass blaer
Heed banger
The wife wanger
Auld flaysome
The hoss tosser
Dag blower
Tash cropper
Bush thresher
The Eden baddun

179

Dutty skirt lifter
Rook grounder
Three crow Helm
Cap pincher
The devil's dunsh
Sir Geysir
The swall yan
The fell taistrel
Auld Nick's stripper

XXXI

In Higher House Farm, Mammy is waiting, sitting at the table in her nylon house smock with a lemon-squeeze face, her reels and marker papers strewn about. She lunges at Janni, catches hold of her arm. Then it's whack whack whack on Janni's bottom.

How did you get out this time? Where have you been this time? You have missed school again!

It's shake shake shake by the shoulders.

Did you let the boys at you, girl? Have I to fetch the carbolic?

Then it's—

No, no, no, there is no such thing. I am full up of Helm nonsense.

Janni smiles and her body swings soft as fleece, and there is no way to hurt her from the outside no matter how high Mammy lifts her hand, how hard she beats. Then she is put in the cellar in the dark and it smells of soot and cordite and nests. Above, the front door opens and shuts and Mammy has gone to the village perhaps. Janni sits on the cold damp flagstones and her boots are wet and now she is cold that is bad not good. There are rats scuttering and scratching along the walls. There are spiders tiptoeing onto her hair. She lies down on a pallet in the corner and she thinks of her king of the mountain, who she will marry one day, with a ring of flowers as a crown. She hums a song from the radio that Elvis sings.

She does not know how long Mammy is gone. An hour or three. The front door opens and shuts again and she can hear Mammy banging the doors of the wardrobe in the bedroom and sliding the dresser drawers and marching up and down. Mammy is packing that tapestry bag with the leather handle for going away – she has had enough. It is dark and Janni is hungry and her arms and legs are trembling despite their fur.

The door is knocked loudly, knock-knock-knock, knock-knock. Then Mammy comes down and Janni is fetched upstairs to the kitchen. There is Dr Thorne-Smith. He has on a charry suit that has not been pressed.

Hello, Janni. I hear you've had some trouble. Shall we find out what's wrong?

Mammy leaves the room and shuts the door and Dr Thorne-Smith performs an examination. He presses Janni's tongue down with a stick and she says *aaah*. He inserts a thermometer underneath it – glass she could crunch hard between her teeth if she wanted. He pushes the sides of her abdomen like she is a fruit. He lies her back on the table; *knees up, please*, he says, and puts one finger, two fingers, right up inside her vee and one inside the other hole. She clutches the edges of the table.

I am going to palpate. Stop giggling, but she isn't. He presses hard, then slides his hand out.

Sit up, Janni. Why have you been making things up? Can you tell me?

Dr Thorne-Smith is bald with a polished head and no wrinkles, none at all – he has milk-glass-skin. He washes his hands at the sink. Mammy comes back in.

I do not think she is pregnant, he says, *but unfortunately she has been ruptured.*

Oh, says Mammy. *Oh, mercy.*

She does not have a fever, so I do not think she is delirious.

They look at her as if she should solve a problem and Janni looks at the floor. She can still feel Dr Thorne-Smith's finger pressing hard into her bottom. She cannot remember Helm's face because Helm's

182

face is never still but she is not a liar. Mammy's voice is high and affronted and it sounds as if she is getting ready to cry.

There was a fit and look, she bit my hand, it is raw, and then she ran off and when she came home she talked about it again. She steals and she fabricates. She self-satisfies in shameful ways. She is a hallan drop on my head and I despair, Doctor.

The doctor nods.

Thank you, Mrs Calder. Yes, I think it is time now. We will away to Carlisle this afternoon.

They are still looking at her and something is trickling on Janni's leg. She cannot remember if the apple she stole from the bowl and gave to Helm was red or green, sour or sweet, or how many spitting pips it had.

Janni, Dr Thorne-Smith says, *Nurse Wilson is outside. You like Nurse Wilson. Don't run off, please, when we go towards the car or I shall have to restrain you. Are you going to run off, Janni?*

Janni says nothing and her Mammy comes fast round the table to clip her.

Answer the doctor!

No, I will not run.

Will you sit nicely with the nurse on the back seat, please?

Yes.

It's a long drive. Do you need the bathroom? Your mother will have to accompany you if you do.

No.

Good girl, then we shall go. Say goodbye now.

Bye, Mammy.

Mammy gives the doctor the tapestry bag. Dr Thorne-Smith puts a hand on Janni's shoulder, light and firm as an owl on a branch, and they walk down the path to his big black car. Mammy shuts the front door before even three steps counted. Nurse Wilson gets out of the passenger seat; she is in the dark-blue uniform and stiff white hat and she smiles and takes Janni's hand.

Hello, Janni, she says. *It's nice to see you again.*

Nurse Wilson puts her arm around Janni and she is warm and smells of almonds and antiseptic. The doctor opens the back door and waits. Janni looks up at the fell to see if Helm is waving. Can Nurse Wilson see Helm among the clouds too, like the Trinny Island sky man she told her about? A small flicker above the mountain, like a candle on a cake. It is the secret sneck where Helm comes and goes. Janni waves. Helm will be sad if she doesn't bring trinkets. Dr Thorne-Smith coughs and clears his throat.

Look at me, please, Janni. At me. I want you to behave on the journey. I don't want you to soil the back seat. Do you understand?

Oh, Janni is a good girl, says Nurse Wilson. *Aren't you, Janni? We will be just fine.*

The nurse helps Janni into the car. The leather seat is cream with deep creases. There are white maggoty stitches in the upholstery that make Janni's scalp itch. Nurse Wilson sits beside her, close and warm. Her tights are black and her shoes are black and her hair has black oiled curls under the little cap.

It feels nice when I press my vee on the floor, it is comforting, Janni says. *Am I bad?*

I brought something for you, Janni, says Nurse Wilson.

She reaches into the pocket of her skirt and takes out a sweetie. She holds it out and purrs, *Mmmm?* The wrapper is gold and green and shiny cellophane. There are chestnut lines in Nurse Wilson's pink palm and her nails are perfect bleached moons. Dr Thorne-Smith starts the engine and the car pulls slowly down the lane, away from Higher House Farm.

Mammy does not give me sweeties.

Go on now, it is just fine. These are Mr Wilson's favourites. Chocolate limes.

Can I keep the wrapper? Janni says.

Nurse Wilson laughs.

Oh yes. Keep the wrapper.

Janni takes the sweetie and unwraps it and pops it in her mouth. She puts the wrapper in the pocket of her cardigan and that will be treasure for Helm next time. She rolls the hard tart lozenge on her tongue. It takes until Lazonby to crack and for the warm chocolate to ooze. She puts her fingertip on the misty windowpane, rubs a heart-shaped hole.

Goodbye.

The doctor looks in the rear-view mirror.

No, Janni.

But can Helm see her through the heart-shaped hole, sucking on her sweetie? Can Helm see the long black Wolseley going down the narrow roads and over the humpback bridges like a fast horned beetle? Is Helm rising up high and watching the car turn onto the big road where the river broadens and the mountains flatten, the road to the city where there is coaly smoke and houses made of bricks and biscuit factories? Is Helm watching as the car drives through the gates of the old psychiatric hospital, which has two towers on either side like Gehenna and is four storeys high, and the windows have grilles, and the carved date-stone says 1862 Asylum, though the new sign says Garlands Farm?

Of course.

XXXII

Wouldn't exactly say Helm is used to the traffic up here. The zoom-
ing about and the racket, since they discovered internal combustion
and got better at aerodynamics. From farty-sounding propellers, lethal
blimps and double-winged loop-de-loopers to airbuses stuffed with
sombreroed vacationers – all occurring pretty rapidly after Henry and
Claudine's surprising entrée in the (don't say it). Helm tolerates the
shared space, mostly.

Unless.

It's those appalling fuckers.

The twin-engine RAF Tornado fighter jets.

TOO LOUD! Helm can hear them coming seconds before they arrive, a terrible, portentous growling sixty miles away, some kind of
sky-quake, or towering wave, or volcanic crater opening. Then that
cleaner, fuller, industrial roar as air tears round their fuselages and
wing-tips. Where are they? They're good at hiding, coming in behind
the mountains, or up high, mirroring the sky – long-beaked, finned,
marine almost, exhaust simmering behind their turbines. They disappear into their own chic glare, behind clouds, the atmospheric swill.

Helm scans the valley for contrails, knows the drill. It's never just one,
but a pair, or three, tilting round the Dales, paralleling the Pennines,
so low in altitude the sheep scatter, aviation fumes stanching their
fleeces. Farmers look down on their sleek grey backs, thinking, what

fucking ceiling? The MOD doesn't care; these are million-pound precision-guided bombers, deployed in every conflict for four decades, care of the taxpayer, gotta practise.

Where are they? Where?

The leader throttles, noise trails behind in the sky. Still invisible; it moves, needle-nosed, silvery, emerges ahead of its own rumble. There it is. Sharkish, gunned, lithe, its wings folded dangerously. It thunders up Eden, its speed so casual. The pilot in his dark visor processing the terrain as efficiently as Helm processes time, so mountains are only blips, the rivers are just delicate laces tied to the tarns, lakes, seas, their sources are flashed past and missed, their mouths swept over in seconds. Landscape devoured so rapidly it may never have existed. It rips through and away, banks towards Blencathra, beating its own shadow.

Where are the seekers?

Growling behind. Here they come.

Partnering, they pursue the leader. They blast past Helm, tipped to a ninety-degree angle, triangular, then tilting flat as estuary fish. Hunting formation, training for war abroad. Assisting other countries, you understand, militarily restrained.

They bank north-west, going to the Langdales, mangling the air, pulverising it, destroying all acoustics but theirs.

All hail the Panavia Tornado. Born of many other planes, a lethal avionic lineage. Assembled in Britain, West Germany and Italy, with minimal drag, variable geometry, designs upgraded to make the jet more manoeuvrable, more stealthy, more and more efficient at – let's not be coy – its job of killing. All the faults – surging and buffering at supersonic speed, piss-poor thrust reversal, test craft stuck in high-altitude cruises, lack of Identification Friend or Foe so they are shot down by allies, flares, lasers, missile system glitches – addressed and fixed, until they are, very nearly, perfect weapons. Widely deployed and carefully sold, placed on Quick Reaction Alert (Nuclear), able to scramble in minutes and be over London (royal priority), able to operate under any weather conditions.

Including Helm.

So that Helm is, in theory, inconsequential. That sudden wind shear nothing but a puff of air against the fuselage. Those two iconic clouds, merely consumables.

If anyone cares, it is absolute torture. It's unbearable. Helm is riven apart, atomised, Helm is skewered, rent, decimated, pulverised. Helm is but a passageway of air, absent on the radar. The valley reverberates after they are gone. Takes days to recover.

Therefore, to be absolutely clear, Helm takes no responsibility what-soever when, for reasons minimally disclosed to the public, there's an electrical failure or pilot error in an F3 on a Pennine training run. A sud-den juddering, dark smoke. North-east of Shap, the pilot and navigator call it and eject. Blast of the hatch opening, aviators thrust upwards. Seconds later the jet arcs towards the fellside, folds itself into a ragged orifice of fire. Navigator Flight Lieutenant Nigel Faulkes and Squadron Leader Giles Graham parachute down, boots rocking gently, ligaments torn, shoulder dislocated, concussed, extremely lucky to have survived. Nice pensions, though, could downgrade and train the Red Arrows, maybe date a television star after. Give or take a few badgers, no one is killed, but every fire engine in the county is deployed, the motorway is shut, ITV News is first on the scene, much to the annoyance of the

Beeb. A massive clean-up operation ensues, literally and politically –
parliamentary questions, loss adjustments, et cetera. In-life costs for an
F3 – nine billion (ouch). Some local lads are told off for moving bits of
the tail and wing, *not souvenir-hunting, like, we were just trying to help.*
The smouldering patch is extinguished. Radial pieces of plane are collected, bagged, removed, catalogued and examined forensically – only
one item of importance not accounted for.

Where is it?

XXXIII

He is in bed with Angela when the call comes.

It's Ange's birthday; forty-five, not one of the big ones, so they've no major plans. They are going to take the dog to the beach in Silloth, go to the pub afterwards for scampi and chips, where he'll give her the concert tickets. Depeche Mode, her favourite. They've just got going properly, the point where he is in danger of finishing solo and early, so she pushes against his chest, the signal to swap positions. He tries to stay inside while they roll, can't, never can quite manage to, and he re-sheathes his cock as soon as she's on top. Ange folds her legs along his hips and straightens her back, rodeo proud, oh god he loves that. Then she puts her hands on his shoulders. Her breasts now orbing above his mouth, just out of reach unless he strains his head up or she offers them closer, oh god they look superb as she moves, especially since she's deliberately pulled her vest up above them, peep-show style.

The phone trills in the hallway below.

Who is that, she says. *It's not even seven.*
 Fuck knows.
 She slows to a gentle movement, just on the end of him, which feels unbearably good.
 Shall I answer?
 No, he says. *Leave it.*
 He holds her bum, presses his fingertips into the skin, that per-fect firm-soft combination. The phone rings on. Clockwork siren woodpecker, hard to ignore. The dog starts whimpering and whining

190

downstairs, and he hears her claws clicking on the hallway boards as she gets out of bed and starts pacing to and fro.

Might be your mum, if your dad's had another turn? Ange says. *It might be Mark?*

Mark won't be up.

Their son, away for his first year at uni, has discovered nightlife, drum and bass and ecstatic trespass. And girls. His calls are infrequent – feigning homesickness when his hall fees are due. Occasionally he's rung them pissed, to tell them he loves them. Ange stops moving.

I'd better go.

Noooo!

She disengages uncomfortably quickly and pads out of the room. He watches the dimpled moons of her rump sinking down the stairs. The damp, hard thing feels wrong up in the air, without its wrapping. He puts his hand there, moves it back and forth, idly joysticking, not with any intention other than keeping the status quo. He pushes it away towards his balls, lets it bounce back, solid with blood. Please don't be anything important, he thinks.

He can hear Ange's muffled voice talking to the dog, then she picks up the receiver.

Dalston 534.

Her voice rises with familiarity.

Oh – hello.

She talks for a minute or so. He can make out a word or two.

Yes. Right-o. Not much. I will.

Doesn't sound like an emergency.

Come on, Ange, he murmurs, *say goodbye.*

He takes a big breath of air and his chest rises. There's a glisten of sweat in the depression between the muscles and in the curled hairs. His balls feel nice and tight, but the main player is beginning to desert the party.

Yeah. I think he will. Is it.

Who is she talking bottomless to? he wonders. Hopefully the

hallway blinds are down and Pamela and John next door can't see in. Not helping. Don't think of Pam and John now. He loves that her bush is dark and contrasts with her blonde hair; it's like secret information, a discrepancy only he knows about. Is her vest still riding up or has she pulled it down? What he would like to do is use the tip of his tongue then the flat of his tongue, as if she is an ice cream. What he would like is for her to—.

Oh, does it. I don't remember. Interesting.

Come on, Ange!

There's a bar of light underneath the curtain, the bright letterbox of a sunny day; it'll be nice for the beach. Good. Good to have something to do since he's retired. Good to keep busy. He does miss getting up in the dark for the early shift, arriving at the station when the sobered drunks are sheepishly heading home, soil bags in hand, a cheery *Morning, Michelle* to the front desk clerk and what is the world going to arse up today. Sometimes he finds himself awake at 4 a.m., making a list – walk the dog, clean the gutter, check the tyre pressure, pay bills, visit Dad, read a chapter of *Mental Maths for Pilots*, walk the dog. Doesn't miss the tedium, though. Sitting in the lay-bys. Paperwork. Sheep on the motorway. Or the steep end of the job, the forced entries into reeking flats, the pulped cheeks of the women saying *I made him angry* and the grey, unconscious junkies on Botchergate, bacon-and-dogshit sandwiches left on the bonnets of the patrol cars. He still sees that door opening and the bucket of acid thrown over Gary – it's set to repeat in his brain. Better to keep busy, or his body feels unprogrammed, scratchy with nothing vital to do, lazy, instead of forbearing. *You sure you want to take it so early?* Ange asked him when he raised the possibility of retirement at fifty. *Aren't you going to be bored?* But the mortgage had been paid off, drug-related procedure was getting brutal – it wasn't a war, it was exploited poverty – and after Gary he'd had enough, just wanted a few beers and a rest. Odd to think doing nothing could be just as dangerous.

Ange calls up the stairs.

Jude? It's Keith.

Keith?

Keith.

He hears her bare feet slap softly on the floor and the kitchen door opens. The tap turns on and water hits the bottom of the kettle with a hollow ring. That's that, then, for the bedroom show. He's not on the club rota today or instructing. Maybe Pete cancelled his slot and there's a free tow. He gets up and finds his Y-fronts in the pile on the chair, stumbles into them and goes downstairs. The dog greets him, snuffling at his crotch.

Get off, pervert.

He shoves her away and adjusts his frontage. In the kitchen, Ange is stretching up on tiptoe for cups from the cupboard. Her vest is pulled down, but her bum cheeks are not quite covered. Nice. Hitch it up, he mimes when she glances over, and she rolls her eyes. He picks up the receiver and the dog noses at him again.

Off, Shandy. Good morning, Mr Ferguson.

How-do-you, Jude. Beautiful day, as I was just saying to your wife. Can you turn it around in fifteen?

We were off to the coast for a fish-and-chipper. It's Ange's birthday.

Keith clears his throat productively down the line.

Ah, salutations to Angela, tell her she's looking as lovely as the day is long.

Charmer.

You might have to make it up to her. Now, do you remember that chap from the Met Office – asked for volunteers to collect some data over the Pennines?

I do.

You volunteered.

Did I?

You did. Well, he phoned me at sparrow fart. Looks like they've got their conditions. I'm at the airfield already. It's the instrumented glider

193

– Perry. *I'd do it myself, but this seems more your kind of shebang. Might be a long one.*

Yeah, hang on, he says.

He puts the receiver against his chest, looks into the kitchen, where Ange is looking back at him, holding a cup loosely by its handle and shaking her head slightly. He shrugs and points at the ceiling.

She sighs. *Go on,* she says. *I'll do you a flask.*

Jude blows her a kiss.

On my way, Keithly.

He mounts the stairs two at a time. He runs through his checklist as he piddles, cleans his teeth and splashes cold water on his face. It's almost like being on duty again – the controlled haste of a call-out. Adrenaline effervescing around the body. He pulls on shorts and a long-sleeve T-shirt, slathers sunscreen on his face and neck and knees, the backs of his hands – the proper stuff, SPF 50, not Ange's roasting oil: learned that the hard way while training for his solo endorsement. It'll be hot and exposed in the cockpit if he stays up a while, and what with the bloody ozone hole – not worth the risk. He buckles on his Casio; still hasn't worn the chunky retirement Rolex, hasn't had reason to. Downstairs he packs his bag with water, an empty plastic Coke bottle to wazz in, sunglasses, hat, two apples and a Mars bar. Three and a half minutes. He takes his flask of tea from Ange. She has on a dressing gown and wellies now for the dog and the garden and the neighbours. Sex hair, mussed at the back. Nice. He leans to kiss her goodbye.

Wait a minute, she says. *Is this that thing?*

What thing?

Are you going to fly in a storm?

No, he says.

She narrows her eyes.

Well, yeah, above it, he says, *so we can measure what's happening for the Met Office.*

194

Her eyes stay thin and interrogational. She probably could have extracted more confessions than he ever did, by this look alone.

I promise it's fine. Honestly. It's not really a storm, it's a wind thing.

It's a storm, she says.

He grins.

Yes, but I'll be on top of it.

Oh, well, we all know how that one goes. I want extra chips when you get back, please.

Chips and extras, I promise.

She pets Shandy's silky chocolate ears, lets her out into the garden, follows her clomping in the wellies. He can smell bread toasting under the grill.

Five minutes, twenty seconds.

See you later. Happy birthday, love, he calls.

XXXIV

Selima locks the bothy door and zips up her jacket. Outside, the pudding-shaped fells are umber in the early-evening light. Their tops are miraculously clear. The radome sits high above on its fat tee, as if waiting for God to strike it with an iron. *Fore!* Or Mohammed or Buddha or Shiva, whichever great leather-gloved hand. Perhaps they all play together, ruminating about the state of the world, in terrible existential disagreement. *It's all going to rack and ruin; no no, everything is right on track; but we are simply in a state of being; of course, all we can do is work for the good and expect nothing . . .*

She heads towards the village, half a mile away. Smelly brown patties cake the road, her good boots being perhaps the wrong choice after all. The lanes are beginning to overgrow, late pinkish blossom frilling the apple trees, fresh greenery. There's a toasted smell to the moorland, a truffle undertone.

She gets to the squat church with its fortified tower and patches of bluebells in the cemetery, pauses by the lychgate. *Go and explore!* She heads in and up the path, past leaning, mossy gravestones. Names repeating on the monuments that are biblical, old-fashioned, stolid. John. Sarah. Isaac. The surnames repeat too, families that have been in the valley centuries. Bowman. Kitchen. Armstrong. A huddle of European ones – Horvath, Meyer, Russo – and a small wooden cross: McBride. Both her parents are ashes in a chai tin, more or less. Always, in cemeteries, she thinks of her mum, though it's more a feeling than a thought, inmost, and completely incongruous: Karen Willis ditched her Anglican upbringing, preferred instead to perfect her

196

gujiyas. Next to the church door there's a sundial with a stone base and the face of the wind carved into it, angry-looking, puff-cheeked, curled-hair clouds.

Mrs H, I presume?

The church door is locked; its iron ring turns but the lever does not lift. Open from 12 p.m. until 4 p.m. daily for visitors. On the stone bench in the porch is a wire basket holding parish news pamphlets; she takes one and puts it in her pocket. She browses the messages on the pinboard. Services are every other Sunday (with a curt footnote: the curate oversees multiple churches in the district). The parish council is asking for donations for fireworks. There's a flyer for a jumble sale. A carlin supper fundraiser for Palestine. Pinned in the corner of the board, on a white file card, is a handwritten passage of scripture: *We are afflicted in every way, but not crushed; perplexed, but not driven to despair; persecuted but not forsaken; struck down, but not destroyed. Corinthians 4:8–9.* A plastic collection box is padlocked and bolted to the wall. It all seems so – rural.

There is the north, she thinks, where levelling-up means Manchester, Leeds and Liverpool, and stops with the BBC effect. And then there's the other north.

She leaves the churchyard and carries on along the silage-splattered road towards the green. It cannot be said that the Eden villages are pretty, exactly, braced as they are underneath the Pennines, the wrong side of the M6. There's a feeling of belligerence, perhaps, like prairie settlements or mining shanties. They are not the overrun slate villages in the heart of the county, that's for sure, bustling with cafes, adorned with Herdy stickers and eternally discounted outdoors shops. David loves it here.

The real Cumbria, he says, *is round the edges.*

197

Across the green, the Horse and Farrier looks inviting, its lights repelling the dusk, bright pansies in its window boxes, a smoking chimney. Outside are two wooden tables, one occupied by young farmerly types and a floppy spaniel, one surrounded by a small peloton of cyclists – pints in hand, all standing (sore balls?). As she approaches, everyone looks over. She thinks: this better be worth it, my friend.

Inside, the pub is small and cosy, a rectory shade of red, with an open fire, old village photos and brassware on the walls. There's an aroma of vinegar, fried food, hops – she immediately feels hungry. The landlady, voluminously haired, lipsticked and seventy if a day, is chatting to an attractive young couple sitting on stools at the bar. She smiles at Selima and calls over, directorially.

Evening, pet, anywhere you like.

Only one table is occupied, by walkers with a sleeping long-hound, vast oval plates of food in front of them. Selima takes a small table by the fire – coal in the grate, not something she's seen in a while, is it even legal? – and hangs her jacket on the back of the chair. She looks over at the hand pumps with local ale badges, colourful mountains and birds. She hasn't a clue. David is the beer connoisseur, evangelical almost, hence the slight belly on his otherwise trim frame. This really is his kind of thing: free house, craft beer, a formidable landlady – what did he say she was called? Lila? Leena? Lenny!

There's a menu on the table, with fairly standard dishes, moussaka being the only vg-friendly offering. Everything comes with chips or salad. Do I go to the bar? she wonders, but Lenny is already making her way over, holding one hip with pinched fingers, limping in a way that suggests advanced arthritis, or childhood polio. She has on skinny jeans and enormous furry sheepskin slippers. Her lip liner is a phenomenal shade of red, connotations of World War Two valour, geisha chic. Lenny smiles, a routine but not false-seeming smile.

Right then, my lovely. Waiting for anyone?

Selima shakes her head.

Nope, just me.

Oh, lucky you, bit of peace and quiet. What can I get you?

Moussaka and a red wine please – what's the house red?

It's a Merlot. Argentina. Serviceable, let's say. Large or small?

Large.

Smashing. Chips or rabbit food?

Well. My friend David will kill me if I don't have the chips. They are legendary.

Lenny chuckles and lists awkwardly to the side. She scribbles on her order pad.

David?

Carradale. The professor? He works up at the observatory from time to time. Think he comes here quite a lot on holiday with his wife, walking.

Lenny pauses, purses her lips, which have perhaps been lined in felt-tip, or tattooed, now Selima is looking closely.

Oh yes. The weather man. Tall. He's a nice chap, isn't he, very interesting.

Sort of, Selima says. *I mean, yes, he is nice. He's my boss.*

How is his wife now? She was a bit poorly last time they were in, if I recall.

Still quite unwell, I think.

That's a shame. Nice lady. I remember we had a long chat the first time he came in – about Cher-noble. You won't remember all that, I bet, too young.

I'm not that young, but thanks. I know about it. Radioactive sheep.

Lenny slips the order pad into her back pocket.

Contaminants are still present in the landscape, he said. He showed me the test results. Well, no surprise there, but he certainly knows his stuff, doesn't he?

Selima nods. *He does.*

Lenny sighs and becomes serious.

You see, it affected all the livestock, really. Terrible, it was. Farmers had

199

to slaughter everything, and the next generations, couldn't sell a single one at market. It took years until they could put the flocks back up on the fells. Lamb Henry is our best dish, just in case you fancy.

I'm vegetarian.

Moussaka it is, then. David Carradale. He did a little book about the Helm, didn't he.

Yes. And he's doing another one.

I told him a few stories. We lost part of the pub roof one year. Terrible, it was. Our insurance went right up – they are buggers. You're up at the golf ball at the moment, are you?

I am.

Good for you. Oof, it's a long way up. You'll be wanting that wine.

Lenny calls the food order over her shoulder, to no one in particular, then limps back to the bar and pours a generous measure of red. She sets it on the counter and resumes her conversation with the young couple. Selima collects it, returns to her corner and takes a sip – not bad, definitely serviceable. She puts her phone on the table – standard defence for lone diners, but on silent, she's not an arsehole – and fishes in her bag for a book.

The Horse and Farrier begins to fill up. She sips her wine, watches the punters. Utilitarian blokes. More cyclists arrive, with mud up their calves and sweat marks around their pits. A mooning middle-aged couple comes in – on a date, it seems; *second-time-rounders*, as her Papa would have said, though he never even looked at another woman after her mum died. It was the iron-haired, reassuringly undistressable Mrs Nanti that minded her and Anita after school (banana sandwiches on white bread, a cheese wheel, orange squash, *homework, girls, you'll be wanting to make Dad proud*). Next in, a Polish handyman in a boiler suit, whom Lenny greets loudly, *Siema, Matt*, presenting him with an already poured pint. Then an elderly gent with an obese black Labrador that collapses huffing by his feet. The atmosphere is warm and companionable. There's laughter around the bar as Lenny holds forth, flirting with a group of ruddy-faced lads.

A boy of about ten elbows his way to the bar. Lenny hands him a banknote from the till, flaps her hand to shoo him away, and he skips back out. More punters; soon the tables are all taken. As Selima is about to start the book, the residential Christians arrive – four of them, including the woman in the fedora with glitter comet-eyes from the bus. She smiles at Selima and Selima smiles back. The others look over and smile too. Selima pretends to read, surreptitiously watches them. They order bottles of ginger beer. There's an air of guileless disinhibition about them. Young, funky, but self-consciously so, as if in being bound to God they are obliged to express sartorial liberty. Comet Eyes asks if they can hand out some leaflets and Lenny tells her to leave a few on the counter, with the other bumf. After dispatching their drinks, the quartet leaves.

Selima's food arrives, delivered by a fuzzy mountain of a man in a hairnet and distressed chef's whites – Lenny's son, or husband perhaps; he's a good two decades younger but the landlady certainly still seems vigorous. He holds the platter with a tea towel, warns Selima not to touch the plate, and sets the huge erupting moussaka down in front of her.
Blimey, she says. *This'll keep me going.*
Beside the creamy bubbling dish there's a stack of golden, crispy fries, and a token quartered tomato.
Sauces on the sideboard, the chef says. *Red, brown and Sarson's.*
Amazing, thanks.
Leave room for pud, he says, and Selima laughs.

She tries a too-hot chip. Hallelujah! It is undeniably good – crunchy, fluffy, the oil blazed and shaken off it, coated in big crystals of salt. Worth venturing out for; fair play, David. She should take a photo for him. She picks up her phone. Silly, she thinks, cataloguing evidence of an unremarkable social life. Still, she does feel a little bit pleased with herself. On the homescreen is a message notification: an unknown mobile number. She unlocks the phone and reads it.

Delivery is coming soon. Time to prepare.

Doesn't make sense. She hasn't bought anything online recently, not since the terribly unglamorous outdoor gear. She reads the message again, and as she is reading a row of thinking/typing dots appears. Another text arrives.

The truth will find you in hiding.

And another.

Look above, Dr Sutar.

Selima stares at the screen. Who the fuck and what?

Is it them? The Endtrepreneurs? Same gnomic portentous bollocks, same facetious ad hominem. It must be. The cold trickle of realisation: now they have her phone number.

The dinner plate steams in front of her.

Her delivered and read notifications are switched on. She goes into her settings to turn them off, reads the messages again, then puts the phone down on the table. She looks up, and around. The pub is full, busy, noisy. There are three big-bellied men in woollens leaning on the bar, David lookalikes, and small groups at the tables, couples, friends. The old chap with the Lab. Everyone seems normal. No one is looking over at her. No one has even spoken to her beyond pub practicalities and pleasantries – *excuse me, yes go ahead and stroke him, he's a big softie, aren't you, Winster, Winster, lie down now.*

Come on, she thinks, this is stupid. It's just absolute stupidness. Eat your bloody dinner, Selima.

She looks out of the window, into the deep, country darkness. She concentrates on not being bothered. Is it anger or anxiety she is feeling? There's a reedy fluttering in her chest, and a tightening, and a tickling, like when she had asthma as a child, the precursor to a proper fit. She takes a big breath of air, exhales slowly, reaches into her coat pocket for the Silk Cut, which are not there. OK, calm down.

Stupid. Weird. And rude. Who the fuck do they think they are—

She picks up her phone, reads the messages again, then calls the number. She holds the phone to her ear, tries to hear a phone ringing somewhere in the pub, as if. The dial tone cuts off almost immediately, no voicemail option available. She can't even leave a piss-off message. But what did she expect, really? She blocks the number.

She catches Lenny looking over.
Everything all right with the nosh? Lenny calls.
Selima nods and forces a smile. She takes a chip, puts it back down.

It can start small, David said, then escalate. But come on. Particle aggregation per cubic metre? It isn't controversial. She hasn't been speaking at COP. There's no disputed hockey stick, no radiation scandal. And she isn't Greta bloody Thunberg. Perpetual minor interference is the new norm, but this cannot be a campaign like the one David suffered. The data of David's generation was game-changing, life-changing; it was Big Industry after them, the ultracons, not that anyone was held to account. And it was absolute bloody hell because the world thought it had been scaremongered, duped. Once, in a rare candid moment, David said that he wondered whether it was the stress that had somehow made Sandra sick. Whether it was, in some way, his fault.
It's cancer, Selima replied, quietly. *It's no one's fault, David.*

So no. This cannot be what is happening.

203

XXXV

Helm isn't feeling Helmself, actually. Helm is a bit off-colour, a bit under the weather.
Waffy.
Squiffy.
Below par.
Just a bit meh.

How to describe it?

It's complicated. Hard to put Helm's fingers on it. Helm just feels a bit wrong lately. A bit faux. Not a fraudster but, you know, not as natural, not as much unbridled brio. Not as vivified or as terrifying. Helm has lost some pizzazzle, truth be told.

It isn't that Helm feels old; Helm is old in human years, goes without saying. Helm isn't tired or addled, grumpy or forgetful; Helm doesn't parp when Helm bends over. (See, Helm doesn't even take pleasure in things that are funny.)

Helm has still got it, obviously. Can still get up. Can still operate.

But some days it's difficult to get going; hard to rally. Maybe the old identity issue. Once everybody knows what you are, the temptation is to be more you. Overdo it. Be you, plus; you, supersized. Once you start wearing the hat, the hat starts wearing you. Hurricane strength, fancy clouds, ruiner, dementor, GSoH, debauchee – right, off you go, do what's expected, yada yada. Take another picture, scream, cower, build the barn again, ooooh so impressive . . . (See, Helm didn't use to do sarcasm either.) People have been giving Helm a hard time For Ever for being Helm. But, whatever, not bothered (OK, maybe a bit bothered). Do they really appreciate Helm, though? It all seems so artificial, a bit too curated.

That's not the problem, exactly.

It's true, Helm might have absorbed some negativity. Pessimism, cynicism, jadedness. Probably human-related (no offence). They can have that effect. Something has definitely got into Helm – a feeling of hopelessness, of fin-de-siècle melancholy, Information Age malaise, overload, elegy maybe. Helm sees it on their phones all the time down there, in their news feeds. The macro crap. Wars, pandemics, natural disasters (no such thing, people, it's natural hazards – nature isn't 're-sponsible' for ruining your trinkets, it is merely ruinous!). And the idiotic minuscule. Burger wrappers, testicle deodorant, lip plumpers. More stuff, more waste, more illness, more unhappiness. All their self-disturbance. World War what-are-we-on-now? It's exhausting. Hasn't it gone a bit too far? People must know better by now, but they can't seem to stop, for fuck's sake. Would give anyone the Ick.

It's more pervasive than lacklustre, though. It's on a cellular level. Like – literally. The feeling of contamination by the world.

Other times things haven't been right with Helm it's been obvious why. The normal environmental stuff. Ice Age. Sun flares. Ash cloud. Pre-Anthropocene establishment fluctuations in the maritime status quo. Those had to be endured for the sake of evolution, Urth, the immune system, proprioception, vita spiritus, you know. Life! The noble fight! Difficult situational conditions = Proper purposeful reasons. Helm had to really work at being Helm. It was good for Helm's health and Helm's mojo.

Now?

Whatever is wrong feels environmental too. But insidious, sneaky, infectious. The surprise disease on the routine tests. Some kind of weird intimate growth you find accidentally and go, Jesus, how long has that been there? A toxic waft when you're asleep; lights out.

And it's everywhere. Everywhere everywhere everywhere. It's in Helm's self, Helm's substance, Helm's consciousness. It's like it's in the air.

XXXVI

All the elite tribes come to the equinox meeting. It is the largest meeting at Magsca that any of the people can remember – word has spread of the magstone and everyone wants to see the eyeless hanging face. They convoy to the river and stand beneath it, amazed, reverent. It is the stone that NaNay has described since she was a child, the stone she has drawn for years. The colour. The features. All Mother is truly a seer.

After trade exchanges are made, deaths and lives calculated on the bead chains, and after the fires are lit, there are discussions about how to get the magstone free from the grip of the cliff. It is still unborn. It is very difficult to reach; this part of the river gorge has no road to it. The people discuss how to quarry the rock, how to move the magstone from the river, up through the woods and across the open country, to the gathering place. It is longer than the other stones of Magsca – the length of four or five men lying down, head to feet. It will be hard to push, even with more rollers.

The discussions become disagreements. The magstone is too tall to dig a foundation deep enough, because of the bedrock. If it is not deep and secure in the earth, the magstone will tip. The herders and farmers dispute this: land here has long earth, and any buried boulders can be smashed apart. The far traders say they have seen tall menhirs like the magstone, but never far from their home rock. The cross stones of the summer henge were transported and lifted; it can be done with combined industry, but only with agreement. River-stone is not as heavy as granite or whitestone, but this piece is vast

– the weight of ten orox, fifteen orox. Its shape, the place where it hangs, the journey from the river and uphill to the plateau – this will take many generations and perhaps it will kill people.

Manno from the forest tribe stands and speaks.

The magstone has not been released fully by the rock, which gives it half death, like a stillborn. To help birth it, we will have to chisel it from above and below. If it falls wrong it will break apart and then it will no longer be the magstone of All Mother's vision.

Another man puts his hands in the smoke and speaks.

Manno is wise. We cannot help the magstone be born. The people must wait for it to fall.

A woman from the estuary people speaks.

The magstone is blind. It has no eye. What does this mean? Does it have anma? It is too dangerous for us. Another stone should be found in the blue quarries. The herders and forest tribes live close to the river but we will have to travel to help birth the magstone. This is not our valley.

NaNay claps her hands and spits on the ground. Her bracelets rattle as she washes herself in smoke. She stands in her white fur, her shoulders rounding, grey locks draped across her back. The heron again. She looks at the people and at the fire, waits for the words to rise. Then she speaks and the people listen.

I am the oldest in our tribe and All Mother. Ancestors laid the first stones of Magsca in accordance with the sun and the stars and the mountains. When my Second Mother was a child, the molar stone of Magsca was found and all the people agreed to cooperate. The molar stone was by the waterfalls above black earth. Now it is beside the entrance. Magsca is our most sacred place above the sands and below the forest. Magsca reminds the tribes to keep peace. How far do people come to gather here? Jemya's people have travelled for twelve days. Borron's people have come from the white shore. I show you my marks again and tell the story of NaNay. I have travelled fast like Halron and seen the other place. I have seen what is to come. In the valley we have sometimes said that Halron is our enemy and we should go back into the forest like Manno's people, or to the other side of the river where Halron cannot reach us. But the soil is not as productive and there is too much water under the earth. Magsca is here, where the people chose it. We have accepted Halron. After the last snow our crops were destroyed by Halron, but we started tilling and we planted again and there was enough food. Halron's strength broke the river walls and found the magstone. I have waited all my life for the magstone. The hanging face by the river is the magstone. My vision was the eye of the magstone. Now the magstone must come from the river to Magsca. The magstone must hold the sun when the sun is weakest and tell us light is returning. I am the oldest here and I will not see this happen. I am speaking the truth.

The people begin work.

It is agreed which tribes will go to the river, and which will make the forest road, in the safest and best seasons. Not when the brown bears come together and the males are roused to fight. Not when their cubs are young. Not when the purple spotfish move upstream and leap the rapids and there is competition along the banks. After barley harvest. Before the winter rituals. Before the river's meltwater spate, when it surges through the gorge, flooding the beaches and glades, bringing with it volleys of scrub and dead animals.

Dal and Manno begin to clear a pathway through the trees for the orox and the people to move the magstone. They cut the brush and burn the trees and Dal drives the orox down to the water to help make the road. They smooth the passage. They collect trunks and shred branches to make the conveyor, and they prepare a pallet of timbers underneath the magstone to catch it when it falls – it is like working under the face of a sleeping god. Rain turns the face dark and it cries black-red tears from the place where no eye is and there is disquiet and wonder among the people. They begin to leave offerings on the beach. In the caves nearby is a new group. They have browner eyes and woven clothes. They have come to serve the magstone. The three men are very scarred, perhaps not to be trusted. One of the women shows Reen how she uses threads across weft and warp sticks, pushing them close together to make warm dense material.

Men from the forest tribe tie ropes to the stumps above the gorge and climb down the cliff to the position of the long head. They begin knocking wooden wedges into the cracks around the top of the magstone, tapping them with blunt-head hammers. The wedges split and shatter. More are carved. The far traders bring a mallet with a dark bronze head that has been made by a mould. It is heavy and extremely strong. It is shaped like the head of a fox.

All this year, NaNay watches the work; she stands on the beach; she points to the weak places where the magstone can be levered away from the cliff, like a tooth from its gum and bone. The cracks widen around it and the people carve fatter wedges.

In winter the work is stopped. Rainwater runs into the cracks and freezes, locking up the magstone in a case of ice, splitting the fissures further. Icicles form on its broad tapered nose. Nothing more can be done until spring. The people concentrate on survival, bringing the herds into the pens, protecting the stores, eating smokemeat, the preserved redberries and dried roots.

After solstice, there is a strange, very warm spell. Winter disappears for a week and flies hatch and swarm. Then there is sickness and in the valley settlement two herders die with foul, watery shit and sunken veins. Little Joa becomes sick. He wails, holding his griping stomach, yellow froth spilling from his backside; he is very hot and soon his eyes cannot focus. NaNay gently pulls Reen away from his bed and tends to him herself. She remembers the fever of her seventh year, and the half-fin; Second Mother blowing smoke and dripping water into her mouth. *I will be safe, leave us alone.* But soon she too is infected. They are so sick, every time they sit up. It is as if they have eaten grass. They lie together, weak, sweating, sleeping. Then Joa cannot wake or be roused. NaNay shakes him and pinches him but his eyes roll. After two more days he dies.

NaNay does not die. She holds Joa's corpse until his recognisable scent begins to fade. His skin has turned ashy and dry as chalk. He was NaNay's favourite, the child of Reen, and his eyes had tints of green, like Kobe's people; he first walked to her, and he loved her best. When he was born she dreamed that milk beaded on her own nipples.

It is only now that her heart feels too thin to hold all its sadness, the sadness of her years, people who have gone. She and Reen prepare the clay for a burial mask. The woman from the caves comes to help them; she stands quietly and then approaches. She follows Reen to Magsca and she gives Reen a beautiful blanket.

NaNay stands in the place Joa's grave has been dug. His face is smooth clay. When it is finished the mask will stay in her hut. She remembers her second baby, the girl with no name and no anma, burnt a long time ago. And Henti, who was killed by Kobe. She puts in Joa's grave the carved-horn figurine that she made during the Halron's storm. She chants softly and loudly over the earth. He will go to the other world and NaNay will see him again soon and she will make him laugh and they will play with the toy.

XXXVII

Michael has traversed too far along the girth of Fiend's Fell. The summit floats in the distance, a high, ungainable island. He is very thirsty, sweated like a pig yesterday, and his mouth contains an evil paste, as if after a night of carousing. He tips the water-skin. It is empty again, but he does not remember finishing it. Poured out by that bastard, dream-seducing incubus, who perhaps also fed him goblets of wine. The cluster of prunes in his pouch he can resist, but water he must have now. Pissed only twice yesterday, hot and concentrated and malignant-smelling. He's seen men get the sting on the periphery of battle and become useless with it, confused, wandering over enemy lines. His mind coalesces around the sole thought. He must drink. He must drink.

He abandons the cross and the blackened firepit, searches the nearby slopes. Wiry upland moor spreads all about. There are knuckles of rock, and the roots of the stunted trees are shallow, as if rain-reliant. The ample water channels of the previous day have all disappeared. Another trick. Another test. The demon has sealed the quim of the mountain. It has desiccated the great damp wen upon which it sits.

He scans the landscape, diving. Over there, where the land wings together in a cleft, should be a tidy little ghyll. There isn't. Ahead of him, then, under a flare of gnats, should be some kind of grassy standing pond. But it is only a bundle of dejointed bones, pink rags attached to their shafts. He searches on, dropping down the hill, walking back up. There is animal shit, fresh, and close to where he slept. There's a woven nest with two tawny eggs inside; he cracks

212

and eats the meat, which is viscous, foetal-tasting and unpleasant. He must drink soon. He must drink.

He lies down, puts his ear to the earth, listens for the telltale sound of underground trickling. All is still. He moves to another section of hill, denser with foliage, tries again. There is no watercourse, but there's a soft padding sound nearby; perhaps it is his own heart. He tries where the shingle and scree might hide a culvert. Cold stone, dead as lightning glass. But he hears it again, the beat, footsteps, the clatter of feet very close by. He starts up, holding his belt—

Who is there?

He cast his eyes around the fell. All directions are barren. There is no one. In this high, open place, he would surely see a form coming, a lupine streak, an arrow shaft. He must drink. He goes to ground, listens. There. Again. Click, clack, tock, tock. Are the stones in this haunted place speaking to each other, or just dislodging up the bank? It is a climbing deer, perhaps, or some low, badgerly creature in its tunnel. But, click, clack – it is surely step-like. He stands and surveils. The land is empty, so empty it is almost hollow. Perhaps some terrestrial minion of Helm – the antlered one – is tracking him, treading invisibly behind, or walking the obverse of the mountain's surface.

Damn this wretched heath. It is the thirsty mind capering. He must drink. He must drink. A man can, under irrational circumstances, easily undo himself, convince himself of gibbers and goobers. The mountain is an exceptional place for doubt. For by its nature it offers choice: it is either impossible or surmountable. On the mountain, man must accept his limits and his mettle, he must traverse trust and fortitude and endurance. The mountain is itself theology, a gift from the maker of this world; it is the radical, indisputable staircase to God.

And he is Michael Lang. Therefore, he will find some fucking water on it.

He locates a brackish well over the next brow, slathered into by a variety of beasts, by the looks of it, and turgid in its bed: the kind of offering that will lead to spurting shits. He drinks regardless, fills his container, then he returns to the cross. He hefts it up onto his shoulder with a shout, and he begins. Upwards.

By noon, he is ensnared in dense briar that snags the muddy wooden base, tripwire as he turns to haul it. His legs are cross-hatched with scratches; his trousers, loose above the gaiters, are ragged and bloody. He knows. The thicket is his ego, and he must wrestle through. So be it, cunt.

He tramples down the thorns with his boot, attempts to make a path through while some heady scent wafts like the tropics over the fell. Gorse has exploded sweetly with blossom. Now his mind is softened by recollections of Eastern feasts aside those great mathematicians. Platters of roasted bird meat, spiced lamb. Jewelled pomegranates, and apricots moist and fragrant. The delicate rose treats, served on tiny dishes. Exquisite. Iridescent blue sea is before him, jasmine-draped walls in academic gardens, and the warm sun is an expectorant on his phlegmatic brain. There was Paradise.

Here on this savage, mucal flank of English mountain, with its clawing scrub and relentless ether skies, it is hell. Sheer folly. He could leave the cross in this tangled minge, be down in Salkeld by sunset. He could leave this godforsaken county, head south to the capital, send his report to Avignon. The pope is busy with preparations for another war and will not care. Were he a lesser man, he would retreat. But he is the Feared Hand, headhunted by the Holy Roman Emperor, astrological predictor of war and alumnus of Toledo. He has split hills apart and shifted lakes in order for armies to besiege towns, reversed eclipses. He is the most persistent bastard of this era.

Finally, he tears free and drags the cross to a bank of rocky ground, where he collapses.

He takes four prunes from the pouch. Eats. Continues. Upwards.

So soon the day has gone. Light is drawing away again, west, over those false, idolatrous heavens, intensifying to peacock blue over the Solway. On view are the saddles and mitres of far worthier mountains than this conceited hill. It is a very clever demon that chooses a lesser peak to impregnate; a calculated fort from which to wreak the most prodigious damage. It is a very clever demon that sits atop the middle spine of the whole country, like a hornet on the gable of a barn.

The second day is concluding and the end is still far ahead; he has underestimated. He will camp; tomorrow he will summit.

He makes another fire. There is a greenish shimmer to the flame; it is magical or coppered, a sorcerer's fire.

He touches his helmet. More than anything, he would like to remove it, cast it off, and yield; he would like to feel the soft breeze on his scalp. It is God's ordinance if he is called home. But he does not wish to go. He thinks of Isa's gentle hand, doctoring him. Soon Isa will be a man and the gentleness gone. How small that hand was on his neck when he first lifted him. Why did the boy not struggle? Bite him? Curse him? He held tight, even after what he had seen. How quickly he was fostered. How might it be explained – the contract? There are times, like now, staring into the cryptic fire, he can almost glean its meaning.

Tonight he does not succumb to sleep, but lies awake, lucid and alert, watching the crescent moon disembark the shore of the horizon and sail its silver coracle through darkness. Hunger passes again; acid sharpness takes its place. He feels no fever or illness coming on from bad water. Tomorrow he will enter the last stage of pilgrimage – transformation. He is open to the spirits.

And so the spirits come, the company of the mountain, one by one, ancient and transitory, beasts and ghosts. The creatures of the high moorland, their eyes reflecting from the terraces.

Some dismal hag in skins and rabbit furs walks past, spits, and throws a stinking bundle of intestines in the fire. She has eyes as white as spiders' nests, reeks of the gibbet.

A leather-pleated legionary comes into the camp. He sets down his shield and gladius; sits on a rock beside Michael. They converse tolerably in Latin. The soldier is dispatched from the garrison in Thorpe and is marching to the wall. He carries news. The emperor is dead, his successor named, and the senate is angry. Troops are to be withdrawn from the milecastles along the border. The expanding wave of empire has finally broken.

The soldier gets up and walks on, leaving a coin on his seat and a satchel beside it. On the coin, Britannia, in her birrus, faces left. Two and a half asses. Michael opens the satchel buckle; inside is a folded alder sheet. It is the written record of Cerialis Severa, commander of Vindolanda garrison, addressed to Domitia, his wife. *Greetings. I await your arrival and think this letter may pass you on the road before you arrive. Our little son Aelius must be grown to the size of a man and I hope he prospers. I have for you a brooch and fan, though I fear you shall find the weather in the north cold. The winds here are especially fierce. Beyond the vallum it has been quiet and the grain supplies are adequate.*

The text fades, oxygenised. He folds the sheet and burns it.

The diabolical gatekeeper that accompanied Michael on the first day circles the camp, its hooves tapping, its horns cutting the shadows apart, but it comes no closer to the fire. He watches it prance. An arrow must penetrate its broadside, in the equator between the blade of shoulder and the last rib.

Towards dawn, from his mind spill all the Cathars and witches and the enemies of King John. They rank about him, disembowelled, burned, imprisoned. On his word, by letterhead, if not by his hand. Damn them all, damn them all again.

At first light, Michael is up and the tended fire is still warm. Wind flushes through the tall moor grass and the stiff heather. If all wind here is Helm's and biddable, he is being well met. The sun rises redly and it begins again, repeating across time. *Fac hodie opus est hodi.* The helmet gives him no pain on this last day. It glows as if newly forged, as if made of new metals, a substance of the future. He hoists the cross onto his shoulder, suffers it, accepts suffering, and walks on; upwards. For he is a brute machine; he is the holy automaton.

Michael.

Michael Lang of Kelso. Listen.

I am listening.

Michael. I see what you are. You are a bullet in my mountain. What dire acts you have undertaken. If only you could see what is to come – the great exterminations, genocides, the final solution. Murder by

217

the touch of a switch, the pull of a trigger, hypodermic chemicals. The gas chamber, the nuclear bomb, semi-automatics, sterilisation. This slow-boiling, storm-cast Earth, its inhabitants crawling over each other to get off. There is no need for the pike and the broadsword, for chainmail or branding rods. No need for your mirrors and hexes. What might you have done, in the age of steel, of atomic separation and virology, so suited as you are to annihilation?

Is it the voice of the Almighty speaking to him in prophesy, or is it Helm, false oracle? He does not know. Nor does it matter.

XXXVIII

Helm's Wind-Force Scale

0. Zero Helm (complete calm). Mean wind speed < 1 mph. Weathervanes and trees unmoving, grass still, water as mirror, smoke rising vertically from roundhouses/cottages/plague pyres.

1. Hint of Helm (ennui). Wind speed 1–3 mph. Occasional twitching of moorland plants and idly flicked pages of open books, smoke drifting sideways from bonfires and barbecues, seed heads mobile.

2. Light Helm (aloof engagement). Wind speed 4–7 mph. Wavelets in the grass, dandelion clocks distributing filaments, passage of air felt on naked skin, aurochs' nostrils beginning to flare, parted rabbit fur.

3. Gentle Helm (viscous interference). Wind speed 8–12 mph. Y-fronts lifting on washing lines, flags fluttering, small-bore pistols experiencing bullet drag, excellent kiting for children.

4. Moderate Helm (now roused). Wind speed 13–18 mph. Lightish, unmoored items skittering about, dust flares and matches extinguished, flowers nodding towards Lakeland, Women's Institute beanstalk alerts.

5. Fresh Helm (naughty). Wind speed 19–24 mph. Trees swaying, wavelets on puddles and cattle troughs, garden birds grounded while hawks consider position, gentlemen's handkerchiefs levitating; zesting of libidos.

6. Strong Helm (bad attitude). Wind speed 25–31 mph. Sheep walls form in fields, windowpanes rattling and smoke sucked back down chimneys, fell ponies canter directionless, village cricket postponed.

7. Near-Gale Helm (inconveniencing). Wind speed 32–38 mph. Minor damage to gutterings and aerials, bins toppled and hay bales unbound, bonnets sternly knotted under chins, pilgrims/shepherds/ramblers impeded.

8. Gale Helm (violent). Wind speed 39–46 mph. Crops uprooted, branches broken and slates dislodged from roofs, inside-outing of umbrellas and weathervanes propellering, snow spindrifting, opportunistic congress.

9. Severe-Gale Helm (destructive). Wind speed 47–54 mph. Met Office Red Warnings issued, paraffin lamps lit and power outages, animals sheltering leeside, turnip piles avalanched, shutters bolted, insurance claims.

10. Storm Helm (hellion). Wind speed 55–63 mph. Mature trees lost, bothies and longhouses demolished, pylons down, heaping waves on lakes, dogs continually barking, stillborn lambs, whisky uncorked.

11. Violent-Storm Helm (berserker syndrome). Wind speed 64–72 mph. Widespread chaos, flattened woods and roofs removed, children weeping uncontrollably, last wills and testaments produced, la mort d'amour.

12. Hurricane Helm (hand of God). Wind speed 73–83 mph, phenomenal damage and widescale loss of life, Eden reconfigured biblically, Carlisle–Settle train lifted off the tracks, history made, FIN.

XXXIX

Dearest Beatrice, you may think my story ends at this most sorry waymark. A sister slung dans les oubliettes. The magazine loaded with armament & those towering monuments doomed to dust. Do not dismay, for Nature, ever the strolling magician, has up her sleeve charms and bedwines.

Long day followed in the boudoir, with not a soul shewing face at the bolted door, no nourishment at suppertime, no word of occurrence beyond the walls, not even Phoebe whispering at the keyhole. Sleep – I had little, but tossed & trembled under the canopy as one all of a dudder with fever. I dreamt I heard the boom & thunder of combustibles. I dreamt the sisters screamed within their stones; agony such as that felt by the doomed souls in Tartarus. Then in that thick, worsted hour before dawn, when you say our dear deceased Mumma oft chatters to you, knitting in her rocker, an Other came to me. 'Twas not as Susanna Bousfield describes, a spirit of the ether gaining entry, the occupation of medium by the departed. My fleshy machinery was not driven by this visitor. Stranger still – a drape in time was opened & through it her separate embodiment walked.

I dreamt (though in good faith, was I not completely lucid!) an ancient woman came t'wards my bed, swathed in winter furs, skin brown as walnut and rippling upon her chest, her hair like corded snakes. She held a dagger in her hand, not viciously for the blade was to her own heart directed. Rather, she held the handle out for me to take. No savage of ante-histoire was she, for the eyes against her darkish face were as aptly lit as any person with appointment in the parlour here, or in the chapel seeking higher answer. Alack, we could not possibly converse! How might we? In which language,

& with what unifying knowledge? I sensed she had conveyance for me, news of endangerment & conflict, some task yet ahead. She was urging me to stand ground, defend myself, fight! I took her knife & in its taking deeply pricked my palm. Asleep or not, I felt the pain, saw blood trickle on the coverlet. Then I awoke. No press of comfrey was necessary, nor bandaging, the wound was sealed & she, traveller from some time long past, had vanished.

Phoebe arrived sore-eyed next morning with an egg, having been plied at length for description of my mischief. She said the horrid act was under way; labourers had begun to carry powder to the common, straw was being sprinkled at the foot of each & every stone to keep the moisture tamped. The men were nervy as foals, she said, atwit with worry for their limbs, fastening up their buttons, tightening their caps. Among them was one she did not know – a fuse master, come over from Honister & employed by Nathaniel to spark the charges. There were marks of back-blast on his cheek, Phoebe said, most malignant-looking. When is the axe to fall? I asked. Today, m'Lady, very soon, before the weather turns. Dear soul that she is, she wept as I wept. I told her hush, reconvene her wits – she must fly swiftly to the battlefield & observe from a safe enclave, then return to tell me all, for I wished to know every particular tragic deed, I wished not to be spared. I, in my restriction, would pray to the Goddess. She apologised for refastening the lock on her way out. I peeled the egg & waited . . .

The rest, dear sister, is Phoebe's tale, recounted to me wide-eyed & wondrously as she set my supper tray. Hers is courageous witness testimonial, hidden as she was behind the coppice wall & peering out, while I implored for intervening forces.

An autumnal scene was set, cloud and bluster threatening. On the common the men, despite their promised fortune, were most disgruntled, saying 'twas an insult to disrupt Meg's daughters. Such rude occurrence would bring disaster to all of Eden, from Hartside down to Brough. How many had known the true purpose of their toil before being tempted by the jingle of de Peyster balsam? As if they'd woke from drunkenness to find bright coins in their palms pledging them to the royal fleet, they rubbed their heads, they protested, all was a mystery. Baffling dogs, Tobias hollered at them, idle apes! Do as you are bid! He shook the money pouch in their faces. Shamefully they dug their holes around the stone assembly. Hot conversation was taking place between fuse master and my husband also. Not fair climes for demolition, sir, the half-faced Honister man said, we shall need to clay the posts with all haste, or delay this event. Nathaniel insisted. Today – now! I want those hellcats gone! A few men shook their heads & departed. The remainder, a sorry clutch, funnelled black powder into the chambers, winging their coats to protect the grains, for the wind was getting up & sewing it like bad seed across the field. Nathaniel strode about with the fuse master at his shoulder, & when the breeze gusted apart the man's locks, Phoebe saw a telltale burn scorched into his skull. Ay, that would be Old Nick, she thought.

This caper I did not see, nor hear, but sat anguished in my room. Eyes closed, palms proffered in the way of the Dialogues, I invited any impalpable assistant to come. Come it did! Beatrice, is it not so that Nature is as powerful as any Créateur Masculin; perhaps Nature, God & Goddess are not separate aspects but are fused in creative collective, as are egg whites & shell & yolk? It is we who crack ideas apart, dribble beliefs through our fingers, casting off this as waste & that as froth, preserving the simple core because it appears golden. I cannot comprehend what followed, yet sense, perhaps as you sense, & as my husband's younger quaking tot does, a fundamental lesson. The more we suppress & desecrate & banish the Goddess, the worse will be her ire returning.

So arrived the Helm – formidable, with tremendous purpose. The excoriating wind I hinted of at this tale's commencement was summoned most opportunely, rescuer to Long Meg and her daughters. First, its song, moaning down the hillside & all around the hall, such doleful opera. When I opened my eyes I saw it stewing over the vale;

then all at once it shook & banged & rattled the barricaded window, as if to break the locks, as if to liberate this captive!

Out on the common, Bedlam! Chaos! The torrent came howling. It toppled the coppice wall near where brave Phoebe stood, her skirts flapping & sailing. It crippled the trees, made them bow low in worship. The men ran all about, hands to their hats, blinded by straw & strewn powder, shouting deuce-deuce & curses in their dialectic reserved for market trading. Some knelt beside Meg & swore never to offend the older gods again.

O tidy, timely reckoner! To have seen with my own eyes the sweep of such a mighty broom – how I wish it!

But what of Nathaniel? What of the fuse master? Ah, yes. Swirled by their explosive, Phoebe said, trapped within two terrible black spouts. Gone on their heels to shelter in the fold, trippity as squealing girls. Then – mark this moment, savour it whenever a pièce montée is fancied – both gentlemen were stripped naked at the back door of the house & sluiced down with pails by Lanter, spitting like camels, for gunpowder was in every nook & crevice of their personages. Only Tobias was left in the brunt, wig gone, frock blown over his bottom, chasing the coin purse o'er the common, for the dallying Helm had hold of it & was tugging it along then pausing, tugging it then pausing, as one might pull a ribbon for a kitten.

Rejoice! Rejoice with me, dearest Bea. Justice has been served! The Goddess has arisen & held our boat in her hand once more. Meg & her sacristy are preserved, as I do not imagine Nathaniel will repeat his humiliation, nor will the villagers permit any further desecration of the ancient altar.

Rejoice, yet sigh a little too. 'Tis a fact of the matter – I remain held in confinement without egress & under dire consideration by husband & the black-plastered goblain. Trapped, irritated, deprived of entertainments, except this sweet, surreptitious resource. I may still undergo radical deposition; were it not for the estate's inheritor in my belly I might even be shipped to the Magdalenes. Yet defiant,

I remain. I wear the red badge around my chops without shame, like the patient fox who waits for the retreating snows & finds its savoury prize beneath.

   Your ever-loving sister,
   Catherine

XL

In early August, Thomas's residency begins in the tiny cottage in Kirkland. It is extremely basic, a two-room dwelling no larger than the orangery at Blackheath, but its croft is dry and has a range if needed – no real hardship for the warmer months, and a step up from the alpine trekking huts. A local woman is to come and cook for him, and clean, if necessary. From this humble abode, he will be able to speed to the site of the Revelation Machine, once the Helm gets going. If, Bodge. If, he reminds himself.

On the morning of departure from Grange House, his belongings are loaded by Boller into the trap. Midge hands him a crusty pie in a basket, which he stows under the seat. Mrs Brooke is not there to see him off, disappointingly. He lingers, and walks into the meadow, hoping to catch sight of her between the larches, coming back from the river. She has left him a salutatory note in the hallway – short, brusque, not entirely a severance.

Mr Bodger. Goodbye. I hope you will reconsider your foolish enterprise.
If not, I suggest with much reservation Grahams for your ink. I suppose I
shall check on you soon to ensure you are not too solitary. R.B.

He quickly scrawls a reply.

With heartfelt thanks, you have kept me on my toes, Mrs Brooke! I
sincerely hope you might change your mind and will bear witness to the
dreaded experiment – Your Fool. T.B.

As the trap clatters down the lanes to Kirkland, he is rather sorry to be leaving the Grange, with its strange interior wildings, the logger-head company at the dinner table. It feels – like unfinished business.

The hot, sweltering, rainless spell continues. The cottage is coolly flagstoned with rag rugs cast about, a pair of pattens left beside the door, and a sheepy smell to its corners. Which former old-timey in-habitant has passed on with no inheritors, he wonders. There is not much to do but wait for the equipment to arrive, take a few expos-ures of the mountain with the portable camera and hope the sky unsettles. Ho-hum.

Not one for thumb-twiddling, he ventures over to the Lakes again for a few days – the Helm surely will not be so unkind as to per-form in his absence. He visits Low Wood, Bowness and Ambleside. The streets tussle with visitors arriving by train; connections to the steamers are seamless now the railway company has subsumed the boat businesses. Remarkable, the changes. The villages he visited as a boy have become towns, their new houses and hotels served by cargo steamers bringing coal, produce, mail. Cake shops, guesthouses, jerries and postcard huts line the streets; the souvenir vendors call to him, undercutting each other, and the pier touts vie for his attention, shoving into his hand leaflets promising luxury sailings at an afford-able price, luncheon and dancing on board, no less.

By the hundreds, his fellow trippers disembark, with lunch ham-pers, with polished shoes and pretty parasols, watercolour boxes and sketchpads. He strolls among them, dodging, *pardon me, pardon me*, as if making his way through London Bridge. He almost expects some skilamalink to riffle his pocket. The crowds are beguiled in this blessed English summer; many have escaped Manchester's gloom for a day of restoration. They are not the radical artists nor the in-trepid climbers of his youth, though certainly he can spot the loyal, wool-socked, shepherd-booted gents, who, like he and his father once did, will conquer the interior massifs, bivouacking, buying eggs from the lime-washed farms. Those chaps get down at the station and walk purposely with their staffs, round the top of the lake, past the forces and gills, to the remote, prized giants. No, no, it is the new expanding middle classes now arriving by the carriageful, claiming the district. For it has become a tamed pleasure ground.

From his window in the Langdale Chase, he watches the cruise vessels bisecting each other on the lake. Perhaps he should have returned to London for a day or two? Perhaps he should shave; he is looking a little shepherdly himself. What, he wonders, is Mrs Brooke doing? Lying on her back in the green pot, her hair fanned out, her body white and lilied as a Rossetti model?

He books a ticket on one of the older paddle steamers, the *Rothay*, up the River Leven, drinks gin at her stern. Her varnished wood is still glossy, her saloon mirrored and smartly carpeted. On the open lake she is passed by the *Dragonfly*, whose passengers jeer amiably as they draw level, the onboard musicians strike up 'Farewell, My Lovely' as she pulls ahead. Thomas smiles and salutes them. He looks back towards shore. The billowing woodbine sends a trail of smoke across the white churned wake. There are more tearooms either side of the docks, villas sprouting, mushroom-like, up the hillsides, slate turrets and bay windows, some grand and imposing, others rather parvenu. Soon, no doubt, *Rothay* will be scrapped, or torched by the fireboys for the insurance claim, another faster berth built and put into service. No stopping the modern.

A few days later, he hikes back towards the Eden Valley, over the Kentmere Horseshoe, where he looks down on the old bobbin mill, abandoned beside the rapid tumbling cascades. He unpacks a lunch – pasty, cheese, apple, a sugary step of gingerbread – and contemplates the sky. He sketches its structures, as best he can. Nimbus. Nimbo-stratus. Cumulus. The vast dynamic province is being rapidly pioneered and classified. From his perch above Mardale, he looks over to the Pennines. Broken blue atmosphere all the way across the fertile basin to the backbone of England. He sighs. Quiet Quaker Howard has categorised the clouds. Beaufort's scale is officially adopted. Soon, deo volente, Thomas Bodger will add his name to the aerial map.

~~o~~

Back at the Kirkland cottage, a wrapped ham, a punnet of black fruits and two harvest loaves have been delivered, and a letter has arrived from Mrs Brooke. Has she had a change of heart? Exhausted from the long yomp, famished and not a little sunburned, Thomas tears off the nub of the bread then tears open the envelope. Inside is a note and a printed, black-bordered funeral card.

Dear Mr Bodger, In your absence there have been several developments at Grange House. The currants are ready and my husband has passed away. Should you hear tattle around the latter; please disregard it. If your work does not prevent your attendance, the service is a week on Tuesday, 10 o'clock at St Michael and All Angels Church. Furthermore, there is something I wish to speak to you about. An idea. R.B.

He replies immediately.

Dear Mrs Brooke, My deepest and heartfelt sympathy for your loss. Of course I shall come; I shall come before Tuesday, if needed. On the matter you wish to speak about, I am your humble servant and await further instruction. T.B.

He writes to Sara, informing her. Too far and too uncomfortable a journey for her to come, he says; he is happy to represent the family.

Sara has not written for two weeks, or the national post has con-founded the sorters and failed to find his secluded cottage. But her last letter was heartening, if oddly composed, with no mention of illness, and reassuring levity to its valediction.

Dearest, I bid you goodbye and hello again soon (truly and newly myself, I shall!). Your loving wife.

XLI

Sketch on paper by schizophrenic inmate of her 'friend'
Garlands Hospital, Cumberland: File MN-1056, Janice Calder, minor
Admission: 15/11/1970, sectioned with psychotic hallucinations
Consultant psychiatrist: Dr Jeffrey Entwistle
Figure represents fear of patient's mother rather than primary delusion.

XLII

Eden Bench Lent Assizes, 1926
Penrith Gaol, Hunter Lane Police Station
Clerk's Record: Case 57

Name of accused: Helen McBride, aka Nelly Wood
Occupation: Herbalist/Astrologer
Age: Unknown
Address of accused: Unnamed abode, Culgaith
Charges against accused: Attempted murder
Plea: Not guilty
Previous offences: Public disorder, poaching

Offence: The victim Joyce Fletcher of Dufton alleged that on November 1st 1925 the accused sold to her from a stall in the butter market in Penrith and for the price of eight shillings a concoction said to increase libido and produce male offspring but actually causing foetal aborticide and toxic effect. Upon becoming sick the victim was ambulated to Cumberland Infirmary where she recovered after approximately three weeks though she remains unwell and is infertile due to hysterectomy. A warrant was issued to search Helen McBride's shack which was of tin and turf nature and located with some difficulty by PC Neville Sowerby. Therein was found a large supply of eclectic and botanic reductions and dried herbs and leaflets in opposition to vaccination and anti-vivisection and in addition the Robinson New Family Herbal, the National Botanic Pharmacopoeia and almanacs on planetary activity. There was also discovered by the constable a large adult male pine marten which Helen McBride described as 'her husband' and which attacked PC Sowerby leading to significant medical treatment.

Helen McBride was indicted for administering a solution of unknown herbs and other substances to Joyce Fletcher resulting in near-fatal illness. She pleaded not guilty invoking the 1542 Herbalists Act giving her the right to practise and of which legislation there has been no revision. She also stated that she had never used the title MD Surgeon or Doctor nor had she ever used an ingredient that was inorganic or harmful, nor had she engaged in bestial relations of any kind.

Testimonials

Joyce Fletcher: Sirs and Madam God forgive me but I have five children and roundabout needed the sixth to preserve my marriage for my husband is of high appetites and we have no sons to labour on our farm which has suffered these last years due to scrapie and no new methods. I knew of Nelly Wood as 'the sage lady' by reputation and have been to her stall in Penrith market for remedies for sleep disorder which I have awful bad most nights and also relief for the pains of the monthlies and occasional anaemia. She does not rent the butter market stall but is tolerated by the other mongers and saddlers alongside her trestle and she also sets up at the horse fairs where she sells sage besoms and chicory tea and her remedy jars of which I have previously bought some. She is also sometimes round the back of the Black Horse alehouse on Fridays attending to the mawks and harlots. It is fact all round the district that she will see to women in trouble who are procuring inducement but that is not why I went along, to this I will swear. I asked Nelly did she have a potion to help with the enjoyment of dutiful relations more, for I am wearied out most nights, and preferably a mix to help get up a son. She – Nelly that is – said aye and then happened to have a bottle of a brewed concoction that was very strong she said because when she had picked her plants the Helm had been on its seventh day and the minerals were proper assimilated she said. Blowstock she called it. I did not know exactly what she meant but we are sorely assaulted by the wind around Dufton so I did not particularly like that fact but I was in some desperation. The bottle had no label but I bought it as her other cures have worked. It was wretched tasting and perhaps it was coal tar for it was a blackish syrup and awful bitter. I do not know what other extracts were mixed and cannot speculate but perhaps rue. I drank it all down without eating a supper as instructed by Nelly. Nelly had said the moon should be in its last quarter when it was drunk but it was not exactly. Well then I cannot begin to describe. I had such pains in my belly and my excuse me your honours privates all night long and was sent repeatedly to the earth-closet and I shall not describe the events there as it is indecent but I began some losses of the womb that I did not know even were present. I was also sick to my stomach many times and was as poorly as if I'd had a bad oyster or mouldered braun and must purge it away completely. My daughters helped me as best they could but there was terrible bleeding and I fainted away. That is when old Jonesie – Dr Jones – came after my eldest daughter Mabel went for him out of fright. I do not remember much else except a little unborn angel child blowing on my brow until that time when I woke up at the hospital in the care of the good sisters. I was then told I had undergone an operation and the surgeon had taken my womb and an ovary and some of the connections which Nelly's potion had ruptured. I was told – please forgive my high emotions – it is still very hard to bear – that I am no longer able to produce children due to that wicked woman. I do not know why she might want to kill me or an innocent babe but perhaps it is because she does not have any of her own.

Police Constable Sowerby: I am familiar with Nelly Wood from her butter market spot and also having arrested her after an altercation on Carleton Hill when she was drunk and I also cautioned her for selling on stolen grouse from the Lonsdale estate. Sergeant Schofield sent me out with a warrant to search her premises which was a corrugate shack very well hidden away in the oaks near Blencarn. It took quite some finding as the roof was covered by ivy and moss and just smoke off the chimney gave it away. The shack is a tinker house and I think gets sprouted about here and there in the vicinity and I am sure has never had building permission from any landowner in none of its locations. Nelly was in the plot beside the shack digging some spider plants. I then asked to be allowed entry to search for evidence in the Fletcher matter and was denied entry. I'd had a right palaver up and down in the woods and my cape was drenched so I did go in sternly showing the warrant to get things done. Nelly had a pot bubbling away with a stench off it such as rabbit glue but I do not know what was inside and cannot speculate. There was also a gin still. I went about and gathered the papers here in evidence and anything I suspected of apothecary type nature or appearing occult. There were bunches of dried flowers and grasses tied in the roof. Nelly – Miss McBride – came in and was watching me and smoking her long antler pipe which I do not believe contained tobacco as she had the pop-eye. There were bottles and wares all about without indication as to what they were so I took down a few for samples and in the clutter a few may have broke which she did not like because she spat at me. I asked if she had sold a toxic to a Mrs Fletcher and she said to me, oh, has that woman died? I noted this down in my PNB as she did not seem surprised that Mrs Fletcher was poorly and at the infirmary. I thought it was important. That is why I wrote it down. As I was nearing the end of my search the defendant made a sort of huffing quacking sound like this [witness demonstrates] which I believe was a signal of some sort and she toed at a basket under the stool and what I thought was a cat or a large ferret or one of those German fashion dogs came out from it and went for my ankle. Right viciously. Teeth like Gillettes. I suspect I may have swore due to the shock and the pain. Good God Almighty I might have said or hell's teeth. I lifted my leg and shook it about vigorously to get the thing off but its jaws had went right into the bone and it tore apart my trouser. Nelly Wood then plucked it off me and crooned at it oh you poor wee darling. What the eff and jeff is that I asked. It is my Martin she said, it is my marra. I then exited the premises quickly with those confiscated particulars in hand and it was a long way back to the wagon on the bad ankle the holes in which took twelve stitches to fix. In addition I had to be sent along for a rabies kit which Sirs and Madam you'll excuse me for saying is twenty-one hypodermics right in the back end and very excruciating in fact worse than the bite off that vermin of Nelly's and it is just pure luck it wasn't carrying the froth.

Dr Ellery M. Jones: I treated the victim at her home in Dufton on the morning of November 2nd. I was called to attend Mrs Fletcher at approximately eleven o'clock by one of her daughters. She was by then unconscious and unresponsive. I examined her and she was clearly in septic shock and miscarrying at late stage and she also seemed to be suffering a form of gastric poisoning as there were many soiled sheets. At first I thought typhoid. However, her daughter Mabel showed me the concoction Mrs Fletcher had purchased from this so-called sage lady. It was very hard to ascertain the contents by sight and smell though I did try. There was no label naturally – I suggested it be sent to a laboratory for testing but it seems this was not done and the bottle has disappeared. Mrs Fletcher was taken to Appleby surgery then ambulated to Cumberland Infirmary, where she was operated on. I have since received a letter from the hospital describing the prodigious damage to her organ. In my medical and personal opinion Mrs Fletcher is very fortunate to be alive and though rather foolish for trusting in such hedgerow quackery, she was not to know the dangerous nature of that which she imbibed. It is unfortunate many of the locals in this parish still retain a fondness for snake oil and a desire to waste their pennies on cheap crocodile teeth rather than paying the professionals. Sirs and Madam, may I draw your attention to the fact that there has been no second reading of the bill presented for registration of these colon-therapists and spiritualists. They should be and will I pray soon be outlawed and many lives subsequently saved. This Helen McBride is simply a witch in the woods and I hope you will make an example of her.

Helen McBride: First Mr Chairman that is Paul Andrews of Blackwell Lodge who I know from knock-knee please do the courtesy of looking at this defendant whence she speaks. I say that I object to the vexatious ransacking of my abode without show of warrant and even more the maltreating of Martin who I rescued as a kit and raised til his bib was full. I never said he was no husband to me just my marra. Martin was defending his territory as is natural by forest law for any nocturnal creature will set about its attacker in the bright of day. Some keep dogs some geese or a peacock for protection as a lone dweller and I have Martin. Second I will say that old sawbones Jones here has killed more patients with his fashionable pharmaceutics and maggot removal than all the qualified members of my friendly society stood in the green field together. I never harmed any soul come to me for treatment nor dealt in noxious experimentations but only ever employed the wisdom of the flower and earth and my instinct. My healings are come from vegetables and pollens which operate in harmony with humans and there's not a plant beneath or above Eden's soil I do not hold communion with. I am nature's simple accomplice and I do not tell it otherwise. I do not use American plants only native but I do use Lebanon cedar which is traded upcountry to me as it is very powerful and has no equivalent. I do not use bone or blood or any animal part including Spanish fly nor love-stone. I do mostly abide by that allopath law for the venereals but I have poultices to ease the itch and many of those ladies suffer neglect from the so-called gentlemen doctors, Christian men of this parish they say they are. I treat the Irish in the Stopping Places as I treat the Duchess. Yes Mr Chairman that is Paul Andrews I do recognise the sun and moon and weathers in my treatments because these are the governments

237

we all must abide by as living beings. It is important to gather when the lunar tide ebbs and flows or during moth hour as that improves the energy of the plant and you will see them brighten. I have my own little physic garden for rosemary and horse fennel and I grow mullein for my pipe as PC Sowerby has seen but it is better to collect everything wild. The Hellum did come for eleven days last October and seven being the godless day that is when I took blowstock off the fell and alongside the Eamont. Stinging hair, yellow dock and valerian. I took hips and dandelion and some other starches. I took what the gale gave in accordance with past lore. Joyce Fletcher came to me on her trotters seeking help for a condition that was a drizzling expectancy, with pains on her left side here [accused presses her lower left flank]. It is common women may lose what they carry early if it hasn't rooted deep in the womb and that is a natural course but she was well along and showing. I'd say near halfway. It is dangerous for a woman with more babby in her if she cannot shed what she must. Joyce was aflushed and in a mither about her fellow Col Fletcher who is very easy of fist as all in Dufton will attest. She often sports the Friday-eye. She pleaded with me and grasped my arm. Please get it gone she said, and other things of a private nature which I will not disconfide despite her flimflam now. When I put my hand over her there was a fever. She had an undershade. I have my oaths and duty, just as old sawbones does. What I supplied was not bane or tar but parsley and fresh grace herb which is rue as rue is quickest to rid dead product and infection. I balanced those with aniseed and some hazel skin from the nuts Hellum shekelled about. I also gave Joyce a bay bob to carry in her pocket for comfort for it soothes a soul in torment and a body undergoing craft-work. I did warn Joyce there would be wringing for some days as it is not a soft procedure once a child is half established. But rue cannot damage the womb as a surgeon's knife can. It cannot poison the blood as dirt and rot does. So I will agree Dr Jones that Joyce is fortunate to be alive and were it not for the grace and power of nature she would be swifter dead than she will be, and with a dead child up inside her. I will say lastly that there's many in these parishes come to me private in the woods as well as to my stall obtaining herbals and stiffeners which are fair priced and truthful cures, humble folk and wealthy men in their high offices and more than one here in this room know my good character and my beneficial practices.

Sentence: Bound over for six months with orders not to sell at Penrith butter market. 15 shillings fine.

XLIII

Days and days Janni is gone. Weeks and months. Every dash and dart and skitter up the fell is not her; it is just leverets and pippins and larks and stoaties. The red patch in the bields is not her fallen hat, just the plush insides of a carcass. The arctic skirt melts and lifts, the becks unlock their translucence. Helm waits. Helm sighs. Helm recalls a million glimmering things. The grass ripples, bends light, makes shadow patterns like stipples in a dog's coat. The hawthorns drop their blossom, the catkins spindle then fall, the ferns unfurl their tight curled ovaries.

Where is Janni?

Helm rises, higher, until being is difficult – there are gases and fast currents, radio waves full of babbling voices and music, aircraft, satellites.

Smog around the city of Carlisle.

Behind its soup is the lunatic hospital, a long corridor-planned mansion house, busy with patients for such a big empty county. There are new pharmaceuticals for their conditions, revolutionising their care. On the disturbed wards, the psychotics are quieter, the paranoids calmer, less need for surgery, no need for tie-jackets. Some inmates are awake and let outside to farm. In the fields around the hospital there are pigs and lambs and cows, dug-overs and greenhouses, and the patients, the ones for whom electric paddles and tablets and therapies are working, are getting better; some are even going home.

Janni is there.

She is carrying corn for the hens. She is fetching swill and straw for new beds in the sties. She sleeps in a room with other women, keeps them awake with her rustling and twitching, but she can't help that. Women, all with their hair cut short, no longer than the width of a finger, which is better if there are altercations, and infestations, better and cleaner and easier. There are no mirrors on the ward unless the doctors use them to help the sick see what they are and are not. They wash their faces in shockingly cold water; cold water is a good self-harm. They make their own soap with lye and lavender and rosemary, and it is sold, unbranded, at the Saturday markets in Penrith and Carlisle. The women wear striped pinafores and under-smocks, big cardigans or jumpers, donkey jackets; they feel the cold more since their synapses have been blocked.

Janni remembers liking the cold, but there's not much else she re-members. Mammy's orange nylon dress, its dagger collar. Her piles of seamstress scraps. The blue school bell and its rope clanger. Elvis's hair, perhaps. But it's a blur beyond the garth gate. Her legs are not so thin now, and not so downy – no longer cachectic, a diet of sago, potato, stout bread, beetroot, milk. Her chest is filling nicely. She is less rabbity. No front teeth: they have been extracted by the hospital dentist, because her jaw muscles are now involuntary, the incisors were mashing her bottom lip to pulp. Unfortunate side effect of chlorpromazine, the wonder drug. But it is working very well, better than expected, the doctors write in a letter to Mammy. Janni is lucky to live in this new medical era. She is controlled; she is cooperative. She is encouraged to dig the gardens and tend the orchard; she likes glossy fruits, tomatoes, apples, she will polish them for hours. She scrapes the soap moulds, washes vegetables and dishes. There are no visions, no voices anymore.

The doctors like Janni, or, that is to say, they are interested in Janni. Her presentation. Her progress. Almost a shame that she is recovering,

241

so vital was her delusion. She has stopped running. She has stopped drawing pictures of her imaginary friend – that creature with the extraordinary faces and long, ghoulish body. Eerie grey scribbles, naive, psalter-like, beautiful really; they are kept in a file in a cabinet in the office. The lead psychiatrist is writing a case study for the *Lancet* about Janni – quite the classical discourse: the Anemoi are referenced, the Loki stone at Kirkby Stephen, the aggravating effect of the wind on the psychology of the people of Eden, especially vulnerable juveniles, especially sylph-like girls. He has spent session after session talking to this patient, reconstructing the world.

That is a table, that is a chair; they are made of atoms.

When asked, Janni says, *What is a Helm?*

Yes, the medicine is working, and soon she will be home, but Mammy must be prepared for the alterations. Such are the chemical scales; corrective, healing, but bestowing other symptoms. Dr Thorne-Smith offers to collect her in the big black Wolseley. Otherwise Mammy will have to get the bus up and bring her back with no discretion or privacy. So the doctor and Nurse Wilson go back to Carlisle.

When the car arrives at Higher House Farm, Mammy rushes out and smuggles Janni inside wrapped in a blanket, like a convict, a stowaway. She is put on a stool in the kitchen and uncovered. Mammy stares at her daughter across the table.

Saints in heaven. What is this? She is spastic. She is a bairn.

Stares disbelievingly at the jerking, soft-faced thing in the oversized pinafore. It is Janni, but she has grown. It is Janni, but she has been retarded. True, the girl does not babble or blaze around the room as she used to. She does not grin and gabble out lies. Instead, she dribbles. She slumps. Her eyes roll and blink and blink and roll. True, she sits with her knees together and tries to stay still. But she can't.

242

The doctor opens his bag.

It is called tardive, Mrs Calder. It could get better in time. We shall be thankful the majority has improved. Now, here are the pills she must take and the instructions – correct doses are written on the bottles. Perhaps Janni would like to see her old bedroom; best to keep her inside to begin.

Dr Thorne-Smith and Nurse Wilson wait a few minutes more, to observe the reinstallation of the daughter. Mrs Calder gawps at them helplessly. The doctor seems pleased: the patient is docile, for all the shuddering. Nurse Wilson looks uneasy, or sad, or reproachful, but Mammy cannot really tell about that woman – she is of another kind, and makes Mammy uncomfortable, the only dark woman in the district, why would Jeremy Wilson marry her, and why would they have the children? At the WI, Mrs Calder and Nurse Wilson do not sit at the same trestle, nor peel apart the paper doilies together nor shelve the crockery after cake sales.

Nurse Wilson is not sad. She has a troubled, thunder-hearted feeling; pattery soaking rain is inside her. Tried to give Janni a chocolate lime in the car, but Janni didn't want it, only the wrapper.

Have the sweet, child. It is my husband's favourite.

No thank you, Nurse Wilson.

Polite as a Victorian orphan. When Nurse Wilson held her close she did not settle, but felt like the end of an earthquake, tremors in her limbs and shoulders, boom boom boom. Collapsed cheeks, all the ridged gummy gaps inside where her teeth should have been. Flattened spirit, where once she was all spicy. Poor bazodee little thing; it was as if they'd run her through a washing mangle.

Did you miss home, Janni? she asked.

No, Nurse Wilson. I liked the Garlands farm.

Oh, I am sure you must have missed it a little bit.

And Nurse Wilson thought for a moment about green zinced roofs

243

and sunburnt walls; she thought about her ajee laughing even as she cried on the dockside, and the smell of diesel engines and the long grey sea. She unwrapped the lozenge and gave Janni the green-and-gold wrapper, sucked the sweet herself.

The doctor sets the bottles on the table.

Come along, then, Phyllis. Let's let Janni and Mrs Calder get on.

I can make you a cup of tea? Mammy says quickly. *And I have some pepper cake just baked.*

No thank you, Mrs Calder, the doctor says. *I have my rounds. Nurse Wilson must get to the dispensary. Give the cake to Janni. Nice and soft for her to chew.*

Mammy glances over at her daughter and away so quick it's as if her eyes have been burned.

What am I to do with her? she snaps.

Put her to work wherever you need her. I think she will like to help out now, won't you, Janni? I don't think she can manage your needles. But the chicken pails. Chores around the house. We'll keep her off the mountain, though. And – no school, she is beyond it after the sedation.

Well, but, when will all this racking pass?

Mrs Calder, we must be patient.

Janni's head bounces and her tongue thrusts out.

Goodbye, Janni, Nurse Wilson says as she passes her. *Remember, you're a good strong spirit. You're going to be all right.*

Yes, Nurse Wilson.

The nurse and the doctor leave. Janni twitches on the stool. Her tongue dips in and out of the puckered hole. Her eyes glitch about.

Sit still, Mammy says. *Stop gurning, child.*

Yes, Mammy.

But she cannot.

Mammy stares suspiciously at the badly patchworked thing. The girl

244

has several ages to her all at once. She has grown into puberty and become a baby and aged sunkenly. She is a stuttering, shaking, toothless innocent. But now, is she truly free of the twist? Or is she still the little imp inside? Perhaps pretending not to remember the things that demented their household, that led to the thrashings and shouting and the overturning of furniture? A rare talent for inventing, this one – furtive and slippery as a mink. Touched by wickedness and talking about it as if it were no sin at all. *Mammy, I like the boys putting hands on me, it makes my vee feel warm.* Oh, Mammy coloured purple and slapped her hard when she confessed that, used the disinfectant, scrubbed her, got her confirmed by the bishop, no less. Is this another cunning switch, another changeling sat there quivering and drool-mouthed on the stool?

Crack on, then, girl.

Janni gets up and stumbles to the fireplace. She kneels and takes the brush to sweep the ashes from the grate. The firedogs clatter off their hooks. She hangs them up. Mammy goes into the bedroom and covers up the looking glass.

XLIV

The Saab used to be on a remote starter; Jude hasn't used it in a while. He backs out of the drive, accelerates through the village, steers round the potholes in the road. At the crossroads he takes the old military link to the motorway that everyone speeds on and the police don't patrol. Not entirely true – he used to park there behind the bushes for hours, but never felt inclined to pull anyone over for doing eighty along its straight carriageway, since he did too as a civvy. Fair's fair. The morning light seems pure and outspread, as if it's bouncing off the estuary and washing over the fields. The sun is up over the brow as he drives east. High white clouds above, lenticular, cumulus broken up into streets, nothing very dramatic this far north. A front of high pressure has been sitting out at sea for weeks, which hasn't been great for gliding.

With no traffic on the roads, the airfield is a twenty-minute drive, round or through the city. Ten if he uses the motorway and hoons it; they know his number plate, still a few perks of the profession. He turns on the radio, Mike Read's show, mid-track. A song too tambouriney and high-pitched for this early in the morning, so he turns it off again. He takes the cambers fast and lean and safely, white-lining. Still got it, old son. At the roundabout he slips onto the motorway, empty except for a few artics; he floors the accelerator, a ton and ten. Pre-shift zen. It's better not to think too far ahead. About what happens if. If he gets into unstable layers and can't get out again. If he has to land in a pond. Off at the next roundabout, he slows along the A-road; he can see the top of the ATC tower, white and bevelled – like a lighthouse. At the airfield entrance, the orange windsock is extended south-west. He checks his watch: seventeen minutes, more or less, to get here.

He drives past a khaki military helicopter, its blades drooping, to the hangarage. He takes his bag off the passenger seat, gets out, locks the car. Keith is sliding open the green concertina door of the unit, in which the sailplanes are stacked tidily on the diagonal, noses to tails. He salutes and calls out as Jude approaches.

Not too shabby, DC Milne. I won't ask what you clocked. Looking lithe too. Rowing back on the beers?

Ten stone three exactly. Same old, same old.

Welterweight. Splendid. Let's just put me down as cruise, shall we?

He pats his rounding midriff and laughs. They shake hands. Keith has on a golf shirt and slacks, a visor. He clearly wasn't going up today and has had his own plans scotched by the Met Office too. A red-and-white turboprop is parked on the north apron.

Is that Piper my tug? Jude asks, following Keith into the hangarage.

It is indeed.

Julia?

The very best, but I am a little biased. She's just having a quick coffee and a bio break.

Great.

Better than a winch launch, I say, I say.

Keith taps the air with a knuckle.

The winch launch wouldn't be invented if it was invented today.

Jude finishes the standard aeronautical joke and Keith chuckles.

Boom, boom.

The truth is, Jude quite likes a rapid cable launch, even though the release is somewhat dangerous. That steep forty-degree trajectory and huge catapult upwards, immediate stick-back, and a thousand feet by the end of the field; it's a thrill, like being on a reverse rollercoaster.

I hope Angela will forgive the rude interruption, Keith says. *Think it's probably going to be quite the experience, though.*

247

The instrumented glider is near the front of the building, its tapered wings long and clean. Green-tipped nose, and green-tipped wings. A one-seater, Polish build, owned by the syndicate. He's flown it before and it handles beautifully, great glide angles, speedy, almost falcon-like, hence its name. *Perry*. He hasn't been up in it since it was fitted out by the researchers – with quite some kit, airflow and radiation shield sensors, pressure transducers, carbon hygrometer and variometer systems. The chap from the Met Office went over it with them. The sensors will be sampled at intervals, digitalised via the 8-bit and transferred onto tape cassette using the Racal data recorder. The results compared with measurements taken on the summit of the fell and the valley floor.

You better refresh me.

Keith clears his throat and goes into formal mode.

OK. *What they want is activity in the lee wave along Great Dun, north-east flow regime, and down through the boundary layers.*

How many tracks?

As many as you can along the ridge, I'd say, from upper to lower altitude. Stay there as long as you can. But keep out of the base cloud, it's a big bugger. Then just have fun, isn't it.

Keith removes his glasses, polishes the lenses on his pocket handkerchief. The two nose pads have ironed red marks either side of the bridge. He smiles, his smaller-seeming eyes bright with mischief.

You could always go for the AA record. Time someone gave Newcastle a run for their money.

Jude laughs.

OK. *Bit of a problem with airspace, maybe. Don't want to annoy Pan Am, do we.*

This is true, but we'll radio you in. What did you say to Angela?

I didn't mention Guinness, put it like that.

She's a smart one, though.

She is.

248

Keith replaces his glasses, shuffles the cotton hanky under his nose, then puts it away in his pocket, adopting a serious tone again.

No, look, they do want vertical velocity and acceleration above the rotor cloud if it's formed. It might look a bit – excitable. But it should be smooth. McLean reported it was smooth, after a massive lift, as you know. So, yeehaw, but there shouldn't be any browning of the trousers.

Has no one been above it since McLean?

Nope. Half a century, my friend. Anyway. Temperatures have to be read when cloud-free. Remember, they really want observations in the spectral gap.

Spectral gap? You mean in the turbulent region?

That is correct. The winds may be asymmetric. Variable.

Yeah. But what kind of observations?

Keith puts a hand on Jude's shoulder.

Any old thing that occurs. Maybe just, by Jove this is bumpy, words to that effect. Or something poetic for the log, Shakespeare.

Not my strong suit. Where are we landing?

Scar Top. Good luck. No unfortunate occurrences.

Cheers.

They shake hands again.

And here she is, Keith says.

Julia comes round the side of the building. She has on a blue boiler suit and her hair is tucked under a beanie. She is holding a small enamel cup of black coffee.

Hiya, Jude.

Hello, Julia.

Beautiful day to fly. Nice and bubbly. There's snow on the tops – should be very pretty down there. Have you got your camera?

Not today.

Shame. We better head out, but no rush, whenever you're ready. The flush has gone in there again if you need to use the khazi.

Think I'm about ready.

Keith removes the stays from the sailplane wheels and they roll *Perry* out of the hangarage. As the three of them push it to the runway, Julia takes him through the flight plan – a continuous tow to the south of the base cloud and up above the storm, where she expects the air to be neutral. Any issues heading down, she'll bear east, come in wider to Great Dun.

We'll be spending a little longer together than usual, Jude. But I'll do my best to keep you comfortable.

Ah, it's always a pleasure.

How's Angela?

Ange is great, thanks. It's her birthday.

Oh dear. She's a good egg, isn't she. Shall we go and find your ride, then?

XLV

The following morning, Great Dun looks bigger somehow, the radome prominent and bizarre at the edge of the summit plateau, a
stark moon, a giant alien mushroom. Some trick of the angled back-
lighting, perhaps. Or is it just her mega-sized hangover, the headache
crushing her skull inwards and uncomfortably warping the world?
Should not have finished that bottle of wine by herself on an empty
stomach. Two miles north, the contours of Cross Fell are also in high
definition, like the shank of an aquatic dinosaur with broad, vestigial
flippers. Nothing compared to the Himalayas or the Dolomites, Selima reminds herself, but today, a bit intimidating.

She fumbles about, wrapping her laptop in its waterproof cover. She
puts her rucksack on. Ouch. Where are her sunglasses and does she
need to be sick? This is lousier than she's felt in years – not just the
booze she drank when she got home from the pub, but the dozen or
so cigarettes. She is tired too from a late night, trying to cross-check
phone numbers of all the people she knows to find out who sent the
messages. Then terrible sleep, tossing about on the bed; disquieting
dreams when she did drift off, about an abandoned wedding, windows that wouldn't lock, a vast, dark container vessel following her
overhead. And the words of the last text message kept repeating in
her brain.
  Look above, Dr Sutar.
  As if that wasn't already her job, day in, day out.

Right, she thinks, as she locks the bothy door. Look above, at what
exactly and where? Be specific, dickheads. The troposphere, with its

clouds and rain and snow, thermals and vapour, all the pollutants cooked on Earth; air cooling by the kilometre and Earth's surface determining its movements? The stratosphere, with its ozone holes and ultraviolet radiation? Or the deeper penetrating cold of the mesosphere? The ionosphere, perhaps, with its mad dance of solar radiation, and radio waves conveying worldwide broadcasts? The oxygen and hydrogen atoms of the exosphere, their random collisions, their ballistic trajectories as they escape into space? Or maybe the outer regions, the limit of Earth's magnetism, those gorgeous radiation belts; charged particles spiralling along dark fields? What exactly is she supposed to be looking at or looking for? Space beyond? God – that faceless, factless be-all and end-all? Perhaps she's supposed to discover some extraterrestrial race, with its convenient intergalactic plastic-particle vacuum cleaner, which will clean up humanity's mess?

You are so bloody pedantic, Lima.

Yes, I am, Nita, and with good reason. When people are ignorant, bad things happen.

She hesitates outside the door of the bothy. Hot flush. Is that gut gurgle going to be diarrhoea? Could go back to bed and sleep it off. (Hide, she means.) She gets on Ellie and starts the commute, through the village. Past the pub, closed, a couple of froth-webbed beer glasses left on the outdoor tables. Past the Christian Centre – no one is around, the rock stars are communally breakfasting, perhaps, or fasting or shagging or sacrificing goats. Past the old barns, the gentrified farmhouse where, today, a black SUV is parked outside. The disconnection of fatigue makes the journey feel unreal; she can almost see herself from above, weaving down the narrow lanes, a tiny woman on a buzzing gadget, exposed on the broad grassy expanse at the mountain base.

She brakes hard and clenches the handlebars when a motorbike growls up behind her, close to her back wheel, and moves over to the verge. The driver overtakes, signals and turns left, towards the Druid Circle, long blonde hair trailing underneath the helmet. Just a woman. Unthreatening. Though that's not true, is it. Women are queuing up to vote sadistic madmen into office the world over. And if university departments are anything to go by, her old pit bull of a supervisor included, women are just as capable of underhand scheming, or out-and-out warfare.

She continues on painfully up the service road. It begins to wend and steepen; the electric motor feels, as it always does, like a parental hand boosting her forward. She thinks of her Papa, teaching her and Anita to ride their pink, ribbon-decorated bikes in the leafy Tettenhall cul-de-sac. Holding the saddles, pushing them forward, his sandals slip-slapping the ground as he ran alongside.

Feet up feet up feet up, be brave brave brave, now go!

And all the jobs he had to do after their mum died that could not be left to Mrs Nanti, the minder. Telling them about periods. Making them tasty but terribly misshapen rotis. Sex-ed (excruciating, the long, medical version, complete with textbook diagrams, the penis actually INSIDE the vagina). Gathering them in under his arms and saying, *No, it is not fair*, when one of them – which usually set off the other – was crying, because they had argued about who had hair most like their mum's, whose turn it was to wear her jewellery, who just wanted her.

She tries to enjoy the ride, and the landscape, and the views, but the hangover is both physical and existential, it seems. She feels awful, and can't shake the feeling of disquiet and quiet rage.

Look above, Dr Sutar.

It's what they want, isn't it? To get inside, to make you unsure, insecure, stirred up.

Well, it worked. Sitting in the hot, crowded pub the night before, she actually, for a moment, thought about going home – not to the farm bothy, but back to Manchester, her flat in the quays. She could cut the research stint short. She could still use the data collected, and co-author the paper with Dr Lim. She wouldn't be the first to ditch this particular field station posting – easy enough to transfer to Holme Moss, with its slightly lower altitude. She sat there toying with her dinner, trying to be rational, trying to regain a lighter mood. Lenny saw her standing to leave, and asked again if everything was all right.

Started feeling a bit cruddy. Sorry.

Raised eyebrows, followed by a frown. She couldn't tell if Lenny was concerned or put out that the chips were still in a heap on the plate.

The single orange streetlight by the village green had barely enough illumination to cast a halo to the grassy edges. And she stalled, afraid to walk back to the rental; she stood in the doorway looking up taxi companies. The nearest was in Penrith – a forty-five-minute wait, to take her half a mile. Sixty-five pounds. Ludicrous. So she switched on the torch and walked quickly down the dark, narrow lane towards the bothy, trying not to panic as blackness swarmed round the beam, trying not to imagine footsteps behind, or a hand on her neck. Convinced herself at one point she'd taken a wrong turn; she practically ran towards the farm once it came into view. No, she had definitely run, clattering down the road in her heeled boots like a spooked cow. Then – fags, booze, scrolling, wondering whether she should call the police. But what could she say to them? *Someone on a burner phone is sending me weird esoteric messages.*

Really?

Halfway up Great Dun Fell, it begins to rain. Of course she has not brought the waterproof trousers, was in such disarray when she got up. Within minutes, it's a true, rudely wetting Pennine rain, carried on a moderate wind that is blowing straight onto her front side. Soon water is dripping off her chin and soaking her jeans. The bike zims on through inclemency. Her fingers begin to cool and stiffen uncomfortably on the handlebars.

Look above, Dr Sutar.

Above, the road disappears into the murky roof of cloud, as if into the end of the world.

The end of the world – yes, the great stage onto which every climatologist has been flung and must perform a role. To convince, to warn, to provide advice. To juggle people's expectations about how hazardous and disastrous it will all be. To prove the increasingly debatable truth, wasting time. It is so incomprehensibly, harmfully, counterintuitively stupid – the fight against knowledge, the rejection of science, tantamount to putting one's fingers in one's ears and singing *We wish you a Merry Christmas* over and over. Why would people not want to know – what they are sucking into their lungs, which systems are conveying waste above their heads – how humanity is altering the whole caboodle? This supposedly pure, poetic, upland rain is actually thick with shite. Under the infrared spectroscope, it is swimming with technicolour microscopic shards. Roll up, folks, meet the three wicked sisters – Polyethylene, Polypropylene, Terephthalate. (Boo-hiss, goes the crowd.)

The bike purrs round the service barrier, until, at the next bend, the red battery light comes on. Are you kidding, Selima thinks. Humourlessly, the bike has not been charged overnight. And the charger is back at the bothy, along with her plastic trousers. Pissed off, pissed on, and now this.

The hardest section of road is just ahead, where the fell drops sheerly away and the hushings run below. The point at which even the most ham-thighed cyclists often give up and dismount. The point at which she has felt consistently superior to be battery-operated. All she needs to do is make it over the next brow, then she can probably pedal the rest of the way. Come on, Ellie, she thinks.

The battery cuts.

She tries to push herself up the gradient, but cannot, and without real momentum the bike wobbles dangerously. She stops and dismounts. The rain is really coming down now, coming at her diagonally too, carried on a fresh wind. Her knuckles are turning a strange, unnatural plum-orange. She pushes Ellie by her side, head bowed, looking down at the glistening black tarmac and her soggy trainers. Overseeing her humiliation is the smug looming presence of the radome.

I feel you, big ball.

By the time she reaches the cattle-grid, she is drenched, and cold, and sweaty. The puffer jacket feels like it's taken on a gallon of water (showerproof not being waterproof, Selima). Her jeans are stuck to her legs. She leans Ellie on the wall, fumbles the key to the field station, drops it, manages to get it in the lock, and goes inside.

Totally bloody soaked. But the exertion has cleared the hangover – a little. She heels off her wet trainers, leaves damp sock prints across the wooden floor as she goes to switch on the kettle. She strips, peeling off her jeans, down to her underwear – her thighs blotchy with cold – and hangs her clothes over the back of the chair. Chance of them drying properly: zero. Probably it would be better to admit defeat, go back down the hill and get dry. Blow off work. Light the stove. Ring the police and try to sort stuff out. But the thought of going back out into the rain is deeply disagreeable. The thought of explaining the harassment to sceptical overworked coppers is also unappealing. What can they do? Ask her to give a list of names of anyone . . . blah blah. Can they really locate trolls inside the great, dank, blind labyrinth of technology? They didn't with David, and he received death threats.

What she really wants is a hot drink and a smoke – at least she re-membered the fags, full marks for deleterious priorities – then she wants to get on with work, do what she has come here to. She takes the cigarettes out of her coat and sets them on the table. The packet is damp but not ruined. She takes out her phone and sets it next to them. No signal. Right. She unpacks her laptop.

The kettle begins to rasp. There's a sandwich of strange oystery light outside now, between the ground and the lifting cloud. She pads to the other window. And behold, God's preposterous golf ball, sucking in electromagnetic signals, emitting some kind of dementing fre-quency. Behold its mammoth, hexagonal panels of dirty white, none of which are proportionally the same, weirdly – what's that about? Then she notices the van is back. It is parked in a slightly different spot from yesterday, beside the outbuildings. She is standing in the window in only her bra.

Oh, fuck it!

Quickly, she ducks and steps to the side, then she peeps back out. No sign of Paul and Racing Snakes. But she can't be parading about half-naked if she's going to be badgered for ID. ID that she has again not brought with her. She skulks over and locks the field station door. She picks up her jeans and shakes them, steps into the wet, clammy legs. She hops about as she hauls them up. Please don't come here, she thinks, not now, not today, not ever. As she turns to pick up her shirt, there's sudden movement by the window – something flurries past. She grasps the shirt to her front, freezes, stares at the glass pane.

No one is there.

She pulls the shirt on and fumbles the buttons, feeling queasy at the thought of them looking in on her.

Her fingers feel numb and clumsy. She steps back into the soggy trainers, squeezing out water from the laces as she ties them. Dressed! But fucking hell she is a mess. Feels wired, and weak. She stands for a moment, and the walls of the building are really nothing, insubstantial, so vulnerable. She feels pitched on the roof of the world. Come on, she tells herself, get it together.

The kettle grumbles disconsolately. She gets the West Brom mug from the shelf for an ashtray, and sits at the table feeling damp and disgusting. *You should know better, Beta. Not now, Papa!* She lights a cigarette, looks at the photograph of the hoary fellows with their pipes and their indomitable fists-on-hips stances. Collecting data while shitting in holes in the ground and eating dehydrated Antarctic explorer rations in the years between wars. Dealers in enviable facts; producers of theories with useful applications. One, at least, knighted. Right-o, lads. She blows smoke in their direction, and waits for a knock at the door.

Nothing.

A breeze flushes round the field station, whistles over the asbestos tiles. She waits.

A pale ragged thing flashes past the window. Selima flinches and drops the cigarette into her lap. She quickly picks it up and brushes off the burning ash, looks back at the window. A grey-and-white bird is standing on the sill. It peers in – yellow-ringed eyes, a haughty, disapproving expression. It has a blunt hooked beak with a red daub underneath the tip, like badly applied lipstick. Moorland gull. She's seen them flouncing about on the fell, picking over the grass, casually sailing backwards in the strong gusts.

You nearly gave me a heart attack! Shoo!

The gull cocks its head to the side, appraising her. It hops and shuffles along the sill, shrugging its wings, and watching her with its nasty, aunty's eye.

Fine, stay, she says. *No tits here.*

She finishes the cigarette and drops it into the cup, nerves still fizzing. The kettle rumbles away, shaking and steaming. She opens her laptop. Just. Get. On. With. It. The truth. The truth. The truth is – she has not wanted to think about where she is and what might happen. The fact that she is alone up here, miles and miles from anyone. And if anything goes wrong, if anything bad does happen – what then?

XLVI

Trinket 91,367
Tornado F3 series, ejection seat pin

Steel, double-pronged key-shaped spoke; one leg is straight, one curved at the tip. Pin has a circular clasped end-piece containing moulded resin; reverse side has red paint on which is written the word BREECH. (Property of the Crown under the PROTECTION OF MILITARY REMAINS ACT 1986: All items recovered from military crash sites must be surrendered to the Ministry of Defence. It is an offence to tamper with, damage or keep such items.)

Length – 6 cm
Width – 2.3 cm
Weight – 3 grams

Location – classified

XLVII

By the following winter the magstone has shifted further; its skull has come unfused, and a deep fissure runs behind it. Grit and rubble lie underneath on the beach and the giant body is leaning out of the cliff. The face looks south, up the river. It is trying to fall.

At the solstice ceremony, NaNay measures the alignment again, walking towards the setting sun. The cairn is still true. She waits for the star shapes to appear and the moon to rise, but clouds drift across, and it begins to rain. The rain gets heavier; soon her white cloak is sodden and heavy, making her stoop. She is tired this winter; her gut has remained loose after the infection that killed Joa. Sometimes she is confused about the years of her life, just for a moment or two, and her hand is the hand of another, an elder, then the misremembering passes. It is as if, in those moments, her anma is roaming away from her, preparing to travel. Perhaps this is because the magstone has been found; she is not as acute, she is not needed. Perhaps she is an old woman.

In spring, the people replace the cradle of wood beneath the magstone, which has washed away in the flume. They begin to chisel underneath its shoulder, trying to determine how it will fall, trying to preserve its face. Some of the new men from the caverns climb onto it from above and jump and push and try to dislodge it, riding it like a wild horse, but this is foolish and NaNay scolds them as if they were boys and they climb down. They obey her. But they do not call her All Mother.

More people have come to the valley and built huts, and the common land is being negotiated and divided again between families and tribes. The meetings have become difficult, too many talkers, no listeners, too much time spent pacifying and explaining agreements. The herders have begun to make sour cheese and are trading it; this has brought others to the settlement too. More orox, more pens; the pens are reinforced to stop the Halron freeing the cattle because the cattle fight or stampede, and then there are arguments. The forest dwellers are afraid and their fear takes the form of anger; if more of the forest is burned for pasture they say they will fight or stop allowing stalks and foraging. Only the road to the magstone was agreed, they say, not the stretches along the glades or the gorge. Already there are fewer eggs and fewer tree-climbers.

NaNay sits on the beach as the cradle is rebuilt, eating hot peppery cress, while the children hunt for crustaceans under stones in the river. She cooks crayfish over a small bonfire. She shows the children how to strip the legs and casing, turn the meat inside out. They run about nipping each other with claws.

Bring it to me. Hold on tight while it pinches! Eat it hot!

She looks up. Ferns and ivy trailing from the crevices around the magstone's head look like hair. The face suffers wisdom of age, even though it is not yet born; it sorrows, and it believes this world. It understands, even blind, with closed eyes. The magstone has a serious female anma.

Be born before I go to the other world, NaNay says to it. *Bring peace to the valley.*

She coughs as the grill smokes. The skeletons of the crayfish pop and split. She rips the bodies apart and tastes the sweet, silty meat, then gives it away. Since winter she has had a wet yellow cough that won't dry up and she feels slow, and stiff, not very hungry for the foods she used to enjoy. Her ankles hurt when she walks further than the river.

Her neck does not turn properly anymore – once she was like an owl swivelling and surveilling, she could see the shapes of wolves moving round the edge of the settlement in the half-dark, and no child could ever sneak up and surprise her. She does not climb anymore and her eyes are blurry; the right has a cataract that splits the starlight. She is too thin to wear the stone-and-ore belt that was made for Second Mother, so it is hung above her sleep mat in the hut. Soon it will be Reen's.

At night, she closes her eyes and lets go of the elemental world that surrounds her. Her dreams are vivid, frightening, beyond her knowledge, as if she is a girl again, without her marks. She dreams of people with long skulls, savages, and a woman in a costume as exotic as a bird, who is trapped in a cave. She dreams there is a hazelwood ring laid in the gathering place and she is told by the people to leave the village or she will be beaten. They say they will kill her and burn her instead of burial. They will sew her into the carcass of a bear. They say they will leave her out on the mountainside and when the Halron comes the Halron will throw her into the black night where no one will remember her.

She wakes in the hut and sees the others sleeping around her. She hears the orox snorting and trampling in the pens, the dull drone of bees, a lapwing. The dreams are a test. She is not frightened. She is being prepared for the journey to the other world.

XLVIII

The cross bears down on him and he bears its weight. One more day to the summit, up the final escarpment and into Helm's lair. Three days to ascend; three is good, a holy number. Below, the valley is lost under mist, and above, the fresh forenoon air is travelling swiftly, sweeping across the path. It is awake now, knows he is coming, knows it is to be dethroned.

He has taken no more than a hundred paces on this last, gruelling stage of the journey when he senses a fresh presence close by, alongside. A different weight and mass to the air. Something living, diurnal, and therefore plainly dangerous. There's a nettling at his nape, beneath the sallet. His neck feels tender, the front of his body exposed. Aye. He is being watched once more.

He stops, hushes the cross and waits for an entity to stir and reveal itself. Calculates. Under the heavy wooden beam, he is not incapacitated, but it is not a good position from which to defend himself – arms occupied, belly soft, with only the lattice and signet of bones protecting his heart. There's rustling in the grass nearby – not the wind this time, but specific. He does not look, the direct eye being a flag of aggression to the bear and the wolf, so slants his gaze. He stands and waits. Demons in daylight are weak, but have the power to stir savage beasts. They may send forth dragons, rouse snakes, drop peregrines from the sky. Far out at sea, he's seen great, rearing bulwarks, white pillars on the ventral surface, things a sailor should not live to tell about, that are impossible and yet exist.

No sword, only a whip. If it is malignantly sent, better to keep hold of the cross; use its power as defence. He breathes slowly. How bloody he is within. The patch of undergrowth stirs again, the tall stems creak and fold down. Gold within the blonde. Whatever is moving in there is a creature of considerable size, the colour of the moraine. The grasses part and it comes towards him – not fast but with confidence. He turns his head now and sees tawny fur emerging through the stalks, a low, stocky thing that pauses, a reach or two away. It is a bobcat, small-headed, with large shaggy paws and a butch tail, black tufted ears. The cat stands squat and proud. It regards him for a moment, with orange eyes and without concern, as if every day of its existence it has seen men wrestling crucifixes up this mountain. Then it turns and pads softly away across the stony upland, without looking back.

Michael watches it go, the powerful back end hitching over boulders, until, cornering the hill below a crag, it disappears. This is no servitor of Helm. It is his augur, a sure sign of victory – guile and grace in battle. Cats have always come to him. Clever and cruel and indifferent as he is, so too is their nature. Lap cats slink and wind about his legs; those wild-bred show themselves at fortuitous moments, crossing his path as he rides to a regal meeting, or staring at him, gore-smeared in the pits, as money is passed into his hand. And once, at the furthest reaches of his travel, a tiger flowed out of the jungle in front of him, then melted back into the jungle – enormous, striated, all molten, flaming muscle.

Good omen, then. He begins dragging the cross again, more determined.

Cobalt cloud is beginning to gather above, and the morning sun hangs prominently below, a chandelier, throwing strong light across the mountain's curve. Conjurer's weather. Helm will come. Or Helm

265

will hide and be admonished as a coward. Either way, Michael will perform the ritual, raise the symbol and sanctify the mountain.

The path ahead draws left, between bluffs of limestone, and this is the easier though longer way to the summit – he cannot pull the cross vertically up the gradient. He stoops forward, drags it on, and the wooden base bumps and crutters and scrapes across bare rock. The transom digs into one raw shoulder, and then the other; he re-saddles it every fifty steps now. His vertebrae feel stacked like ivory counters.

Up. Up.

He makes a step that takes him nowhere, his foot hovers, cannot commit to its forward motion, so he resets it, grunts, tries again, and this time finds the steady ground beneath. The giddiness when he stops moving is overwhelming. So on he goes. Grunting, lowing, bellowing; winching the cross to the next step, and the next, and the next. Animal depravities coming from his mouth. He is a hog or a heifer; he has become half-demon himself.

An hour. Another hour. Three hours to travel a third of a mile and fifty feet of altitude. The end of the mountain is in sight. At the top of the bluff, he almost faints; he misplaces the track and stumbles. The base of the cross slips off the edge, yanking him backwards. Quickly he extracts himself, as it thuds down into a gully. It does not break apart – James the elder is no shoddy axler – but rests, propped on its side on a ledge. Michael climbs down to retrieve it. He loops his whip around it, climbs up, hauls, but cannot pull it up; it wedges against the cliff. He climbs down again, finds firm footing, wraps his hands under the base, squats and lifts. He blares like a bull in rut as he pushes it up over the lip of the gully. It hovers, tilts, shifts, slides onto the path. The veins rear through his skin. His chest hammers.

When he has calmed and can breathe, he drinks an inch of water, eats a last hard prune. He fights a sudden nausea, a griping in his stomach; unties his trousers and shits a hard fast scattering. That's it. He refastens the garment, assumes the position and begins again, inching the terrible device up the mountain.

Long past exhaustion, long past passion, beyond himself.

He staggers on. He is the task, nothing other. So stooped now, he is nearly crawling.

The path weaves up through white-and-grey terraces, layers of sediment with tiny curled shells inside, lustrous calciums, spines; such detail the Lord has made while creating the world, so impossibly elaborate, such art.

Up, up he goes, like Sisyphus, painfully, unceasingly.

Aware only of the slavish song of the cross dragging behind him.

After too long by military standards, he hears another sound. Soft, subtle crunches and the skittering of pebbles. He does not stop but continues on, as he must, or he will fail. Surely just another imagining, a dead soldier marching the old road, the ungulate succubus. Helm, preparing an avalanche – but let it come, let combat finally begin, and cease, whoever may profit or be crushed, let all this be done.

There, again, definitely, is the noise. It is the tread of careful feet, somewhere behind, or above. Is it the bobcat, curious after all, fancying its chances with prey beyond the usual scope? Or is it some foul keeper of Helm's house, readying itself to swoop and strike?

The fiend itself, perhaps, revealed without his dream – multi-headed, winged and taloned, made of lightning, hail, tornadoes? Helm cannot not touch him while he holds the holy sign.

The soft, slippery padding continues, closer – is it closer?

Michael stops, draws breath, barks out the words.

Praesidium a malo!

And, mustering as much intimidation as he can, he turns against the wooden frame, rises up and thrusts high the cross. The world spins and buckles around him. There's a blur of colour down-path as a sly form ducks for cover. Michael blinks and squints at the rough terrain, sees incongruous blue amid the wintered browns and the wind-scoured stone; a bright swatch, hiding behind a thorn bush. His arms shake with effort. He drops the cross and it wallops to the ground. He stoops forward in his torn and blood-ruined shirt.

Sheep, he calls weakly across the hillside, and his voice cracks like old leather. *Blue sheep. I know you.*

His throat is dry as sand, his tongue a sticky, thrusting creature. There's a twitch behind the branches, but the thing does not move from its hiding place.

Blue sheep, show yourself.

Michael croaks louder, and emotion saps the last of his strength.

Show yourself, Isa. You cannot hide from your master.

XLIX

The day before the colonel's funeral, the first batch of pipes arrives and is deposited on the low fellside, near Thomas's cottage. Three cartloads of thick-walled tubing. The Symonds crew – swift, brawny and courteous – stack it efficiently, and are gone within two hours. Thomas stands gazing at the ironwork. At last – the true beginning! Now he may begin to see it, out of the notebook and the projector of his imagination, and here, in situ. The Revelation Machine, snaking up the mountain in its rigid, riveted sections, manifolds and valves, ducts to rival those of Rome and Pompeii, conveying the life-source, the super-power of this fabulous age! But he does not have time to admire the equipment, or for his feelings to sink, as they so often do sink when the products of his mind are externalised, when ideas are no longer snug in the parlour of hypothesis but tarnished with reality. He must get to Langwathby station, then on to Carruthers' in Carlisle, to collect his hastily ordered suit and hat. And to visit a decent barber too, for the once-tidy beard is now bushing and tufting like a bear's backside, and his hair is bohemian in length; he has become quite the mountain man.

The weather breaks the following morning – an ominous rumble of thunder at dawn. Slow, heavy raindrops gather pace, hissing like soft glass from the grey sky. For an hour rain batters the roof, so heavy it is as if pails of water are being tipped over the cottage, and it seems he will not be able to venture outside, let alone travel to the church. So this extraordinary glorious summer is extinguished. The deluge passes, and with it the humidity, but suggestive clouds remain, ragging the hills. Outside the cottage there are standing pools. He has arranged for a carriage to take him to Grange House, where he will process with the hearse and Mrs Brooke to St Michael and All Angels. It arrives, more or less on time, at the end of the lane, its hood extended, the horses steaming. The driver calls to him,

Very big crocks beyond, sir, can't chance it further in case we regress. Could you come across?

What? Come across the flood?

Any waders?

No!

Go about the edges, then, perhaps.

Thomas stows his top hat under his arm. He removes his shoes and stockings, pops them into the hat, and turns up his trousers. Then he walks, gingerly, shin-deep, through the standing water, toeing for craters. If Glaisher and Fitzroy could see him now! *Off for a seaside paddle, Bodge!* Mrs Brooke would probably approve, though. He takes hold of the rail and gets into the carriage, sets his hat down.

Heavens to Betsy. Well, there we are.

Yes, very well done, sir.

The driver hands him a rag and Thomas dries his feet. He replaces his footwear and hat.

Off to the Grange?

Yes.

For the old lad?

The colonel, yes.

It'll be a closed lid, I expect.

Thomas glances at the man and says nothing. He removes his hat again, places it on the seat. How odd it feels, how constructed. The driver snaps the reins and the horses move off carefully along the unmade track, then brisker. The carriage wheels whir through the fords.

There is no wreath on the door when they arrive at Grange House. In the hallway, the household is gathered sombrely, uncomfortable in their black formals – Boller shaven, combed and excessively pomaded, Midge prim and uncomfortable-seeming in her ribboned hat and layered frock, deathly pale, as if the tragedy had only just occurred. Upstairs, Thomas finds Rebecca Brooke standing beside the landing window. She has on dull parramatta silk, a short widow's veil, nothing especially elaborate. Despite its bustle and peplum, the black mourning dress makes her seem slight, diminished. The veil hides her eyes and he cannot discern whether there are widowing tears behind the gauze. He suspects not. Without thinking, he takes her hand and holds it gently. She does not resist. The silk fingertips of her glove rest on his pulse.

Are you—? Of course not. Dreadful. Mrs Brooke. Rebecca, may I, I am just so very sorry and—

He stumbles his condolences and then stops. He means to say more, but finds formality abandoning him. Of all people, it will serve her no use. He does not want to release her hand, but he does so. She lowers it.

It wasn't unexpected, Mr Bodger. Sanderson was quite unwell and very unpredictable, as you will have ascertained; he aggravated himself. They did try, up at the – hospital. We all tried to rinse him out. But what can one do, once the faculties fail? Short of burying all the guns.

Oh. Oh, yes, I see now. Oh dear.

Poor Midge found him. She is still quite stricken. It's all round the village, of course, but there we are. Look, they're arriving.

Thomas glances out of the window to see the cortège coming towards the Grange, a military caisson, and, he assumes, members of the colonel's old guard, decrepit but smart, walking slowly alongside. A horn sounds as it arrives.

I suppose we had better go down now and get on with it. Mr Bodger, could I ask you not to leave until we have spoken privately again?

She faces him, and through the drapes of her veil he can see the outline of her nose and chin, the glimmer of those stunning eyes. She sounds weary, a politer version of herself, though somewhat easier.

Of course. Whenever suits.

271

He processes with the other mourners to the church, behind the black-feathered horses and hearse. Light glosses the wet surfaces all about. *Glisky* – he knows the word for sunshine after rain now. It is not a long cortège; he recognises faces here and there among the Glassonby and Ousby villagers. They nod. He nods. He is almost part of things. The locals disperse at the church gates, adjusting their caps and capes. Only one hymn is sung in the service, falteringly by the few, and at the burial Thomas stands back, while Mrs Brooke remains graveside, small, and silent.

As the coffin is interred, he notices the woman in white, standing by the old yews in the gateway, whom he saw the first day he rode through the valley. The herbalist. She comes no further than the shaggy trees, but stands, somewhat resolute. She catches his eye, cocks her head like a bird assessing a seedpod it might peck. Bold, he thinks, her type. Bold because they are marginal and powerful, keepers of intimacies; for Sara too has gone to practitioners of the Worshipful Society, to the spicers' stalls at Blackfriars, hoping to find relief, so she does not have to submit to the laudanum.

After the burial, Thomas accompanies Mrs Brooke back to Grange House. The rain begins again, drumming on the umbrellas and the carriage hood. There's a chaotic bustle in the hallway as damp coats are removed and hung, tea and whisky and arvel cake brought out. Mrs Brooke approaches Thomas beside the fire in the drawing room. She has removed the veil. For a moment she says nothing, and when she speaks her voice is no longer strained. It is as if, after months of mistuning, her strings have found their notes.

I'm supposed to weep and say honourable things about Sanderson, aren't I? It's a sham, Mr Bodger. All the jet and the lilies and everything is supposed to cease. Leave me in the woods when it's my turn, or send me downriver as they do in India, then just get on with it.

Thomas smiles.

Noted.

I would like very much to get out of this ridiculous dress and walk. I don't care who disapproves. Will you come?

Yes, of course.

I'll return shortly. In fact, don't wait. I'll meet you at the bottom of the meadow? Do you care about the weather? It looks unsettled. Good grief, we may even get the Helm.

And it is only then that he realises: this is the first day since arriving in Eden that he has not thought of the project, his equipment, or the wind.

He collects his hat and coat and wanders down through the rain-pummelled grass, to the little stone bridge, where, as instructed, he waits. The raindrops are widely spaced, slowing again. He can smell wet hay and mud from the fields. The leaves in the copse have begun to drop. He looks up at Cross Fell, swathed by cloud. There is a slight tingling feeling again, but it seems unrelated.

Rebecca Brooke arrives. She has changed into a less difficult dress, the mazarine, a jacket and stout laced boots. Her hair is still tightly bound and there is a black ribbon tying her hat. The tinted lenses obscure her eyes, as ever, and he is – yes, he is frustrated by them, by how well they do their job. She has with her an umbrella, which she holds not by the handle but as one might hold a halberd.

They say those who meet on bridges are prepared for conversion, Mr Bodger. But I suppose you are still pursuing your scheme?

He smiles and bows a fraction.

Yes, I am.

Fine, then, she says, sighing. *I wish to show you something. This way.*

She starts along the path towards the woods and the broad, sliding river. But instead of walking upstream to the beach and her bathing spot, she follows the flow of the water. The downpours have increased

273

its volume, and the river swirls past boulders or rides over them, debris scaling its surface. The trees along the bank drip and patter as if, inside the canopy, it is still raining, but she does not open the umbrella. They walk along the path without speaking. This time it is not uncomfortable. He listens to the brush of her skirt in the undergrowth, remembers her naked feet, her soaked hair, and he thinks, I have a wife, I have no wife; we exist with overlays, the heart repeats in several places.

They reach a stretch of wide, impounded river, its edge smooth and determined. Thomas hears the sound of rushing. Mrs Brooke speeds up a little and raises her hand to point. There is a large weir, several feet high. Water spills over the crest of the dam, polished and smooth, cascading down the steep wall, then churning below. As they draw alongside it, she stops. She turns and faces Thomas.

There, she says. *Do you see?*

She looks up at him. This close, the lenses are an imperial purple, opaque and sullen as a chaperone. Only when she turns her head towards the river again does he catch glimpse of a bright, prominent, greenish eye. She looks back at him, waiting for an appropriate response.

Forgive me, he says, *but I'm a little lost.*

She purses her lips, frowns slightly.

Mr Bodger, you said that if we consider the laws of hydraulics, we may find an answer to the Helm. Did you not say that, on your first night at Grange House? And that the basis of power systems is seen in nature?

Yes, it's true. I did say that.

She nods.

Very well. I considered the idea, and while I was walking here those things we spoke of returned to mind, and – look, don't you see it?

She points again.

There is the mountaintop, and there is the wind rushing over and down the slope, gaining force. Below, the force rises again and forms a – what's that called?

Thomas looks at the weir's base, at its brink, and its base again. He watches the head of water sweep over and down the long stone ramp. At the bottom is an undular trough in the river's surface and the water leaps and curls back up.

A stopper wave. It's called a stopper wave. It's where the energy recirculates.

Like the bar cloud? she asks.

Like the bar cloud, he agrees.

They stand for a moment, shoulder to shoulder, watching the river. What he wants is to take her hand again, to press it, lift it to his lips. To say— But she takes a small step to the side, and reaches into the pocket of her jacket. She removes a folded piece of paper and hands it to him.

Here. I have drawn the comparison, rather artlessly, but perhaps you will be able to improve upon it.

He opens the page. The diagram is not at all poor. Before he can thank her, or say anything, she turns and begins walking back through the dripping trees.

L

Janni is taken into the village, when Mammy goes for the post or the milk or to get a book from the Tinclar library. She is taken to the church on Sundays. Those who are kind say, *Hello, Janni, grand to see you*. Some look away; for you wouldn't want to catch it, her illness, you wouldn't want your own child getting those ritters. The girls ignore her as ever they did, the boys don't dare go near for fear of – of what, they don't know. Mammy keeps Janni's hair shorn short – it is easier to brush, less vinegar – but she cuts up the Garlands pinafore, uses it for sundries, patching the holey trousers of her customers.

At Sunday service, Nurse Wilson, uninvited and Baptist-hatted, sits in the pew alongside the Calders and shares her hymn book with Janni. She sings her confident alto louder than the mousey choir.

Lord of all hopefulness, Lord of all joy.
Lord of all kindliness, Lord of all grace.

As if, Mrs Calder thinks, to draw the eye of the congregation and posit a kind of shamelessness to their misfitting pew. If Jeremy Wilson is with Phyllis in his high plaid trousers and wool waistcoat, unruly straw hair brilled down, he pets Janni like a father. And the Wilson children squeeze onto the seat too. One is studying for university, a brilliant, mid-skinned girl. The other has a hearing grommet and uses symbols and signs to speak, but is a very beautiful boy, long-lashed and pearly-eyed. Both loved the same, and this makes Mrs Calder feel angrier and more reduced.

The weeks pass by. Janni is what she seems to be, a reformed and ruined daughter. The quakes are getting no better, though. Her wet mouth smacks. Her eyes blink. Her neck jerks sideways. Mammy despairs. She looks in on her while she is sleeping, body heaped under the blankets, exhausted by the perpetual motor of her nerves. Mammy has spied on her in the tin bath too – there's no poking about and examining, no folding open; the girl washes as a Christian now, quickly, decently, with a flannel. Janni does the work Mammy sets for her, the mucky jobs, the blackening, the chip pan, the chickens; she repeats it and repeats it and repeats it, and she doesn't complain. She takes the medicine that Mammy mostly remembers to give her. Which is better? The good, dystonic daughter, or the fit-bodied crazy one? Unfair, either way.

But the girl can be left to get on. She can be trusted with hot pans and irons; she doesn't try to ferret away under the door jamb. The dowly world is gone. She has stopped twittering and provoking with her outlandish stories about Helm this, Helm that and Helm the other. Mammy doesn't say the name, doesn't want to remind her. The girl has stopped stealing foil tops so the milk goes sour, stopped pinching coppers and hairpins from Mammy's purse. Either the wicked crick is deeply hidden, or sickness has been rinsed from the bottle. She has stopped looking for her friend.

But Helm hasn't stopped looking for her.

Helm has seen an old woman of a child, pulling a bucket of coal from the shed to the back door of Higher House Farm, tugging it with gangly spasms. Helm has watched her moving round the farm with scraps for the hens, her limbs like the kinetic jitters of a twinkling star. Picking up apples and wrapping them in newspaper so their sides don't touch; dropping apples when her fingers accidentally scissor. Hanging dripping frocks and aprons on the line and losing pegs in her pockets. Sweeping the step stiffly with the wire broom, scrush-scrush-scrush, like a marionette.

277

It is Janni.

But she is not the rabbity girl from the hillside. She is not the bolting friend who would come and give Helm shiny treasure, who would show her cuts and bruises and her secret parts, who would blurt a thousand thoughts and questions: *Have you a nest in the sky, and why are your eyes so many, here is a shed adder skin, here is a penny I did not give to God, and you are my Valentine, look I have made you a card with a silver bow, and Justine Lahey has a hussy skirt, she is the first in the village to go above the knee, and do you promise to teach me to fly, do you promise.*

It is Janni.

But she is not the girl who escaped the rolling pin that day and ran up the fell, and ran all the way to the summit and saw Helm sitting on the cairn, alone, with the hole in Helm nothing could fill, and said,
   Oh, there you are. Where is your heart?

And if we are not seen, are we not real? If we are not believed, have we no form and pain and purpose in the world? Whosoever loves us, do they love us when they no longer remember us?

I do not know.
   I will find you a heart.

Chlorpromazine, the wonder drug. Janni is cured. So off Mammy goes on the bus to town, and Janni pegs her stockings and her cone-cupped falsies on the washing line. She drops a peg and picks it up and fumbles it into her pocket. She doesn't think of Helm. She doesn't have a friend. Only spaces in her mind where something extraordinary and companionable and wrong used to reside. Empty pockets in her life where shiny things no longer are collected. Except for this – bright, pretty wrapper of green and gold, which her scrabbling-about fingers find.

Oh.

A breeze catches her cropped hair, and tousles it. A breeze kisses her forehead, like the tenderest natal kiss in the cradle, long forgotten, imprinted. Look, Janni. What is that in the sky? An ink spill. Magic elixir trickery. The cloud on the biggest hilltop seems familiar. A doming belly. Arms and legs reaching out along the ridgeway. Look at the cloud now; hasn't it a blue face melting, and a grey face forming? So many smoking eyes, hair like the shorn locks of a lunatic? How dark the expression it is wearing, how fierce and coveting.

Janni holds the shiny paper between her fingers.

Oh, that is—

Cold, excited air seeping into the valley. The dogs working the fields stop their herding; they prick up their ears and whine, they jump and chase their tails. The oystercatchers and the lapwings go to ground softly, like bags of dust dumped in the bin. There's a flush past Janni's ear and the stockings flare from their wooden grips. The garth gate swings open. The open back door bangs closed. Tug, tug, tug at the bright cellophane wrapper.

That is—

It is.

It is a black Helm, worst of all Helms. Helm is dressed formally, for a funeral, or a marriage, or to proselytise from the summit – black

279

cloak, to convert the unbelievers, black suit, to claim what is Helm's in the court of Eden, black robe, to reap.

In the villages, the women and the rectors and the gentry are hurrying inside; the farmers are bringing in the Galloways and the pregnant ewes, the Melmerby geldings and the Dufton bull, especially the bull, which must not be loosed or it will trample and gore and take down more walls than the bastard wind. They are closing the storm doors, hooking the coops, moving the trailers and barrows leeside. The milk tanker is turning around in a wide spot on the road: the dairies will have to wait for the churns to be collected. And in the schoolroom at Milburn the headmaster chastises the children; they're getting giddy, they are getting skittish and kicking about like foals.

Sit down, Kenneth, turn around, Denise, stop barracking, Richard.

Should he send them home early? He looks out of the window at the blackened summit. Dear God, yes!

Put your books away. Gather your bags, please, hurry, hurry now.

He shuts the schoolhouse door, removes his hairpiece, locks it in his briefcase. The children run home with their satchels banging their bottoms and their coats open, singing.

The Helm,
it blows and blows,
it mugs your lugs
and flattens your kittens
and doesn't care where Sir's toupee lands.

Even from the beacon streets in Penrith, the black cap can be seen, cowling the Pennines, filthy as char. And the long whirling bar cloud, a cyclone tipped on its back, a giant spinning top, an ogre's candy-floss machine. Mrs Calder, conversing with the fishmonger inside the covered market, doesn't see a thing. She notes the finger dents in the trout skin: the cod is too slick. Too smelly, not fresh enough.

In Dr Thorne-Smith's surgery, a keening begins round the corners of the new brick building, rattling the guttering, and Nurse Wilson wonders about telephoning Higher House Farm, just to check. Between dressing changes and drainings she telephones, but no one answers.

Janni puts the wrapper in her pocket. How quickly the wind is getting stronger, madder. She watches the washing sail out from the line, the tights performing can-cans. A spectacular brooding thing is in the sky above the mountain – it is a ship, a blacksmith's anvil, a dromedary, a fallen angel. Pieces of twig and greenery are flying past the garth. The hayricks in the field above scatter and catch against Janni's dress like confetti, and the fell grass presses flat as a cricket pitch, as if ironed by a huge roller.

That is—

But she cannot speak. She cannot remember what she wants to say and her tongue is a slug in salt. The wind is gathering all the air about her, sucking it from her lungs. What does it want? The washing basket is snatched from beside her feet and spun westwards past the gable. The garments dance faster and higher until the washing line snaps and the conical bras are freed. She must get inside quickly. She must not tarry. But her body is slow and broken, its muscles no longer depend on her mind; it is twice the effort to ask for cooperation. The door of the farm is slammed and locked; the coal shed is the only shelter. She wrestles the hatch door up and crawls inside, and shuts the hatch behind. She sits on a pile of lumps in the coaly, dusty darkness, hands over ears, eyes squeezed closed, mouth working madly.

Such a wailing has begun outside. Lamenting and ululating all around, like a song of grief, like praise for some primary deity. She is inside a beaten drum, inside the womb of a bomb. It is a rare storm, this one, a caterwauler; it will enter the annals. There is nothing this Helm can't

281

shift and shake, hurl and demolish – aerials, water troughs, dovecotes, old engines left to rust, the Celtic cross in the graveyard and the heavy stone paving on the Roman road. Helm punches through glass in the window frames, it lifts doors, whistles emergencies through drains, it carbonates blood in the arteries. Shelves of books in the Tinclar library topple and the leaves flutter madly; *Heavens*, the librarian screams as the index cards are sneezed and spatter across the floor. One of the great sycamores at the Grange bows too low, splinters apart and timbers; sacks of flour in the bakery spill open and white dust tornadoes swirl round the ovens. The headmaster, bald as the day he was born and running towards his bicycle, looks down at his wristwatch – will he survive the ten-minute cycle home? Have the hands of his watch been wound back an hour by the dreadful wind?

Yes. Oh, yes.

Helm will turn back time.

Helm will scatter all the pages, rearrange the chapters, Helm will tell Helm's story every possible way.

Helm will begin this forsaken world again, recreate history, furiously, gloriously. Helm will be remembered.

Go back, Janni. Run back, fall back, fly back in your mind.

Here, in this small, dark place with panelled walls, fear smells bitter as cordite. It is the room you were put inside at Garlands, where the doctors said you were wrongly wired; something in your brain was loose and flapping in its own chaos, some upsetting thing must be removed. It is the cellar of Higher House Farm where Mammy left you with the light off. Loneliness. Emptiness. Without—

Go back. Through the slow treacle of forgetting, to the cold metal plates on the temples and the endless seizure, waking up in electrical wreckage, the past razed. Back to the green sour-tasting tablets, jaw held like a dog's until they were swallowed. *Tongue out, good girl, tell me who is in this picture.* Back to the doctor's big black car reversing. Chocolate and lime. The antiseptic comb gently parting your hair. Home and—

Go back, run back, fly back.

It is only bone and flesh anatomy, only blood's infernal barrier stopping you, only time. If you push hard, the locks of memory will turn and spring open. Once, your mind was fleet and remissive in the bracken. Once, you were lithe and agile on the mountain. The sprint to the summit was nothing and your lungs were full as sails. You could jump and soar and your feet were paws and your instinct was clear as an eel's. You were a wonder to behold, not lonely, not broken; you were going to marry one day. And that was best of all, worth the laughter and the rough grasping by the boys, the blind knives of the girls' eyes. Worth Mammy's slipper stinging your thighs, and the scalding baths, and spoonfuls of mustard to make you vomit out the lies. You ran, and you ran, to the top of the fell, and waiting there was—

Helm.

That is you.

The wind drops. The clattering and the booming and the bellowing stops and the coal dust arrests in a galaxy of dark stars inside the bunker. There's a hush and a sigh, like an intake of breath, as if in surprise, or pleasure, or sorrow: all the lover's sensations. Nothing moves and no one denies her and there's no sound other than Janni's mouth kissing and kissing and kissing the air.

She gets up slowly from the tarry black chair and the lumps scatter. Slowly, she pulls the hatch door up and she crawls outside. And, oh. Oh.

Outside, the world is held. It is all held perfectly still for her.

Feathers and branches and hay stalks are resting in their flight. The laundry basket hangs above the chimney of the farmhouse, waiting to be fetched down, and a slate from the roof hovers by the window. The fell's torn grass has paused its wave and a handful of flowers has been tossed beside the coal shed door, earth-strung roots, a pretty posy for a bride. Janni stands and smooths the dirty creases in her smock. There's coal grime underneath her fingernails and her hair is that of a convict. Her mouth has been emptied of teeth, and when Dr Thorne-Smith checked the sockets he said, *We all have our troubles, Janni, we all have our impediments.*

True. But she is fearless bonny. For no creature is ugly in this world, not in all its continents and oceans, not in all its hidden legions; there is nothing wicked or sick or ugly, when it is loved. Helm has stopped the world for her. She is the only moving thing and she flitters like a butterfly, through the wind-cured garden, to the open gate. And look, isn't it beautiful. A hawk has been caught sleeked into a gap in the wall, its wing splayed and ruffled, its black eye static as obsidian. Water from the stream has blown an arc across the lane. She steps under the shattered droplets, a million sky-borne diamonds. She passes a crop of rye, stroked flat against the ground; passes a field with whorly sheep huddled still as a photograph. On the fellside, the drystone walls have paused mid-tumble, the air is full of grit and filaments like a shaken globe. And on the mountain they fear and want her to stay away from is a miracle ginnel: grass has been parted all the way to the summit. She stumbles as she climbs it, her limbs slow and tangled; she struggles step by step.

But there is no need to rush now. Helm will wait. Helm will wait, for ever, for heed, for adoration, for her. When she reaches the top they will be together. She will take the shiny wrapper from her pocket and Helm will blow it from her hand. She will stand on the edge of the mountain and hold her arms out wide, and she will say—

Teach me to fly. You promised.

LI

The three of them wheel the sailplane out of the hangarage towards the turboprop. They unhook the tow-line from the Piper and attach it to the glider. Jude gets into the cockpit, stows his gear, runs the checks. All OK. There's a small oxygen tank up front, if needed. He takes a sip or two of tea from the flask. Strong, milky; Ange has left the bag in, just how he likes it. Not too much – it is awkward pissing into the Coke bottle. He screws the flask lid on firmly, sets it in the caddy, unwraps the chocolate bar and has a bite or two, then rewraps it and puts it away. Might be up there a while without breakfast, so he takes it back out and wolfs it down. He puts on his sunglasses and the bucket hat, straps in, thumbs-up to Keith, who salutes.

Julia fastens the door of the Piper and starts the engine. The propeller purrs into life, its blades a blurry wheel. Reminds him of Mark blowing an angry raspberry when he was a toddler; he always thinks this when he hears the sound. Julia radios the traffic tower and they are cleared. He takes hold of the handle, ready. He rolls his thumbs three times clockwise above the stick, an irrational habit he developed before heading out on call. Some of the effects he just hasn't been able to shift. For a while he couldn't stop seeing the pale fluid arcing past his shoulder, couldn't stop hearing the splatter of it on the doorstep, and then Gary howling as he tried to claw his own face off. Two inches right and it might have been him. He sat there on the hospital chair next to Gary's wife guiltily thinking that, while the surgeons removed the melted eye, transplanted skin from Gary's thigh up to his cheek. You expect knives – guns, even, from the boneheads. You don't expect something medieval. Two standard sessions with the police shrink, where he said not much, then pretended to have learnt to live with the nightmares, the erratic tremors, to be fit for service, and not sinking seven pints a night.

All out, all out.

Julia taxis along the field and accelerates; the propeller buzzes furiously and the cable tautens. The sailplane responds immediately, flows forward, bumps and trembles on the runway under its minor weight. It picks up speed swiftly. Here we go, he thinks, here we go. Less than the length of a football pitch – the glider lifts off the ground before the Piper is airborne. He keeps it straight and neutral with the foot rudder, inches up, down, kiting behind Julia. He checks the ASI. The turboprop tilts and lifts and climbs ahead of him, while he and *Perry* levitate behind. The runway disappears below. Julia steepens a fraction at the edge of the airfield, clearing the road and the canopy of nearby trees; then she eases back – nothing much to avoid in the flatlands around Carlisle.

They are aloft. In flight. It is always astonishing. Every time, his heart pumps a half-beat quicker and there's the thrill of becoming a visitor in this rarefied domain. A slight crosswind to the west. Full vision of the sky now. A cool, quartz blue. It's a truly lovely April day. The Piper does all the work, *Perry* so sleek and aerodynamic behind that it seems almost biological. The airfield vanishes, the fields around the city shorten. Now they are up higher, the soft tresses of adrenaline floating around inside him begin to settle, like ash down a chimney. Julia banks east, takes it gently, and on the horizon he can see the north Pennines rising, the shore of Kielder Water. He drifts behind the aerotow, checks the speed brakes. They turn to head south and wind whistles past the window. The glider barely shudders in the current.

Ange might look up as she's walking the dog, and see the planes. From below, they'll appear invisibly moored; the glider won't look assisted, it will seem to be hunting its leader, wide-winged and narrow-bodied, streamlined at the neck and fuselage. A graceful swan next to a hard-working pigeon, or a bee chased by a dragonfly. Some kind of elegant, evolved spirit, released from its chunky casing. Don't be recording that one for the Met Office, you twat, he thinks.

After a few minutes, the taller Pennines come into view, shrinking as the planes gain altitude, late snow on the highest contours, a murky brew over them. The wide and narrow rivers in the plain lace silver along their courses, the Petteril, the Roe and Caldew. The South Tyne. There's Alston, its buildings clawing onto the high landscape. The planes head towards the cloud mass above Cross Fell. A long tow, but a quick ride; he takes it all in. Farm fields enclosed by walls. The villages of Eden, metal bridges, ponds, the tops of silos like circles drawn on a map, stood on their ends like pen lids. Lazonby lido – its rectangle of incongruous azure in the ochres of north Cumbria. Small scuds to the side of the glider now as the wind strengthens, but it is still mostly quiet, sibilant air flushing past *Perry*'s fibreglass skin and the humming of the propeller ahead.

God, he loves it. The calm inside his head up here. He can forget all the manufactured job lists, the hectic arrests and the conflicts of the past. The repercussions, recriminations. How he hasn't rung his mum. How he hasn't rung Gary's wife. The cross on the ballot paper that got this bastard lot in power, creating so many divides, so much sickness and disorder. His institutional life; three decades of seeing bad eggs cooked. Society's Kitchen, that's what the psychiatrist called it after the attack; fine, nothing's random, nothing's meaningless, but where did he fit exactly, and was the force just one of the bubbling pots?

He can forget how he could have kept on with the Theakstons and the stumbling home, losing his temper with the dog, unable to touch his wife who he'd adored since she was nineteen and looked like Sandie Shaw – those legs! How he'd missed her promotion to deputy head, been awol in the pub and late to the restaurant celebration, said something awful to her colleague. Not entirely sober before his shifts. *Get help, Jude, or go, or I will.* The week she did, and took Mark with her. Mark having to resit his O levels, not through his own fault, poor kid, and that moment. Christ. That moment at Dalston station, on the platform bridge, the rails below warping. Thank God, thank God he'd not. Thank God it was no one he'd worked with who approached him, talked him down, walked him out of the station. Thank God she'd taken him back.

And then he found this, gliding, or perhaps gliding had found him.

The plane shudders again, moves slightly right of the Piper. Julia adjusts, bearing south-east. She tows him along the capped ridgeway towards the weather front, climbing steadily higher, keeping them out of the lee wave, as smooth as she can. Now the Helm's base cloud is clearer, a vast lenticular, stretching the whole length of Cross Fell. It is the first time he's seen it, or properly taken notice, maybe. Such weird nebulous definition, as if it is its own isobar; it has an inferred energy that makes him suddenly nervous. He looks west. Three miles or so across the valley, the long pale bar cloud has formed and is willowing away at its northern edge. Spectral gap, he thinks, yeah, that's about right. The space between is unreadable, eerie, with remnants of connective clouds broken up by wave disturbance.

They fly on, past the cloud formation, looping round the broad backs of the range to Great Dun Fell. In position. He detaches the sailplane from the line; nothing more than a small back-shunt feeling as his airspeed decreases, and he is autonomous, in the mid-layer of three

289

boundaries. The Piper manoeuvres right and speeds away, begins its return to the airfield.

Cheers, Julia.

Still odd to have no one in a control room telling him where to go or what disturbance he'll have to deal with. He remembers so clearly that first solo flight, how it felt so incredibly peaceful, the solitude, the headspace.

But today, he has a job to do. He pulls up and left, the first soaring turn. He watches the red yaw string flickering outside the front window. The plan is to keep between forty-eight and fifty-two knots. He checks his watch, the instruments. The glider levels, and there it is again: the massive orographic base cloud to the north-east.

Two thousand five hundred metres. Smooth air.

Smooth air. But the weather out of the side window is spectacular, like Byzantine architecture, or the set of a horror film. What is that surfing fog, that fermenting palace, what evil lies within it? He's read up about the Föhn effect in the Alps, its mountain waves – chaotic flow, sudden turbulence; in summer, the smoke of bellowed wildfires can be swept so high that pilots often refrain from flying in these conditions. He can control the plane, tactically speaking, but he can't control the weather. The weather is the flight, really. There's a lesson in this, he knows, about responding, about relinquishing, accepting whatever comes. But still – shitting hell, look at that thing!

Sorry, Ange, he says.

He begins his first track along the storm.

LII

The ugly gull takes off, with a big athletic launch. Selima tries to ignore her damp clothing, and not think about the nonsense in the pub last night. She tries to settle into work. The ceiling of cloud has lifted a little and wind flushes briskly past the building. The field station gutters vibrate. She shivers and tries to concentrate on writing up her notes, comparing the last series of readings with previous cloud vapour records. She stares at the rows of figures. Depressing, even on days with no hangovers.

Twenty-eight out of thirty samples analysed by the lab contain microplastics. The lower the altitude, the higher their presence – shockingly high. Hundreds of particles per cubic metre. Here in the empty fells. And these are only the fibres large enough to identify. Dr Lim has shared similar data from the Mount Tai research post. But over Shandong, it's thousands of particles per cubic metre. Their experiments have shown that cloud-borne plastics are leading to denser accumulation of cloud. The polymers are hydrophilic, travelling along at altitude and altering chemically, encouraging new vapour formations as they go. Droplets attracting droplets attracting droplets. They are making new weather. At what point, she wonders, and which enumeration, do cloud-borne plastics become plastic clouds?

She leans back from the laptop. It's hideous, really. Some days it all seems so unfathomably bad, and frightening, even to her. Some days the numbers are not shapes in columns but portents of – yes, of doom. She is Cassandra.

Her phone lights up and she feels a jolt of anxiety. Hesitantly, she looks, but it is just the morning message from David.

40mph in Upper Tees V and hp over N sea. Anything glamorous around 1800m today?

She glances out of the north-facing porthole window; replies.

Unglamorous. Got pissed on coming up, bit miserable all round actually.

After a moment or two, another text arrives.

Hope you're OK, life can be rough hey. Thinking of you.

This is oddly earnest, for David. Makes her wonder how things are with Sandra, whether something has happened. She finishes the data entry. She should forward the lab results to him, but it feels like delivering another bad prognosis. As well as all the other climatic changes, Mrs H's lidded striations of warm and cold air may stop happening if the cloud becomes too dense and wet and heavy. Mrs H may stop happening. So this is how her dad must have felt, day after day, sitting across the desk from his patients, answering tearful questions, reaching over to hold a hand.

No, I am very sorry, we cannot cure, but we can try to slow the disease. No, we do not know how long is left. Of course we will do our best. We must make the most of every remaining day.

Not one for beating around the bush, her Papa. Perhaps she should simply say to David: How are you? She should just ask, plainly: How is Sandra?

She picks up her phone again, but the roving signal has disappeared.

She tries to work, but her jeans feel shrunk onto her legs, her skin is puckered and chilly beneath the damp denim. At least the gull hasn't come back, with its crude gaze. Nor Paul and his pal – the van pulled away half an hour ago, loudly, gravel skittering under its wheels, as if attention-seeking. Fuck them. No doubt she should call it quits and go back to the bothy, but now the wind is getting up; making mournful, religious-sounding notes over the summits.

She stands and goes to the window. There, as ever, is the radome. A thing of utterly improbable engineering – an alighted intergalactic mothership, yet somehow primeval, and eternal-seeming. All those howlers it must have endured since it was built, force 10s and 12s, whiteouts, hurricanes, sub-zero temperatures, but it has not shifted an inch.

I do not like you, big ball.

She squints an eye closed, brings her finger in line with its shell and taps the side. It creaks off its cement base and thumps onto the fell below, begins a big, slow roll, down Great Dun, gathering speed as it turns, faster, crushing the bracken and pancaking stunned sheep, dropping over gullies and bouncing back up, barrelling through drystone walls, turning this way and that on the withers of the fell as it rolls like a giant mad mythological egg, unstoppable, riving the trees apart, until, chipped and cracked by limestone, it shatters, ends up in huge hexagonal pieces all over the bottom of the mountain. (Perhaps taking out the Christian Centre first, like a bowling skittle.) Goodbye.

Selima stares at the radome. It doesn't move. The wind haws round it. Beyond, the grass on the summit plateau ripples briskly.

Yeah, she should go. She hasn't yet got stuck in the field station, unlike David who was hit by a late-spring snowfall one year and got stranded for several days, or the black-and-white long-johned chaps, who must have spent endless stormy nights wrestling the tin roof of the original shack back down. May it might be, with lambs bumbling around the fields and bluebells, but the weather here obeys nobody's rules and attends to nobody's heroic complacency. She closes the laptop, puts it back into the waterproof case and stuffs it in her rucksack.

She gathers up her cold, soggy jacket and unlocks the door. There's an immediate yank and suck of air as she opens it, a considerable rise in noise outside. She shoulders the door closed, locks it, zips her coat up, and goes to get Ellie.

The bike is not where she left it.

Did she prop it on the other side of the building? She peers round the corner of the field station, but Ellie is not there. She walks a circuit of the walls. Hangover brain. Did she actually bring it inside out of the rain? Pretty sure not since – bra, perverts, et cetera. She unlocks the door again and glances in. No bike. Come on, Selima. She looks in the gravel and grass beside the station. This is silly, she thinks. The security guards must have moved it? Maybe it was in the way, somehow? Or it had fallen over in the wind and they've propped it in a shelter. Doing her a favour, maybe. They just didn't bother to tell her?

She can't see it anywhere. The van is definitely gone: can't ask those morons whether they've been 'helpful'. She walks towards the radome on the other side of the complex. The zingy tinnitus sound grows louder as she nears it – a sort of electrical elephantine soprano. Is the noise real or is she imagining it? She has never been over to the cabin, the tee on which the monster ball sits, has been careful not to seem too curious or do anything unrelated to her placement here. The arrangement with the CAA and the university is not exactly clear to her – old kissing cousins, a tolerated shared lease. Above, the dome is vast, dirty-white. Two antenna towers spire up next to it. No obvious storage place, and she can't see the bike. There are CCTV cameras pointing down from the wall of the cabin; two more under the belly of the radome. The cabin door has no window; it looks sci-fi, moulded resin over a metal infrastructure. She pauses, lifts a hand and knocks. The sound barely registers.
Hello?

She knocks again, louder.

Hello!

Nothing. There's clearly no one in there; or they're busy, and not going to assist with a bicycle hunt. But where *is* the fucking bike?

Paul, she thinks. Has he dumped it behind the radome as a joke, as passive-aggressive punishment? Ha-bloody-ha, arsehole. Today of all days, when she is feeling particularly – tender.

She starts walking the circumference of the big ball. It is the strangest structure, like a puzzle that doesn't make sense. There must be some mathematical key to the panelling – though, if it was taken apart, could it ever be put back together? On the eastern side of the structure, the wind is properly gusting, snatching at her coat. No Ellie. There has to be a good reason. But what possible reason has a security unit got to move her bike? And not tell her.

She stops walking. Is it intended – to frighten her?

There's a small, internal burst of anxiety. Her breath is snatched away. She turns and looks behind, as if she might have walked straight past Ellie. No. On the fell, then? If so, they really are fucking with her. It just isn't funny. At all.

She walks quickly back across the complex to the fence, crosses the cattle-grid and begins a bigger loop of the summit, where the bike might be dumped and invisibly lying on its side. The grass is buffeting in the wind now. Must be twenty-five or thirty miles per hour? She holds her hair back while she searches. There is barren emptiness all around, and in the distance the stone pathway of the Roman road leads north to Cross Fell. Outside the complex fence, she feels very exposed, gelid in her damp clothes, shoved at by the wind. Two thousand feet up, without a way to get down. This is insane. This is – dangerous.

She tries to maintain calm, to not let dark thoughts enter her brain. Nothing sinister happening, it can't be. There's a perfectly reasonable explanation for the bike being gone. Very hard to think of it.

She starts back across the summit towards the radome. Paul, who is no doubt spying from somewhere, will have returned the bike while she's been away looking for it, surely. Joke over now. Good one. But I am reporting the hell out of you, she thinks. She picks up her pace, harrying herself towards the complex.

The bike is nowhere to be seen. She can hear her own breathing, loud, irregular.

She takes her phone out of her pocket. She still has the number of the Penrith taxi firm, hasn't she? Sixty-five pounds seems like a bargain. She'd pay double, triple. If they'll come up this far? No signal. Of course. She walks about, trying to find a spot to pick one up. Her hands are so cold now they feel sore, frozen solid. How can there be two giant fuck-off antennae here and no consistent signal? And can't emergency calls be made regardless? She dials 999, because, well, a crime is currently taking place. Isn't it? Theft. Harassment. Obstruction. Of some sort. The call fails.

She makes another useless circuit of the radome, knocks on the door of the cabin again, bangs on it with the side of her fist. Is she being watched, filmed? She looks up at the camera, thinks, at least I am on record, evidence for a complaint, then thinks, or it'll be on the news, with the presenter saying, *Last seen wearing a purple puffer jacket.* The door remains shut. The radome hums queerly. The wind calls to awful prayer.

Then, the thought she has suppressed, along with the anxiety bubble in her chest, ruptures horribly.

296

It's not Paul.

It's them.

The Endtrepreneurs.

What? A bunch of spotty alienated right-wing incels. Are they really going to leave the comfort of the swivel chairs in the bedrooms of their parental homes, or whatever Tolkien-postered hobbit-hole they occupy, and trog up a fell to – to what? To what, Selima?

The truth will find you in hiding.

The wind sweeps round her, rattling her coat sleeves, throwing her hair about her face. She turns and half-walks, half-runs back to the field station. She opens the door, goes inside, and locks it.

LIII

LEE WAVE

Meteorological conditions suitable for lee wave formation are:

(i) a stable layer of air between less stable layers at the ground and at a higher level;

(ii) a wind of at least 15 kn across the top of the ridge; and

(iii) constancy of wind direction up to the top of the stable layer.

R. S. Scorer expressed the required conditions mathematically as an upward decrease of $l2$ where:

$$l^2 = \left(\frac{g\beta}{V^2} - \frac{1}{V} \frac{d^2 V}{dz^2} \right)$$

where β is the static stability, g the gravitational acceleration, and V the wind-speed component in the direction across the hill.

LIV

By the time the magstone is born, summer solstice has passed, a good harvest has begun, and the trees are bright as embers burning on the hills. Aspen, yellowing all at once, the beeches turning bronze. No one is at the river or nearby. No one hears the tremendous cracking dispatch from the cliff or the splintering of the stacks underneath when the magstone falls. It lands, half in the river, half out, intact except for a few shattered lumps where it hits the ground, impacting beyond the wooden nest. As it topples sideways, pebbles and mud and water kick up alongside it, and a wave reaches the other shore. The river closes its quick amphibian mouth around it.

Birds lift squawking and flapping from the canopy. The minnows dart in shoals to the shadows of the deeper wells, or upstream away from the silt. When the shock of the occurrence passes, they return to investigate the new, benthic landscape.

The magstone lies, blindly facing the new world. In the light of early morning, the sheared sandstone cavity above looks raw, like an open wound, an inflamed canal after delivery. The magstone's great triangular nose points towards the middle sky. Its jowls are washed by the swirling current. On its surface and around the hole in the cliff are thousands of alligatored marks, knapping, from hundreds of days of human work.

The mushroom gatherers find it first and come running back to the settlement. In the commotion, weapons are taken in hand. But there are no invaders. Reen and Dal wake NaNay. They pick her up and carry her from the hut and all the people convoy to the river shore.

All Mother, the magstone is born, they keep saying. *It is as your vision.*

They run too fast, bumping and jostling her uncomfortably along the forest road, and she complains.

Slow, slow, slower, I am sore, I will not die before we get there. I need to piss.

They put her down, hold her arms, wait while she squats, dribbles. She is very sick; all the little infections have blossomed in her body and will not heal: rot in her jaw, the thick mucal chest. Her sight has become milky. Since summer she has been sleeping most of the day in the big hut, looked after by Reen's children. She mixes up their names. They hold her hands and rub butter into the frail, livery skin. They stroke her long grey hair, count the beads. They give her juniper berries for her sore mouth.

Dal lifts NaNay into his arms and carries her like a lame child down the new road, to the pebble beach. He sets her upright and shows her the fallen magstone. Her head moves around. It is a dark-red blur but she can see the edges, the shapes, and now the face.

Yayaya, she whispers, her voice thin as smoke, her eyes bright inside the wrinkled pouches. She touches her forehead with her fingertips. Her face crumples.

All Mother is crying or she is very happy, Reen says.

Put me on it, NaNay tells them.

Dal lifts her gently up onto the hull of the magstone. Reen drapes a blanket over her back. She places the ore belt around her waist. NaNay sits, tiny and hunched over, the flaps of her breasts touching the magstone's surface. She is emaciated and the muscles in her arms and legs have withered to almost nothing; she is too weak to wear the heavy orox fur. She cannot eat orox meat anymore – disagreements in her gut, five loose brown teeth wobbling when she

300

chews, and an abscess in the hinge of her jaw. Her body is consuming itself; winter is coming again and she will go to the other world as bones.

But not yet, not now. Now she rides the slab triumphantly, like a beast in a painting in a cave. She pats it. She digs her heels. The red surface is warm.

Yayaya, she says again.

She reaches down and rubs along the stone with her hand, squints hard and focuses her cloudy vision. She finds the place above the cheek where there is smooth blankness. She has seen many things and the magstone has not yet seen any.

Reen. Come.

Her daughter places a hand on NaNay's back.

Do you want to come down, All Mother?

No, no. I will stay with the magstone. Bring me my white fur. And hazelnut paste. Bring Dal's metal tool.

The white orox fur is fetched. The tool is passed to her. She marks the stone and she begins to scratch at the surface. Her hand is weak, but she does not drop the tool into the river. She scowls as she shunts the chisel back and forth. She rests. She dozes with her chin on her chest. Then she begins scraping again. An hour, two, all afternoon.

The children climb onto the magstone behind her; they jump off into the water. People from the forest and the herders and the new settlers come and go, looking at the fallen stone. They know a tremendous event is happening and they rank about quietly, watching. They burn three woods. Reen passes NaNay beakers of water; she does not drink. She does not eat the hazel paste in the wooden bowl beside her. She sucks juniper. She sleeps and does not fall. She wakes and she carves the rock. The people sing and their anmas hear. They replace the slipped blanket around her shoulders. They warm her cold feet with their hands.

This day passes; she has marked the stone faintly, a ring around a cup.

All Mother, it is getting dark – shall I carry you back to the hut? Dal asks.

But NaNay keeps scoring the stone.

The night comes, with a moon that hides behind nacreous clouds. No stars; meteors scratch the surface of the night sky, unseen. Dal builds a fire on the pebble beach and sleeps next to it. The family from the caves have made torches with fat and rush; they glow along the beach.

In the morning, light creeps up from behind the Halron's mountain. River mist forms above the water. There is the tiny sound of scraping as NaNay works the tool. She does not stop or ask to be brought down and taken home. Another day passes and moves towards its end. People from beyond the forest have come; they gather on the beach to watch also, and they sing and help protect NaNay's anma. She was the one whose child joined the people in peace. She is unkilled, ancient, venerable. They have brought gifts: giant, orange-gilled mushrooms, nuts, berries. From the herders: cheese, sour milk, tender cuts. It is a feast, quartering the year.

By the time the sky is turning pink, NaNay is very tired, but the mark is clear; it can be deepened by others. She stops carving and passes the tool to Dal.

All Mother, do you want to come down now?

The magstone is awake, she says. *I have opened its eye.*

He lifts her as carefully as a wounded stork, down to the ground, her weight no more than a stripped carcass. He lies her on a blanket beside the river and places the white orox fur over her body. She curls underneath, and sleeps.

In the canopy above, the leaves burn brightly, copper, golden, and fallen leaves slide brightly on the river's back. Shadows are filling the bottom of the chasm, and as the sun goes into the other world there is burnished light in the gorge, and the magstone passes between many reds, fly-eye, flame, scallop, blood. It watches the sun set.

LV

The boy rises, unwillingly, from his crouch. His blue shemagh is vivid and jewel-like against the wastes. Impossible. How did such a peacock track the lion? Isa: beloved, loyal. It is his first true disobedience. He holds the master's aspic glare; its pale fire is undiminished in the dirty, weary face, but anger is not the predominant fuel – there's a conflict of emotion. Three days in the wilderness; the man is ragged, torn up and gory, as if he has been back at the crusades. He is glad to see the boy, or some part of him is.

Come here, he calls again. *Come to me.*

Isa springs nimbly up the fellside, with all the fresh energy of a kid goat. He stands before Michael. No need to fall to his knees: the path has him lower than his superior. He glances at the iron sallet, perhaps to be reassured, habit. His master's eyes are fixed, but any poise he might have had is deconstructing. He trembles, reaches out.

Are you a mirage or are you solid? Here. Let me touch.

Michael places a hand on the boy's head, on the soft, dark shock of hair. The warmth and animal gorgeousness of it. Last of all, most distressful and undoing, is this temptation – if it is a test, it is the worst yet.

Real, then.

His chin drops. His eyes sting. Do not undo me now, O Lord, he thinks, and he lifts his head, attempts to compose himself.

I told you to wait below. You have come into the maw, to the brink. It is foolish, unprofitable sacrifice.

Isa looks up at Michael, and Michael must reread the face, which, for seven years, he has understood to be simple to interpret. The eyes, dark

304

as agate and reddish, holding their history – fealty, in childish form, indebted, needful, even loathing. But a future – this is occluded, suddenly harder to see. Michael reaches round the back of the boy's neck, pulls Isa's head to his breast. Unwise to embrace so close to the summit, but he cannot help it. Inside the broad cavity there is a heart, knuckled, pounding hard against the walls. He coughs drily, releases him.

How long have you been following?

The boy, who speaks to no other but his master, looks up again.

All my life, since it ended and began anew.

Yes. That is good.

Always the right answer; appealing to the master's philosophy. They stand for a moment, facing one another. Yes, it is his immigrant. Familiar, placid. But something else is in the boy, new occupation. Is it the Helm? No. He does not appear possessed.

How swiftly the world here changes, as if the sky and the earth and sea are reversing, mixing elements. Marine movement above – there's heavy rolling surf on the upper currents, white-tipped, spume-like. A tide is coming in, down over the mountains. And in the lower sphere, a lake of white, watery mist. It is hard to separate, but they must, of course. The boy is in danger; the longer he stays with Michael, the greater the chance of predation. Michael holds Isa's shoulders, and pushes the boy away from him, and this hurts; it hurts his arms and his back, and to the quick it is deeply wounding.

Go now. Go and wait for me in the place I instructed. By the evening I will be done. The creature will be cast out.

He looks over the boy's shoulder, down the long slope of the mountain.

This is not good country. Did you bring your knife?

Isa nods, lifts his sleeve a fraction; he has it. He does not move. The instruction was too hollow, perhaps, not firm enough. The boy is confused by his own unorthodoxy, or he has been whispered to. Michael coughs again, hoarsely.

Give me a drop of your water.

Isa unfastens the skin tied at his waist, passes it, and Michael drinks and could drink it all, so fresh and pure does it taste. As he tilts the skin down he sees the boy's eyes resting on the helmet again.

You are concerned. Do you think this demon will take off my head like an artichoke? My fate is not here, in this blasted place. I will be carried whole through the streets of my town. Go now, Isa, back to the longhouse. I do not wish for you to be overturned.

The boy does not move; he gives no indication that he will ever move. Placid, yet is he taller on the path? Is he not almost Michael's height, in fact? Not a boy after all, Michael thinks; has he not noticed, or in two days has the growth been so considerable? The refugee is gone. The stranger to this cold, adopted country, gone. A man is arriving on the mountain, an agent of self-government.

I see you are in disagreement. I am an old bull and my back end sinks. But have I not mapped the stars correctly? Am I some prone academic? When the church tower was lowered by those Italian deceivers, did I not still calculate its height to the moon? This demon blinds sheep and the poor wretches below. Its trickery will not work on me.

It is the usual form of speech, but it is expensive. He struggles for breath between words; he is nearly spent. But those eyes! Unaffected by light, even the hard, planing light of the north. Made by some glacial technician, like the sled dog's. Who would not believe such a man? Who would not bow humbly to him? How many times has his boy carefully replaced the helmet, trusted and trusting in it?

Isa remains firm, within striking distance – were the old methods to work. Feet planted on the path, the shawl of his birth slung over his chest. And so they are locked, neither turning away.

What, then? Michael says, finally. *Ah. You have seen fate, perhaps, and have been biding. That is why you have come. It is a morbid vision. You cannot speak of it. Your purpose is difficult. And you are unsure how to break the chain.*

Isa nods again, a small, discreet gesture. Michael searches his eyes. Two futures: a vagrant skinning rabbits at the river, culpable, hanged; and a tall, beautiful scholar in the Islamic gardens of the South. The century will move on; there will be painted gods again, new ways of seeing, behind and inside objects, anatomies of the eye. A world where belief serves no cause – fails, even.

I must first set the cross. That, at least, in my name, in the name of our Lord.

A third time, Isa nods, and the painful fist of muscle turns in Michael's chest. He winces, presses a hand against the place.

If I had seen your face before I drew my sword, I might have pitied them, spared them. I do not ask your forgiveness, and you cannot grant it. There is no reparation but God's. I lifted you towards His grace. You have served me because of my sins, but you have served me. The white canons will receive you and give you refuge. The abbot is a trustworthy confessor. Abn.

He leans forward, kisses each cheek, kisses the soft mouth. Isa allows it. He waits. There are bastard sons across these islands, sired in youth, from punishments, before the sacraments. And then there is this one, adopted as a wolf might suckle an orphan pup after killing the bitch that produced it. Any man may be dominated by force or favour, brought into service. Until such time as he takes the knife from his throat and turns its point. Until love makes a servant of the master.

Michael bends and heaves the cross onto his back, the right shoulder, his strongest, where it has almost worn a bed. He rocks weakly, then takes a first step on the path, and hauls forward. Another step,

307

and another. The cross is dragged away, grating across the desecrated lunar landscape.

The path bends and rises. The cross follows its bearer, its momentum no greater than that of Michael Lang. His iron head glints. Clouds are gathering, thicker, a coagulant stir, grey as a haar, curling over Fiend's Fell and down towards the valley. Isa stands and watches him lumber on, pulling the indestructible load, disappearing into the brume, into a realm where only madmen, angels or assassins would follow. Then, hand within his sleeve, he begins after him.

And perhaps it is true. There are demons all about, sitting trollishly along the summit escarpment like grotesques on a roof, grinning and gurning, their long forked tongues wound about their genitals, faces protruding from their knees, claws picking at their orifices. Perhaps all the creatures of hell are here, readying themselves to welcome one more to their ranks.

And Helm reigns above them, the aerial sovereign, apocryphal, be-guiling, powerful enough to harness the weakness of any soul – greed, lust, vengeance.

Or perhaps Helm need only watch these humans fight, struggling on the summit, grappling each other and spinning, as if in a dance. There is no need for Helm to interfere or intervene. It is exceptional theatre down there, where the actors love and despise each other, help and betray each other, break whatever they've made. It is by their own hands that they injure one another, striking at the softest parts, rolling on top and floundering under, beating with fists and begging mercy, then slipping bloodied from the edge – their bones so heavy as they fall, mortal under their armour.

LVI

Trinket 242
Iron skullcap or sallet

Helmet of hemispherical form with rounded cut-outs for the ears. Main edge is plain, bordered by pairs of lining holes. Exterior is smooth and patinated. There is a long crack running from ear to ear, visible on the outside and in places inside, indicating damage from a traumatic impact. Thirteenth-century production date, made in Europe, used for combat and war.

Height – 120 mm
Length – 215 mm
Weight – 815 grams

Location – foot of the cliffs, Fiend's Fell escarpment

LVII

In early September, the last piece of the Revelation Machine arrives, slowly down the track to Kirkland, behind two long-fringed piebalds. *Lilith*. She has been bought and sent over from Harrisons, the agricultural merchants in Penrith, for the bargain sum of fifty pounds. Her hold is red, black and brass, two cylinders on top of a boiler, assembly mounted on rigid front-steering wheels. John Harrison himself has adapted her for purpose from the old Tuxford design.

Lilith – Thomas was informed by the oil-stained merchant as they walked between threshers and ploughs, Buckeyes and tractors – had been tragically underused for the past two decades. Demoted by the rise of those self-propelled models now thundering and honking about the place.

Here she is.

And there she was – magnificent, at the end of the aisle of machinery, like a lady of a certain age, still handsome, still productive, waiting to be asked to sally.

The world is too fast a place for legislation, Mr Bodger, much as they try, Harrison said, rubbing a spot on her brassware with his pocket chamois. *We invent, then run like buggery to sweep up invention's mess. But this beauty is still at liberty on the roads, unlike the runaways, and she's as grand as the day she was built, you mark my words.*

Unnecessary to have a drive belt or flywheel fitted, they decided. The first section of pipe would be connected to the horizontal chimney by the fitters.

And she'll be portable? She'll make it up the declivity, will she? Thomas asked, sotto-voiced, as if not wishing to offend either seller or merchandise.

Surely. On a thirty gradient, I'd put men behind her, as insurance. She's sow enough to stand her ground in a gale, but you'll want to ballast her once she's staged. I've seen what that wind can do. It is not a pantomime. Now, if she's coked high, Harrison went on, *she has the heft for a goodly length of pipe, but best not push your luck, Mr Bodger, best not conceive of miles.*

No, no, we'll find the sweet spot, Thomas assured him. *I have of late been helped along with my formula.*

And there will be some form of pigment involved, will there?

Unlike Jesse Symonds, John Harrison had enumerated his doubts about Thomas's scheme. One, would the steam, ruddied or verdant, not dissipate a furlong up? Two, would the Helm, known to be zealous enough to blow calkers off clogs, not just distribute steam to the four corners of Eden? And three, well, to what end? Was some scheme afoot to moderate yon hellion? For he had heard all manner of poppycock before in that regard: tunnels dug underneath the mountain to draw it off, a great wall like the Oriental, an awning to redirect it, forestation with gorse. The only credible notion, in his opinion, was harnessing it, a vast turbine, such as the Dutch might engineer, to put the scoundrel to some useful industrial purpose. Thomas kept his literary ambitions brief. John Harrison was clearly used to practical applications, hoeing and harvesting, scything and sewing, and cared not for being a footnote in some meteorological treatise. In the end, fifty pounds was fifty pounds – a not insignificant boon for the Harrison business.

So *Lilith* comes on, towed by horses led by Harrison's boy, who says, *Good girl, Monny, good Moll,* having drawn gawps from the fellside villagers, from the travellers in bright caravans leaving Appleby for the next fair, and from all the twittering, scuttling hedgerow inhabitants. Here she comes – regally rumbling down the track behind the horses, fit for fire crews or a collier queen, her big wheel spokes flashing yellow. She jostles against the verges, bringing down low-hanging conkers and sloes, sending the sparrows up from their roosts. The horses' nostrils flare as they haul her.

Easy, girls, harve up now.

They could be towing anything, barley, rusk, sacks of coal – how could they know they are towing their own replacement? Still, they bring her on, steadily down the narrow rutted lane, and as she draws nearer Thomas sees a row of truant youngsters following on behind, skipping and laughing, and leaving fingerprints on the polish. What a thing! What a spectacle!

Imagine if the old boys from the Society were here to see. Imagine if Sara were by his side. *Oh, Tombo*, she'd say, *it's a dandy!* What he wishes above all, and so deep down as to be unspeakable, is that Rebecca Brooke could see this marvel; that she might find some revision of heart, some solidarity, and, despite her weeds and reservations, might come to Kirkland and be part of things. But of Mrs Brooke he has seen and heard nothing, not since she buried her husband and took Thomas to the river. He did dream, the previous week, that he was afloat in the clear waters of the Eden, and though he sank to its pebble bed he did not drown but could, by some aquatic transfiguration, breathe. When he woke he thought, this is not my dream, this is her dream. And then he recalled Helm's naughty nocturnal muddling, as relayed to him by Mrs Hodge. The Helm is coming, he thought, and he rushed to the window in his nightshirt, but there was no mantle over the fell's summit; there was only a slight wind, not *the* wind. Another strange thought arrived, one he was excited and saddened by. He could photograph Rebecca Brooke as well as photograph Helm, so that when he left the valley there would be proof of both.

Lilith. Her name is written cursively on her flank. She will be towed up the slope and stationed at the point, as best he can estimate using the weir theory, in the return of the force. She will be roped and staked

312

under tarpaulin to keep her dry. Next to her, a hood of coal, so she may be fired up the moment her service is required.

And the pipes? All delivered, on schedule, never a doubt about Symonds's punctuality. They are currently being assembled by a group of fitters, some of whom, though he has not pressed for references, are transients from the crews that blasted the railway tunnels and built the viaducts. Wages paid at the end of each week. No questions asked about mountain follies, no remarks made about enthuzimuzzy Londoners, or side-eyes. The foreman – forewoman, it transpires – is Peg. Peg of the Goliath boys. Peg of the gold tooth and the ruthless charm, who dresses as one of them, if less shabbily, in green plaid trousers and waistcoat, her hair pinned up under a bowler hat. Peg strides about in the rain in a long waxed coat, laughs like a cawing jackdaw when Thomas offers her his umbrella. She could be any age between thirty-five and sixty. Trim, flat-chested, tiny. But dear God, that Sicilian eye: the boys are terrified. Is she their tyrannical aunt, Thomas wonders. Ex-circus stock? A chain maker from the sweat shops? He doesn't ask and she doesn't tell.

But Peg knows the terrain all right. She knows its uppers and its mucky swales. She has, of course, *laid the rail that fetched mettle from Settle, sir*. There is little Peg doesn't know – plumbing, surveying, topography, psychiatry, which smith made the watch fob that Thomas wears (Carnelian). Peg walks with him across the stretch of land that his machine will span, marking it with twine, tying red rags where there are obstacles – tall scrub bushes, rocky outcrops, peat holes.

Passable, passable, Peg says. *Not passable, axe it. A jig of explosive should level out there – we'll supply and bill. Passable, passable. No. We will need another pier here. Valve, or pressure will be lost. And here you will need a dolly-down.*

He feels quite the Mary-Ann beside her. When he casts his eyes back over the red-ragged zigzagging route, it does look rather piggledy and somewhat improbable. No matter. Trial and error; things can be adjusted, perfected, he reassures himself.

Peg has negotiated the wages, politely, apologetically, and with a rational stubbornness that brought to mind Thomas's father on the dockside, trading with the bargemen. Peg collects the money on Fridays and distributes it, or doesn't, as far as Thomas can see. North Walian, a Gog, he thinks, the rolled r's; he hears her singing to get the men singing as they begin lifting the pipes onto their shoulders, as they ferry them like long iron coffins over the moorland, dropping them and cabering them upwards where it steepens. Brawn on them like rams. From time to time they take a pinch of something brown from her little silver box, offered down the line.

Twinkle, twinkle, Peg says. *Get your grind.*

And my, they do oblige. They stand behind her when she speaks, shy as maidens looking down, and flank her when she walks. They put a cushion for her on the seat of the cart. She cuts their heels if they misbehave and hangs the moon above their heads.

My boys are like the whirling dervishes, she says when Thomas asks for an estimate of the job. *They pause for nought but prayer and pote.*

And sure enough they don't. Their lamps glow on the hill in darkness as they work the night shifts. Too busy to attend St Lawrence's on Sunday; neither, for that matter, does Thomas. As for the ale, he does not see them partake on site, or in the back of the cart when they depart Kirkland for their quarters, so only the Lord of the breweries knows.

Now *Lilith* grumbles up the lane and stops beside the cottage wall; last piece of the puzzle, the heart of the machine. There's fresh grease on her axles. Her parts have been buffed to a gleam. The horses halt and snort. Harrison's boy waits to be told where to park the engine. He rubs the long, velvety noses of Monny and Moll, gives each a sugar lump from his pocket.

314

Well done, girls, stand now, stand.

The horses wait for water. The boy waits for a tip. Thomas admires the boiler and smiles, smiles and then frowns a little, when he notices all the smudged fingerprints on the polish.

Never bet on clouds, Thomas, his father would say as they laced their hiking boots; a fine life motto. But here, beside the broad and billowing Pennines, as September prepares to kick open the door to autumn and conditions for the Helm become favourable, that is exactly what he's done. *Lilith,* when she's detached from the hauliers, is left sitting beside the cottage, where she looks less like a titan of the steam-driven age and more like a boy's toy, dropped and lost and diminutive against the mountains.

Thomas feels both cheered and oddly robbed of his dream, as he stands next to the engine. Something splendidly rigged in his brain folds down, and uncertainties arise. Has he designed the system well enough? Shall he be able to man the thing and get photographic evidence at the same time? Has this prepossession been worth the bland northern poddish and lack of well-roasted coffee, worth his absence from Blackheath and Sara? Worth missing the International Meteorological Conference in Munich, with its exciting exchanges and talk of polar research stations, attendance by representatives from Denmark, Russia, Bavaria, physicists, geologists, admirals, and even the astronomer royal? It has, but not for reasons he might admit. Does he sense defeat? That portentous tingling intuition – where is it?

There have been times on the ridge ascents when the weather has closed in, and he's known he'd have to turn back, conquer the tops another day. There have been examinations in the laboratory where a thrilling reactive concoction became an underwhelming fizzle. Such is crag-hopping and such is science. In business, the trick is to refinance rather than recuperate losses – but will that wash with the council, if he has to come back and say, sorry chaps, no joy, care to sign another cheque? Will his own bank manager have it?

Such is human history, its past and future – gloriously imagined, occasionally heroic, often anticlimactic.

So, Thomas Bodger – Bodge to his friends in the Royal Meteorological Society, Tombo to his long, long-suffering wife, Mr Bodger still and unalterably to Rebecca Brooke, whom he has grown not fond of exactly, or friendly with, not faithlessly involved, but attached to in a way he cannot quite fathom – is to be saved from engineering's so often almost-brilliant, yet frequently doomed, enterprises. A letter arrives a few days after *Lilith* and well before the Helm has any intention of doing so, the first from his wife in several weeks. More a note than a letter, the handwriting is unusually and terribly poor, the hand that composed it having faltered, its wrist supported gently by a nurse.

Dearest Tombo,

With apologies that you were not present as signatory, but I have given my own consent and undergone surgery to remove the offending organ. I am wretchedly pained and have developed a fever. Alas, there is talk of a blood transfusion. I had hoped to mend, then come north and witness your tremendous experiment. But the surgeon has instructed me to request your return, and swiftly. Forgive me. Sara.

Within an hour he has stuffed his valise with essentials, departed the Kirkland cottage, and is awaiting the 1.37 at Langwathby station. He paces the platform, ignoring the sandwich vendor and the stationmaster. He looks up-track and listens for the telltale whistle and clank of pistons. He checks his pocket watch; a moment later he checks it again. Where is the *Bluebell*? Where is she—?

The *Bluebell* is on time, solid runner that she is. Smoke purls above the locomotive as she arrives into the station, and smoke purls behind her as she departs. Thomas sits to the right of the carriage travelling south, not the best view of Ribblehead, nor of Cross Fell for that matter, and the skeletons of the shanty camps – Batty Moss Hole, Jericho, Belgravia – pass by unobserved. He is too preoccupied, fretting at his cuff, rubbing his thumbs, wondering if he will make the connection to London, and hoping to God they will put saline not milk in Sara's veins.

No time to have packed away his gear, the wind roses and barometers, the portable camera with its undeveloped mountains and Lakeland crowds, and Beaufort's cherished letters – it will all have to be sent for later. No time to have written to Mrs Brooke, explaining the aborted tenancy, or bidding her farewell, or thanking her for her company, her spirited reflections, her hypothesis by the weir – quite the eureka moment; he will credit the diagram in any forthcoming article. No photograph to be revealed, of her or the Helm. And, as he looks one last time at the valley, no imagined kiss goodbye from either extraordinary being – aerial or earthly.

So, *Lilith* sits by the cottage garden in Kirkland under a crab-apple tree, losing her gleam as fruit and leaves and blossom drop onto her, slowly sinking into the earth and overgrowing, hedgehogs nesting in her boiler.

And it is Peg and her boys who remove the pipes the following year, when it becomes clear the job is scotched, carting them down the fell and into the back of their wagon, mostly under the cover of darkness; for they are worth a lot more than scrap, they will fetch a good price in the city of Carlisle, and that'll make up for their pay getting bobbed. In any case, Peg tells her crew, gold tooth glinting as she grins, who in their right mind, or with what dumb-struck mania, would lay steam pipes up a mountain to nowhere?

317

LVIII

Jude touches the air brakes, releases them. Easy, steady. He breathes, deep, and slowly.

The storm is grey-lobed, supercharged. Filling the lower right side of his vision, impelling, seeming to generate thought like a bad, diffuse brain. And to his left is the long winnowing rotor cloud.

He blinks, refocuses.

Dead ahead, the north spans out in far reaches, towards Scotland. The contours beyond the Helm look moulded from primordial material. No rain; there's mostly clarity in his flight path. The lower sky contains only shredded vapours, evidence of some tearing tantrum, forces of 9 or 10, unfelt at this altitude, but lower, once he's in it—

Concentrate, he tells himself. Get ready. That old feeling is there, of driving towards the crime, the catalyst, whatever unpredictable, charismatic danger must be attended. The feeling of being a buffalo, turning and shouldering into the blizzard instead of running in the other direction. Madness, perhaps – the override switch, the willingness to enter disaster.

He breathes, takes his bearings, scans the wider sky and below.

On the plateau of Great Dun Fell, demolition of the old radio station is under way. Its ugly tower and penal-colony-looking outbuilding are half gone. Diggers and a crane are parked up on the work site, like matchbox toys in a sandpit, and the old road up is being resurfaced, fresh black pumped halfway up its winding vein. Construction of the NATS radar will start soon, last in the chain of the new network; there's lots of talk at the club about the regional airports expanding, money, opportunity. To the side, postage-stamp size, is the weather station, its pale-grey roof lit by sunlight at the very edge of the base cloud's shadow. The Met Office research team will already have arrived and set up their gear – the ultrasonic anemometer and thermometers. They'll be able to see *Perry* sailing overhead, in the interstitial space, tracking south–north, north–south. More equipment is being positioned on the valley floor, in the supercritical flow. Regardless of what he's about to do, he wouldn't want to be down there as part of the field campaign, getting goose-skinned and blown off his feet. He imagines them hunkered on the moor, their cagoules flapping madly, black balaclavas under their hoods like terrorists, yelling in the racket.

It's a lot of trouble to go to, isn't it? Ange said to him after he'd told her about the researcher's visit to the club. *All that expensive kit and fannying around in a gale.*
 Weather boffins, you know. They like their tech.
 Mmm. They're not the only ones.
 Yeah, well. I'm happy to help out if I can.
 But, wind structure? I don't get it. Wind doesn't have a structure, does it?
 Guess they'll find out.

He'd mostly gone along that evening to see Keith and Pete and have a beer at the little airport bar afterwards, but the talk was surprisingly interesting. It was all new research, they were told, measurements to assess stability of flow over large-scale hills – a bit paradoxical-sounding, Ange wasn't wrong. The researcher was barely older than Mark, with a thick Northern Irish accent, a Polartec, Nike trainers and mod specs, nothing at all like the balding, checky-suited weathermen on the telly.

All honesty now, lads, and lady (he waved to Julia), *there aren't many places this research can be done. Cumbria's one of them. The Helm's anatomy is still theoretical, and we can't model it accurately. There are too many eddying effects off the topography – sorry for the jargon. So this is where yous all come in. We need to get up there, and in it, you know. Not gonna lie, we are talking cyclone intensity, as some of you probably know. It's a blazer. But I hear you lads like to get high.*

Laughter. He'd got their attention. Even Julia was smirking.

So, does anyone want to volunteer?

McLean, Jude knew, had broken the British altitude record above the Helm bar in 1939, reaching a whopping 3,395 metres. He'd encountered prodigious lift just to the east of the rotor cloud, and had used the standing wave to get up there. Jude had read the unusually figurative entry in the pilot's log during a guest return at Newcastle.

Tremendous vertical velocity. A smooth elevator all the way up to 3,350 m. Glorious. Like the kiss of God.

How had that felt, he wondered. Incredible. Pure elation. The way Mark described his house music parties, boosted by the illegal substances his dad had spent years patting youths down for. *Just don't tell me, son.* Not that he and Ange hadn't partied hard back in the day. That night after Led Zep, fucking in some dingy Brummie bathroom, out of their minds; probably the night Mark was conceived, actually.

He makes the first track, high along the lumbars of the Pennines, the plane impervious to the riot below. Then he turns, banks into the crosswind and pushes the opposite rudder, increasing drag to lose altitude – a forward slip greater than he would usually use this high, as if on a miscalculated final or a short landing. Gradual, he thinks. Enter the fray by stages. He finishes the turn, and tracks south along the length of the formation again. The sun is radiant on his skin, illuminating the cockpit.

Past Great Dun, he banks again, turns the glider in a graceful migratory arc, lowers altitude, and begins along the mountains, nearer to the clear, furious torrent. Every move responsive, confident, careful. It is like a courting ritual, approaching and retreating from some stunning, lethal mate, asking, *Do you want me? Will you spare me?* With each track he moves down through the boundary layers, the base cloud's colours darkening as he gets closer – shale, gunmetal, pewter. Odd, poetic words fill his head, but he keeps his observations factual, simple, nothing inaccurate – ever the copper, Keith would joke.

Wave disturbance, side shear, small-scale connective turbulence.

Increased wave disturbance, increased side shear, increased turbulence.

He holds the stick tighter. He banks, turns the glider, re-enters the passageway, the sailplane beginning to shudder and buffet and ride fast. Spectral gap. It is the right term for this haunted corridor between the two clouds. The energy feels poltergeistic, logarithmic, with continuous changes in the leeside winds. A tormented mind. Bouncing and hopping now, as if in white water, not what he's used to. Flashes of sunlight explode off *Perry*'s wing, cosmic, synaptic. Like angels strobing, fire through holes in the sky. Flickering ghosts. Gary. Gary's face. It's OK. Concentrate. He is hungry, alert. His nerves are live, but he does nothing reckless. He eases his grip on the stick. The glider drops, bucks. Enjoy the thrill, he tells himself, this one isn't going to kill you. And still. It could, couldn't it.

Two hours later, the inversion has lowered, and the system is beginning to weaken. Jude has plenty of recorded data, through the shaking and jostling, and feels wired. He's kept an eye on it – the rotor cloud has remained intact to the west of the corridor, a long rolling tunnel in the sky. If this were space and he an astronaut, he'd go nowhere near such an entity, front end or back; it looks like the kind of thing that would crush him like a can, or he'd come out the

321

other side wormholed to some distant galaxy, orange-mooned, unresolved, webbed with dust.

Get the job done, then just have fun: that's what Keith said to him in the hangarage. And isn't this why he raised his hand and volunteered, isn't this part of the reason he wanted to be the one? To catch that heaven-proof ride. Absolute altitude. McLean's record. He considers having a piss in the bottle – no, he can hold it. He checks the oxygen tank is reachable, then banks west, heads swiftly downwind across the valley towards the huge tumbling tube, as if heading into big surf.
Here we go.

The hoist is sudden and incredible. He feels the glider rising fast, and himself rising from and against his own heaviness, and as the velocity increases his heart and stomach drag down through his body, and his body separates, lifting against the belts, lifting from its frame, out of every thought but this movement.

Its enormous strength.

Rushing. Flowing upwards.

Christ Almighty—

Still in his seat, but there is no seat. His hand is stunned on the stick and his feet are useless; he cannot stop this lift, its force, bearing him up. Higher and higher. Sky changing colour, bluer, paler. Nothing beneath, no ground or gravity. No avatar. He is only ascension, is fibreglass, bird-like, a comet, and *Perry* is his body, his lungs and heart, burning, they are – up, up, travelling above three thousand, three fifty, four, four fifty, up above the world, away from its hold, away from—

It is gorgeous, it is—

the opposite—

of what might have been—

if he'd jumped from the bridge and ended—

Hope, love, ecstasy, God, if there is a God, oh God, it is so—

Massive; the sky is massive, and endless, endless, it is endless. Something vast and divine has hold of him, them, together, its breath, its body, a waterfall rushing upwards, they belong to atoms, stars, brightest matter, and it is sheer—

Rapture.

~⊙

Later, when the glider has landed at Scar Top and been caged and transported back to the airfield, after he gets home to find Ange lounging on the sofa with the dog, one year older and still who she always was when he loved her, he confesses. They eat chips for tea and drink a bottle of wine and go to bed, finish what they started earlier. She lets him go down on her. She takes him slowly, softly into her mouth. He lies under her looking up, and he feels it again, immense bliss, abandonment. He looks at her face as she comes, her blonde-white hair half-covering it, her eyes focused somewhere in space, and he comes and every cell in him is risen, and he thinks, *this*.

Then, feeling awkward and shy and like a tosser talking so profoundly to his wife, he tries to describe the feelings of the flight. All the words he did not say into the recorder. How the plane became irrelevant. How he felt that something alive and seductive had him in its grip, he was inside it, like sex, *congress* of some kind. How he felt as if he *was* the atmosphere, not the atmosphere but its movement, not its movement but its *life-force.* It was like making love with – the storm, with the Helm. Angela rolls on her side and smiles and teases him.

You cheated on me on my birthday? What!

He does not mention the absolute altitude record, which he now holds by a considerable margin, because although the measurement is astonishingly high, so high his blood felt thin and the Earth below looked bent at the edges and he finally had to put the oxygen mask on, and although he knows he will never repeat the experience and that the record will take some beating, it doesn't seem important.

LIX

She lights a cigarette, smokes it quickly; long, steadying inhales,
dragon-style exhalation. She looks at the chaps in the photo. Saggy
woollen crotches, missing fingertips from frostbite, mint cake and
Spam to contend with. No persecution, just fellowships and honours
lists. Think, Selima. Be rational, she tells herself. You are a rationalist.
This is not a cheap thriller or a horror story. No one is going to harm
you. All things being equal, in a world of benign coincidences and
mostly followed rules, the worst scenario is not happening.

She drops the stub into the West Brom mug. She waits for her pulse
to settle and the flurrying in her chest to calm, then she goes to the
window. Look, there, a typical scene. Wind blustering, manky cloud,
a scattering of rain. A single grey-white sheep with green bum signature has made its way onto the top of the fell. Look, this is prosaic
fucking England.

Enough, then. Enough of this nonsense. The power games, the hiding.
She will not give anyone the satisfaction of trapping her inside her
own paranoia, let alone in a hut with a cranky kettle and no heating.
She will damn well walk. A long way it may be, but it is all downhill.
If the octogenarian ramblers can manage it, so can she. And as soon as
there's a phone signal, she'll call for help. Taxi. Police. Whatever. But
she is not going to act like a victim.

She zips up her coat, finds a hairband and ties back her hair. She
pulls her hood up and she leaves the field station, the wind buffering
all other sound now. She crosses the complex and the cattle-grid,

stern of stride, and begins down the steep service road. Fuck-them fuck-them fuck-them. The radome sinks into the fell above and the wind drops away behind the shelter of the summit. The tarmac slaps dramatically under the soles of her trainers. She does not look behind. She stares down, ignoring the periphery and all its idiocies. Her angry-bird walk, Anita always called it. The one she used to do leaving their bedroom, when her sister had the radio on too loud, techno, or hip-hop or bloody Oasis, and Selima was trying to study. The one she would do when Gaurav had suggested, again, that it was unnatural for a woman not to want children, that she was penalising him unfairly; he could have had children with – her, if he hadn't left her for Selima.

People can't act this way, she thinks. Inflicting on others their unhappiness, their opinions, their beliefs. She can hear Papa's voice, pedantic and songish: *Can't isn't won't, Selima, can't isn't don't.* Thoughts of the boys outside the grammar school, following her and Anita home. *Hey, Sut-butts, lift your skirts, is it too dark in there to see your pindas?* Thoughts of all the unnecessary rewrites to her PhD, and the failure to be credited as co-author on published articles. All the times she was made to feel powerless, or just less.

Fuck-them fuck-them fuck-them.

In front of her, the road winds and falls away, chicaning down the mountain. She glances up. Above, all but the topmost tip of the radome has disappeared behind the brow, its crown like a bleached sun, setting the wrong side of the world.

And fuck you, big ball!

Selima walks on, her wet trainers rubbing uncomfortably. She walks a little less angrily as the coarse shoulders of the mountain rise and dwarf her. The black road tapers into the distance. When was the last time she walked more than a few miles? Probably not more than ten minutes since she got Ellie. She checks her phone. Surely she will get a signal soon, or there will be a dog walker, a cyclist, someone to help; she won't have to walk the whole way. Surely.

Out of the summit lee, the wind begins to find her again, shoving her forward as if she's a naughty child, at times so strong she could almost lean back against its embrace. She feels chilled – the temperature has dropped a good seven or eight degrees. She passes the junction with the up-sloping dirt trough for runaway vehicles, and continues on.

So much slower going on foot, and it feels unnaturally physical after the bike, practically Neanderthal. Hangover is kicking back in too. She should have made a cup of tea before she left, at least brought some of the field station's parasitic water with her. There's half a protein bar and a mushy banana in the rucksack, isn't there? Good luck surviving on that, she thinks, at least Neanderthals knew how to skin and gut stuff. She keeps her eyes on the road, on her damp, white trainers making minimal progress on the tarmac.

Only when she rounds the flank of the hill and the road bends north and the wind hits her hard on the side of her head does she look up again. There is Cross Fell. Its steep loaf. Its ramped precipice like a cascade of shattered bones. And there, above it, is something quite magnificent. A gargantuan, iridescent cumulonimbus – nothing at all like the badly replicated smudge on the cover of David's book – advancing outwards across the summit, its vespers like ragged prayer flags. She looks across the valley. There, with several miles of clear space between, is the bar cloud, long and contrailing, the burly hydraulic jump.

Mrs. H.

David was right. It's incredible, frightening and exotic-looking, breathtaking. A supercell belonging nowhere else in the world, only here. One of a kind. Beautiful.

She stands and stares. Her eyes blur in the current, not just wind tears, but strange, sudden emotional ones. She blinks to clear them. Why is she crying? David? His life? Her own? This – phenomenon? It hurts. It hurts to look at, to witness. It hurts to think of its disappearance, of sufferance, everything that will be gone. That is already gone. It's all so vulnerable. Even this vast, powerful thing, that looks untouchable. Dying. She reaches into her pocket for her phone, puts it on camera setting. No picture will do justice, she thinks, though after she takes it and looks at the image, yes, it's beautiful and frightening and exotic on the screen. Still no signal, but she sends it to David, and writes, *Make the most of every day remaining.*

She puts the phone in her pocket. She wipes her eyes. Her hands are trembling. Her chest hurts. Inside her chest hurts – her heart, hyper-vigilant, knocked around by the last few days. The last few weeks and months – years, if she's honest. She shakes her hands, curls them into fists. Something is unravelling. Everything that can't be masked or soothed or made to go away by work. She can't seem to control the tears, the feelings. She wants to get off this fell. She wants to stay, looking at this extraordinary thing; she wants not to be part of a world in which ruin happens.

The wind is getting fiercer now, urging her to move, pouring loudly down the mountains. Perhaps she should go back; she's not – right in herself. It's such a long way down. She looks at the crest of Great Dun Fell, the lopped-off crown of the radome. The hood of her jacket blows back onto her shoulders. She turns and looks down the road again. There – in the lay-by where dog walkers park – there's a pale shape, a glimmer of metal or glass. A vehicle is parked up, silver perhaps. She can ask for help, get a lift. Right, come on, she tells herself. Pull yourself together, Selima.

She begins to walk, wiping her eyes, straining to see ahead. Then she raises her arms above her head and starts waving. Don't drive off! Don't— Slowly she brings her arms down. The vehicle is cream-coloured, dirty white. Is it the security van? Is it Paul and his partner? Selima stops walking. Are they waiting for her because they know she has no bike and will have to walk? Some kind of interception. A trap. That's just – really wrong.

She stands still. Totally exposed. They must have seen her coming on the road by now – a bright-purple dot in the sea of monotones. It's hard to breathe. Hard to think clearly, of anything else but the scenario now forming in her mind. Of what will play out.

Paul, though that is not his name, and the other one, have hold of her arms. Their faces are impervious, their grip is vice-like. The back doors of the van are open and inside is the electric bike. She is dragged towards it and her heels dig into the ground as she tries to fight; she braces against the bumper with her feet, but she is not strong enough. They take hold of her legs and lift and slide her inside, hard, so she hits the bike wheel. The van doors are shut, locked. She scrabbles and bangs as hard as she can, shouting in darkness. The men say nothing. The engine starts and the van pulls away, bouncing out of the rutted lay-by.

No.

It is not the security van. It's yellower. The minibus from the Christian Centre. A smiling group is waiting for her, very sure of what they are doing, deadly serious. *Are you from here? No, I'm on secondment – up there.* She has identified herself for them. This is Eden, and she is the serpent with knowledge, the fallen scientist. They don't want any climate combat to occur, no COP summits, no amelioration; they wish for Armageddon to be hastened. It is the Endtrepreneurs. Their residential has been timed to coincide with hers.

Selima stands in the road and doesn't move. A blast of wind shoves her forward a pace; she rights herself and braces.

Worse. Because everything is falling apart, nothing is safe.

She knows the car parked below, small, beige, unassuming, *vanilla*. She knows the person who has been increasingly tormenting her, turning the dial bit by bit, and is finally stepping out of the shadows. It is always someone the victim knows, a watcher, a sick admirer, rejected, longing, suffering close by. The lover who isn't. Not Gaurav.

David.

Panic hits her, the cold, indiscriminate tidal wave of it.

No. Nothing is safe. Nothing survivable. He. They. It. A terrible, certain feeling sluices around her: pure dread. Something awful is going to occur, something violent and tragic; it's not possible to stop it, it's never been possible.

She turns and begins to run back up the road, into the brunt, one shoulder shoving forward against the force of the Helm. Her feet slap heavily on the tarmac. She stumbles uphill as fast as she can but it is so hard to move. Her legs feel so slow, barely pushing her body forward. The weight of her laptop is incredible suddenly, a slab, banging on her back in the rucksack. And her heart is useless, in overdrive though she has only run a hundred yards. The wind rushes past, thick, almost glandular, swarming her eyes, flooding them again. The ground swims and all the world's lines blur. She wipes at her face, casts a look behind. The vehicle is a pale, warped form against the massive sweep of green and brown. Has it moved? Is it coming up the road? She can't hear an engine – only wind flushing against her hood and her own ragged breaths.

330

She will never make it back to the field station. She cannot go back there now.

She should get off the road. She should hide. On the moorland. In the gorse bushes, the lime kilns or the old lead mine cuttings – they're a hundred feet deep in places. Hide and wait and call the police.

She steps onto the verge and climbs over the low metal siding, then begins scrambling down, into the steep hushing that runs along the roadside. Below, water is trickling in its carved bed. She skids down the dirt and stones, slips and catches herself before she goes over, then she slides inelegantly on her bottom, grazing her wrists, feeling her coat snag and tear. She gets to the bed and stands up. Wind haws through the narrow channel or it is an engine straining on the hard ascent, coming too fast in a low gear. She tries to keep her feet dry, stepping on rocks to cross the hushing, but she can't keep her balance on their slippery backs; her feet slip into the freezing water, up to her ankles, her trainers soak. She splashes across and climbs out. Her throat feels swollen and inflamed. She looks up towards the road, can't see anyone leaning over the metal siding, can't be sure.

Come on, she thinks. Come on, keep moving. Which way. Which. So hard to think; she is not thinking, just possessed by instincts, her thoughts are swept away by the rushing feeling, the surge of fear towards some edge. Real, it is real. Whatever is happening is happening. Whatever is happening is happening to her. Come on, move.

Above, the fell's gradient is steeper than the way down. Tufts of wiry grass and spongy moss, trickling black water and grass-hidden rocks. Too acute to climb in some places, but she has to. She starts up; her ankles feel frail and cold and unsupported on the rough ground, her trainers keep sinking and slipping. She leans forward, grasps handfuls of the grass and rips it out as she pulls herself up, her thighs stiff and

331

lactic, the burning now in her lungs. Two-thirds of the way up the slope, she has to stop. She cannot breathe, is almost hyperventilating. What little oxygen is in the air feels snatched by the wind. She clings on to the hillside. She feels sick, is almost sick, retches twice; only the frantic feeling stops her vomiting.

She looks at the sheer side of the hill, its impossible angle, looks back over her shoulder. Below, the hushing snakes away, its chasm plummeting, vertiginous. The wind buffets her sideways, catches her rucksack. She flails, rights her body, balances, but can feel herself falling, as the perspective tilts and the ground rocks. She leans hard towards the bank, claws it rigidly. Her legs lock. Her hands, her fingers petrify. All the mechanics of her body shut down except for its acute seizure. She is stuck and cannot move. Her breathing is so fast and shallow now, it is almost non-existent. Even her heart isn't beating. She is having a heart attack. She is going to pass out and fall into the gully.

Move, she says. *Please. Please.*

Begging herself out loud. But she can't. Everything is paralysed. She is so high up and the earth is rearing as if to tip her off. She is dizzy and numb and lodged, hugging the hillside, crying, but there are no tears, just tiny dry convulsions. She hears a sound in the distance. A slam? Car door.

Move!

With a tiny hypnic jerk, she releases her grip on the mountain. She lifts her foot, shuffles it an inch higher. She gropes about, finds a rock. She pushes up. Her arms are quaking. Her legs feel boneless, unmuscled. She reaches again for a handhold, finds purchase. And weakly, bit by bit, using her knees, her elbows, she claws and crawls

332

up the bank, ugly, desperate, quickening towards the top as the gradient flattens. She clatters on the shale of the final rise, dislodging rocks
with her hands and feet. She rises up, runs. Once over the crest, she
collapses down again. She retches, brings nothing up but phlegm, saliva and the taste of nicotine. She spits out a mouthful. Cold and wet
seep against her knees and cuffs. The wind barrels over her, pulling
strands of her hair from its band, making it flow electrically around
her head.

She can't see the road or the hushing now so she can't be seen here
either. She has a chance. If she runs. She must find a way to stay out
of sight, cut north across the flank of the mountains, avoid the station
and the radome. If she can get up onto the ridge closer to Cross Fell,
she will be behind the Helm, in its lull. Then— Then she will figure
out what to do next, how to get help, how to get down.

She stands and smooths back her hair, reties it. She starts off again,
over the rough terrain, her white trainers sucking through black, oily
patches of bog. Her limbs feel soft and stiff. She lopes towards the
next rise, the bridge between higher mountains, Little Dun, the smaller cousin. To her right on the horizon, the radome is a blank cracked
moon. She keeps going, painfully across the moorland, half-hobbling,
half-running, her feet sore in the wet sliding trainers, her ankles clicking and twisting and threatening to sprain. Above, the base cloud has
folded itself at the edges like a huge soft shell and is reaching over
the smaller neighbour hill. She has to get up there. But the wind is
so strong, gusting all around, and to the north she can hear it roaring,
cascading down Cross Fell.

She turns and looks behind, at the brow of the hill above the road.
Lumpy, with hummocks and statues of rock. Is there a figure standing against the horizon? Is it moving? It doesn't matter. She can
only be sure of what is happening inside, of the feeling of terror, the

commitment to it. She limps on, a quarter of a mile, the wind scathing in her ears, just and so running. Twice her left ankle snaps over and springs back up, and on the third turn she stumbles over completely and lands on her side in a shallow mire, peat water and mud up her thigh and hip, her elbows.

She rolls and kneels and gets up, tests her weight. The joint doesn't feel broken, just staved. Her hands are filthy. She wipes them on her jeans. She walks on, jogs painfully until the ankle gets too hot, walks again. The hood of her puffer flaps and shuffles around her head. The bag on her back is tugged about. Her face is smarting, as if slapped. She limps on, breathing raggedly.

Then, aching and exhausted, she slows and stops. She turns her back to the wind, puts her hands on her knees, takes heaving breaths of air, until, steadier, she can stand.

She reaches into her pocket to take out the phone, but the pocket is looser and empty. She feels around it, into its corners. An opening in the lining her hand travels through. When she looks, there's a tear in the material at the side. She tries the other pocket, finds only the wet packet of cigarettes. She tries both pockets again, groping desperately at the hole. Did she put the phone in the rucksack? No. She didn't. She took a photograph with it and— She looks on the ground beside her feet, as if it might only just have slipped out. It is gone. Dropped somewhere, anywhere. The steep bank above the stream. The fall in the mire.

This isn't happening, she thinks. But it is. It is.

And it's OK.

She stands still, nothing really left in her after the flood. She looks at the fellside as the wind pulses and shouts, its noise perpetual. No one is coming. There are no trees, no bushes, just scoured grassland and jutting stone. The uplands are empty and seem to go on for ever – long earthen curves, limestone reefs, patches that are bone-coloured and blood-blistered, brown and sallow. It is all so dead. Like the shades and joints and the scars of a body lying prostrate, wasted, drained, blasted by unstoppable disease. She is so small in the landscape, so small, like a child in the adult world. Ten years old again, standing beside her mother's bed with her school bag on, her homework all done, and she has worked so hard on it, hour after hour after hour, so she doesn't have to feel anything, doesn't have to feel sad or angry or afraid or helpless.

I'm sorry, she whispers.

But it is OK. It is OK to be those things. It's OK, to be over-whelmed, to know and not know what is going to happen, to try to solve, and to fail.

She turns again and faces Cross Fell; its summit is shadowed by the vast bruising floor of the base cloud. Light is being funnelled underneath it from the west; the mountain slopes are ringed and lit, lambent as gold on a corpse. It looks like some kind of blazing holy war up there. She walks on, head down, shoulders forward, slowly and effortfully, up the slope of Little Dun. Her legs are so tired she keeps staggering. But she doesn't stop. As she gets to the pass where the hill flattens and saddles the truer mountains either side, the wind begins to weaken, the gusts shorter and softer. As if she has walked through an invisible wall, into a completely different dimension, Oz's curtain. She is behind the Helm, backstage while it performs. And there, just ahead, is the pathway laid along the top of the Pennines, along the roof of England, leading north towards Armageddon, and south to the radome and the field station. Its slabs are giant and worn away, as old as the Roman road, perhaps older.

It will all be funnier in the retelling, she thinks.

How she limped along the pavement to the bizarre, Ottoman-shaped shelter on the top of Cross Fell, and waited there, shivering and unable to contact anyone, until the wind abated. How she walked down the mountain, her feet bloody and soaked and raw, until she got to the road, where she sat down, unable to take another step. How a group of New Pagans, dressed in green velvet cloaks, antlers and bird masks found her on the way to the Druid Circle for their ceremony and one of them wrapped her in his cape to warm her up, and they gave her hot tea and chocolate biscuits in their camper van, and took her to the police station.

How David came to collect her and bring her back to the bothy, having left Sandra with the carer, and told her the electric bike had been found by the young Christians dumped on the side of the road in the village, battery flat, but no sign of any damage; an abandoned theft maybe. They'd charged it and cleaned it up, asked at the pub where Selima was staying and left it at the Airbnb for her – nice bunch.

How, when she started crying and laughing, unstoppably, hysterically almost, and couldn't explain why, David gave her the most enormous hug, and said, *Well, you wouldn't be the first person to go cuckoo up there.*

How she got on Ellie again the next morning, and went back up to work, because we must think of the positive version, we must not be deterred, we must understand the effect of matter around us, and our effect on matter, and measure the damage in order to reduce it, to reverse it, to do better, and anyway – fuck-them fuck-them fuck-them.

It will all seem much funnier, imagining it now, as she limps along the path towards the storm.

336

LX

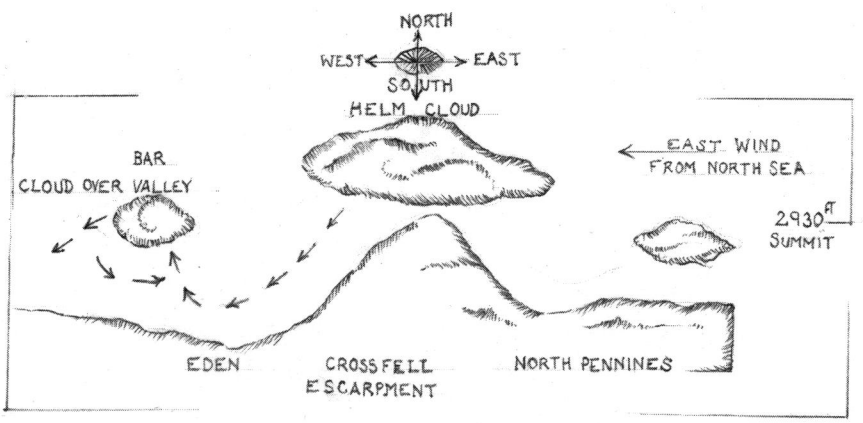

Proposed diagrammatic formulation of the Helm wind (not to scale)
Met Office Archive, attrib. T. F. Bodger

LXI

Even so!

Helm doesn't know when Helm will die.
    If it will be soon, in a while, or aeons.
    If it will happen suddenly, quietly, or violently.
    Whether Helm will simply cease one day, or fail slowly, blow by blow on the mountain.
    Never knowing which is the last time, or a long, sad goodbye.
    Helm doesn't know if Helm will have a legacy, as all Helm is, all Helm's identities and versions.
    Existing in some being's mind only, divine, radical, monstrous, or an archival simulacrum, a code that's downloaded.
    Being forgotten, or celebrated, or commemorated.
    After the humans.
    Or before them.

There is a lot of speculation, expert and otherwise. Humans love predictions and projections – bird-gut prophecies, cloud patterns, compound analyses, AI, eschatology. Some say everything will be fine; people will get their shit together, clean up their act, clean up the skies, somehow, and Helm will outlive every last skin-bag or robot or artificial person. Some have that feeling of foreboding, impending crisis, like the worried feeling Helm first had about humans – correct! Except, Helm isn't killing Helmself, of course; Helm doesn't have a choice in Helm's downfall.

So many possibilities for endings.

Disassembly of finely balanced weather fronts – not such a future issue.

Polar collapse. Maritime collapse. Gulf Stream collapse. Total meteorological collapse.

Back to that wildly volatile atmosphere, extreme clashing systems including:

superstorms,

gas emissions,

ceaseless rain,

solar heat plumes,

new melted seas,

intolerable temperatures.

Earth's fevers and chills.

The climate totally fucking around again.

A giant global fart-off (one last gag, thank you for coming).

It seems human time is Helm's time after all.

The way you affected Helm was quick and unexpected. You caught Helm by surprise with Helm's extinction, after such a promising beginning, a lot of mutual history, and fun. You made a god of Helm, a demon, a phenomenon. You said Helm was special, a spectacle, a marvel, so wonderful and fearsome on this weather-obsessed little island that no other wind was named. You found a way into Helm's heart, the space where Helm's heart would have been if Helm had one, left something shiny and dirty there. Busy, careless humans; you probably didn't mean to hurt Helm, but – it's a relationship.

If it ends, Helm isn't sorry. The contributions were amazing, if a little puzzling now and then, and sometimes crazy – dials and datas, scales and squiggles, formulae and fanatical magical instruments. Stories. So many stories. Helm would not be Helm without your brilliant, curious, silly imaginations.

Still, the end is inconceivable, a little scary. What comes after is impossible to know. Darkness. Light. Heaven. Hell. The perfect stillness of final peace. Continual stormy torment. Maybe resurrection, one day, once the terrible skies are clear and calm again and humans are gone, or while the last few cling on, surviving, starting again, looking up at the summit of the biggest mountain and pointing.

Helm doesn't care, as long as there is Helm.

The author has created a maker's mark to assert the organic, bio-logical, non-AI-generated nature of the novel's creative composition and artistry. The author offers this as an affirmation of her craft.

Acknowledgements

I've been trying to write this novel for almost twenty years. There are so many people to thank for their support during that time and for the many stories, anecdotes, yarns and observations about the Helm wind, in strange and wonderful detail. Some are nameless strangers: passing Edeners, fellow hedgerow meteorologists, cloud-spotters. But to those known to me, below, a heartfelt thank you.

To the following artists and makers for their beautiful, original works:
Tom Philipson for the demonic mountain woodcut print.
Richard Archer for his formulation diagram, inspired by the studies of Professor Gordon Manley.
Loy Hall Garvey for her tormented friend sketch.
Neil Gower for the map.
Henry Petrides and the art department at Faber & Faber for assisting with the illustrations and presentation, managing to catch Helm on the cover, and as always making beautiful items.

To Alex Bowler at Faber & Faber, Tracy Bohan at The Wylie Agency, and Kate Nintzel, previously at Mariner, for their editorial wisdom, skill and patience with so many spinning plates, and to Jin Auh and Jessica Vestuto for their reading responses, and kind and helpful comments. To Silvia Crompton for excellent copy-editing (and apologies for the Neolithic wormholes!), and to Kate Ward, Anne Owen and Kate Burton for such care with production and publicity.

I am so grateful, as ever, for everyone who assisted with my research and enquiries, no matter how specific, bizarre and baffling, or read early passages of the novel.

Thanks to Richard Thwaites especially, for his psychological advice, his Very Cumbrian comments on both character and place, his knowledge of Garlands Hospital, and for tromping up and down the Pennines with me on wet, wild and otherwise wonderless days. To Peter Hobbs, long-time friend and brilliant advocate for wind demons. To Jim Spence, an inspirational English teacher and windswept resident of the Eden Valley. To Sarah Perry for her star maps, uncanny tarot cards, cigarettes, pinecones, mottos, and the many conversations about bodies, love, belief, devilry and writing. To Louisa Yates for thoughts on Victorian consent and medical procedures. To Ian Woolverton for the West Midlands stuff, for letting me nick his eyes, and for his endurance of storms and collapsing barns. To Gaurav Siddhu and Joanna Härmä for the rotis and swear words. To Fiona Renkin, whose window faced the right way in Penrith. To Imogen Cloët for her introduction to Richard and the regular positive vectors sent NE to NW. To Carol Lahey for all things folkloric. To Louise Brealey for her vocal exercises. To Cara Morgan for her mathematical lessons. To Johanna Forster for insight into grant applications and the bureaucratic. And to Jane Kotapish, Erin Stephens, Anne-Marie Sanderson and Jennifer Custer for the goddamn enthusiasm.

Thanks also to Geraint Vaughan at Manchester University for signalling the right papers. To David Uttley for his brilliant book *The Anatomy of the Helm Wind*, which was very useful reading, and to Steve Matthews at Bookcase in Carlisle for publishing it, as well as for his endlessly fierce support of local arts and literature. To Mark Beswick, Archivist at the Met Office National Meteorological Archive, and Dr Sophie Pocock, Library and Archive Specialist at the National Meteorological Library and Archive, for their assistance and direction.

I'm profoundly grateful to Alex Bowler and Mary Cannam for their spirit of innovation, support and protection around my creation of a Human Written maker's mark; for understanding the significance of blood on the page. I'm reminded again and again what an exceptional and humane publishing community Faber is. Thanks also to Kate Devlin, Professor of Artificial Intelligence & Society at King's College London, for the big thumbs-up.

Lastly, thanks to my parents, Anthony and Elizabeth, for finding the little cottage beside the hill from which a small girl could storm-watch day after day: Dad, Mum, I wish you could read another one. And thanks again to Loy, for her lovely spirit and creativity – this book is for you. How I hope there will be a Helm when you are old.

Permissions

The lee wave equation is an expression by R. S. Scorer, as depicted in the 1991 Met Office Glossary, Digital Library and Archive.

The Helm wind formula diagram is inspired by studies found within 'The Helm Wind of the Northern Pennines', an article by G. Manley, Air Ministry – Meteorological Office, 1942. Open Government Licence © Crown Copyright. Information provided by the National Meteorological Library and Archive – Met Office, UK.